JESSICA ANN DISCIACCA

WITCHES *of* TRIORA

BLOODLINE

DARK FLAME
PUBLISHING

JESSICA ANN DISCIACCA

BLOODLINE

DARK FLAME
PUBLISHING

NOTE TO READER

CONTENT ADVISORY: This fantasy novel contains elements that may be unsettling for some readers, particularly those who may be sensitive to themes of emotional or mental health. Within the realms of this fictional world, some depictions and discussions touch upon such challenging subjects. The intention is to weave a compelling tale while being mindful of our readers' wellbeing. If you anticipate that encounters with these themes might be triggering or discomforting, we recommend exercising caution and considering whether to continue with the story. The fantastical nature of this narrative does not diminish the potential impact of these elements, and we prioritize the comfort and mental well-being of our readers. Thank you for embarking on this fantastical journey with us, and may your reading experience be enjoyable and mindful of your emotional boundaries.

*To the women who lifted me when I
stumbled,
who believed in me when I doubted,
who spoke courage into my silence and
kindness into my storms —
this is for you.
Your strength, wisdom, and love have
been the light that guided me through
every shadow.
I am who I am because you stood beside
me.
Thank you, from the deepest part of my
heart.*

Chapter One

"Home, sweet, home," murmured Belz.

"This is fucking absurd," stated Gor, stepping through my portal. "I can't wait to tell you all I told you so."

Mammon appeared beside Gor and patted him on the back. "Thee of little faith, brother," Mammon said. "How disappointed Father would be to see you now."

"Leave Him out of this," Gor growled through his teeth. Mammon laughed, walking towards the others.

I watched them through the small doorway to Hell I had opened with my power. It was my first attempt at being a whispering traveler, flexing my goddess powers over death, and so far, everyone had crossed over and lived. I looked back at my cousin, Frankie, and the remaining demon brother, Levi. He tightened his arms around her, as if afraid she would be torn away.

"Please reconsider," Levi whispered to her.

Frankie looked up at him with love. She drew the back of her knuckles down the side of his face.

"The two most important people in my life are going through that portal," she said, looking from Levi to me. "There is nothing and no one that could stop me from going with you."

Levi's eyes pleaded with me. She might never forgive me for it, but I agreed with the demon prince of Envy. If Frankie accompanied us to Hell, she would be another weak spot that would draw my attention away from my goal: getting to him. To my demon prince ... Asmodeus.

I gave Levi a small nod as he held onto Frankie. His shoulders relaxed. I approached my cousin.

"Ready to go make a mess of things, per usual?" she asked with a smile.

"I'm always up for a challenge," I replied, pulling her into me. I held her tightly, tears threatening to escape. I took in my beautiful cousin, her bright green eyes and dark curly hair. She was my soulmate; but this, I could not ask of her. I could not risk her life. Not when I had almost lost her once before. The memory of her dead body in my arms still haunted my nightmares.

Levi bent down and kissed her as I stepped away from Francesca.

"I love you," he whispered, tracing her lips with his thumb. She furrowed her brow, looking between us, puttting the pieces together. Levi took a step towards me, towards the portal.

"No," she said in disbelief. "You aren't leaving without me," she said, moving forward. I threw up my hands, trapping her in place with my tendrils of dark shadows. Red flares of light now danced through my dark magic, a gift from the power of my mate, Deus.

Frankie fought against the restraints, trying to break free. "No!" she screamed.

"I'm sorry, Frankie," I said, tears flowing freely. "I can't risk your life. If I die, the Salvos must go on."

"No!" she yelled, yanking and pulling at the shadows, but I was too strong. "You can't leave me. You won't!"

"I love you, cousin," I whispered. I turned to Levi, taking his hand as we made our way to the portal.

"I will never forgive you for this! I will never forgive you," I heard her yell as we stepped through. Once we had crossed, I absorbed the energy of the gate within myself, placing a permanent barrier between Hell and Frankie. I could still hear her screaming as the zapping sound behind me finally silenced.

I felt sick. But I did what had to be done. She would remain safe. Frankie was a powerful witch, but she wasn't a demon, and she wasn't a god. She was the weakest link, and I knew Lucifer would exploit her to manipulate me. I had to focus on Deus. He was the only thing that mattered to me down here. I gripped the key to our home back in Romania that still hung around my neck—a reminder of what was at stake.

I felt a hand on my shoulder. I remained silent, torn up by guilt at what I had done to my best friend.

"Thank you," Levi said, rubbing his thumb against my shoulder. "She's safe. Even if she never forgives us ... she is alive."

"I know," I replied. A sick feeling wrenched through me as I looked at the four princes of Hell who had agreed to help save their brother.

Gor's brow furrowed. "What's wrong, Seren?" he asked.

I shook my head, refocusing. "Nothing. Just adjusting is all," I replied. I had willingly agreed to venture into Hell with four demonic princes of sin who were known for the horrors they had each unleashed on the mortal world. And somewhere in this harsh realm was Lucifer, the most powerful demon of them all. His conniving mind and sadistic behavior were the thing I feared the most.

This entire plan rested on my shoulders. Finding Giana would be my first priority. Hopefully, she had found Deus as we had discussed. That would save us time. Then, I had to find a way to free him of whatever shackles Lucy had placed on him. I was everyone's ticket out of this horrific place. I couldn't fail.

I pushed the thought from my mind. I knew the risks that were involved when I came up with this plan. My end goal would remain the same. Either I walked out of here with Deus, or I would remain here for all eternity.

The land surrounding us was crimson and barren. Red and orange sand glided across the ground, thanks to a harsh wind that whipped around us. The heat was excruciating, though I couldn't find the sun above us. The light bounced through the sparce clouds without a clear source of where the yellow beams originated from. No sign of life was visible for miles. The horizon blurred from the heat that seemed to steam from the ground.

"Welcome to The Desert of Desolation," said Belz, the Prince of Gluttony, moving to my side.

"This isn't a part of one of your territories?" I asked. I hadn't ever inquired as to how Hell had been divided between the seven.

"That would be correct," answered Mammon. "We needed a place to put all the riffraff that we created when we were younger and more ... experimental with our new gifts."

"Plus," interjected Levi, "this part of Hell has always seemed to have a mind of its own. None of us could ever bend it to our control, not even Lucifer, so we all decided that it would remain unclaimed."

"How big is it?" I asked, regretting that I hadn't packed a few more bottles of water.

"It's infinite," answered Mammon, Prince of Greed. "Hell is ever changing. This realm feeds off its victims' worst fears. It transforms into their torments and break down the souls that are trapped here. That is what feeds our power."

"I don't understand," I admitted.

"Hell fuels us," answered Gor, *sloth*. "Without us, there is no Hell, and without Hell, there is no us. The souls that end up here act as an energy source that keep this plane alive. Their energy feeds our power. In return, we tempt souls to this realm through our sins."

"So, what happens if Hell no longer exists?" I asked.

"That will never happen," Levi said in a flat tone. "There will always be good, and thus, a need for evil. Even if we die above, we will be trapped here to continue what we were created to do. It isn't pretty, but it is a necessity. That's how Father designed it."

"So how do we get out of here?" I asked. "Can we shift?"

Belz huffed. "Not unless you want to send up a big arrow signaling to Lucy where we are," he answered. "We're in his sandbox now. With the power that he draws from this place, he will be able to sense us the moment we unleash our magic."

"We use our legs, sweet Seren," said Mammon, leading the way into the dry desert.

"The plan is simple," stated Belz. "Get to friendlier territory, locate Deus, avoid Lucy, and get the fuck out of here as fast as angelically possible."

I stuck close to Levi and Gor. Everything around me felt off. My skin crawled with disgust yet, deep inside, something screamed home. I wondered if it was because I possessed a part of Lucifer's soul—the part he had used to save me from the car crash he orchestrated before I was even born.

I could feel the souls lingering nearby. They were hesitant to make contact, but I knew they wanted to reach out. To ask for help. I could feel their despair and their pain as if it were my own.

Within three hours into walking, I was unsure if I would make it out of this plane alive. The heat was nothing compared to the pain that now tore through my body thanks to the spirits. I fell back a few feet from the princes. My limbs felt so heavy as my boots dragged through the sand. The heat only became more excruciating and the air around me felt thick and tasted of ash and blood.

My vision grew fuzzy as the dehydration took hold. The horizon shifted unnaturally. I tried to focus, willing things around me to stop vibrating. A pulsating black figure far in the distance caught my attention. It flashed in and out of sight. I stopped and rubbed my eyes.

When I opened them again, the figure had jumped closer, disappearing and reappearing closer and closer with each blink. A growing scream accompanied the specter, rising in pitch with each shuddering flash until an image of a woman flared in front of me, bellowing a painful cry.

"Help ... me," she whispered, and disappeared.

A heartbeat later, something slammed into me. My entire body lit up and I froze. It was a soul. I felt their pain and heard their screams as their skin was peeled from them layer by layer like a potato. Their skin tore from their muscles as a demon in front of them laughed with amusement. The demon brought the skin to its mouth, slurping it up like a noodle.

The invisible spirit finally let go of me, slithering from my body. My knees hit the hot sand. I looked up just in time to see a white fog rushing towards me. It smashed into my chest, sending another zap of memories through my nervous system. This spirit had been suspended in the air by two hooks driven in either shoulder. Ever so slowly, the spirit was lowered into a pit where rats eagerly waited to feast on his flesh. The first rat leaped, digging its claws and teeth into his thigh, causing a stream of blood to trickle down his skin. The blood called to the other rats and the swarm of rodents unleashed on the man, tearing into him like an all-you-can-eat buffet.

The spirit left, only to be replaced by another, and then another. My body and mind were overwhelmed with horrific memories of torture. Body after body was dismembered, burned, spiked, impaled, dissected, and eaten. The experiences made horror films back on earth seem like fairytales.

Finally, I was able to cry out just before another spirit took hold. A flash of pain seared down my back; the spirit had his spine ripped out of his flesh by a pair of sharp claws while he lay strapped to a cold metal table. I screamed, the pain electrifying every nerve ending in my body.

The spirit let go quickly and I fell helplessly forward. Gor caught me before I face-planted into the sand. My body was completely exhausted. Even though they hadn't been my memories, I felt every bit of their fear, sorrow, and regret. And God, the pain. This was their future. To endure this type of torture for eternity.

"Seren," I heard Gor's voice. "We have to keep moving."

I took a deep breath in, forcing my body upright. I sat in the hot sand, allowing my body time to stop shaking. "What was that?" I asked.

"They fed off your humanity," answered Belz. "For a moment, your body was a haven for all they've endured here. That is why humans are not allowed into Hell unless they've died."

"I don't understand," I whispered.

"Your soul is not damned," explained Mammon. "Not yet at least. You are a connection back to earth, back to life itself."

"So," I said softly, "when they are inside of me, they no longer feel the pain and torment of this place? Because I am still alive?"

Belz nodded. "Exactly. Just like we feed off their souls once they're here, they were feeding off yours. Using you as a blockade."

I felt sorry for them in a way, to know this was what they would endure for eternity. I forced myself to stand on my weak legs. The brothers surrounded me, assessing my wellbeing.

"I'm fine," I said. "Let's keep moving."

I felt Mammon's eyes on me as I forced myself to drag one foot in front of the other. "What?" I finally said.

"You feel bad for them, don't you? The souls?" he asked.

"How couldn't you?" I replied.

"Don't," he said coldly. "Some of the souls here deserve every ounce of suffering they will endure." He focused on the horizon up ahead. "I'm fully aware of what I am and what Father cursed us to be. But the things I've done ... after thousands of years, the havoc I've caused dims in comparison to what some of these souls have done in their short human lifespans.

"I've watched them rape, murder, torture, steal, all without a single influence from any of us. The souls that end up here ... some make us look angelic. The pit where Deus most likely is holds some of the worst." He paused, looking at the ground. His face was haunted by his own thoughts. "Some of the things I've seen them do ... to children ... even I won't repeat." He inhaled, recentering himself. "They deserve every moment of pain, and then some."

He strolled ahead, leaving me to trail behind the group once again. I looked at the white wisps of souls, no longer feeling the pity I felt a moment ago.

Chapter Two

I lost track of time. The light, whether it was a sun or not, never set. I could feel my skin blistering under the unbearable heat. The princes didn't seem to mind. They must have been used to the brutal climate, since it was their home.

Levi gave me his shirt, which I wrapped around my head for protection from the rays. The brothers only took small amounts of water, leaving the majority for me. I was even more confident in my decision to leave Frankie back home. I wouldn't have wished that climate on my worst enemy.

My body screamed from exhaustion. Finally, we stopped in the middle of the desert and made camp. Mammon pitched our tents and we all gathered inside, taking comfort in the small reprieve from the heat and light. We nibbled on our rationed food. I wasn't hungry, but I forced the food down, knowing my body needed the energy. Without a single word, we slept.

As my mind drifted into slumber, the memory of Deus's death consumed me. The tenor in his voice just before he spoke his last words rang through me like a symphony. His lifeforce transferring into my body had felt like a warm wave crashing through every part of my being. And then, I saw his lifeless body again, only inches from me. How beautiful he remained … even in death.

I jolted awake, refusing to have those memories be our last. I would do whatever it took to get back the future we had been robbed of. Even if it meant I would have to cheat death itself.

It felt like we walked for days. God, how my body craved the crisp winter wind of Deus's balcony. After this, I would shift there immediately and bury myself in a heaping pile of soft, white snow. I escaped into my own fantasy. Deus next to me, brushing the small specks of snow from my hair. His smile, and the way his dimples accentuated his beautiful, sensual lips. The feeling of those lips on my skin. God, how I missed the taste of him.

"Finally," I heard Belz say.

I snapped out of my mind. A clearing of tall trees and vegetation lay before us, resembling a rainforest. The smell of soil and greenery replaced the scent of blood and ash.

"What the …" I said, not knowing what I was looking at.

"Hell shifted," answered Levi. "We're leaving one brutal climate and entering another. The Forest of Azlon."

"I hate this part," whispered Gor.

"Why? What's in there?" I asked.

"Remember I told you there were demons and monsters that were hard to kill?" Gor asked. I nodded. "Well, that's where most of them reside. Yay us."

"Come now, brother," said Mammon, pulling Gor into him. "I do recall a few good memories within those trees, back when we had just fallen."

"And what, per se, would those be?" asked Gor. "The time you all used me as bait to catch a hashon, or the time you all left me inside the hive with the tremonite?"

The brothers began to laugh ... even Levi.

"You're all assholes," snarled Gor. "Complete. Fucking. Assholes."

"What type of creatures are those?" I asked.

"You don't want to know," answered Belz.

"Just stay close and try not to make a lot of noise," instructed Levi. "They're going to smell you regardless, but the less noticeable you make yourself, the faster we can get through this part."

"Got it," I said, removing the shirt from my head and stuffing it in my pack.

The forest was an oasis: one of the most beautiful and alluring environments I had ever laid eyes on. It reminded me of the rainforest Nonna had brought me to for my first birthday dinner that we had all shared together. God, how things had changed since then. That memory felt like another life entirely.

Leaves and branches crunch underneath my feet. No matter how silent I tried to remain, nature seemed to make it impossible. The air was moist and damp. My skin welcomed the drink of water. The trees stretched miles high. The green canopy of leaves and vines twirled and danced above us. Flowers in different colors and vibrancies opened as we passed, seeming to watch us.

Birds sang alluring melodies high in the trees. Light from above bounced through water droplets that ornamented the large green leaves of the rainforest.

Thunk.

I went still. Slowly, I brought my hand up to my neck, where a sharp stinging began to pulsate from my skin. I wrapped my fingers around a small, needle-like thorn and pulled. A yellow, sticky substance dripped from the tip of the black shard. My body began to warm. The light around me played with my vision, creating beautiful spectrums of colors and shapes.

"Uh, guys," I managed to say, before the world around me began to spin like I was on a rollercoaster.

"Shit," said Levi, rushing towards me. His beautiful pale hair and the sharp angles of his face appeared in front of me just before I plummeted to the ground. In an instant, Levi threw me over his shoulder and began to run.

"Where is it?" I heard Mammon yell.

"The fuck if I know," answered Belz.

"It marked her," added Gor. "We have to kill it."

"No shit, little brother," said Belz.

Faster and faster Levi ran. My numb body bounced against his back as I tried to regain control of my extremities. I looked down at my fingers. Rainbows of colors and little balls of light drifted across my skin like stars. I laughed, enjoying this peaceful high. I had never done drugs before, but this was what I imagined it felt like.

In the right corner of my vision, a large green shape burst out from the foliage, hurtling towards us. The creature was massive, with the body of a lion, but the skin of a scorpion. Black talons stretched from its paws, digging into the earth, lending the creature momentum as it lunged forward.

Its scales shimmered from green to blue and then black. It could camouflage itself. The creature's teeth dripped with yellow venom as its jaw unhinged. Two more sets of razor-sharp teeth extended, growling and snapping. Behind its body, a tail thrashed and rose high in the air. A large black pod like a flower bloom opened, revealing hundreds of razor-sharp needles, undoubtedly laced with poison.

"A ... gg—ru," I tried to warn Levi, but my mouth was numb and uncooperative. I patted him on his back as hard as I could, which must have felt like a friendly tap.

"What?" he yelled.

"Looouuuuuoook," I slurred, now drooling on myself. Levi slid his eyes over his shoulder.

"Fuck!" he yelled, "Shields," he ordered, dropping me down in front of him. The princes formed a protective barrier around me, slamming their hands up in front of them. The small needles released from the creature's tail, slamming into the invisible wall of the princes' magic.

The beast slid to a halt on the other side of their shields. It lowered its eyes and growled, pacing slowly in front of us. Through my fuzzy vision, I watched it arch its long, scaled neck into the air before a barking sound echoed through the air. It repeated the action again.

"Fuck," growled Levi.

"We need to kill it, now," demanded Mammon. "Before his pack finds us."

"We can't use any more of our powers," said Gor. "The shields are small, but it could still be enough for Lucy to find us if he was looking, and we all know, he probably is."

"We only used a small portion," said Belz. "He doesn't know we're here. Not yet, at least."

Mammon unsheathed a sword from his belt. "Well, I guess we do this the old fashion way." He stepped up to the barrier and nodded at his brothers. The shield lowered and before I could blink, the creature attacked. Talons ripped and tore through the air. Mammon swung confidently, severing one of the creature's arms clean off. The thing yelped, raising its tail, dozens of little black needles zipping through the air.

The princes threw up their shields. Levi stayed close, protecting me with the small amount of power he was able to use. Belz and Gor joined Mammon, finally killing the thing before it could fire another batch of poisonous needles. Levi hauled me over his shoulder as we continued to run through the jungle. My lips buzzed and tingled, but my vision began to clear.

"We need to find shelter and clear our scent," said Belz.

"And how do you suggest we do that without using our powers?" asked Gor sarcastically.

"Well, what do you suggest, *brother*?" spat Belz.

"We need to get to water," answered Gor. "That way, they will lose our scent. We need to travel downstream for a while."

"You do remember what are in those waters, don't you?" asked Mammon, sporting a devilish grin.

"How could I forget," snapped Gor.

The other three brothers laughed while continuing to run. The faint crashing of water in the distance grew louder. Levi set me down by a large boulder.

"Can you move anything yet?" asked Levi.

"My ... my feeenguurs," I slurred, wiggling them slowly.

"On it," said Mammon. He and Belz gathered broken logs near the edge. Levi pulled rope from his bag and threw it at Gor. He wove the rope between each log, creating a small raft.

The princes snapped their attention to the clearing along the edge of the shoreline. The trees and bushes began to rustle. Something was coming.

"That's our queue," said Mammon, hauling the raft over his head.

"Up you go," said Levi, pulling my numb body from the ground.

He placed me on the raft as the brothers each entered the water, holding onto the corner of the logs. The water was rough and rapid as the currents carried us down stream. Four creatures, similar to the one the princes had just slaughtered, barreled through the tree line, stopping before their paws hit the water. They raced down the shoreline, pursuing us from land.

"What are they?" I asked.

"Numatras," answered Gor. "They hunt in packs and are known to tear apart their prey limb by limb."

"I think I prefer just a normal lion to that thing," I replied.

The brothers laughed.

"Welcome to Hell, goddess," said Mammon.

"Where your worst nightmares are surely going to come to life," added Belz.

"How long will they track us?" I asked.

"Not sure," said Levi, dodging a boulder. "They won't jump in after us though."

"And why is that?" I mumbled, still trying to wake my lips up.

"Because there's something far worse and bigger in this river," answered Belz. "The hashon."

"And if I recall," added Mammon, "it has a taste for Gor."

Levi, Belz, and Mammon started laughing.

"I despise all of you," spat Gor.

"Which leg did it take again?" asked Belz. "The right?"

"It was my left arm, but thank you for your concern," replied Gor. "The damn thing hunted me for a week and none of you even attempt to assist. You just left me, per usual."

"Oh, we didn't leave you," answered Mammon.

Gor froze, forcing the whole group to stop and look back at him.

"What do you mean?" he asked.

Mammon and Belz snickered to themselves.

"Leviathan?" asked Gor.

Levi grinded his back teeth together, attempting to hold in his amusement. "We were up in the trees," he finally answered, "watching the show."

Mammon and Belz lost control into a fit of laughter.

"Oh Father," Mammon gasped, "When that thing almost bit off your ass on the third night when you were sleeping. I almost gave away our position. I couldn't contain my laughter. Thankfully, your scream covered any other sounds."

"At that point," said Belz, "we were unsure of if it wanted to eat you or fuck you."

"Deus swore the thing wanted to mate with you," added Levi. "The way it toyed with you and took its time."

"It probably kept your arm as a reminder of your time together," Mammon said softly, reaching over and pinching Gor's cheek.

Gor swatted his hand away. "After this, I never want to see any of you again," he growled.

"And how many times have we heard that?" asked Belz.

"At least a few times a decade," answered Levi. The brothers continue to laugh together, sharing stories and memories as we drifted down the dangerous river, Gor's lover lurking somewhere beneath.

CHAPTER THREE

Thirty minutes floating in the rough river and the numatra creatures finally gave up their pursuit. Thankfully, sensation was returning to my extremities, and we had yet to encounter Gor's girlfriend.

We finally banked on the side of the river, where we made camp and took turns resting from the rigorous swim. I trailed away from the group, looking for Giana. It had been days, and I had yet to see any sign of her. I hadn't just promised to save Deus, but also my former fiancé's sister. I felt a comforting hand on my shoulder. I turned to see Gor towering over me.

"You shouldn't stray too far from the group," he instructed.

"I know," I answered. "I was just looking for—" I cut myself off. I hadn't told him my plan to bring Giana back to the living.

"For whom?"

I bit the bottom of my lip. "For ... Giana. She was supposed to find me once we entered through the portal."

"She crossed over?" he asked, surprise lacing his voice. "I thought she ..." he trailed off, but his disappointment and sadness were plain.

I reached out, taking Gor's hand in mine. "I'm bringing her home with us when we leave," I said softly.

His eyes went wide. "What?"

"She crossed over to help me find Deus. She's going to help us all get out of here and she's coming back with us. That was our deal."

"Seren, you can't just steal souls from this place. It's already going to be challenging enough to get Deus home."

"Are you telling me you don't want Giana to come back with us?"

"Of course, I am not saying that, but ... there is a process for a reason."

"Gor, this place ... this life has stolen enough from me already. Giana was an innocent. I don't know why she ended up in this place, but I am not leaving her down here for eternity. Especially not after what I experienced back in that desert. I don't care about the stupid rules anymore. As I've proven time and time again, they don't apply to me."

Being a tribrid—genetically witch, goddess, and demon—had done nothing for me except put a target on my back and endanger the ones I loved most. After everything I had endured and lost, the universe owed me. If I wanted to use my powers over death to create a gate and bring someone back from Hell, then that's exactly what I was going to do, rules be damned.

Gor smiled, dropping his head. "I can see why Deus loves you so much." He pinched my chin between his first finger and thumb.

"Save the complements until I get us all out of here. Then, you can stroke my ego all you'd like."

Gor laughed softly, pulling me into a side hug. "Let's get some rest. We're going to need it for what comes next."

"And what new challenges does Hell have in store for us?"

"We'll have to travel through Satan's territory. Wrath. A lot of killing, torturing, and brutality. It's not a place for the faint of heart."

"I would expect nothing less," I said, wrapping my arm around his waist as we walked back to the others.

That night, I didn't sleep. I had an eerie feeling I couldn't shake. I tried to focus on Deus, reaching out through our mental bond, but I remained alone in the darkness. Over the past year, I had grown accustomed to his presence inside of my head, the soft caress that would push against the walls within my mind. The sound of his laugh. The softness of his voice. God, I missed him. He was my reason for being. My reason for breathing.

After an hour or two of sleep, Levi woke me and we continued our hike through the jungle. We stayed close to the shoreline and followed the river out to a large waterfall. I stepped up to the edge of what could have easily been a thousand-foot drop. Memories of my attempt to end my life flashed behind my eyes.

I looked over the waterfall, feeling a tightening in my stomach. The trauma and torment I had endured during my time of depression still haunted me. I shook my head, pushing those moments deep inside of a box I kept in the dark.

Across the horizon, Satan's territory was visible. Black smoke and fog billowed high in the sky. The horizon looked like it had been painted with blood.

"How are we getting down?" I asked.

Levi pulled out a rope, wrapping it around my waist and then his own. "We're climbing down."

"You've got to be kidding me," I replied. My body was already weakened from the past few days of constant walking and fighting off the creatures of Hell.

"Father, I miss shifting," Belz murmured before he began his decent.

"Deus owes us at least a few centuries of debauchery after this rescue mission," added Mammon.

"If I don't see you lot for a few centuries, that will be the best reward I could ask for," said Gor, climbing down the side of the rocky cliff.

"Always whining, little brother," said Mammon.

"Stop with the act and just admit that you love us," added Belz.

"Not a chance," Gor said, moving down the wall. Mammon and Belz chuckled.

I sat on my bottom, hesitant to take the first step down. Levi slid his hand comfortingly down my arm. "If you fall, I got you," he said with a soft smile.

"You promise?" I whispered.

He nodded. "If anything happened to you on my watch, I don't know who I'd be afraid of more: Deus or Frankie." We both laughed at the memory of the two people we loved the most. I nodded, finding the first foothold as we began to descend the side of the waterfall.

The brothers all climbed at my pace, staying strategically positioned around me to assist if I missed a step and fell. We climbed forever. My arms were numb and my fingers cramped from the constant bending and strain they were forced to endure. Sweat rolled down the back of my neck.

Mammon sang almost the entire way down. I focused on the sound of his voice while my wobbly legs scraped across the rocks. My knees grew raw from the sharp edges of the stones. Warm blood seeped through the fabric of my pants, but I forced myself to continue.

I was concentrating on my breathing, moving to the tempo of Mammon's song, when a massive gust of wind slammed me against the hard edges of the rocks. I flattened my body against the surface, a cut ripping on my face with a sharp sting. I looked over my shoulder to see a massive bat-like creature soaring through the air, circling around towards us.

"Move now!" demanded Belz.

The five of us climbed faster down the mountain. My body yelled in protest, but the adrenaline quickly kicked in, bypassing my sore and tired muscles. The creature screeched and flew towards us. It had the legs and arms of a praying mantis, but the physical body of a bat, covered in short, black hair. Its eyes were yellow, and it had sharp pointed ears. Its wings looked to be made of leather.

The creature slammed into me, causing my grip on the rock to falter. I fell back away from the wall. I went to yell, but the rope around me cinched on my waist, causing a flash of pain to ripple through my body. Levi secured himself to the side of the wall, bracing my weight. Mammon reached down, pulling me up by my arm, holding my sore body against his.

"Keep moving," Mammon instructed.

I forced myself back against the wall and obeyed. The creature circled back around, closing in on our group. In a flash, Gor pulled a sword from his belt and swung, taking off the flying bat's arm. Black blood splattered across my face, but I didn't stop moving.

We finally made it to the ground. Levi and I detached the rope that connected us before falling into a circle with the other princes. I turned my focus to the sky. A dozen bat-like creatures now surrounded us above.

"Weapons!" yelled Belz, pulling his sword and taking a stance. I pulled a gun from my hip, but Levi shook his head.

"The sound will attract more of them," Levi explained. He handed me a spare sword and I hunched down, my palms beginning to sweat. In the blink of an eye, they soared to the ground. One landed in front of me, slashing and nipping at anything it could get its claws and teeth into. I swung, but it backed away.

Another creature flew low, attempting to grab hold of me, but I ducked, rolled on the ground, and sliced the leg of the creature in front of me. It yelped, and I brought the blade through the air, down its wing, cutting the leathery material in half. Blood sprayed my face. I closed my eyes, only for a moment. Two claws buried into my shoulder and I was hoisted into the air.

I flailed, screaming from the pain. If he got me any higher off the ground, I was a goner. I wrapped my hand around the gun at my hip, pulling it free and pointing it towards the creature. I fired twice, hitting it in the chest. It let go, sending me crashing back towards the hot, brittle dirt. Gor opened his arms, breaking my fall before I hit the ground.

"I'm sorry," I gasped, fighting the pain that radiated from my shoulders. "I had no choice."

"I know," Gor said. Another dozen creatures appeared in the sky. We readied ourselves for battle. My mind refocused. I pushed the pain aside, just as Mal had taught me, and swung.

Creature after creature. Limb after limb. I no longer felt or thought. All I did was act. We were surrounded by their black leathered wings and hairy bodies. The sound of their thin, membranous wings would haunt my dreams forever. My skin bore repeated slashes from their talons, but I didn't stop, not even for a moment to catch my breath. I didn't know how long we fought, but time no longer mattered. All the mattered was surviving.

When the last of the creatures retreated in the air, I took a cleansing breath and looked at the destruction before us. At least three dozen of those things lay at our feet, motionless. I collapsed to my knees from sheer exhaustion.

"Looks like were having bat for dinner tonight," Belz joked. We all laughed, breathing heavily.

"Are you alright?" asked Levi, making his way towards me.

"I'm alive, so that's a plus," I answered.

"I'm very impressed with your sword skills," commented Mammon. "Who taught you?"

"Malphasia," I answered, pressing my hands to my shoulders. I was still bleeding. Levi pulled some cloth from one of the packs and wrapped my wounds.

"Mm, she is an exquisite demon," replied Mammon. "And that beautiful red hair of hers is—"

"Not the time to get a boner, brother," interrupted Gor.

"Just reliving a delightful memory," Mammon said with a wink.

"Can you walk?" asked Levi.

"Yes," I answered. "Just needed a minute."

"There are caves up ahead," said Belz. "About four hours from here. Let's head that direction and make camp there."

"Agreed," said Levi.

I forced myself up and followed the brothers, leaving the wake of our destruction behind.

Satan's territory was barren, a lot like the desert. The soil was made of some type of red clay. The air was hot and thick, and the tangy smell of blood stung my nostrils. We found a cave on the outskirts of his land and made camp. I was exhausted, too tired to even eat. I found a corner of the cave and passed out without a single word.

Too soon, I felt Levi's hands shaking me back into consciousness. I opened my eyes and his beautiful face tensed. He brought his finger to his lips, signaling me not to speak. Night had fallen in this territory, and we were surrounded by darkness. The cool embrace was something I had missed. Mammon, Belz, and Gor were standing towards the mouth of the cave silently.

"Scouts," Levi whispered.

"Shadows would be nice about now, goddess," whispered Mammon.

I let a small trickle of my power go, folding us within the darkness. Two reptilian creatures on their hind legs entered the cave. Their eyes were offset to the sides of their heads. Only holes appeared for ears. They had razor-sharp teeth that hung out of their mouths. Their bodies were lean and looked fragile, but they were armed.

One sniffed. "Smell that?" It said in a deep voice.

"Ya ... magic," the other replied.

Mammon and Belz surged forward, tackling the creatures to the ground. They slashed and fought, but before the scouts could harm the princes, their heads were removed from their bodies.

"Time to go," instructed Belz.

I gathered my pack and fell in line with the others. At night, Satan's territory roared. Firearms and cannons exploding in the distance. Bright bursts of light sparked and flashed over the horizon. Pillars of fire sprung from the ground into the air, forming funnels like tornadoes. We headed towards a grouping of rundown buildings.

"How fast can we get out of here?" I asked.

"Our goal is to find some horses," answered Gor. "That should cut our travel time in half. So, I would say a few hours if we don't run into any problems."

I peeked inside one of the windows of a building. Souls, in the shapes of people were huddled together, cowering in the corner. One of the figures looked to be no more than thirteen years old. An elderly woman looked up at me, her mouth quivering.

"Please," she gasped. "Please ... help us." I was frozen, unable to formulate a sentence. She crawled across the floor, reaching out, taking my arm in her hands. Before my eyes, the elderly woman turned into a decaying shell of a human. Her cheeks hollowed out; her eyes turned black. Blood stained her wrinkled, loose skin.

She smiled wickedly at me. "Here!" she yelled. "I've found something the prince would—"

A hand slammed into her neck, grasping the woman's throat.

"I don't think so," Belz said. He opened his mouth wider than I had ever seen one of them do before. His eyes blazed orange as her soul turned into a black fog, funneling into his mouth.

The other two souls attempted to make a run for it, but Mammon and Levi stopped them, doing the same. Gor placed a soft hand on my elbow. I jumped, confused and terrified by what I had just witnessed.

"They absorbed their energy," Gor explained. "Their very essence. A mercy really. They no longer exist. No more pain or suffering. The ultimate end."

"Then why not do that to all of them? Why leave them here to suffer?" I asked.

"Hell needs them to exist, and we need Hell, remember? If we did that to all of them, there would be nothing left. It's all a system of checks and balances."

"If Hell has checks and balances, then why is Lucifer more powerful than the rest of you?"

"It hasn't always been that way," said Belz, making his way over to us.

"In the beginning," said Mammon, "when we first fell, we were equals. Our realms were balanced. We weren't forced to trick or tempt people into committing travesties to fuel our realms. Everything worked in unison."

"There was a natural peace," added Levi, "for Hell, at least."

"When Deus broke away from Lucifer," continued Belz, "and we began to go our separate ways, Lucifer sought ultimate dominion over this plane. I think it was some pathetic attempt to keep us all close, to make sure we could never truly leave him. But it threw off the balance we had known."

"Pride's territory began to expand into each of ours, consuming and possessing what it could," said Mammon. "But Hell still demanded a balance."

"Thus, our venture into the earthly plane," Gor chimed in. "Tempting Father's precious creations was easy enough. All they seemed to need was a little push, and over the edge they would go, helping us balance the needs of our home in return."

"So," I said, still processing the history lesson, "if Lucifer was eliminated, returning his territory to its normal size, Hell wouldn't be so ... horrific?"

A deep laugh rattled in Belz's chest. "Hell will always be a place of torment where the worst of mankind will spend eternity for refusing Father's love and grace. But yes, in a way, if things could return to the way Father had originally intended, I suppose the necessary torment would lessen. Though, no one can interfere with another's free will. There are some souls that are beyond saving ... even for you."

Come on," said Gor, extending his hand out towards me. I took it, allowing him to pull me along.

I tried not to focus on the war that surrounded me. The brothers quietly scurried from hiding place to hiding place, going unnoticed.

Souls were caged, being tortured by creatures so hideous, I couldn't find the words to describe them. Bodies were impaled on long wooden spikes, Vlad-style. People were being cut apart with swords, chainsaws, and other sharp objects. Wrath was a constant war zone. Day and night. There was no peace, no rest, no surrender.

It took everything I had inside to remain silent. At times, I wanted to scream in fear. My instincts yelled to save those being castrated and chopped limb from limb. As we knelt behind a massive stone wall, I buried my face in Gor's chest, trying to block out the living hell that surrounded us.

As we made our way into a barren section of the territory, we stumbled across four horses that were tied to wooden post. The horses were black and gray, but they were ... decomposing. I could see the flesh falling away from their hides. Their manes were patchy, and I could see holes that went clear through one of their necks. One of the horses huffed and turned its face as I approached. I stumbled back in shock. There were two empty eye sockets where there should have been eyes. Half of the creature's jaw was missing, exposing his teeth fully.

"Hell," whispered Gor, "remember?"

"How could I forget?" I mumbled. Gor got onto the horse, reaching down to help me up. I settled in behind him, wrapping my arms around his lean waist as we took off through the night. We rode hard and fast, not stopping for anyone or anything. I closed my eyes, resting my head on his back, trying to tune out the cries and pleas for help that I knew would haunt me for eternity. Small tears escaped my eyes.

Chapter Four

"Ah, home at last," I heard Belz say.

I sat straight up, realizing I had dosed off against Gor's back. There was some type of invisible belt that kept me fastened to him so I wouldn't fall off.

"Did you have a nice nap?" Gor asked.

"Yes, thank you," I replied. I felt the invisible belt loosen. "Where are we?"

"Crossing into Belz's lands." I looked over his shoulder. A golden road waited ahead. A ripple of power radiated around me as our horses left Satan's territory. Immediately, Mal appeared, holding Giana by the arm. My heart leaped.

"Giana," I yelled, tumbling from the horse, rushing towards her and embracing her. Being able to touch her ... it was unreal. I pulled back, smiling from ear to ear. Her body was tense, her smile weak. "What's wrong? What is it?"

She opened her mouth, but Mal stepped up beside her.

"Prince Resnov has summoned you," Mal said in a demanding tone. At the sound of his name, I stopped breathing. Every neuron in my body fired. It took everything I had not to yell and jump for joy. I reached through my mind towards him, but I felt nothing.

"You found him? You found Deus?" I asked Mal, not able to contain my excitement.

"He is at his castle, where he belongs," Mal said. She was cold. There was no sign of the demon warrior who had trained me for all those months.

"Mal, what is going on?" I asked, searching for the friend I thought I knew. "Are you okay? Where's Hashen?"

She ignored me, focusing on the princes.

"What do you mean he's back at his castle?" asked Belz. "He should be in the tormentor's pit."

"I am sure the prince will explain everything once you arrive," Mal answered. She turned and made a circling motion with her hand. A portal opened, revealing a luxurious room on the other side. She pulled Giana with her. "Follow me."

"Something isn't right," said Levi.

"No shit," added Mammon.

"There is no way Lucy would allow Deus to return to his lands," said Belz.

"Maybe ... maybe Lucifer gave up," I said hopefully.

"You don't know him like we do," said Levi. "That will never be a possibility."

Mal appeared on the other side of the portal. "Are you coming?" she asked.

The princes' faces were streaked with worry and confusion. Levi stepped up next to me.

"Stay close to us," he instructed. "You go nowhere without one of us. Do you hear me?"

I nodded. One after another, we stepped through the portal. The room had a large bed adorned with a thick comforter and pillows. Dressers made of rich red wood stood along the walls, below some very graphic artwork of people in compromising positions. I looked at Mal. Giana was gone.

"Where did Giana go?" Gor asked.

"To her own quarters, for now," Mal answered. "Lady Salvo will stay here. I will show the rest of you to your chambers, unless you wish to return to your own territories."

"That won't be happening," answered Belz.

"We stay where Seren stays," snapped Gor. "Nonnegotiable."

"Either you can trust your brother to keep his mate safe, or I can escort the rest of you back to Gluttony's territory where I will alert Prince Morningstar of your arrival," Mal said, staring the brothers down with dead eyes. They each looked at me for direction. I nodded, assuring them I would be safe.

"Good," Mal said, turning her attention back to me. "You will find clothing in the armoire. Please bathe and freshen up. Dinner will be served at seven." She nodded before heading towards the exit. Levi stayed planted next to my side. Mal froze in the doorway as the others passed into the hall.

"Prince Whitelore," she said. "I assure you; Prince Resnov will not allow any harm to come to Lady Salvo. Now if you'd please ..."

"I'll be fine," I whispered, smiling up at him.

"I don't have a good feeling about this," he said.

"I'm not exactly helpless anymore, Levi."

He smiled down at me. "No ... you're not. If you need anything, yell."

I laughed. "Got it."

He hesitantly left my side.

"Mal," I called once the others had gone.

Her body stiffened. She turned her head slowly towards me. "Yes, Lady Salvo," she replied.

I moved towards her to stand face to face. "Lady Salvo?" I asked. "You haven't called me that since the first time we met. What is going on? Did you accomplish what we planned?"

Mal and Hashen had agreed to ready Lust's armies, just in case we needed backup. They were my mate's right and left hand, two of the most deadly creatures I had ever known. I hadn't seen Mal for a few days, but I had full faith in her abilities and cunning wit.

She took a deep breath, removing her eyes from mine. "I serve the prince, Lady Salvo. You might do well to remember that." Without further explanation, she shut the door.

I stripped out of my soiled clothing and quickly showered, scrubbing the blood from my skin. I rebandaged my shoulders, attempting to cover the bruises and scratches, but took little care. The only thing I could focus on was finding Deus.

I threw the armoire open, pulling a dress of sheer fabric off the hanger. Every option was revealing and would have been better suited for a brothel. The dress wasn't going to be on my body long enough for me to care. I rushed into the hall, searching behind every door. This castle was nothing like our home back on earth. Red infused into everything—every rug, pillar, tapestry, wall.

Sounds of passion came from various rooms. Moving pictures of sexual acts hung out in the open, coming to life as I passed. The low lighting was tranquil, creating the perfect ambience for a tryst. I turned a corner to find two massive wooden doors at the end of the hall. It could only be his room.

I rushed towards the doors, pushing them open. My heart was racing like it might explode out of my chest. I searched until my eyes found what my heart desired. What I had been robbed of. Who I had been missing.

His shirt lay casually open in the front, revealing his toned, tanned, muscular chest. His midnight dark hair was tousled and unkept and his pants hung low on his hips. Strongs hands braced his forearms on the table where he studied a piece of parchment.

Then his eyes rose to meet mine, those beautiful crystal-blue eyes that I had fallen head-over-heels in love with. Everything about this man, I craved.

His back straightened as I stood in the doorway. My emotions roiled: relief, joy, happiness, love, and an overwhelming need to cry. Or scream. The thought of a life without him ... it didn't make sense.

I barreled into him, wrapping my arms around his neck as I smashed my mouth against his. I needed to feel him more than I needed to breathe. Relief exploded from me. I felt him pull me in closer. This was my home; here, with him, my savior, my love—my mate.

He picked me up by my ass, slamming me onto the table. Papers went flying everywhere, but neither of us seemed to care. My hands roamed along his toned, firm body, needing more. I ripped the rest of his shirt off, tossing it to the floor. My mouth moved to his neck, then his shoulders, then his chest.

His fingers tangled through my hair at the nape of my neck. He pulled my lips away from his skin, forcing me to face him. I whimpered, still needing more of him. His eyes swirled a vibrant shade of red. He smiled down at me and I nearly came undone. That beautiful, bright smile, with those long canines I loved to feel scrape against my skin. Those deep dimples that shaped the edges of his luscious lips.

"Well, hello to you too," he said in a deep, sensual voice.

"I've ... I've missed you so much," I gasped, fighting back the tears that welled in my eyes. "I never thought I'd see you again. After everything I—"

"You've missed me, have you?" he asked. He bent down and nipped my bottom lip between his teeth. "Why don't you show me just how much?" he whispered along my ear. I pulled his lips back into mine, moving my fingers to the button of his pants. I felt his hands slide up my dress, finally grazing my skin.

Heat pooled between my legs. My desire threatened to shatter me. I needed him and I needed all of him. I forced his pants down, reaching for him, but before I could pull him free, a force shuddered through the room, ripping him from my arms. His beautiful body went flying into the nearest wall, freezing in place.

Gor stood behind me, his hand extended out to Deus, Giana at his side. Mammon, Belz, and Levi rushed in, looking between their brothers and me. I straightened my dress, sliding off the table.

"What in the hell do you think you're doing?" I snapped, marching in front of Gor. "Let him go, now."

"Not a chance," Gor growled. His eyes were glowing a shade of golden brown. Deus laughed behind me, still glued to the wall.

"I have a feeling you've discovered something you'd like to share with the class," said Mammon.

"Tell them," Gor instructed Giana. He threw out another hand towards Deus, fighting to hold him in place.

Giana's big green eyes turned to me. I could see the sadness behind them. "Deus, he's ... he's not whole," she whispered.

"What are you talking about?" I demanded, stepping towards her.

Belz inhaled a sharp breath. "Fuck," he said, dropping his head.

"His soul … it's not there. It's not intact," Giana explained.

"What is she talking about?" I demanded, but the brothers all stood silent. "Someone answer me before I light your asses on fire!"

"I can feel him, Seren," continued G, her face twisted as if she were in physical pain. "There is nothing good inside of him. All there is … is darkness and lust."

"Lucifer can separate our souls from our physical forms," explained Levi. "He must have ripped Deus's soul from his body. That's why he was allowed to return to his lands."

"What does that mean?" I asked.

"It means," Belz stepped up, "this isn't your mate. This isn't the real Deus. It's the pure demon version of him. The original Prince of Lust … before he found his soul. Before he rediscovered his humanity. His heart."

I looked back at the man I loved, feeling an emptiness there. "Where is his soul?" I asked.

"I'm assuming the pit," answered Mammon.

"Then I'm going to the pit," I said.

Deus laughed again. I looked back at his beautiful face. He shook his head as if amused. "That, I would pay to see," he said, winking at me.

Mal barged into the room. "Release him," she ordered. The princes did nothing, unfazed by her demand. "Release him now, or this entire realm will destroy you."

Gor looked back at Levi. Levi nodded. Gor dropped his hands. Deus landed gracefully on his feet.

Gor turned to face Mal. "You really think this realm can take four princes of Hell?"

"No," she said smugly. "Not on our own. But with Prince Lucifer and Prince Satan … easily."

"Now, now," interrupted Dues, strolling towards us. "There will be no need for that." He stopped next to me.

I looked up at him, searching for the passion and love I had always seen behind his eyes, but Giana was right. There was something missing. He winked at me with empty eyes, then turned to Gor, one eyebrow arched. "Now, that is no way to say hello, little brother."

Gor stepped up, chest to chest with Deus. "Don't you fucking lay another hand on her, you disgusting filth."

"I was not the one who initiated our wonderful reunion," Deus said, smirking down at me. He turned back to Gor. "And who are you to tell me what I can and cannot do with my *mate*."

Bam! Gor's fist landed on Deus's jaw.

"She is not your mate," growled Gor. "She is nothing to you when you are in this state. You do not touch, look, or speak to her, unless one of us are with you. You stay out of her fucking head as well. And I swear to Father, if any harm comes to her, soulless or not, I will destroy you and everything you've built."

Belz came to Gor's side, placing a hand on his shoulder. "Belphagor, I think you've made your point."

Deus's eyes blazed with fire. "Little brother," he said, grabbing Gor by the throat. He lifted him off the floor. To Gor's credit, he stayed completely still, no panic visible. "How dare you come into *my* house, into *my* room, and lay *your* hands on me." With an effortless thrust, he tossed Gor into the wall, splintering the stone into an impression of a body. Gor fell to the floor, gasping for air.

Giana and I rushed to his side, checking him over. "Gor," I whispered. He nodded, letting me know he was alright.

"Would anyone else like to take a shot?" asked Deus, throwing his arms out in an inviting manner. "No ... no one? I didn't think so. Apparently, we need a few rules set in place. Rule one: you don't lay a hand on me, nor do you use your power against me in any fashion. Rule two: do not tell me what the fuck I can and cannot do. And rule three," he paused, looking at each of us, "enjoy the debauchery, ladies and gents. It's been far too long since we've all been in Hell together at once. Time to make a few new memories, wouldn't you say?"

"That's enough, Asmodeus," spat Belz. "You've made your point." At that moment, two demon females, one with red skin and the other green, stepped out from another entrance at the back, which I assumed led to his bedchamber. They were sinfully beautiful and adorned in only underwear. My heart fell into my stomach. Gor took my hand and squeezed as we rose to our feet.

"Prince," one of them said sweetly. "Have you brought more guests to join us?" Deus smiled at her.

"Any takers?" he asked, looking at each of us for an answer. When his eyes met mine, I looked away, fighting with every ounce of control I had not to break down in front of him.

Mammon went to step forward, but Belz stopped him, grunting his disapproval.

"Looks like this crowd is a bit dull, my loves," he called back to them. That was *my* title. He was using it for those whores.

I began to shake. Gor squeezed tighter while I fought to hold back my abilities, but the emotions were too overwhelming, the pain and the anger too great. The power welled inside of me and I threw my hands out, unleashing my white flame towards the two women. Black and red sparks flashed between my flames. They screamed in agony as their bodies quickly incinerated to ash.

Deus watched, laughing. "Well, someone appears a bit jealous," he said smugly.

I stormed over to him and slapped him across the face. He adjusted his jaw, his smile now holding a sharp edge. "Do I have to remind you what rule number one is?" he said, tilting his head to the side.

"I don't give a fuck about your rules, you selfish prick," I said behind gritted teeth. His eyes began to glow red, his anger taking hold. I stepped closer, unafraid. "What are you going to do *prince*?" I said mockingly. "Send me to Hell? Too late."

I unleashed my power again, blasting him backwards into the table I had been ready to take him upon only moments before. I turned and stormed out of the room, stopping next to Mal.

"That is not the Asmodeus you pledged yourself to," I said to her. "Where is your honor and devotion now, Malphasia?" I pushed past her and stalked down the hall. The other princes and Giana followed until we were behind closed doors.

"Now that was impressive, goddess," said Mammon, patting me with pride on the shoulder.

Giana rushed towards me. I wrapped my arms around her. "Are you okay?" I asked. "Did they hurt you?"

"I'm fine," she said. "Really. I was caught snooping a few days ago and they've kept me locked up in a room until now. Seems like they knew you'd be on your way." She paused, her eyes filling with tears. "Seren, I am so sorry he—"

"Don't," I stopped her. "I'll find a way to get him back. I didn't come all this way for nothing."

"That's impossible, sweetheart," said Belz. "Only Lucy can put his soul back. And knowing him, he isn't going to want to lose his favorite brother anytime soon."

"This is a trap," Gor said, looking lost in thought. "He's going to notify Lucifer that we're here, and he has Seren. We need to leave, now."

"I agree," said Levi. "Even though you're more powerful, he can still take it. He can still consume your soul, and your power along with it. He will make the torture you went through back home look like child's play."

I thought over the details of all we had learned. As my mind raced, a plan began to form. "Lucifer's power," I whispered.

"Excuse me?" asked Belz.

"Lucifer's power," I repeated. "If Lucifer can separate and return a soul back into a body, that means I can do the same."

Mammon threw his hands out in an exasperated manner. "See ... this is why I don't fall in love. It makes you reckless and stupid."

"Oh, shut the hell up," said Belz. "Must we remind you of Trinity a few decades back?"

Levi chuckled. "If I recall," he said, "you were the cause of the Great War. All because you fell in love with the enemy's wife."

"Both of you shut the fuck up," growled Mammon, turning away from them.

Belz stepped forward. He looked down at me behind his brown lashes. His blue eyes twinkled. "I've watched you overcome so much in the small time I have had the honor of knowing you. I'd be prideful if I didn't admit I was impressed. How young you are, yet how powerful you've become. If anyone can save our brother, it would be you, Seren De Salvo.

Witch, goddess, demon ... whatever you are, I stand by you."

"Thank you, Beelzebub. Truly," I said with a soft smile.

Belz nodded with a small grin before turning to his brothers. "We still have time. Deus might be soulless, but that also means his ego is cranked up to one hundred."

"He's unpredictable in this state," Gor said. "We don't know what side he's on or what game he's playing. Too many unknown variables for my liking."

"I just need a little more time to formulate a plan," I pleaded. "I know I can reach him. He isn't lost ... he can't be."

"And what do we do about Lucy?" asked Mammon.

"We entertain Deus's ego," suggested Belz. "Stroke it, if we must. No one do a damn thing to piss him off. If he thinks we're solely here for him, ready to go along with whatever plan he might have, that may deter him from calling in big brother."

"And if you're wrong?" asked Mammon, rubbing his brow in frustration. "If Asmodeus has already notified Lucifer of our presence ... then what?"

"Well, in that case," said Levi. "Looks like we'll have a dinner to prepare for. It will make The Consort look like Christmas."

"I do love a good dinner and a show," said Belz, smiling widely.

Once everyone left, I casted a protection spell around my room, unsure if it would even do me any good down here. I sat on the edge of the bed, thinking over everything that I had endured to get to this point. I touched my lips, still able to taste him. God, how good he had felt ... how familiar. Finally, I let free my emotions. Tears spilled out as I cradled a pillow. *Let it out now*, I thought. Tonight was sure to bring more disappointment and pain.

CHAPTER FIVE

"**A**re you ready?" asked Giana.

"Does it really matter?" I replied, looking at my reflection in the mirror. I had chosen a revealing red dress that covered only small amounts of my skin. The fabric was light and sheer and flowed when I walked, the shoulders falling sensually across my arms.

"I wish there was something I could do," she said, standing behind me.

"You being here is enough." I gave her a small smile. "So, tell me, how was it to finally be able to touch Gor?"

She smiled bashfully. "Better than I could have anticipated. He's so gentle and kind."

I laughed. "He is the tamer out of the seven, I'll give him that."

"I tried to kiss him, but he stopped me. He told me he didn't want that memory tainted with the vileness of this place."

"Ever the romantic, that one."

"He's right ... but honestly, I don't care. I just want him so badly. I've never felt this way about anyone before. I never really had the chance before I got sick."

"Take things slow, G. As soon as we get home, you'll have your time with him ... I promise."

She reached out, taking my hand. "Thank you," she whispered softly. "For agreeing to bring me home."

I touched her face gently. "You don't belong here. I don't know why you're here, but this isn't your fate. It can't be."

She laughed softly. "Most people wouldn't—couldn't—have done anything to change my fate. I can see why you have so many suitors: my brother, Orion, a prince of Hell."

My heart tugged at the mention of Orion. I dropped my gaze.

"Is ... is Orion here?" I asked. If he was, I'd bring him back too. I'd stop at nothing to—

"No, he's not. I think he went up instead of down."

A part of me was relieved, but another thought cut through me painfully. I could never bring him home to Delphine.

"Well, at least he made it to a better place than this. He deserved that."

"I agree," she said. A knock came at the door. Gor peeked inside. Giana's face lit up.

"Am I interrupting?" he asked.

"Not at all," she said, rushing to him. She took his hands, lacing their fingers together. He smiled down at her. A true and loving smile: one I hadn't seen on him before.

"Well," I said, slightly uncomfortable. "I guess it's showtime. Where are the others?"

"Already in the dining hall," Gor answered.

I turned back to the mirror. I felt like there was a weight on my chest. I missed my family. Frankie, Nonna, and Aunt Thora were always my strength when I needed it the most. "I can do this," I whispered.

"You can," replied Giana. "You're his mate. If anyone can reach him, it's you."

Gor's face was unreadable.

"You think it's pointless, don't you?" I asked.

He looked away from me. "I know firsthand what is feels like to be without a soul," he answered. "The unlimited power. The carelessness. The total clarity of mind. I would always choose to have a soul, to love, and make true connections. It's worth the challenges that come with it. But ... once free of that burden, it is very hard to convince one of us to take on a soul and all the regret and repentance that follows.

"In Deus's case ... he died, Seren. He believes he's trapped here forever. Why would he take back his soul, if it only meant feeling the pain of this place? Living a life without the joys of earth. The pleasure and the beauty of it all. A life without you."

"But I can bring him back," I answered.

"It's a risk. It's never been done before. What if he takes his soul back and then is stuck here?"

"Then I will stay with him," I answered.

"Who are you staying with?" Deus said, entering the room unannounced.

I gave him a small smile. "No one," I answered. Gor rolled his eyes at him, pulling Giana against his side.

"Found a pet, have we, brother?" asked Deus. "Could have picked one that was alive, though. That would probably be more beneficial when you're top side and all. Someone you can actually touch and feel."

"Fuck off, Asmodeus," snarled Gor.

Deus laughed. "Always so emotional this one." He assessed Giana, then smiled at me. "Antonio Simonelli's sister, yes."

"I am," Giana answered before I could.

"Would you two please give Deus and me a moment?" I asked politely.

Gor looked at me with a warning expression. "I'll be fine. I am sure the Prince of Lust wouldn't mind escorting me to dinner, being the gracious host he is."

"Seren," Gor whispered.

"Oh, for Father's sake," snapped Deus. "Stop playing guard dog and fuck off." Deus raised his hand. With a swift snap of his wrist, Gor and Giana flew backwards out of the room, the door slamming shut after them.

Deus's eyes blazed with hunger. The dress had affected him as intended. He slowly approached me, his gaze drifting over my barely covered form. My breasts perked in response to him. I craved his touch ... his mouth ... the feeling of him inside of me.

I licked my lips, trying to stay focused. "You look very handsome tonight," I said softly.

"Thank you. And you look absolutely delicious."

I smiled, unable to contain it. I looked up at him, feeling my heart swell. "Deus," I whispered. "I want you to come home with me."

"I am home."

"I mean ... back to earth. Back to Romania. Our home there."

He looked at me with a puzzled expression. "If I recall correctly, I died in order to save you, stripping any chance I have of ever returning to that plane. How do you plan to do the impossible?"

In that moment of desperation, I took his face in between my hands, caressing his soft skin. I pulled his head to mine, succumbing to my own desperation. "Come back to me, my love," I whispered. "Please. I can take you home. Just come back to me." I pulled away, looking up into his haunting eyes. "I love you, Deus. You died because you loved me. We are mated forever. Two parts of a whole. I can't live without you ... I won't.

Please don't give up. Fight. Fight for us, and for the future we haven't even begun to explore. Please, Deus. I love you. I love you so much it hurts."

He gently gripped my wrists and pulled my hands from his face. "Sweet little witch," he said softly. "I remember everything. Ever conversation. Every look. Every touch, kiss, laugh. All of it. I remember the way it felt to be inside of you. To feed off your pleasure as I found my own. And though it was satisfying ... it is not worth the headache you've been since our first encounter."

My heart broke at his words. I stepped back, unsure of what to say. I had to remember: this wasn't Deus, not completely. He couldn't remember how much he loved me. I had to hold on, for the both of us. I raised my eyes to meet his. He stepped forward, reaching his hand out towards me. He gently trailed his fingers along my jaw, down my neck and to my chest. Everything inside of me relaxed at the contact.

"Let me pleasure you, Seren," he said softly. "It would be mutually beneficial. I remember every caress ... every lick ... every bite that sent you over the edge."

I inhaled, collecting my emotions. "And when was the last time you engaged in a mutually beneficial sexual encounter?" I asked, tone unfaltering. He smiled, dropping his hand from my chest. "Was it this afternoon?" He looked away. "Ah, before you came to collect me." I nodded, allowing the pain to flare only for a moment.

"You know who and what I am, Seren. I've never lied to you about that."

"You're a demon," I said, taking a step towards him. I took his hand in mine, bringing his red ring closer to my face. I ran my thumb over the smooth jewel before bending down to kiss the top of his hand. "But this version of you ... it isn't my demon." I dropped his hand.

He licked his lips. His eyebrows arched as he closed his eyes, seeming to collect himself. I studied his facial expressions. Was that ... annoyance? Was he aggravated that I had rejected his offer? I held back a smile at the small triumph. It may not have been love, but it was an emotion all the same.

I straightened. "Now," I said, "we don't want to keep your other guests waiting, do you?"

His smile crept to the side of his face, and he extended his arm towards me. I took it, relishing in this simple touch. I saw now how I had taken small moments like this for granted. We made our way to the dining hall and were greeted by the others already placed around the large round table. The room was magnificent, yet the entertainment was not to my liking.

Servants, both males and females, were scattered around the room. They wore nothing but thin leather straps that left their entire bodies on display. A large window overlooking Deus's lands stretched to the ceiling on my right. Outside, every sexual act you could imagine was taking place. Some seemed to enjoy it, while others ... I turned away, unable to watch the suffering occur.

I flinched at a pair of hands on my arms and turned hastily, ready to obliterate whoever it was. Levi's eyes met mine. I couldn't hold back tears any longer. I looked back at the window, a panic rising deep inside of me. I needed to stop to this. I needed to save those people.

"Seren," Levi said, snapping me out of the horror.

"This isn't him," I whispered desperately. "He wouldn't do this. He wouldn't allow those people to ... to suffer like that. To endure those torturous acts. No one deserves this type of violation. I don't care what they did. No one deserves this."

"This isn't the Deus you know, but the demon inside of him. Seren, this is a part of—"

"No, I don't want to hear it," I said, turning away. I closed my eyes as tightly as possible, trying to gather myself. I heard footsteps approaching, then fabric fluttering. I looked up to see red velvet curtains covering the heinous acts outside. Mal stood to the side with the rope still in her hands.

"Thank you," I whispered. She nodded, expressionless.

"Oh, come on, Mal," Deus's voice said behind us. "How am I supposed to entertain myself now?" I heard a girl giggle. A stranger sat in his lap, running her hands over his face and down his body. "Prayers answered."

Levi took my hand, leading us to the table. I exhaled, sitting in between him and Belz. I gathered myself, trying to focus on the crazy experiment I had cooked up in my head only a few moments ago. As the first course was served and I was forced to watch the females of the room touch and lick all over my mate, I leaned into Belz.

"Question," I whispered.

"All ears," he said, cutting into his salad.

"Earlier, Deus tried to get me to sleep with him."

"Never mind," he said, pulling away.

I hit him under the table. "I rejected him and that seemed to aggravate him, or ... hurt his ego. I couldn't tell which, but something was there."

"So, what's your question?"

"Even though he can't feel, is it possible that playing off his power could trigger an emotional response?"

Belz turned his head slowly and smirked. "You are a very clever cookie, little witch," he replied with a prideful smile, chewing on his salad. "I suppose it's possible. We are our sins, after all. If they are manipulated, soul or not, it could trigger a reaction or even, as you say, an emotional response. Deus has never been told no before, nor denied. His power takes over and he gets what he wants. You being his mate and all … it might work a little differently."

"Worth a shot," I said, pushing my chair from the table.

"You're going to try now?" he asked with surprise.

"I'm not wasting any time." I walked over to where Deus sat. The two girls on his lap didn't even look up as they continued to kiss and stroke him. "Move," I said in a firm voice. All four princes turned their attention towards me. The girls laughed, ignoring me.

"Would you like to join?" asked Deus.

"As I'm sure you remember, I don't share," I replied. I turned my attention back towards the girls. "I said move."

The blonde laughed. "Or what?" she said flirtatiously.

I allowed my darkness to seep around me, the part of Deus I carried shining brightly as the sparks of red whipped and lashed violently.

"I'd go look at the piles of ash left in the prince's room," I said with an evil smirk. "They might look familiar to you two sluts. There was a blonde one with red skin and a brunette with green, if I recall. Didn't get that good of a look before they combusted." White flames began to lap around my right arm. I held it up as a demonstration. The girls shuddered in fear, pushing off Deus and scurrying away.

"Well, aren't you the worst wing-woman ever," Deus said, taking a drink of wine.

I slid myself onto his lap, wrapping my arms around his neck. He stilled and gave me a suspicious look. I crossed my legs, letting the slit in my dress reveal my bare thigh. As if he couldn't control himself, his hand instantly slid along the exposed skin until he reached my hipbone and tighten his grip. His thumb made small circles against my skin in a teasing fashion.

"If it's alright with you," I said softly. "I'd like to take my dinner here."

"Mm, you will hear no complaints from me," he said, leaning down and kissing my shoulder gently. My body went into a frenzy. My core warmed and heat welled between my legs. He pulled away and smiled. He could sense my arousal. My need for him.

The second course came, and then the third. Deus continued to stroke my skin, his fingers taunting me in the most alluring ways. The rest of the princes ignored us. I caught glimpses from Gor while he tried to assess what the hell I was up to. I kept my mask secured. I flirted with Deus, stroked his ego, and teased him. I didn't have much experience in this department, but I had watched him enough times that I had picked up a few tricks of the trade.

Dessert finally came. Belz and Mammon were teasing Gor as usual. Deus sat back in his chair with me still perched on his lap. He watched the others, laughing along with them. My heart stung. There were so many familiarities about this Deus, even though he was missing a key ingredient.

My self-control was beginning to slip. Being this close to him, smelling him and hearing his laugh: all things I never thought I would experience after he sacrificed himself to save me. His eyes turned then, studying me in a predatory manner.

His fingers trailed up my thigh until he found the evidence of my desire, sliding across the moisture that was seeping between my legs. His nostrils flared and a smile crept across his face. He gently traced the outline of my underwear before sliding underneath the thin fabric. A wave of magic was released from him. I took a deep breath, feeling the ripples of lust and desire, but as his mate, his magic couldn't overwhelm me.

The brothers silenced, looking down towards us. "Everyone out," demanded Deus, not taking his eyes from me.

"I don't think so," said Gor.

"Out!" Deus's voice boomed. His eyes were feral.

I looked back at the others and nodded.

Levi looked worried, but he understood, placing a hand on Gor. Once they filed out of the room, I turned back to Deus. Without another word he forcefully brought his mouth to mine in a passionate kiss. He stood from his chair, pulling me with him as his power sent all the plates and glasses from the table shattering to the floor. He lifted me up until I was perched on the edge of the large wooden surface.

His hands ravaged my body, rough and intense. He parted my legs, sliding his hand between them until he reached my soaked underwear. With one tug, the thin fabric snapped apart, allowing him full access. He slid his fingers down my wet slit. I pulled away and moaned. It was too much. I was coming undone. I had lost all control, and I loved it.

His teeth sunk into the tender part of my neck, sucking, and licking his way down until he got to my chest. He pulled the fabric aside, taking my full breast into his mouth. I laced my fingers through his hair, pulling him harder against my body. As if he could read my mind, his finger slipped deep inside of me. I moaned, arching my hips towards him. My body began to quiver as he pumped forcefully inside of me.

He pulled his lips away from my chest, claiming my mouth with his, absorbing the sounds of pleasure that he coerced out of me. He pressed closer against me. My hands explored him, reveling in the feeling of his perfect body. He hooked his fingers up, pressing against my g-spot and sending me tumbling over the edge.

I let out a cry, my body shaking. The heat in between my legs was overpowering. I held onto him, riding out the orgasm until my body finally stilled. I was panting, trying to clear my head. He pulled away from me, his beautiful deep eyes smiling as he brushed his thumb over my bottom lips.

The emotions inside of me welled to the surface. As if I had no control at all, I whispered, "I love you."

Deus laughed, pressing a soft kiss to my brow. "Lust can feel like love, Seren, but I assure you, that was all this was … lust." I swallowed, holding back tears of disappointment. "Now," he took my hand, pulling me from the table, "we can either continue on the table, or we can return to my chambers. What would you prefer?"

I pulled my hand from his, feeling sick to my stomach. "No thank you," I said softly.

He made a huffing noise, smiling down at me. "Excuse me?"

"I said no, thank you. I do not want to fuck you, Deus."

Deus dropped his head. When his face rose, all signs of the playful prince were erased. His expression was tense and full aggravation. His eyes blazed red as he moved towards me, pinning me between his body and the table. "You fucking tease," he growled.

"Not used to being told no, are we?" I said, matching his temper. I felt another release of his power, warm and comforting. My body tingled in response, but I held onto my control this time, not allowing my heart to cave in. I laughed at him, tilting my head to the side. "That's cute."

He looked surprised, pulling back. "What the—"

"I'm your mate, Deus. Your power is my own. It doesn't work on me the same way as it does others ... or did you forget?"

He growled, swiping a hand towards his chair, sending it smashing against the wall. With another release of power, various pieces of furniture around the room exploded into small shards. The windows blew out of their frames and the lights and chandeliers around the room flickered and shook.

After he calmed, I walked over to him, close enough to hear his rapid breathing. His eyes still blazing with anger.

"You do not deny me," he growled. "No one refuses me."

"But I just did," I replied sweetly. I stood silent, studying him for a moment. "You feel that, Deus. It may not be love or compassion, but it's a feeling nonetheless. You aren't lost. Not yet. I will get you back."

In the next heartbeat, he had his hand wrapped around my throat, his fingers squeezing. I squirmed, struggling to breathe and fighting the shock of his aggression. He brought his face down to mine, baring his teeth.

"Get this through your thick, daft skull," he said in a voice I didn't recognize. "I will never accept my soul again. I am done telling you. Whatever future you hoped to have with me is gone. I do not want to love you. I do not want to need you, and I sure as fuck don't want to be tied to you for the rest of my life."

With a smooth motion, Deus threw me across the room like I weighed nothing. I landed on the floor, my body screaming from the impact. I gritted my teeth, fighting through the sharp pain that shot through my right arm. I pushed myself up on my good side, but fell again, still reeling from the pain. Tears filled my eyes, but I didn't let them fall.

I felt hands on my shoulders. Mal hunched over me, pulling me to my feet. Deus poured himself another glass of wine in a chipped cup, downing it in one gulp. He looked over at me, his face emotionless. Mal remained at my side. I cradled my arm, trying to look unfazed by the pain he had inflicted.

"Take her back to her room," he instructed and turning away.

Mal kept her hands on me until we were safely behind my doors. She sat me on the bed, checking my arm. I winced as she pushed and moved it.

"You've dislocated your shoulder," she said.

She went to the dresser, gathering some material before returning to me. "Here," she said holding out a soft piece of wood. "Bite down."

I did as I was instructed. Before I could inhale fully, a loud pop sounded, and my vision blurred. I screamed out in pain, unable to keep the tears from falling. Mal wrapped my arm, securing it to my chest. She then checked my neck and the rest of me.

"Thank you," I said softly once she had finished.

"I'm—" she started, but cut herself off. She seemed at war with herself. "I don't know what to say."

"There's nothing to say. That isn't Deus. Not my Deus, at least. He would never ..." I felt the pain in my throat where his hand had been. I reached up, rubbing the bruised flesh.

"You were right," she said. "That isn't the prince I devoted my services to. He would never hurt you, Seren ... never."

"Where is Hashen?" I asked, using this opportunity to gather answers.

"In the dungeon. He refused to serve the prince in his current condition, so he was punished."

The guilt pummeled into me. "I ... I don't know what to do," I admitted. "I don't know how to reach him."

Mal sat next to me, wrapping an arm around my shoulder. This was the first sign of compassion I had ever seen the demon warrior express. We sat at the edge of the bed for a long time in silence. I processed that night and then filed it away, trying to come up with another solution that would reunite me with my mate.

Chapter Six

The next morning, my neck was purple and blue. My shoulder was swollen and bruised, matching the mark that appeared on my hip where I had landed on the floor. I wrapped my shoulder back up and dressed just in time for the knock that came at my door.

"Come in," I said, figuring it was Gor or Levi. I didn't know how I would explain my current condition, but I'd find a way. The door clicked shut. I came around the dressing curtain, still fumbling with the arm brace, and froze.

He held out his hands in a surrendering fashion. "I didn't come here to hurt you."

I took a step back. "Then why are you here?" I demanded. "You made yourself clear last night. I don't need another demonstration."

Deus folded his hands behind his back and approached. I moved back until I hit the wall, pinned between it and the Prince of Lust. The rage that had flickered behind his eyes last night was gone. His face was blank. His eyes trailed along my face, stopping at my neck and then my shoulder.

"I came to fix you," he said plainly.

"What?"

"I came to heal you. I figured since none of my brothers had stormed my castle in an attempt to avenge your honor, you hadn't told them about our little … transgression last night. I'll fix you up and we can just agree to keep this between us."

"And why would I agree to do that?"

He tilted his head, smiling softly. He reached towards a piece of my hair that had fallen in front of my face, but I reared back, afraid of his touch. He froze, studying my reaction.

"Usually, women don't recoil from my touch. Quite the opposite."

"Well, is it usual for you to crush their windpipe and toss them across a room?"

"Not unless they ask," he said. He inhaled, lifting his head to look at the ceiling. "You *are* going to let me heal you, because you love me, and you don't want my brothers to kill me. You're still hoping there is a way to save me. Is that reason enough?"

I battled my desire to punch him and kiss him all in the same moment. I relaxed a bit, still uncomfortable, but he was right. I didn't want the others to know what had occurred. This was easier than making up a believable story to explain my broken body.

"Fine," I said softly.

"Good," he replied with a smile. "Your neck first then." I arched my head up. The skin was tight and slightly burned. He gently placed his fingers along the bruises. His thumb caressed the skin softly. I held my breath as the warming sensation began. After a few moments, the discomfort was gone.

He removed his hand and reached for my shoulder. I winced in pain at the contact. He pulled back.

"I got it," I said, removing the sling. He lowered my sleeve gently, his hand cool on my swollen skin. As the healing began, I gritted my teeth.

It was painful, to say the least. Tears fell silently, but I focused, trying to keep myself centered.

When he finally finished, I took a deep breath, closing my eyes. The pain was gone, but my body was sore, and my heart hurt from the strain of this situation I now found myself in. I felt his fingers wipe the tears from my cheek, and pulled away, startled. He retracked his hand. I slid my sleeve back into place, standing.

"Where else are you hurt?" he asked.

"That was all. Thank you," I said, moving to step away from him. His hand slammed against the wall, preventing me from passing.

"I can feel your discomfort," he said, making a disgusted face. "An inconvenience of our ... connection, I suppose."

"It's just my hip," I answered. "No one is going to see that, so I'll let it heal naturally."

"I'm here, offering to take away your pain. Why not let me just heal it?"

I faced him, our chests almost touching. "Let's just say it's a good reminder of what you're actually capable of," I stated firmly.

He smirked, arching an eyebrow, then slammed me against the wall, drawing my dress up until his hand touched with my hip. His warm healing power surged through me. I pressed my hands against his chest, unleashing my power, blasting him across the room. He slammed into the bed, sitting straight up as soon as he landed.

"I said, no thank you," I blurted.

He began laughing. "Now who's being dramatic?"

"At least I didn't slam you into the marble floor."

"I apologized for that."

"Did you? I don't remember hearing those words come out of your mouth."

He stood to his feet, striding gracefully forward. As he towered over me, his jaw tensed. That fire I had witnessed last night began to ignite. I allowed my flames to flicker around my fingers. My shadows seeped from my feet.

He appeared unfazed by my display. "You're not going to kill me, little witch," he said confidently.

"No, but that doesn't mean I won't hurt you. Especially if you try and pull the shit you did last night."

"Then maybe you should have thought twice about refusing me," he growled.

"Aw, did I hurt your little demon ego?" I taunted. "The big bad prince doesn't like rejection?"

"I felt you last night. You wanted it just as much as I did."

"No," I said, taking a step closer to him. "I wanted Deus ... my Deus. Not this half-assed version in front of me."

He huffed. "Suit yourself, witch," he said, and left my room.

I took a moment to gather myself before heading to Belz's room. When I opened the door, he was in a bed surrounded by three beautiful demon females. "Oh," I said, startled by the sight. The females didn't move, but Belz's head popped up with a lazy smile.

"Here to join?" he asked.

"Why do all of you princes assume everyone wants to bed you?"

"Because they do," he replied, tapping two of the demons to move. They got up, lazily sliding their dresses over their naked bodies before sauntering out of the room.

"Enjoying the pleasures of the realm?" I asked.

"I thought I'd indulge a little while I was here. Gluttony and all."

"Yes, I'm aware." I fell into a seat in the corner of the room.

"You look troubled," he said, sliding a shirt over his toned body.

"Observant, aren't you," I replied.

He poured a glass of wine and handed it to me before pouring another for himself. "Plan didn't go as you'd hoped?"

"Not exactly." I weighed the pros and cons of telling him the truth. "Can you keep something from Levi and Gor?"

He smirked, bringing the glass of wine to his lips. "Keeping things from your besties, are we?"

"Levi and Gor are too focused on protecting me. My focus is Deus. Their worry will just get in the way of what needs to be done."

He nodded, gesturing for me to continue.

"Deus is capable of feeling. He feels hate, jealousy, aggravation."

"And how did you discover this?"

"I flirted with him until he lost control. Then, when he offered me his bed, I rejected him. He wasn't too happy about that. He ended up choking me and throwing me across the room. I dislocated my shoulder and gained a few extra bruises."

His face showed no sign of concern. He took another drink. "You don't look very banged up to me."

"Deus showed up at my door this morning and healed me … well, most of me. My hip is pretty banged up, but I didn't let him touch me there. I figured it could heal on its own."

"I see." He leaned forward, placing his cup on the table. "May I?" he asked, gesturing to my waist. I stood and crossed over to him. He lifted my dress gently, still seated. His healing power felt light and feathery. There was no warmth like when Deus used his power. Belz's power felt like a cool gel sliding across my skin.

"Thank you," I said as he pulled away.

"My pleasure. So, what is your plan, now that your little game of cat and mouse has ended?"

"Honestly, I have no clue. If I find his soul, maybe I could—"

"That's not going to happen, sweetheart. His soul is in the pit. No one willing goes in and comes back out."

"But someone like me has never tried. Cecilia ventured to Hell, but never the pit. What if I could?"

"Are you willing to risk an eternity of pain and suffering on a 'what if'?" he asked.

I dropped my eyes, hopelessness beginning to swell inside of me. "My life is over without him, Belz."

He exhaled, running his finger along the rim of his glass. "Well, I guess we need to find a way to get you into Lucy's territory then."

"But I thought you all said the pit wasn't in his territory?"

"We lied," he said, slamming his wine back. "We didn't want you getting anymore crazy ideas. Yet, here you are ... crazier than any of us anticipated."

"You'll help me? Really?" I asked.

"The others aren't going to like it," he answered.

"Levi and Gor, no, but what about Mammon?"

"He'll help us."

I smiled, a spark of hope ignited. Belz suddenly stiffened, his eyes going wide.

"What is it?" I asked. "What's wrong?"

A moment later, Mammon burst through the door. He looked panicked. "Belz," he said softly.

"I know," Belz answered. "Lucy and Satan just arrived."

"This could be our chance," I said, looking to Belz.

Mammon looked from his brother and then to me. "What are you two planning?" he asked.

"Shut the door before the others arrive," Belz demanded. Mammon complied, and we filled him in on my diabolical suicide mission.

CHAPTER SEVEN

The plan was simple. Distract Lucifer. Sneak onto his lands. Find the pit. Find Deus's soul. All while somehow surviving and making it back to the earthly plane. My palms were sweating as our group made our way to the throne room. Deus had requested our presence to welcome our new guests. Mal waited in front of the closed doors. Once they opened, the princes and Giana entered. I stepped to her side, trying to be discreet.

"I need to ask you for a favor," I whispered.

"What are you planning?" she asked, walking alongside me.

"I'm going to sneak onto Lucifer's territory and find the pit," I admitted.

She grabbed me by the arm, digging her fingers into my skin. "Seren, that's a suicide mission."

"Do you have a better idea?" I asked. "I was hoping you'd accompany me there. I know what I am asking, and you don't have to come, Mal. You have a choice."

She took a deep breath, examining me intensely for a moment. She bowed her head slightly. "It would be an honor to assist you, Seren De Salvo."

"Thank you, Mal. Truly," I said, and took my place next to Belz.

We stood at the edge of the room. Deus sat in a large wingback chair, leaning across the table towards Lucifer. The princes were engaged in, apparently, a comical discussion, as they laughed uproariously, seeming completely oblivious of our arrival. Satan sat across from them, expressionless, clearly the third wheel.

Mammon cleared his throat. "Brothers," he said, giving them a small smile. "You requested our presence?"

Lucifer's eyes finally turned towards us. His smile, most beautiful and elegant, glistened in the soft lighting of the room.

"Now isn't this something," Lucy said in his smooth, rich voice. "The seven demons of Hell, all home at the same time. And two moon goddess vessels. What are the odds?"

My breath caught in my throat, but I tried to hide my panic from my expression.

Belz laughed softly. "Brother, I know you're getting up there in age, but unless my eyes are failing me, I only see one goddess vessel." A petite figure with lush white hair and olive skin stepped from the shadows. Her exquisite, soft features and sensual lips lit the room. Victoria.

She placed a hand on Deus's shoulder, looking down at him with love in her eyes. He took her hand and kissed it gently, rubbing his thumb against her skin. His eyes then met mine. His lips curved into a sinful smirk.

Rage. Hate. Fury. Jealousy. Pain. All my stupid emotions stirred within the pit of my stomach. I felt Giana's hand run down the center of my back in a calming gesture. She must have felt the turmoil raging inside of me like a tsunami. It seemed her emotional telepathy was still active in hell. I didn't know a soul could still possess their powers even after death.

Focus, dammit, I told myself. I forced a smile on my face, nodding my head towards her. "Victoria," I said plainly, "nice to see you again."

She looked at me with hatred. Without a word, she made herself at home on Deus's lap. Goddess vessel or not, I would one day deliver her the ultimate death.

"Now, I am curious," said Lucifer. "What has brought you all to this realm?"

"They hope to restore my soul and bring me home," answered Deus as he drew his fingers down the column of Victoria's neck. I tried to ignore it, but my efforts were useless.

Lucifer appeared surprised. "Is that so?" he asked. "And how are you all going to do that?"

Belz attempted to answer, but I stepped forward first. "Asmodeus has made his desire to remain soulless perfectly clear."

Lucy chuckled. "Yes, and without me," he said, "you can't put his soul back, so your efforts are futile, little goddess." He rose and sauntered over to stand in front of me. If I hadn't know better, I would have found him charming and alluring. His light hair framed his beautifully constructed face.

He reached out, softly trailing his fingers along a strand of my hair. I remained still. Deus watched the two of us intently. Lucifer's fingers traced the exposed skin at the edge of my neckline. Then in an instant, his hand was around my throat, squeezing the life out of me.

The others moved to attack, but Satan and Deus stood from their seats, throwing their hands out, preventing them from retaliating. I lit my fire, blasting Lucifer with my power, but the flames seemed to do little damage. He just laughed.

"Oh, sweet Seren," he said, bringing my face closer to his. "You're in my realm now, you little bitch."

I pulled at the power deep inside of me, the untapped magic that was dark and dangerous. Lucifer himself had imbued me with his magic before I was born, tricking my mother in his desire to possess the next moon goddess. I had never touched that power, in fear of what I would become.

With one massive release, he, Deus, and Satan flew across the room, slamming into the opposite wall. My friends were freed from their restraints, coming to my aid. A mixture of shadows, fire, and something that felt like pure, untapped potential flickered through me in the most delicious combination.

I closed my eyes, rolling my neck, allowing the forbidden magic to seep through my veins, tainting my blood with its malice and promises of death. I shifted my shoulders, licking my lips as a smooth weight coursed through my body like a warm shot of liquor. I felt ... different. Careless. Powerful. Reckless. I laughed, indulging in a moment of pure bliss as I basked in my own glory.

"Seren," I heard a voice from behind me. I turned to see Gor staring at me in shock. "Your ... your eyes."

The table in front of us blasted to the side of the room. Lucifer stormed forward while Deus and Satan rose to their feet, dusting themselves off.

"How dare you use my own power against me?" Lucifer roared.

"Aw, is someone's pride damaged, Lucy?" I mocked, making a pouty face.

"I will rip it out of you!" he screamed. "Along with every ounce of power you possess!"

The other four princes made a stance at my side. They threw out their hands just as Lucifer sent a wave of dark magic that ate through everything it touched, turning it to ash.

"Go!" Belz demanded.

"I won't leave you," I replied.

"Go now, or there won't be another chance to do what needs to be done," he groaned, using his strength to hold back Lucifer and the others.

"What are you talking about?" asked Levi.

Gor put the pieces together before I had a chance to respond. His face grew worried.

"No, Seren," he said, grunting as his magic held. "You can't. You won't survive."

"I have to, Gor," I replied. "There is no life for me that doesn't involve him."

Mal appeared at my side. I took her hand, looking back at the four princes of Hell that had become my family, then to Giana's beautiful face. "Survive," I said to them all.

"You too, goddess," replied Mammon.

I closed my eyes imagining the maps of Hell that I studied before arriving. I pictured Lucifer's territory and shifted.

We were greeted by a massive force of wind and heat from the towers of flames that surrounded us. Tornados, hundreds of stories high twirled and blazed with blue and red flames, shifting and traveling through the lands. Pits, full of trapped souls screamed and cried out, reaching through the grates praying for a miracle.

Souls were strapped to crosses, some hung upside down. They were beaten, tortured, and burned. Black crows ate their flesh as they cried out helplessly. Body parts littered the ground. The smell of blood and burning fat singed my notarial turning my stomach until I couldn't bare it any longer. I leaned over and vomited, sickened by the sights, sounds, and smells that surrounded me. This was what I had imagined Hell to be. A burning, torturous pit of nightmares. And somewhere in this horrific land, Deus was suffering.

"Makes the other realms look like a vacation doesn't it," said Mal.

"I wouldn't go that far. Do you know where the pit is?" I asked.

"Not exactly, but if I had to guess, it's somewhere in his castle. He wouldn't just leave it unguarded."

"Fan-fucking-tastic," I said, turning in the direction of the black, monstrous palace that stood before us.

Lucifer's castle was easily the largest structure I had ever laid eyes on. It reached high into the sky which swirled with black and gray clouds. Blue and yellow lightening blazed through the atmosphere. Dragon-like creatures flew overhead, making the worst screeching sounds I had ever heard. I covered my ears, lowering my head in defense. The sound was horrific. I pulled my hands away, revealing blood now dripping from my ears.

"Noctori," explained Mal. "If they get close enough, they'll be able to rupture your ear drums.

"Let's not give them the chance," I said, refocusing on the structure of nightmares in front of us.

The castle was made of some type of black rock that looked to be … bleeding. Moisture covered the surface and seeped into the ground around it, creating a weblike effect that reminded me of veins. Anything the branches of the black liquid touched turned to ash and decayed.

"I'm guessing we avoid the black creepy stuff?" I asked.

"That would be correct. Though, now that you've accessed Prince

Morningstar's power, I wonder if it will even have an effect on you?"

"What do you mean?"

"He's a part of you. This is his land created from his power which you possess and now wield. It's just a theory, but I am willing to bet that this realm will respond to you the way it does him."

"Well, that's comforting," I replied sarcastically.

"We've never had a Queen of Hell," she said with a smile that seemed to hold secrets. "Could be fun. Come on, before he realizes what we're up to."

We took off through the lands, avoiding the pits of souls. I kept my mind focused, trying not to divert my eyes to the suffering I was surrounded by. After this experience, I was unsure if I would ever sleep again.

We made it to the castle doors where two guards were stations. Their skin was black like tar and plagued with boils and oozing sores. They bared their razor-sharp teeth. Demons. They lunged and attacked. Mal pulled two short swords that were strapped to her back. She swung and sliced through the air, cutting through them with little effort.

I stopped at the door, looking at the deadly oozing substance that trickled across the dual, rough, black stone. I looked down at my hands and without another moment to talk myself out of it, I pressed them against the surface. An illuminating blue light shot through the carvings and grooves of the doors, engulfing the entrance in light. A moment later, the door clicked, opening to reveal the inside of the castle.

"Theory proven," Mal said, still griping the swords. "Now, the search begins."

We entered the long hall of the entryway. The walls were covered with paintings depicting Lucifer in all his glory. Some were of him fighting battles, others were more relaxed, reflecting his beauty and grace. Mal grabbed a hold of my arm, pulling me into a dark corridor off to the side. She pressed our bodies against the wall, signaling for me to be silent.

A group of females and males passed by. Servants or guest, I had no clue, but I knew if we were spotted, they would report back to Lucifer and my chance to find Deus's soul would be gone. Once we were in the clear, the hunt began.

Mal led me through the halls as if she was intimately familiar with the layout of the castle. I followed closely, taking in my surroundings as Orion had taught me during our training sessions that now seemed so long ago.

Lucifer's mansion was indeed extravagant and massive. We turned down a new hallway every few feet, then descended a wrought iron staircase that seemed to plummet deep into the earth. We came upon a servant who startled at the sight of us, dropping a tray of wine and glasses. Before he could yell, Mal drove a dagger into his throat, killing him in a moment.

"We need to move faster," she instructed. "Someone else was sure to have heard that."

"And how do you know where we're going?" I asked.

She shrugged, stepping over the dead demon. "I may have not been fully truthful when I said I didn't know where to find the pit."

"Mal!" I sneered, following after her.

"Here," Mal said, halting at two intricately carved onyx doors. "The hallway of mirrors."

"What is it?" I asked, examining the figurines crafted into the surface.

"The gateway to the pit."

"Gateway? What—"

Before I could finish, Giana appeared out of nowhere, covered in blood and ash. Her face was streaked with tears, her eyes bloodshot.

"Seren," she said, then collapsed. I caught her before she hit the ground.

"How did you get here?" I asked. "What happened?"

"I'm tied to you ... through your power. Remember?" she said, painfully sitting upright. "Lucifer and the others are too strong. They're suffering. Gor is hurt. We need to leave ... now."

"Giana, I can't," I said, the pain of her words settling in my chest. "We just found where the pit is located."

"If you don't," she cried, "Deus won't be the only one stuck here. They all will be confined to this realm. Under Lucifer's wrath."

"She's right," added Mal. "If he removes all of their souls, the end will be upon us." I allowed myself a moment to think. The right thing would be to go and save them, but my heart ... I was so close.

I took a breath, looking at Mal. "Fine," I said. "I will open the doorway back to earth, but once everyone is safely through, I am coming back to finish what I started."

"You will hear no objections from me," Mal replied.

I held onto Mal and Giana, shifting us back to Deus's realm. We arrived in a room now layered with ash and fire. The walls were falling apart. The ceiling no longer existed. Windows were completely shattered. Everything around us had been destroyed. Blood was splattered along every surface.

A torrent of acid shot passed my face. It hit the wall, the cinderblocks sizzling and melting into nothing. I turned back to its source. Levi and Belz stood side-by-side, firing away towards Lucifer, Deus, and Satan. Satan was badly hurt, blood pooling from his abdomen. Mal took a deep breath and then disappeared from my side.

Deus was bleeding from his head and stood on unsteady legs. I turned back to see Mammon cradling Gor's body. G and I rushed to their side. Gor was missing an arm. His leg had a massive slit on his upper thigh. He was bleeding from the mouth, coughing up blood.

"Oh my God, Gor," I said, reaching for him.

"We need to leave now," said Mammon in a weak voice. A bright beam of fire shot overhead, slamming into the wall next to us, setting the remaining piece of tapestry on fire.

I stood, allowing my power to well inside of me. I focused on the door I had spent months creating. I rotated my arms and hands, pulling my power from within until I was able to project the doorway that would be our salvation. The portal opened, revealing Deus's throne room back home on earth.

"No!" I heard a scream from the other side of the room. I turned to see Lucifer's raging face. He sent his deadly, dark power into the portal. I could feel his magic begin to eat away at the gate. I held firm, pushing everything I had into keeping it open.

"We need to go now!" I yelled. "I can't hold it much longer!" Mammon picked up Gor's limp form and rushed towards the portal. Giana took a deep breath and followed, stepping back into the world of the living.

I felt Lucifer's power overriding mine. He was too strong. I may have had an ounce of his power—a drop compared to a tempest. I yelled in pain, forcing everything I had into the door.

Levi stepped through. My vision began to tunnel. I was burning out. I could feel the sweat on my brow. My arms began to shake, but I held firm. I felt two arms around my waist as they hauled me towards the gate.

I held onto the magic as we stepped through the doorway.

Everything inside of me was screaming not to let go of Deus ... of hope. "No," I cried, fighting to free myself from the strong arms that restrained me. I pushed and shoved, the memories of my mate becoming my strength. "No," I mumbled, as the gate's energy dissipated with each passing second.

I could hear Lucifer's screams of anger on the other side. I turned back just as Deus stepped in front of the portal. His face revealed nothing. There was no love. No empathy. Just ... darkness. Focused on only his beautiful face, I fought harder to get back to him.

The portal began to constrict. Black veins of death devoured the door that had taken so much of me to create.

"Seren!" A deep voice behind me yelled with desperation. My vision began to tunnel. The humming of the power that danced around me heightened. A burning sensation ripple underneath my skin. Something inside of me was building, begging to be unleashed.

I took one final breath and gave in to the pain inside.

"NO!" I screamed with everything I had. A massive wave of energy blasted from me, blinding my vision. My heart constricted and I fought to breath, but the release ... oh, the release was well worth it. All the emotions inside— fear, anger, resentment, sadness, guilt—billowed from me. Everything went silent. Everything felt ... numb.

CHAPTER EIGHT

Bam! I slammed into a hard, cold surface. My head was spinning. Exhaustion set in, spreading through every limb. I forced myself up from the cold floor, assessing my surroundings. Portraits of Lucifer hung from the walls. Rich tapestries and furniture littered the room around me. I held my breath in horror. I had shifted back to Lucifer's castle. I was still in Hell.

Two young demon girls looked at me with shock and horror.

"Where is the hall of mirrors?" I demanded.

They just stood, huddled together in fear.

"If either of you want to live," I said, "I suggest one of you take me there now."

"I can," a small girl with golden blonde hair whispered.

"Good," I said, grabbing her by the arm and heading towards the exit. When I flung open the door, two demons were passing in the hall. They took one look at me and lunged. I blasted my power towards them, setting both of their hideous bodies on fire. The girl began shaking.

"Move," I instructed.

We took off down the hall and descended flight after flight of stairs. Demons appeared every few moments, attempting to hinder my plan. I slashed through them with my shadows, setting others ablaze when they got too close. They whined and squealed as their flesh melted from their bones.

The girl came to a halt in front of the same onyx doors Mal had led me to.

"I ... I can't go in there," she said.

"Why not?" I asked.

"The hall of mirrors ... it ... it forces you to truly look at yourself. I won't go in there. Not after—"

"I got it," I interrupted, heading for the door. "Thanks."

I pulled on the handle and stepped inside. The door shut with a loud thud behind me. The lighting was low, but the room's name was no exaggeration. It was made entirely out of mirrors. I stepped softly on the glass surface. The floor whined under the weight of each step, threatening to shatter at any moment.

Mirrors were suspended in the air, hung by invisible cords, just ... floating. The ceiling towered twenty feet high, made from the same reflective material. Gray fog swirled and twisted around the open space. I turned and looked at my reflection. I was still in the gown that I had gotten from Deus's castle. My hair was a mess. My skin was marred with bruises and scratches. I looked like I had been through Hell ... fitting.

I took a few steps, trying to find my way through, but no exit could be seen. I turned around to discover the onyx doors had vanished. "Shit," I whispered, continuing deeper into the room.

I turned down an aisle of more mirrors, larger than I was. A memory flashed across the mirror, playing like a movie. It was me, back in Montecassino. I was walking with my crutches down the hall, dressed in typical nun fashion. Sister Francis came up behind me, placing a hand on my back for comfort as I dragged my dead legs across the polished floor.

I turned from the image and came face to face with Sister Odette. Her face had been slashed by the claws of the hell hounds that had killed her. She tilted her head, holding her rosary in her hands.

"I should have listened to my sisters and ended you the night your evil sire brought you to me," she said, her eyes filled with disappointment. "We would all still be alive doing God's work, if it weren't for you."

I forced my eyes closed, shutting out the face of the nearest thing I'd had to a mother for so many years. "This isn't real," I whispered to myself. "It's only an illusion."

"Are the signs of my death not real enough? Was the forfeit of my life to protect yours an illusion?"

"Am I an illusion as well?" came another voice to my right.

I turned my head, eyes widening. "George," I whispered.

"You trusted the enemy," he said, taking a step towards me. "And because of that, I am dead. You chose someone who had proven that they couldn't be trusted over your teammate. Over an innocent."

"I'm so sorry," I cried, looking at his marred and torn body. He appeared as he had when he died, ripped apart by demons.

"Did you not think your actions would have consequences?" he continued. "I was just starting my life, Seren. I was even younger than you."

I turned away, not wanting to relive another moment of my deepest regrets. The next mirror was a picture of Nonna: our reunion. The next of Aunt Thora. Of Frankie. Then ... Orion.

My heart fell into my stomach and tears threatened to fall at the memory, frozen in time. I was pressed against Frankie's dresser while he stood in front of me. It was the first time we had met. I watched as his face searched mine for answers. Beautiful curly brown hair, toned body: he was the very sight of perfection. Tears slipped out as the sound of his voice echoed through the hall.

"Orion," I whispered, feeling a pain in my chest.

"Sometimes," I heard behind me, "I wonder what my life could have become if I had never stumbled across you that day."

I swirled around, now facing him in the flesh. I cried out in shock and excitement.

"What are you doing here?" I gasped, now shaking. "Giana said you weren't in Hell."

"I've been in Hell since that day," he said. His face was hard. There was nothing loving or caring about him. "You took everything from me, little dove … everything. My future, my heart, my life. Yet here you are, going to the ends of Hell in order to save a demon prince. Where was that determination for saving my life?"

"I tried, Orion," I cried. "I am so sorry. There hasn't been a moment since—"

"Oh, spare me the bullshit," he said. "I loved you. You were my soulmate. Be honest, you never even gave us a chance. You were always looking for something else. What? Was I not damaged enough for you? Not evil enough?"

"You are perfect. You always have been. And I did try. You know I did. That part of our love never clicked into place for me. But you knew how much I loved you. I would have given my life to save yours."

"Well, maybe you should have," he said. "Why was I the one that had to suffer? If you had given Lucifer what he wanted, I'd be home with my fiancé, planning our wedding."

"I would have traded spots with you in a heartbeat. How could you question that?"

"Because I've come to realize that you are selfish. What Aradia saw in you, I will never know. The reality is you deserve to be here … in Hell. I hope your demon prince never recovers and you get to live your long, pathetic life watching him fuck his way through Hell while you suffer. You don't care about us; you only care about yourself and what makes you feel good."

"That's not true," I cried.

"Isn't it?" said George, approaching my right side.

"I devoted my life to being your caregiver," added Sister Odette. "I loved you like my own, and look where that got me."

"A one-way ticket for all of us to Hell," said George.

I cried harder, falling to my knees while they surrounded me. Orion bent down beside me.

"This needs to end," he whispered. "If you die, this is all over."

"It won't bring us back," added George, "but at least it will protect the ones that are still alive."

"You're too much of a liability, child," whispered Sister Odette. "Your life, for the lives of those you love. Those that you can still save from the evil that follows you"

Orion reached out, wrapping his fingers around my hand. He opened my palm and then placed a dagger inside. I looked up at him, tears still falling down my face. He smiled softly.

"This dagger is special. It can deliver the ultimate death. You can finally find peace and protect those who still have a chance at living. It's time for you to join me, little dove," he said, brushing a strand of hair from my face. "We belong together. We can be together. All you have to do … is let go. You chose me once, during the rite. Choose me again. Make this right. Make everything right." He leaned in and pressed a tender kiss to my lips. "I love you, little dove. I always have."

It would be over. All of it. The pain. The suffering. The fighting. With my death, it would all end.

I thought back to that day in Romania. The feeling of my toes hanging on the edge of the cliff while I pondered over my life. It had seemed like the answer then, and could be the answer now. All I had to do was take a leap and pray that God would forgive me for all the wrong I had brought into his world.

I closed my eyes, bringing the dagger into position. "It will all be over," I whispered, taking a deep and brave breath. "I just have to sacrifice myself. Correct the wrong that was allowed to live." I drew out the dagger, aiming for my heart. I gritted my teeth together, preparing to be set free.

I positioned the tip of the blade for a final blow when the clink of metal pulled me from spiraling thoughts. My necklace shifted against my skin as the knife made contact with the small, welded key. I froze, and for a moment, my mind cleared.

I reached into my shirt, drawing up the cold silver chain. My fingers wrapped around the familiar pendant. The token that my mate had given me ... the key to our home. I relaxed and began to cry, smiling to myself as a rush of happiness and love overcame me.

This key represented the life I wanted. A home where my mate and I would live in happiness. A safe place to explore our passions and interests. A place where our family would meet and create memories. A home where I was loved, desired, and cherished. My home ... Deus.

My eyes snapped back up to the three figures. I looked at Sister Odette and then George, studying their faces intimately. No matter how long I lived, no matter how much happiness I might experience ... I would never forget them. I would always feel the weight of their deaths on my conscious, but it was time to move on.

"I'm sorry," I whispered, watching their faces study my own. "I am truly ... sorry." I let out a breath of relief, forgiving myself and letting them go. They disappeared into the gray fog that floated throughout the room.

I turned my eyes to the man I had come to deeply care for. But this wasn't Orion, no. This was my test. This place knew I carried the most guilt about not being able to save him. I took a few deep breaths and then stood, stepping closer to him. His face tensed.

I stretched up on my toes and kissed his cheek, then pulled away, looking into his dark eyes.

"I love you, Orion. I will always love you. And I will find you ... maybe not in this life, but the next." His face relaxed. The anger and pain evaporated, Orion along with it. I took a another breath and swiped at the tears on my cheeks.

A doorway opened at the end of the row of mirrors. Red, brown, and yellow light poured into the dark hall. I moved towards it, feeling a tugging sensation I couldn't explain. I stepped over the threshold and into the tormentor's pit.

Loose objects crunched under the soles of my shoes. I looked to the ground and realized I stood upon thousands of bone fragments. The air here was dry. It smelled of mold and something foul and grotesque. For as far as my eye could see, there was nothing but bones and body parts.

I ran my hands across my face, defeat and exhaustion taking hold. I was almost there ... I could do this. I took a step forward, flinching at the sound of smashing bones beneath my feet when a white, wispy soul slithered from the ground. It danced through the air, slowly at first, seeming to study me, assessing if I was a threat.

I froze, then raised my hand to touch it, but the wisp swerved away like a scared animal. I remained still, allowing the thing to feel me out. Without warning, the soul lunged forward, invading my nostrils and mouth while wriggling inside of my body.

"Please, no," a man's voice cried while his arms were ripped from his body. I opened my mouth to yell, but no sound came. I could feel my skin burning, my bones yelling in protest. My heart slammed against my chest so hard, I wondered if I was experiencing a heart attack; until finally, my arm was pulled clean off.

I came back to my own body in the pit, falling to my knees as I vomited from the memory that wasn't my own. The soul wisp squirmed away frantically. I lifted my head, wiping my mouth as I looked out into the horizon. The ground beneath me trembled, signaling I wasn't alone.

A decaying gray hand shot up from the pile of bones. The hand was missing its ring and middle finger and fought to pull the body it was attached to from the pile of ivory. One by one, humanoid figures ascended around me, crawling and glitching in the same fashion as the possessed Obsidian witches. Their skin was melting from their skeleton, oozing with infection and rot. And the smell was unlike anything I had ever encountered.

As they began to lurch towards me, I bolted through the first opening I saw, leaving no time for them to catch me. I peeked over my shoulder as they began to follow. Their bodies were stiff and slow, yet the more they moved, the faster they became. Dropping to all fours, some began to run after me like wild animals in pursuit of their prey.

Something wrapped around my ankle, slamming me into the ground. A sharpened piece of bone speared straight through my hand as I reached out to catch myself. Before I could scream, a pair of dull teeth sunk into my calf. I yelled out in pain, kicking my other foot into the creature's forehead over and over until it finally released me. I forced myself up, blood streaming. I cradled my hand into my chest, the wound pulsing around the bone that protruded from my palm.

Wisps of souls began to emerge all around me, seeming to be drawn by my presence. I kept moving. I was unsure what would happen to me if the decaying creatures caught me, but I wasn't going to stick around to find out. I raced to the top of a hill, unable to see what awaited me on the other side, then tripped and tumbled headfirst down the prickly mound, landing face first.

The souls descended. Pain, suffering, and sadness consumed me. I fought to force them out, trying to focus on what I had come for.

"Deus," I whispered. The torment of this place seemed to fuel Lucifer's powers deep inside me. I lay on the mound of bones while the souls drove through me, one by one, seeming to take a piece of my humanity with them with each possession.

The darkness inside of me began to slither across my being like a blanket of silk, traveling up each limb like a smooth caress. Unable to move, I lay there and felt each soul's penance, while something far darker threatened to consume me entirely. The magic welled deep within the pit of my stomach, feeding off each soul that entered, until finally a massive wave unleashed, sending every soul and dead creature flying away from me with one powerful surge.

Air rushed into my lungs as my nerves screamed to life. Everything hurt, but the darkness inside of me had provided an opportunity. I wasn't going to waste it.

I pushed up and continued forward through the plane. Massive pits began to appear around me. Red hot lava wove like streets through the cracks in the ground. I reached the edge of one pit, only to see skinless shells of humans, crying out while they suffered. They had no eyelids, nails or clothing. They scratched at the sides of the pit, attempting to pull themselves from the hole.

I moved onto the next trench and the next, searching for Deus. The farther into the pit I went, the stronger the tugging sensation became. I stopped fighting and allowed it to guide me. I ran and ran for what felt like forever. The creatures were gaining on me, but I needed more time.

I approached a small pit, separated from the others. The screaming here wasn't as loud or overpowering. The air was thick, and the scenery was eerily quiet. I looked down into the hollow ground and saw a wispy soul, stagnant against the side of a wall. Something inside of me calmed in its presence. Could this be—

I jumped into the pit, instantly regretting the decision. My legs screamed as they hit the hard ground. I examined the wisp, praying to whomever was listening that it was my mate. It seemed to watch me hesitantly.

The bone fragment still protruded from my palm. I took one deep breath, wrapped my good hand around the thick base and pulled the spur free from my flash, biting back an excruciating yelp. I ripped a piece of my tattered dress, using the fabric to bandage the wound.

I refocused on the spirit in front of me. I stepped only inches from the white, billowing fog and reached slowly towards the entity. It flinched, then flowed through my fingers cautiously while it assessed me. I let it linger, knowing what came next would be painful. I closed my eyes while the cool, soft presence circled me. Finally, I felt a tickling sensation slide against my chin. I opened my mouth, taking one deep final breath.

The wisp slid inside, nestling into my essence with a sense of familiar gentleness. Then, without warning, my entire body burned like it had been set on fire.

Memory after memory of horrific scenes flickered through my mind. Sexual traumas, crimes, and moments too monstrous to be true. I could feel it then ... feel him. His trauma, pain, and regret for his part in it all. Drowning in the horrors he had orchestrated, I could feel his mind slipping into the darkness that surrounded him.

A flicker in one of the memories caught my eye. I fixed on it, honing my senses. And then again, a flicker of Deus's person flashed ahead of me before fading out of sight. I moved forward in my mind, determined to reach him at all costs.

"Deus," I called out, as a strange wind around me began to pick up. His person flickered again to my right and then again to my left. "Deus," I cried. "I am here for you. I am here to take you home!"

Gray, misty funnels above me swarmed into a tunneling vortex that slammed into the ground, erupting into a spiraling tornado of fire. Massive twisters, one after another, surrounded me, setting everything they touched ablaze.

I continued to move towards Deus, following the flashes as he went in and out of sight. I covered my face while the wind tore at my skin. I called out, determined to save him.

The flashes began to appear quicker, hopping randomly in front of me until, finally, his likeness ran straight for me, screaming in a deep, haunting roar. When the being made contact, it absorbed me, and everything went silent.

I shook with fear, my eyes squeezed together so tightly I felt sick. The sound of my pounding heart began to calm, and I opened my eyes. I was in the pit; yet, everything was quiet.

Deus sat against one wall. He wore a pair of brown pants that were torn and tattered. Blood seeped through the fabric. His beautiful, sculpted torso was bare, covered in bruises and cuts. The soles of his feet were bloody, ripped to shreds. His arms covered his face as he rocked back and forth, crying.

My heart broke. I approached slowly, kneeling in front of him before reaching out to touch his arms.

"Deus," I whispered. He flinched away from me, scrambling farther back into the dirt wall. His face looked terrified. His eyes were full of pain. Sweat and tears streamed down his face, making small paths through the dirt that covered his skin.

"No!" he screamed, pulling away from me.

"Deus," I whispered, trying to find a sign of the man I loved. "It's me ... Seren."

He looked at me for a moment, trying to put the pieces together.

"I've come to take you home," I said, reaching out slowly, touching his knee. "Back to earth, back to Romania. Remember, our home there?"

He shook his head violently. "No, no," he said in a weak tone I didn't recognize. "I will never go back. I belong here. For all the things I've done. For all the sins I've committed. It's better to leave me here. So I don't hurt anyone else."

"No, Deus," I said, leaning in closer towards him. "You're good. You're kind. And you're loved." He began to scratch at the skin on his arms anxiously. "Deus, please," I whispered, now crying. "I need you, baby. I came all this way to find you. So we could be together. Remember ... you're my mate. My other half."

His big blue eyes looked up at me, full of pain and sorrow. "I am so sorry you got stuck with me. You didn't deserve this. All the pain I've already put you through. The doubt I sowed inside of you. The women I took when I ... when I had already fallen in love with you. I can't stop who I am, Seren. I've tried in the past. Nothing has ever worked. Nothing will ever change."

I stroked the side of his face. "But you've never found your mate before. The person that was designed to complete you."

He removed my hand softly. "Go home, Seren. This is where I deserve to be. For all I've done, this is my price to pay."

"No," I said, shaking my head as I tried to remain coherent. "I came to retrieve you, and I am not leaving until you agree to come with me."

"That's not going to happen."

I sat down beside him, pressing my back into the warm dirt. "Then, I guess you just earned yourself a pit mate."

His eyes widened in shock. "You are out of your mind," he said.

"Maybe. But I know my limits, what I can and can't handle. And I know I can't live without you, Deus. Nor do I want to." He was worth it. To me ... he was worth every bad thing I had endured. The light this man created in my life was indescribable. Nothing would ever compare. I loved him completely. "Tell me every terrible thing you ever did, and let me love you anyways," I whispered, reciting the poem we once shared.

His eyes met mine, and his lips turned up, just a hint. "And I would ask you to show me your flaws, but I fear it would make me love you ... more than I already do."

"You have done horrific things in your long life. I won't deny that, but you've also done extraordinary things. Like sacrifice your happiness, your power, your life for those you love. Someone who is capable of love, and is loved in return, is worth saving." I took his hand in mine. "You are worth saving, my love."

In that moment, the months of torture this place had inflicted upon him came rushing to the surface and because of our bond, I could feel every horrific thing he had to endure. We embraced each other, and I promised myself, I would never let go. I held onto him as he allowed the pain of his past to escape. I buried my head in his dark hair, holding onto his trembling body like he was the most valuable thing in this entire world. He was, to me.

Finally, he pulled away, reaching out to touch my face. He was hesitant, but I leaned in. "We need to go," I whispered.

"But how? There's no way out. Only Lucifer can let me out of here. And then there's the issue of returning my soul back to my body."

I smiled. "I've got all that taken care of," I said, pressing my lips to his gently. I willed his soul into mine. Two parts of a whole, finally reuniting as one. Instantly, my power flared to life. A heat, an awakening burned inside of me, that I had only experienced for a brief moment when Deus had admitted he loved me. Right before I had died.

I opened my eyes and Deus was gone. I carried the most precious part of my mate inside of me. Now, it was time to end this. I closed my eyes, imagined Deus's palace, and with a burst of red and black smoke, I shifted.

CHAPTER NINE

"Well, well," I heard his voice say behind me as I appeared in Deus's bedroom. "Miss me already?"

Deus lay in bed with three demon women, naked. One sprawled across his lap, another curled into his side, while the third kissed down his neck. A sick feeling rose inside me while I fought to remain calm. I would bathe him in a vat of bleach when we were both topside again. I looked away, not wanting to break.

"You must have a death wish," he said, sliding off the edge of the bed without regard for the women. He pulled on his pants and moved toward me. His eyes bore down on me, but I couldn't meet his gaze—not when he smelled of them.

He laughed. "Come all this way to give me the silent treatment, did we?"

I took a deep breath, gathering myself. I wanted to burn this whole place to the ground. I clenched my jaw, trying to remain calm, and looked up at him. Before I could say a word, his hands were around my throat. He picked me up, pinning me to the wall. His fingers buried themselves into my skin as he flashed his teeth. His face was full of rage.

"You stupid cunt," he growled. "I was naive enough to play along with your game the last time, but I won't be that complacent again. My brother will have the power that he is owed!"

I grabbed at his wrists, trying to force him to release me, but he was so much stronger. The girls on the bed laughed, propping their heads up to watch the show.

"I ..." I tried to get out words, but he was crushing my windpipe.

He leaned his lips closer to my ear. "What was that?" he said sarcastically. "Oh, now you have something to say?"

"Yes," I managed to get out. He loosened his grip on my throat, still pinning me to the wall.

"Make it fast," he growled. "I've already alerted Lucifer you're here, so you have mere seconds before you're dead."

"I have one last request," I said, choking, trying to breathe. My throat was already beginning to swell.

He laughed, arching an eyebrow at me. "The balls on you, little witch. What is this request?"

"A kiss," I said, trying to appear meek and timid. "I want to feel your lips on mine one last time ... before I die."

He smiled. I watched as his pride got the better of him. "I suppose I can do that for you," he said, licking his lips sensually.

"Thank you," I replied with a small smile.

Still pinning me to the wall, he lowered his head. I took a deep breath, allowing the power inside of me to rise. His lips caressed mine softly, testing the waters before pressing firmly against mine. I wrapped my arms around him, forcing his face harder into me. He tried to pull away, but I held firm.

The part of him I carried latched onto the connection I had made with Deus's body. Something heaved deep in my chest as his spirit unraveled from mine, one now becoming two, returning to its original vessel. I pulled away slowly, my mouth stretched open as a red and black fog transferred from me to Deus. His eyes were wide in shock, his body convulsing.

The girls on the bed were shaking, huddling together in fear. The lights in the room flickered and the entire castle shook with power. Finally, his spirit let go of me. I fell to the ground, weakened and breathing heavily. I didn't dare open my eyes. If this didn't work, I was dead, and Lucifer had won.

Finally, I look up at Deus. His body was still shaking slightly as he stumbled backwards. I sat back on my knees, waiting for a sign to indicate which Deus had won. His eyes lifted slowly from his hands to where I sat on the floor.

"Seren," he whispered, shaking his head. The sound of his voice. The emotion in each syllable that formed my name. My head fell into my hands and I began to cry. It was him. It was really him. My nightmare was almost over. I had done it.

Deus looked around the room and at the females in his bed. He closed his eyes in shame, turning from them. "No," he whispered, covering his face.

I stood and rushed to him. I pulled his hands away, looking up into his haunted eyes. "I need your help," I said in haste.

"My love," he cried. "I am so sorry. I—"

"We don't have time. I need you to focus. I need you to push your power into me through the bond. I need to form a new gateway as fast as possible before your brother arrives."

He looked away, his face confused and tormented.

I took a deep breath, placing my hands on either side of his face. I turned him towards me. "Deus," I whispered. Pain and guilt shone through his eyes. "I love you … every part of you. The demon … the angel … the man. Even in your darkness, I love you. But now, I need you to focus, so we can go home. Back to our family, and our future." I paused, rubbing my thumbs down his cheeks. "Can you do that for me?"

He nodded, unable to say a word.

"Good." I leaned in and kissed his cheek tenderly.

A white fog appeared in the corner of the room.

My heart dropped.

Lucifer.

"Deus, now!" I yelled. Deus held onto me as I focused. I threw my hands forward, forcing our power to become a solid entity. His power was overwhelming yet comforting; intoxicating and smooth like a drug. I pooled our powers together, merging them with the essences of Lucifer and the moon goddesses that I carried. The gateway began to form, blocks constructing in a matter of seconds.

"What do we have here?" I heard Lucifer's voice behind me. I stayed focused on building our escape. "When will you learn that you are no match for me, little goddess?"

"Stay the fuck away from her," Deus growled, removing a hand from me. There was a moment of silence, but I didn't dare turn around to see the shock I was sure had overwhelmed Lucy's face.

"She restored your soul," whispered Lucifer. "Using *my* power."

"You're no match for her," Deus snapped.

Lucifer laughed. "We'll see about that," he said. I heard a blast and felt Deus's body stiffen as he took the blunt force of the attack. I continued to focus on the gate. It was almost complete. I was so close, but I was approaching burnout. Even with all this power, a bridge to another world was not designed to be created at this pace.

More explosions sounded from behind me. I saw the girls rush towards the exit as furniture and shattered glass flew around me. In the corner of my eye, a sharp spear of wood impaled one of the girls, dropping her dead before she could reach the exit.

Sweat began to pour from my brow. My hands and body shook. I fought to breathe, but I didn't let go. Just another few moments and we'd be home. I willed the power to mold itself into an arch. I focused on the door and what would be on the other side. I closed my eyes, imagining Frankie, Aunt Thora, Nonna ... even my mother. I still had so many questions. We had lost so much time, thanks to Lucifer. I wasn't going to let him take one more thing from me.

"Deus!" I yelled, adding the finishing touches to the gate. I needed him close for the final surge to activate my magic. In the next breath, his arms were around me, barreling us both towards the portal as fire and ice flew towards us. I reached for the door, feeling the cold bite of the metal handle. I pressed my thumb down. *Click.*

Deus lunged forward, falling through the gate, hauling me with him. He spun to take the majority of the impact as we crashed into the floor. I sat up, throwing my hands towards the archway, absorbing the magic back inside myself before Lucifer could follow us through. I screamed with pain, opening myself up, siphoning my own power at a pace that would have killed any normal witch.

I heard Lucifer yelling in a fit of rage on the other side. The portal began to dissipate.

"I will kill everything you love, Seren De Salvo," he yelled. "Everything you hold dear, I will take from you. You will watch as all those around you suffer because of your incompetence. I will destroy you. I will have what I am owed." And with that, the portal closed.

I collapsed on the floor next to Deus, my heart racing. We both gasped for air. I relaxed, allowing a smile to escape. I looked at my beautiful mate, finally whole, beside me. I rolled to my back, brushed my hands over my face, and laughed.

The doors to the room flung open. Belz, Levi, and Frankie ran through, looking like they had seen a ghost.

"Oh, thank Aradia," Frankie said, hurtling towards me. She gathered me in her arms, squeezing so tightly I thought she was going to crush my ribs.

"Mammon owes me money," said Belz with a smile on his face.

Deus sat up, his face expressionless. He went to the table, pulling an old shirt over his body without a word.

"Asmodeus," Levi said, approaching him with caution.

Deus turned slightly, not making eye contact with anyone. "Yes, brother," he replied softly. "Soul is intact. No need to worry."

"I'm glad to hear that," Levi said with a smile. "It's good to see you back on this plane."

"Is it?" Deus replied, fidgeting with something on his desk.

Frankie looked at me with confusion. "You didn't come through the gate with the others. What happened? Where did you go?"

I took a deep breath, my thoughts and emotions still spinning. "I really don't know how," I admitted, standing, "but when I was going through the gate, I couldn't stop thinking about Deus. That ... if I left then, there may not be another chance to save him. Then bam, I shifted to where I needed to be."

"Your power is seriously amazing," Frankie whispered with a soft smile.

"How's Gor?" I asked.

"Bitchy as ever, but alive nonetheless," said Belz.

"And Giana?" I asked.

"Fully materialized, and hasn't left Gor's side yet," said Mammon.

Dues took a deep breath. "I'd like to be alone," he said, still not looking at the others.

"So, I should cancel the welcome home party I have waiting outside, then?" asked Belz playfully.

"I said, get out!" Deus yelled, his power rippling from him.

Levi approached Frankie, taking her hand in his. My cousin looked at me with worry in her eyes.

"I'll be okay," I reassured her.

"I know," she said, pulling me into another hug. "But I can't promise you will be after the lashing I have prepared for you." I laughed softly as she pulled away.

"I thought you may have forgotten about that."

"Never," she said with a wink. Everyone exited our room, closing the doors behind them. I walked over to my mate cautiously. I knew he had literally been through Hell, but the thought of being away from him, even in the next room, felt worse than death right then. I placed my hand on his arm, but he pulled away, like the contact physically pained him.

"Please," he said, unable to look at me. "I just … I need time right now."

I paused, assessing the man I loved.

"No," I replied flatly. "I'm not leaving you. Not even for a moment. Not ever again."

"Seren—"

"Deus, I said no."

He finally brought his eyes to mine, and I saw the guilt of reliving his sins was eating him alive. "I'm going to shower," he whispered.

"Sounds like a good plan," I said, heading to the bathroom. "I need one as well." I started the shower, the steam soon filling the room. He stood in front of me, hesitant to remove his clothes. I took the hem of his shirt and slowly removed it, then his pants. I allowed my dress to fall from my body.

I took his hand and led him into the warm streams of water. I lathered a sponge, gliding it over his body, making sure to be considerate of what he had been through. I washed his hair, and then mine. My heart was relieved he was home, but shattered for the suffering he had endured. He was a shell of himself.

I rinsed my body and then his, being respectful of the space he clearly needed. I turned him around to face me, sliding my arms around his waist. His eyes finally opened, looking down into mine. He tried to smile, but failed. He broke.

Deus buried his face into the crook of my neck, wrapping his arms around me. His knees gave out. I took the brunt of his weight as we slid down the wall of the shower. He cried against my skin, holding onto me so tightly it almost hurt, but I didn't let go. I kissed his head, pulling him into me as closely as I could. We sat there wrapped in each other's embrace, completely bare and exposed. Raw.

CHAPTER TEN

That night, I slept beside him. I woke up every few minutes, making sure he was still next to me. Deus barely slept. He tossed and turned, tormented by his experiences in the pit and what he had done when he was soulless. I placed my hand on his arm, letting him know I was there, but I didn't say a word … I didn't know what to say.

I was dealing with my own trauma from what I had endured and seen in Hell. The smell of blood and burning flesh seemed to be permanently singed into my nose. The cries of those lost souls woke me during the quietest moments of the night. I could feel the claws of the flying bat creatures still latching into my skin. The sound of the noctori haunted me, blood pooling in my ears. My mind was wrecked.

And then there was the emotional and physical abuse I had gone through at the hands of my mate. Even though the horrors the I had witnessed and endured in Hell weren't truly done by the man I loved, the memories and feelings still weighed heavily. I had accomplished my goal. He was safe, lying next to me. I just didn't know what came next.

The next morning, after he finally dozed off, I managed to sneak out of the room, going to the kitchen to gather food. Giana was in the kitchen with Frankie, preparing breakfast. They looked at me with small smiles.

"Good morning," I said softly.

"Morning," both echoed.

"How's Gor?" I asked.

"Better," replied Giana. "He's awake and his arm has grown back. Still a little red and tender, but he's assured me the hard part is over."

"That's great to hear," I said, the weight of my worry lessening. "I'll stop by this afternoon to check in with him, if that's okay."

"Of course," she said, putting two plates on a tray. "He has quite the lashing prepared for you, so I know he'll be thrilled."

I laughed. "Good to know. Have you reached out to your family?"

"No," she said hesitantly. "I'm not ready for that yet. I'm just going to focus on Gor and his health right now."

"I understand," I replied with a smile. "One thing at a time."

She took my hands in hers. She was holding back tears as she forced a smile.

"Thank you ... for saving me."

"Don't mention it," I replied, rubbing the top of her soft hand with my thumb.

"I wish there was some way I could repay you."

"Live a happy life. Make each other happy. That's all I want for you and Gor."

"We are eventually going to have to go home," said Frankie, popping a grape in her mouth. "Nonna has been blowing up my phone."

"I know," I huffed. "I'm just ..."

"I feel you," G said, her brow furrowing, "and for what it's worth, you're handling all of this with an amazing amount of grace."

I nodded my thanks. "I just can't deal with anything else right now."

Frankie ran her hand down my arm. "I get it," she said. "I'll go to them tomorrow and explain everything. In the meantime, you and Deus focus on healing."

"How is he?" asked Giana.

I shrugged. "I don't even know where to begin," I admitted. "I don't know how to help him, or what to even say. I was so focused on the saving part that I didn't really give much thought to what happened after he came home."

"The love you share will aid the healing," said Frankie. "Right now, you both need time."

"Here," said Giana, pushing the tray of food and beverages towards me. "Take this and go to him. The best thing for the both of you right now is to be together."

"Thank you, guys," I said, picking up the tray and heading back to our room.

When I opened the door, the bed was empty. I set the food down and followed the sound of running water to the bathroom. Deus was showering again. I waited patiently at the table, sipping my coffee. When he finally emerged, his skin was red and raw, like he had scrubbed off the first few layers. His heavy eyes landed on me, sadness still lingering.

"The water bill is going to be outrageous this month if you keep these habits up," I said teasingly.

He threw the towel in the basket and sunk into the chair in front of me. "I feel ... disgusting," he admitted, taking a cup of coffee off the tray.

I allowed my eyes to roam over his handsome features. The skin under his eyes was bruised and swollen. Even though he was suffering, it couldn't diminish the happiness that he was sitting in front of me ... alive and breathing.

"What can I do?" I whispered softly. "Tell me what I can do to help you."

"There's nothing. You've already done enough."

I got up from my chair and sat softly on his lap, wrapping my arms around his neck. He didn't touch me. He hung his head in shame. I rubbed his cheek softly, and his body tensed.

"I hurt you," he whispered. "In so many ways ... I hurt you."

"I knew it wasn't you."

"But it was. It is this vile, horrible part of me that deserves to suffer."

"Deus," I said, forcing his eyes to mine. "Anyone would have acted the same way without a soul. This isn't your fault. None of it is. I don't hold anything during your time in Hell against you."

His eyes drifted to my neck and then my shoulder. "I—" he tried to say.

"Stop!" I demanded, pressing my forehead against his. "It wasn't you. The Deus that I love, that is here now ... you died for me. You gave your life to save mine. You risked everything so that I would live." I pulled back, looking in his beautiful eyes. "So that we could live. I want to live with you ... my mate."

"How can you forgive me?" he whispered.

"There's nothing to forgive. Your actions weren't your own."

"But I remember," he admitted. "I remember the thoughts, the actions, the ... women. I remember all of it, and it makes me sick."

"Then let's forget it. Let's replace those memories with our own happiness. Don't let Lucifer win, my love. Don't let him take away this special bond that only few get to experience. We've only begun to explore what we can do together ... what we can be."

He didn't look at me. His hands remained at his sides. God, how I craved his touched. "What Lucifer said at the end," he whispered. "He's coming for you. It's no longer just about your power. His pride is damaged. He's going to attack everything you've ever loved."

"I'm no longer afraid," I said confidently.

His eyes finally met mine. "You should be, Seren. You should be very afraid."

I left Deus after breakfast to check on Gor. When I opened the door, Giana was snuggled into his side, grinning from ear to ear. Gor's laughter filled the air, possibly the most beautiful thing I had ever heard—except for the laugh of my mate, that is.

I knocked, feeling like I was interrupting something intimate. "Hey, it's me," I said softly. "I can come back if it's not a good time."

"Oh, no," said Gor, wincing as he sat up. "I've been waiting for this visit, you little kamikaze witch."

Giana laughed, kissing him on the cheek before getting up from the bed. "I'm going to the kitchen to get more food," she announced. "Does anyone want anything?"

"All you've done is eat this morning," stated Gor. "Where do you keep it all?"

"You try being dead for a few months and see how hungry you come back." She stuck her tongue out at him, shutting the door behind her.

I walked to the bed, smiling down at my friend softly. "I'm so sorry you got hurt," I whispered.

He shrugged. "Isn't the first time, won't be the last. Come sit," he said, patting the bed. As soon as I did, he pulled me into him, crushing my body against his chest. Safely engulfed in my friend's embrace, I broke. I cried while the demon of sloth soothed me, rubbing his hand down my hair and back, kissing my head softly.

I lay there in his arms for what seemed like forever. It was the first moment of peace I had experienced since being tortured by Lucifer all those weeks ago. Everyone was where they should be ... except Orion.

I forced myself to bury the memories from the hall of mirrors deep in the back of my mind. I wasn't ready to process what I had confronted within myself.

"How are you," Gor asked softly.

"Honestly ... I don't know." I pulled back, looking up at his soft brown eyes. "Deus is suffering, Orion is still dead, and I pissed off Lucifer to the point that he is now not only after me, but everyone I love."

"So, just another Tuesday then?"

I laughed, laying back next to him. "How do I help him, Gor? How do I heal him?"

"Being there for him, so he knows he's not alone, would be a good place to start. When I first had my soul returned, it was years before I could look at myself. Granted, I was without mine for centuries, but still ... the pain and regret is potent, especially with how powerful we are."

"I miss him so much," I admitted.

"I know, but look on the bright side; now that we know you are part demon, you'll have all of eternity to heal and find joy together.

I pulled away, looking at him in disbelief. "What?"

He shrugged. "I still want to run some tests. Mammon is the one we need to see about that, but since you have Lucifer's powers and DNA along with being Asmodeus's mate, it would only make sense you have our life span ... you're immortal, Seren."

"But, if that's the case, how did I die—" I froze, putting all the pieces together. The moment Deus died, he'd sacrificed his lifeforce in exchange for mine. And then there was what I had seen the brothers do in the underworld with the souls and how they had consumed them entirely. My mind spun and swirled with the possibility.

Lifeforce, even for a prince of Hell, was fragile. Not enough and you died ... too much, and you would suffer the same fate. In this universe, each plane has a balance. If I could somehow overpower Lucifer, gain the upper hand, maybe I could tip the scales, use my lifeforce to overpower and burn him out. Though, if I was right, it would mean sacrificing myself in the end.

"What is it?" Gor asked. His brow furrowed while he studied me.

"Nothing. It's just crazy to think of myself as immortal."

"You deserve a long life full of happiness, Seren." He smiled at me endearingly. "You are my favorite of any of them, you know."

"Who?"

"The vessels. Even Cecilia. I am honored to have spent time with you, and to call you my friend."

I laughed softly, wiping the tears from my cheeks. "A girl from a nunnery, best friends with a bunch of demons. Sounds like the beginning of a bad joke."

"Or maybe a really good one."

After I left Gor's room, I found Frankie and told her I'd return home with her to Castle Salvo. I needed to talk to Nonna. I prayed she would understand and support me when it came to my plan on how to be rid of Lucifer for good. Frankie would not. Aunt Thora most likely would side with Frankie. It didn't matter. I had started this war with the devil, and I was the one that needed to end it.

That afternoon I took a walk through town and worked out how I was going to end Lucifer, and the dominos I needed to set in place to make that happen. Late in the evening, I returned to Deus's room. He was awake and standing on the edge of the balcony.

He was so beautiful. I couldn't have created a man more perfect even if I tried. The thought of having eternity with him ... I embraced the joy of it, even if only for a moment. That eternity would never come. Not in this life, at least.

"Are you going to say hello, or just stare at me?" he said, turning his head slightly.

"I was just enjoying the view," I replied, stepping up next to him.

His hands were in his pockets, and I didn't dare push it with physical touch. Even though I wanted to spend the remaining few moments of my life wrapped in his arms, taking in every feeling, smell, and taste.

"Thank you," he said softly.

"For what?"

"Coming for me. I know you suffered because of that decision ... but all the same. Thank you."

"And thank you for sacrificing your life to save mine."

"I would have a hundred times over again. Your life is worth more than mine."

I paused, feeling the weight in my heart. "Don't say that Deus. You're amazing."

He looked at me then, offering a half smile. "How can you say that, after all you've witnessed?"

"Because I know what it's like to love and be loved by you. And I'd take those moments of happiness with you over anything else this life has to offer."

"You're insane," he said, shaking his head with amusement.

"I know. I'm mated to a Prince of Hell, for heaven's sake." We both laughed, and my heart lightened at the sound. "I missed you so much." I turned to face him fully.

He allowed a few moments to pass before he spoke again. "When I saw you … felt you die, it was the worst feeling I have ever experienced. Like a part of me had been torn out of my soul, just when it had finally been made whole. I was foolish to deny what was so evident between us before. It took you being kidnapped to get me to admit what I knew I'd never be able to escape." He laughed softly. "Sometimes, I wonder if pride is Lucifer's sin or mine.

"We made it, Deus. I'm alive, and so are you. Against all odds, we made it."

He finally turned to me. "Seren, I need you to be honest with me, even if it's not the answer I want to hear." He paused, licking his lips as he dropped his eyes from mine. "After everything, you truly, without hesitation, still want to be with me? You can overlook who or what I am, and what I've done?"

I smiled, drawing my hand down his face and neck. He stiffened. "I love you more than my own life," I said. "I am honored to be your mate. I know you better than you know yourself, Deus. I'm never letting us go."

His body relaxed and he smiled, truly smiled, for the first time since he had returned from Hell.

"Well, in that case, I promise to love and cherish you for eternity. My heart, soul, mind, and body will belong to you and only you. Forever and always."

My eyes filled with tears. I had wanted to hear those words so many times before. And now they came from the lips of the most extraordinary man I'd ever known.

"I am honored, my prince."

He stepped closer, his smile remaining as he looked down at me through his thick, black lashes. He trailed his fingers tenderly along my jawline and down my neck, then pulled back hesitantly. I caught his hand, placing it on my face.

"Don't you ever hesitate to touch me," I said, reveling in his caress.

He smirked. "I'm working on it."

I took a breath of relief at the breakthrough, knowing it would be short lived.

"I'm going back to Triora tomorrow with Frankie. I need to inform my family and coven about what's coming. Would you like to come with me?"

His eyes fell. "I ... I'm not good around people right now."

"I know, but maybe a change of scenery would help with that."

He hesitated. "I'll think on it."

I smiled. "I can live with that."

He looked out over the balcony, and I followed his gaze. The beautiful landscape of the massive mountains was captivating. Small snowcaps had formed on some of them as the winter winds were beginning to descend. I smiled at the peace my home provided. I felt his eyes on my face. When I met his gaze, he was smiling down at me.

"I was thinking about going for a ride," he said. "Care to join me?"

"I'd love nothing more."

Chapter Eleven

We rode most of the night through the thick forests that surrounded Castle Resnov. The crisp, fresh wind cleared away any thought of what was to come. We rode fast and hard, not stopping until our horses demanded rest.

When we returned, we followed the sounds of laughter and glassware clinching until we stumbled upon our family, crammed around a table in the dining kitchen, eating supper. When Deus entered, the room went silent. All eyes turned to my prince. I felt his unease ripple off him like waves of heat. He stiffened in the doorway, looking at those who had risked their lives to save him.

He cleared his voice, taking a brave step forward. "I want to first thank all of you for everything you did to rescue me," he said. "I owe each of you a life debt, which I am sure none of you will let me forget. I also want to apologize for any pain or trauma I caused when I ... when I wasn't myself. I would never willingly hurt any of you. Your dedication and loyalty mean everything to me. Thank you."

There was a moment of silence before Levi finally stood. He approached Deus, stopping as he stared his brother down. Then, Levi threw his arms around Deus and embraced him fully. The tension released in the room. Mammon and Belz were next, then Gor. He walked slower than normal, but he was up and moving, that's what mattered.

Deus's eyes filled with regret as he looked down at his youngest brother. "Gor, I am so so—" he tried to say.

"Don't," interrupted Gor. "All is forgiven." Gor turned to me and smiled. "You're a lucky man, brother. She never gave up on you ... not for a second."

Deus turned and smiled tenderly at me. "I don't know what I did to earn the love of this amazing woman, but I plan to show her how thankful I am for her every day for the rest of my life."

"Enough with all the emotions," said Mammon from the table. "Sit, eat, drink."

"I have to agree," said Belz. "We've outsmarted big brother. That deserves a toast."

"Seren outsmarted Lucy," Levi clarified.

"To Seren," said Giana, holding up a glass. "For always extending a hand to those less fortunate."

"To Seren," added Frankie, "for being the most loyal person I've ever known."

Levi held his glass up. "To our goddess, for overcoming every obstacle."

"For outsmarting and maneuvering the smartest and oldest thing in this world," toasted Mammon.

"For being fearless, without any thought of her own wellbeing," added Belz.

"To our little witch," said Gor. "As reckless and as careless as you might be, I'd have you no other way. Your bravery is a testament to everything that you are."

Deus picked up a glass and turned towards me. "To my mate," he said tenderly. "For being everything I am not, and teaching me that everyone, no matter how scarred and flawed they may be, deserves to be loved."

My eyes filled with tears as I looked at the family that I had found and the home I had chosen.

"To all of us," I said, taking in their beautiful faces. "Together we stand. Together we fight. Together ... we survive."

Before we completed the toast, Mal and Hashen strolled through the door, looking more badass and devious than ever. I stood and hurtled into Hashen's arms. He returned my affections with a simple pat on the back.

"There, there, little witch," Hashen said in his deep voice. "All is well."

"Are you okay?" I asked.

"Wouldn't be the first time I was locked in a dungeon in Hell," he replied.

Deus stood from his chair. Regret washed over his face as he stood looking at his two most trusted generals. "Hashen," Deus whispered.

Hashen held out his hand, stopping him from continuing. "I've known you for many centuries, my prince. A few months of being locked in a dungeon isn't going to change the grace you have shown me, nor the respect and loyalty I have for you. Though, I must say, I prefer this version of you over the other bastard."

We all began to laugh, including Deus. He moved to stand face to face with Hashen. "Thank you, my friend," he said, extending his hand.

Hashen took it with haste. "Of course, my prince."

The rest of the evening was filled with love and laughter. We drank and ate around the table as if there wasn't a potential apocalypse on the horizon. Towards the end of the night, Mal caught my attention, signaling for me to follow. I slid out of my chair while Belz retold the story of Gor and the tremonite creature from Hell.

I followed Mal out into the hall. "What's going on?" I asked.

"I thought you'd might want to know about what has been transpiring in Hell."

The heavy feeling in my gut returned. "I'm listening."

There was a long pause before she finally said, "Nothing."

"I'm sorry, what do you mean nothing?"

"Lucifer has done nothing but throw a temper tantrum since you took the prince and returned to earth."

"That can't be right. He vowed to destroy me and everything I love. He must be planning something."

"As of right now, there have been no movements on his part. Things are more peaceful than they've been in decades down below. Hashen has agreed to return to Hell to keep an eye on things."

I tried to think through what Lucifer could be planning, but my mind was exhausted, as was my body. I looked back to Mal. "Any word on where Victoria scurried off to?"

"I can look into it," she replied.

"Good. And Mal, let's just keep this between us. Deus is finally coming around. I don't want to burden him with Victoria or anything regarding Lucifer right now."

She bowed. "As you wish, princess."

I laughed. "What did you call me?"

Her head tilted, her eyes confused. "Princess. That is what you are. The Princess of Lust."

I examined her to determine if she was serious and then ... I laughed and laughed hard. Harder than I had in weeks. "Me ... the Princess of Lust?" I gasped, trying to catch my breath.

"That is who you are," said Mal in a firm voice. "If you are his mate, then you are my princess. I serve both Deus and you, Seren De Salvo. You have more than earned my devotion."

"I think I have enough titles, don't you? Witch, goddess, demon ... princess seems a bit excessive."

"If you are with the prince, then you are *our* princess. That is how this works."

"So does that make Frankie the Princess of Envy?" I asked.

"No. Not unless she ends up being his mate or they marry, and she gifts her soul to him."

"Excuse me?" I asked.

"I will leave Prince Resnov to explain the fine print of how our kingdoms work. All the same, I am honored to serve you. You are a great addition to House Lust."

"Well ... thank you ... I think," I replied with a small smile.

The door opened behind me, and Deus stepped to my side.

"There you are," he said, assessing the situation between Mal and I. "Am I interrupting something?"

"Not at all, my prince," answered Mal. "I was just explaining to the princess here how formalities within the houses work."

Deus's brows rose, his eyes settling on me as a smile stretched across his face. "Princess," he said with a hint of surprise. "I never thought—"

"She is your mate, correct?" asked Mal sharply.

"Yes," he replied.

"Then, that makes her the princess of our realm."

"I suppose it does," he said.

"You didn't know?" I asked.

"I mean ... I know how the hierarchy works, but none of us have ever found mates or taken wives. This matter has never needed our attention before."

"Don't worry, *mate*, I will willingly sign a prenuptial agreement. The kingdom of lust is all yours," I said in a sarcastic growl.

He laughed, sliding his hands into his pockets, shaking his head.

"If that is all," interrupted Mal, "I will be retiring for the evening."

"Thank you," I said before she headed to her room.

Deus pulled me into him, closer than we had been in a long time. "And what was all of that about?" he asked.

I shrugged. "Just girl talk."

"Hm," he growled, moving a piece of hair from my face. "Funny how this bond thing works. I can actually feel a little twist in my gut when you lie now. That is going to come in handy."

I rolled my eyes. "Doesn't mean I am going to tell you the truth," I replied, pulling away. Before I got too far, he tugged me back into him, holding my arms in his strong hands.

"Love, I'd rather not have to go deep diving into that beautiful head of yours."

I squared up to him in challenge. "I'd like to see you try."

He arched an eyebrow, assessing me before laughing softly. Concern replaced his amusement. "Just promise me you aren't running headfirst into danger."

I forced a smile on my face. "I promise," I lied.

He studied me a moment longer, as if he knew the truth. To avoid any further questioning, I decided to divulge a little of what I had learned, to throw him off my tracks.

"Mal told me that Lucifer has been quiet since we left. No gathering of armies or such."

"Yes, but for how long?"

"Does it matter?" I asked. "If that means we get a few moments of peace and quiet, shouldn't we take it?"

His face softened. I felt his finger gently rub along my arms—the first loving affection he had shown me since being back. "You're right. After we check in with your family, why don't you and I disappear for a few days? How does that sound?"

A smile stretched across my face uncontrollably. "Sounds like heaven."

He rubbed the back of his knuckles down my face. "You're my salvation, Seren. I never thought ... I never knew what love could be, until you."

I smiled, holding back the tears that fought to be free. "Everything I've had to endure has led me to you. My best friend. My lover. My mate."

Deus cupped the back of my head gently, leaning down just enough that I could feel his breath on my face. His eyes searched mine, taking in every detail. "May I kiss you?" he asked.

"Always," I replied. His lips slid across mine, testing the waters before softly pressing against my mouth. I inhaled, feeling a rush of joy, relief, and *lust*. I pulled him into me, needing more ... needing everything. Everything he was willing to offer.

He pulled away, too soon for my liking, but I wanted him to be in control. If he needed time, I would give him that, no matter how little I might have left.

"So, tomorrow we face the Salvo women," he said, taking my hand and leading us back to our bedroom.

"You've decided to come?"

"If it makes you happy, then yes."

"I don't think they're going to be thrilled about my recent travels."

He laughed. "Your nonna will be furious, but she will also be proud as hell. No pun intended."

I smiled, thinking about the one situation I still hadn't resolved that waited for me at home.

"What is it?" he asked.

"My ... my mother. We really haven't had time together since her soul was returned. I was too busy mourning you, and she was busy trying to live with all she had done."

"Take it from one that knows, it's no easy feat."

"I know, but after everything, I think I want time with her. To get to know the real Annalise, not Lucifer's puppet."

"Then take that time, my love. Take all the time you need. You have it, now that you've tapped into the demon part of you," he said with a grimace.

I stopped walking and pulled him back. "What was that?" I asked.

His gaze fell. "It's just ... Lucifer. A part of him is in you. It's unsettling."

"Well, is that something you can live with?"

"Do I have a choice?"

I took a step back in shock. "You sure as hell do. Mated or not, I can leave right now if it's that big of an issue for you," I said, turning to walk away.

He pulled me back against his torso, laughing, holding me close. "If the only good thing Lucifer does in his long existence is saving your life, then enemy or not, I will always be grateful to him." He bent down, kissing me again. This time, his lips weren't as hesitant. I breathed him in, the stir of desire awakening in me.

This time I pulled away first, resuming our path towards our bedroom. "That also means I won't have the lifespan of a human. Or at least, that's what Gor presumes."

"Which means I am stuck with the most stubborn witch I've ever met for eternity. Lucky me." He kissed the top of my head.

When we got back to our room, Deus showered, his new favorite pastime. I wanted to join him, but I didn't want to push. After I showered, I found him standing in front of the fireplace, lost in thought. I approached with caution, touching the back of his arm softly. He jerked away, turning quicker than I could register.

He grabbed onto my shoulders, slamming me forcefully into the nearest wall. My head hit the bricks, my vision tunneling. I whimpered at the impact. Deus's eyes were full of rage, but at the sound of my cry, his aggression dissipated.

He instantly released me, stepping back and looking at his hands in disbelief. "I'm so sorry," he whispered, his voice full of pain. "I didn't…" He fell to his knees in front of the fire.

I dropped beside him, placing a hand on his shoulder. "It's okay, Deus. This is to be expected. What you've been through—"

He pulled away from my touch. "Don't make excuses for me. I … I lost myself and hurt you. There is no rational reasoning that will ever make that okay."

I grabbed his face between my hands. "Deus, look at me," I demanded. He obeyed. "You've been tortured for what must have felt like eternity. You were stuck in a pit where your darkest moments and deepest regrets plagued you, ripping away everything that was good. Healing will take time. I know this, and I am here for it, but you need to give yourself permission to take the time to heal."

He rubbed his thighs with his hands. "You're right," he whispered.

"I know," I said playfully, relaxing a bit.

He smirked. "I'm sorry you have to go through this with me. I didn't imagine this is how we'd be spending our first few months as mates."

I scooted closer, looking at him playfully. "And what did you think those first few months would look like?"

He smiled at me. "You ... me ... never leaving that bed," he said in a sensual voice that rolled through me in the most delicious and arousing way.

"Sounds like a dream."

He turned his eyes back to the fire. His head hung in shame. "Seren ... I want to wait before being with you in that manner. Until I have a grip on all of this."

"What about your powers?" I asked.

He shook his head. "If it becomes a need, then we'll deal with it, but ... I want to be with you completely. Not like this. Not when I still can't even stand the sight of myself."

I leaned my head on his shoulder. "I understand," I replied, pushing down a ping of disappointment.

"Thank you," he said, kissing the top of my head. "I love you, my princess."

I chuckled. "And I love you, my demon prince."

Chapter Twelve

Darkness engulfed me. I tried to move, but something was restraining my arms. Claws dug deep into each wrist. Warm streams of blood trickled down my forearm. I began to panic, trying to see through the clouds of darkness. A flickering image of a woman appeared. The details of her person remained cloaked in the shadows, but something about her seemed ... familiar.

The outline of her mouth came into view. Her lips pulled away from her white teeth, mimicking a scream, but no sound came from her. She vanished and then reappeared closer. The figure reached out a pale, white hand towards my face, but before she made contact, she disappeared.

Screaming yanked me from my dream. All the horrors of my time in Hell came flooding back to the surface. I jolted up, my heart racing and my power ready to attack.

Deus screamed again, so powerfully it pulled him from his own slumber. I reached out to comfort him, but he recoiled, as if my very touch pained him. I felt useless. I didn't know how to help him recover from this trauma.

He sat on the couch the rest of the night, eyes drawn into the flames as they licked and lashed against the logs. When I woke the next morning, he was gone.

I took a shower and prepared for my trip home. My heart felt hollow. I was lost. Deus was in so much pain, and I was useless. I missed his touch, his kiss, his playful remarks.

I drifted down the hall towards the kitchen where I was surprised to see Gor cooking. I smiled at him, some sense of normalcy returning. He grinned back, flipping a pancake in the air.

"Where's G?" I asked.

"Still sleeping upstairs," he replied with a wink and a devilishly handsome smile. I laughed at my friend, happy to see him with such light and life flickering behind his eyes.

I slid into the stool at the edge of the island. "Long night?" I asked.

"Very ... now that I'm fully healed." He slid a plate of food across the marble countertop and poured me a cup of coffee. "You?"

"Yes, but my evening wasn't as pleasant as yours, it would appear." Gor's brow furrowed.

"He ... he woke up screaming last night. I tried to comfort him, but that did little good. He didn't come back to bed and when I woke this morning, he was gone."

Gor reached underneath the island and pulled out a bottle of brandy, poured a shot into my coffee, and then took the stool next to me. I huffed in amusement.

"And how are you doing with all of this?" he asked.

I shrugged. "My feelings aren't important right now."

He took my hand in his. "Yes, they are. What you experienced and went through down there is just as real and important."

I held the warm mug of coffee in my hand, watching the steam rise into the air as the sweet liquor wafted underneath my nose.

"I feel ... lost. Depressed, even. My chest hurts, constantly, like it's hard to breath. I can't focus on much beyond Deus." I paused, taking a deep breath, letting the reality of all we'd experienced settle onto me.

I covered my face with my hands. My entire body trembled, tears spilling over while I released the fear, the stress, the pain ... all of it.

Gor held me against his chest, running his fingers through my hair. I willed myself to stop, but once the floodgates had been opened, there was no going back.

I lost track of time. Folded in the arms of my friend, all I knew was that I felt safe. I felt understood.

I told Gor about the gallery of mirrors and what I had seen there. The people who I had let down, who had died because of me. I told him every detail about Orion, and how I still longed for him, and for the part of myself that had died alongside him.

Then, I got to the pit. Without betraying Deus's trust, I told Gor what I had gone through to bring him back. The women I had seen in his bed, knowing what he had done with each of them.

When I was finally able to gather myself, I pulled away slowly, feeling foolish for losing control. Gor poured me another cup of coffee without saying a word. That, among other things, was what I loved about my relationship with Gor. We didn't need words.

I picked up my fork and ate.

"Nonna and Mamma are going to kill us," remarked Frankie.

I sat on the edge of her and Levi's bed as my cousin frantically found things to clean, trying to distract herself.

"They're going to be more pissed at me than you," I replied.

"Oh, no. That's not how Nonna works. I'm going to get the brunt of the blame, because I'm the oldest and I should have known better. I'm responsible for talking you *out* of doing crazy shit like going to Hell and taking on Lucifer and his legions. I can hear it now: *'Francesca Rose, how could you let your cousin, our beloved moon goddess, make such foolish choices? You know better, bambina. When will you learn? Why has Aradia cursed me with such a foolish descendant?'*"

I laughed, unable to ignore the eerie similarities between Frankie and our sweet nonna. "Well, I'm notorious for doing things I shouldn't."

"You will hear no argument from me," she said, tossing a decorative pillow at my face. I laughed, catching it.

Levi appeared in the doorway, looking elegant and handsome, as usual. He took one look at Frankie in her frantic state and smiled. As she passed, carrying a pile of clothes, he caught her in his arms, pulling her into his body. As if under a spell, she locked eyes with him. All tension, worry, and panic faded away. Her arms relaxed, dropping the clothes to the floor.

He ran the back of his knuckles down her face, gazing at her tenderly. She closed her eyes, breathing in deeply and leaning into his touch.

"That's better," he whispered.

Something in me tightened. I fought to hold back tears of jealousy, and longing.

Frankie took another deep breath, gathering herself. "Alright," she said with confidence. "It's now or never. Let's get this over with."

I popped off the bed just as Gor and Giana appeared in the doorway behind Levi. G's face was panic-stricken, but she forced a smile and said, "got room for two more?"

"You're ready to see your family?" I asked, surprised by her decision.

She hesitated, looking at Gor for confirmation. He smiled down at her, running a soothing hand down her back and nodded. She shrugged at me.

"I suppose I should see them before Lucifer decides to attack again. After dying, I've realized how precious each moment is and I don't want to have any regrets moving forward."

I took her hand and smiled at her. "I'm proud of you," I said softly.

"Where's Deus?" G asked.

I swallowed. "He didn't get much sleep last night," I said, trying to hide my discomfort at his absence. "I figured Frankie and I could handle our nonna."

I had waited for Deus to return to our room after breakfast, but when he hadn't, I figured it would best if he sat this one out. I wrote him a letter, letting him know I understood him needing time alone, even though it pained me to be parted from him.

Frankie huffed with amusement. "Yea," she said, "like anyone has ever *handled* Lucia De Salvo and lived to tell the tale."

The truth was, I wasn't doing Deus any good by being here. It killed me to leave, but he needed time to process and heal. And on top of that, I needed a distraction: something to solve or fix. Handling the Salvo women would be easier than looking into his eyes and knowing he was suffering and there was nothing I could do to fix it.

"Okay," said Frankie, "if we don't do this now, I might back out."

I took her hand and gave G my other. Gor and Levi completed the circle. I looked around at my family and forced a smile. "Home sweet home," I said.

Wind whipped around us as dark, red-laced tendrils of my magic lashed and grew, engulfing us in a funnel. We landed in the center of my room back at Castle Salvo. The group stumbled back, gathering ourselves from the sudden travel. With the addition of Lucifer's power—my demonic side—shifting no longer taxed me as it once had.

I looked at Giana, who took a deep breath, then nodded. I pulled out my phone and called Antonio. He picked up on the second ring.

"Seren," he said in a worried tone. "Is everything okay?"

"Hey, yes. Everything is better than okay, actually. Can you ... can you come to my room?" I asked.

There was a pause. "You're home?" he asked in surprise.

"Just arrived actually. I have ... a gift for you."

Another pause. "I'll be right there." He hung up.

"I think he's going to be disappointed with the gift when he arrives," said G with a playful smile. "He's probably thinking he's getting laid."

Frankie and I howled with laughter. I elbowed G in the arm.

"You're awful." I shook my head.

"What?" she said. "I'm serious."

"We'll gather Nonna and Mamma," said Frankie. "Meet in Nonna's room in ten minutes?"

I nodded and she and Levi took off down the hall.

Giana looked nervous, fidgeting with her hands. She glanced at Gor and then at me in a silent plea for help. Gor nodded with understanding.

"I'll make myself scarce until you're ready for introductions to be made," he said, kissing her on the head and vanishing into thin air. A knock came at my door.

Giana froze, her eyes large and her hands trembling. I placed my hands on her shoulders, trying to soothe her.

"Hey," I said softly. Her eyes met mine. "He's going to be over the moon."

She laughed, some tension releasing. "That's funny, coming from the moon goddess."

I shrugged. "What can I say? I am a jack of all trades."

"You're something, that's for sure."

I went to the door, opening it just a little to make sure it was Antonio. His handsome face peeked around the crack and smiled at the sight of me. That smile met his hazel eyes as his dark hair shined in the light. I pulled the door open to allow him entrance.

Before I could shut it, he gathered me into his arms, burying his face in the crook of my neck and hugged me. I returned his affection, savoring the feeling of another's embrace. He pulled back and gazed at me with gentle longing.

"I'm so happy you're safe," he said. "We were beginning to worry when we—"

He stopped mid-sentence, his eyes snapping behind me. His mouth gaped open as his hands slid from my arms. Tony took in his sister from head to toe, completely speechless.

Giana shifted uncomfortable and smiled. "Hey, big brother," she whispered, unsure.

Tony looked back to me with questions and confusion in his eyes. I shrugged. "Surprise," I said with a grin.

"How?" he said, still in disbelief.

"Long story short," I said. Tony slowly approached Giana. "I took a little trip to Hell recently, and decided to bring your sister back with me."

Tony studying every detail of his sister's face. He reached out, hesitant to touch her as if she might disappear, but before he could make contact, she slammed into him, wrapping her arms around his waist with a death grip. Her sobs filled the room as tears of joy ran down her face.

"I've missed you so much," she cried out. "Out of everyone, I've missed you the most."

Tony's cheeks were now wet with their own streams of tears. He wrapped his arms around her, bending to kiss the top of her head. He laughed, and my heart bloomed in response. I softly made my way to the door, trying not to disturb.

Tony turned to me, Giana still in his arms. His face shone with happiness.

"Thank you," he mouthed. I nodded in reply and left them to their privacy.

I walked the halls, recognizing coven members I hadn't seen since before the elders had kicked my family out of our home—our birthright. They nodded and smiled, but whispered as I passed.

I didn't care. I was done trying to earn their approval. I had more than earned it. If they only knew all I had done and sacrificed.

I had decided, in those weeks I had lived among them after Deus's death, that I would not accept an elder position when it was my generation's time. I would pass that to Frankie, allowing her and her offspring to carry on our traditions. Though I was the daughter of Nonna's eldest, I would not accept the title and position.

But now ... after discovering what must be done to put a stop to Lucifer, I had to accept that I wouldn't be alive long enough to even be offered the mantle.

I took a deep breath as I approached Nonna's door and knocked.

Frankie's face appeared on the other side. She gave me a grave smile and allowed me to pass. Nonna, Aunt Thora, and my mother all stood near the fireplace. I strolled into the room, taking in my beautiful family—the lineage that had sired me. The powerful, unmoving, and devoted women who had given up so much for each other.

Nonna stepped forward, opening her arms to me. I dove into her hug, savoring that sense of happiness and love only a grandmother could give. Aunt Thora ran a hand through my dark hair, and I pulled away from Nonna to hug her tightly. My mother stood off to the side, uncertain. I walked over to her, offering a small smile as I reached out and embraced her.

She hesitantly placed her arms around me, her fingers flexing as her body shivered slightly.

"I'm glad you're home, little bean," she whispered.

"How are you?" I asked, pulling away to look at her familiar face.

"Better," she replied. "Every day is better, but I have a long way to go."

"I'm proud of you," I said. "And happy you're healing."

She nodded. Aunt Thora stood by her side, placing a hand on her back. The similarities between the twins were uncanny. Besides the different fashion choices and hair, they were identical, even in their facial expressions and mannerism.

"Freaky," said Frankie, coming to my side. "Right?"

"I was just thinking the same thing," I admitted.

Both Aunt Thora and my mother gave a small laugh as they looked at each other. "I'm glad to have my soulmate back," said Aunt Thora.

My mother leaned her head into her sisters. "I'm glad to be home," she replied.

Frankie took my hand. I looked back at Nonna, and her eyes filled with tears of happiness. She wiped them away before anyone could comment.

"Right," Nonna said, gesturing us towards the seating area by the large bay windows. "Now, what is it you have to tell us, bambinas?"

I told my family what I had discovered, where I had gone, and all I endured. Frankie sat by me in silence for support. I told them everything ... almost. I left out how I would kill Lucifer. That was a conversation I would have with Nonna alone. Only she would understand.

When I finished, they sat stone faced. Nonna finally rose, focusing on the world outside of the window. My mother had tears running down her face. She held her head.

"I am so sorry I've brought this upon you," Annalise said. "If I would have known all those years ago, I—"

"There's no point in looking back now," I interrupted. "Without those actions, I would never have found my mate, and that is something I wouldn't change for the world."

"You actually went to Hell?" Thora said, still in shock.

I nodded. "I wouldn't recommend it as a vacation spot," I said.

"And you brought back Giana Simonelli? Just that easy?" she asked.

I nodded. "She didn't deserve the life she was granted. This way, she has a real chance."

"And now she's involved with the Prince of Sloth?" asked my mother.

Frankie nodded. "Seems like our generation has a type," she said playfully.

"This is no joke," Nonna said. "You may be a goddess, Seren, but you don't get to play God. It is not up to you to choose who lives or who dies."

"Isn't it?" I said boldly. "What is the point of having all this power, all these abilities, if I can't protect the people I love? Has the universe not put our family through enough?"

I took a moment to look at each of them. "I am done playing by any set of rules others have created for me. I am the most powerful witch there has ever been, and if I can stop those around me from dying, then I will, whatever the cost."

"Seren," whispered my mother. "This isn't the life I wanted for you."

"It's the life I was born to," I replied. "No one can change that now."

"What's it like?" asked Aunt Thora. "The demon portion of your power?"

I paused, the darkness inside me flickering alive as if it had heard her question.

"It feels ... different then our magic. Ancient, and darker. Heavy. It's addictive, and all consuming. When I tap into it, I almost lose myself. Like I'm walking on the edge of sanity and complete hysteria. But when I use it ... it feels good ... too good," I admitted.

"It will consume you," said Nonna. "If you use it, it will destroy everything that you are, leaving you no better than the Morningstar."

"I don't believe so," I replied. "I think my bond to Deus is an anchor of sorts. Even in the blur of the power, I always seem to have a lifeline back to him. To my home."

Nonna stood and paced, fuming. She glared at Frankie and me.

"How has this happened?" she asked. "The heirs to the Étoile coven, in love with *demons*. Is this some cruel joke? Some ... some final test the universe has burdened me with?" She pointed at Frankie. "Is he your mate?"

My cousin looked at me and then back to Nonna nervously. "I ... I don't know," she admitted. "If he is, the bond hasn't clicked into place."

"Well, hopefully it doesn't—"

"Regardless," Frankie interrupted Nonna smoothly. "I won't leave him. I belong with him, Nonna. I am sorry if you can't see that, but—"

"Enough," Nonna blurted. She turned back to me. "And where is your *mate*?"

"He is recovering back home," I answered.

"*Home*?" repeated Thora.

I looked at her and nodded. "Yes," I said. "My home."

"This is your home, Seren," spat Nonna. "Don't be ridiculous. You are a Salvo. You have responsibilities, and one day you will be an Elder."

"No," I said softly. "I won't." Everyone looked at me as if I had just grown another head.

"What?" Nonna gasped. "You would give up your ancestral right for a demon?"

"Little bean, please stop and think," said my mother softly. Even Frankie looked at me with question.

"I would like to speak with Nonna privately," I said. They didn't budge. "Please."

Franke squeezed my hand, standing and heading to the door. Thora followed, and finally my mother did the same, never taking her eyes off me.

Once the door was shut, I stood and approached the window. Nonna's jaw was tight, her expression full of rage and pain. I ran my hand down her arm, but she didn't move.

"Nonna," I whispered, "there's more." I waited. Her eyes turned to me, full of exhaustion. "I won't become an elder because ... because I won't live long enough for the title to pass to me."

Her mouth fell. "What are you talking about?" she asked.

I took her hand, leading her to the sofa. I rubbed the back of her soft skin, taking my time to form my sentences.

"I've figured out how to kill a Prince of Hell, but before I tell you, I need you to swear to me you will never speak a word of this to anyone. You will never write or share with anyone how to kill them. I need to make sure Deus and the others remain safe."

Her eyes searched my face, but she nodded, tightening her hand around mine.

"Only another demon prince can kill one of the seven. They all have the ability to absorb souls. That is how they remain powerful and alive. It is also how Hell functions ... on the life forces of those who have died and been sent there. When Deus sacrificed his life to bring me back"—Nonna grimaced at the memory—"he killed himself in the process. They are bound to one another and can't repeat how they can be killed, but Deus died. Truly died. When I went to Hell with the other princes, I watched them consume souls. They're able to transfer their life force while taking the life force of others. I think ... I believe the princes can only be killed if another prince is willing to sacrifice himself, forcing his own essence into the other to override their system which leads to their death."

Nonna's brow furrowed. "How does this concern you?" she asked. "You aren't a demon prince."

"No ... but I have Lucifer's magic inside of me. I am also the mate, the other half, to another prince. Because of this, I am immortal, according to Gor. I'm part demon, Nonna. I can use his own power to destroy him. But I am going to need your help ... and the help of our family."

"They will never agree to this," she added.

"I know. That's why I am meeting with you now, in private. I know this is hard for you, but I also know you're logical. Lucifer vowed to destroy everything I loved, including this family and the coven. He needs to be stopped."

"Why doesn't one of the other princes volunteer?"

"I wouldn't ask this of them. Not when I've seen firsthand what would become of them down there."

She paused, looking away from me. "Why you, bambina? Why must it be you? You've barely had a chance to live."

"I've made peace with this decision."

"And your mate? What does he have to say about this?"

I bit the inside of my lip, feeling a pain go through my chest. "He doesn't know... and he won't."

Nonna exhaled, dragging her hands over her face as she thought. "What do you need the family to do?"

A sense of relief spread through me. "I need you and Mother to siphon Lucifer's power into me. I need him weakened for this plan to work. I only have a fraction of his power, but if I can access more, I should be able to burn him out. Since we're all connected by blood, I should be able to act as a conduit for you and Annalise's siphon abilities, linking our powers to draw in Lucifer's magic and send back into him."

Nonna looked at me with heavy eyes. "You're brilliant, bambina. Truly brilliant."

I smiled. "Thank you. Pretty good for being raised in a nunnery, I suppose." I laughed softly. She cupped my cheek with her hand. Her face was filled with pain and sorrow.

"All the years we were robbed of," she said softly. "There has to be another way." Her hand dropped away.

"There isn't. Believe me, I've thought of nothing else."

"I hate this plan."

"I know. But I need you to help me with a cover story for Mom and the others. They can't know."

"I … I can't do this, bambina."

I took her hand in mine. "Nonna," I said firmly. "I am the only one that can do this. If I don't, millions of people die, along with everyone we love, and he wins. He gets the power he wants and then the world ends. What is the value of one life compared to billions?"

"Everything, Seren. You are everything to me," she said, desperation lacing her voice as tears fell.

"I love you so much, Nonna."

She pulled me into her. "And I you." She ran her hands through my hair. "You're no demon, my baby. You're an angel."

I smiled, tears welling. "Hopefully, I've done enough good to end up in the right place once I go. Maybe … maybe Orion's waiting for me up there. It'd be nice to see him again."

"I'm sure he's looking down on you right now, thinking how crazy this all sounds."

I laughed. "I don't doubt it. So, does this mean you'll help me?"

Her lips tightened into a straight line. "I will do what must be done," she answered with a nod.

"Thank you, Nonna.

CHAPTER THIRTEEN

I returned to my room feeling as if a weight had been lifted. Nonna had agreed to my crazy plan, even though I knew it had killed her. I shut the door behind me softly. Antonio and Giana had left, which I was thankful for. I needed some quiet.

The doors to my terrace were open, the cold breeze shifting the curtain panels. A figure strolled into the room casually. He was dressed in his normal black tailored suit with a red tie. His hair was perfectly parted on the side, the dark strands glistening in the sunlight that followed him.

Deus.

I smiled softly as he examined me from head to toe. "You left without even telling me goodbye," he said in his deep and sensual voice. "To say I'm offended is an understatement." He looked down at me with those crystal blue eyes.

"I wrote you a note. Plus, I didn't want to add more to your plate," I replied, fiddling with my hands, trying not to reach for him. "I figured you'd want some alone time, to deal with everything."

"And why would I want that?"

I shrugged. "I just haven't felt like I've been much comfort for you. I didn't think my absence would be noticed."

His brow furrowed before his eyes softened. He reached out, running a hand down my arm. I shivered with a sudden weakness at the contact. "We've been separated long enough," he said softly, pulling me in closer to him. "I don't want to be without you. Not for one more moment. And you have been comforting. Being close to you ... it makes things easier and reminds me I'm alive."

I smiled, looking down at my hands. "I miss you," I whispered.

His fingers slid underneath my chin, bringing my eyes to his. "I'm sorry I haven't been there for you like you've needed. I know none of this has been easy for you either."

I swallowed, trying to refrain from breaking in front of him. "After everything we've both been through, I just don't want to waste another minute. I don't want to look back and regret the time we didn't take advantage of. I don't want Lucifer to take another moment from us. He's stolen enough."

He smiled at me. "I agree. But just so we're clear," he said, sliding his arm around my waist, tangling his other hand in the nape of my hair. He gently angled my face up to his, expression full of love and passion. "I plan to spend the rest of our existence worshiping the very ground you walk on."

The tears came fiercely at his declaration. I ran my hand down the side of his face softly. He turned into my touch, closing his eyes. Little did he know, my life already had an expiration date stamped into it.

"Can I kiss you?" I asked, needing any part of him he was able to give.

His smile faded into hesitation, before he leaned down ever so slowly. He brushed his lips against mine, soft and testing.

The feeling of him—the taste—it was overpowering. I needed more. I needed him. I needed my mate.

I pulled him closer, claiming him with my mouth. My fingers tangled through his hair. I slid my tongue along his lips, and he parted them slowly. Frantically, my hands slid across his body, needing more. I pulled his jacket off, dropping it to the floor as I moved my fingers to the buttons of his shirt. I undid one, then two, before he stopped me, pulling my hands back.

I whimpered, staggering back from him. I was being selfish. He had asked for time and here I was, forcing myself on him. But there was something inside of me that just ... needed the intimacy. The connection. I needed him.

I couldn't look at him as I pulled my wrists from his grasp. I ran my hands over my face and through my hair.

"I'm sorry," I was able to choke out, wiping the tears from my face. I stepped away, trying to find something else in the room to focus on. My gut twisted with embarrassment, desire, frustration, and anger. I didn't know what emotion to focus on or which was more aggressive. My cheeks warmed as my hands shook slightly. Embarrassment. Embarrassment had won.

"Love," he whispered, taking a step towards me.

I held out my hand to stop him, still unable to look in his direction.

"This has nothing to do with you," he said, his shoulders slack. "Please believe me when I tell you that. There is nothing for you to feel embarrassed over."

"Stay out of my head," I snapped with more vigor than I had intended.

"Seren," he whispered. I focused on the fireplace, fighting to hold myself together. Everything I had been through was now threatening to send me over a dark edge. I was bound to leap off sooner or later. "Seren, please look at me."

"I ... I need you to leave," I admitted, feeling myself come undone.

"No, love. I'm not going anywhere."

"Deus, please," I said, forcing myself to look at him. I was trembling, tears falling freely. He didn't know that our time was limited. He didn't know what I was feeling. Even with our bond, I had walled away enough of myself to keep my impending death from him. "I need to be alone right now."

His face was wrecked with guilt. "I'm ... I'm so sorry," he said. "I'm trying. Please know that I am trying to get back to who I was."

"I know, and I don't blame you for any of this. It's just ... I need to heal myself, and being around you, I—"

He wrapped me in his arms, holding me close against his chest. "I'm right here," he said, his voice now trembling. "I will do better. Please, don't push me away." He kissed my head softly. "Let's go away ... right now. Just like we talked about."

"I just got home," I said. There was so much I needed to do before Lucifer decided to come out of hiding and make good on his threat.

"I know, but we need this. We are stronger when we're together. Being apart, it isn't the answer."

His eyes were so full of desperation. He was right ... maybe we both needed time in a new place. Just the two of us.

I smiled softly and nodded.

He grinned. "Good," he said. "I know just the place. We can leave now—"

"No," I interrupted. He looked at me with confusion. "I need to talk to my family first. I don't want to leave them again without saying goodbye."

He nodded. "Understood. Tonight then?"

"Yes, tonight."

"You talk with your family, and I will get some things prepared."

"And what is it that you are preparing?" I asked.

His eyes narrowed, focusing on my lips. A soft kiss followed. I left my hands at my sides, unsure of what parts of him I could touch. He pulled away with a smile.

"You'll just have to wait and see." With that, he disappeared.

My emotions raged. Everything inside of me was on edge. The torment of the past months slammed into me like a wrecking ball. Losing Orion. Being tortured. Losing Deus. Going to Hell. Finding out I'm part demon. Lucifer's threats. And now, the knowledge of my impending demise. In the next breath, I shifted myself to the top of a snowcapped mountain, where I knew I'd truly be alone.

I slammed a shield around my mind before unleashing everything inside of me. A loud boom and snap sounded like thunder as fire, ice, darkness, and everything in between exploded from inside of me. I howled at the top of my lungs, falling to the ground, my knees screaming from the impact. The mountain shook. Piles of rock and snow tumbled down the sides.

Finally, I let go of my magic, exhausting the rage inside of me. Quiet. Everything was so quiet. I allowed myself to fall into the soft, white pillow of comfort. Tears ran freely, even though I no longer felt myself crying. My body was still blazing with heat. The white dusting around me melted, seeping into my skin as I fizzled out. I screamed some more, allowing everything inside of myself to come to the surface.

"Why?" I wept, between each inhale of breath. "Why is this my life? Haven't I gone through enough?" I asked to no one. I lay there, the wet snow cooling my burning heart. I closed my eyes, drifting into a soothing darkness of my own making.

When I woke, my skin was frigid, and my teeth rattled together. The wind had picked up. A storm was coming. I stood, my power already replenishing as I shifted back to my room. I stumbled when my feet hit the solid surface, my head dizzy and vision blurry. My hair dripped on the carpet. My clothes clung to my body, half frozen.

"Looks like I have impeccable timing," a voice came from my doorway. Tony shut the door behind him and took me in from head to toe. "Did you just get back from a swim?"

"Not exactly," I replied, wrapping my arms around myself, shivering. "Can you give me a second?"

"Of course," he said, showing himself to my seating area.

I pulled dry clothes from the closet and took a quick, smoldering hot shower to defrost my frozen skin. I slid the warm sweater and leggings on before returning to my room. Tony sat causally, one leg crossed over the other as he stared into the fireplace.

"I thought you and your family would be together tonight," I said, taking a seat next to him.

"We have been," he answered, giving me a small smile. "Thanks to you."

I smiled back. He took my hand, leaning close to my face. I looked into his hazel eyes, still seeing fragments of the man I once loved.

"How will I ever repay you?" he asked.

"I don't want anything. I just want G to be happy."

He huffed, pulling away. "Right ... about her *happiness*," he said, looking back into the fire.

"I'm assuming you've now met Gor?"

"My sister in love with the Prince of Sloth. My ex-fiancé mated to the Prince of Lust. And her cousin in love with the Prince of Envy. I'm living a nightmare."

I laughed, hitting him in the arm. "They aren't that bad. Gor especially. He's my second favorite."

"Good to know you approve. My father about had a heart attack. My mother is beside herself."

"Nonna and Aunt Thora had the same reaction. Once you get to know him, you'll feel differently. I'm sure of it."

He sat silent, studying my face. "You found your prince?" he asked.

I nodded.

"And you brought him back. Against all odds?"

I nodded again.

"And to think, a little over a year ago I found you so helpless inside that prison you once called home. I never could have imagined how remarkable you'd become."

"You can stop now," I said, shifting uncomfortably.

"Are you happy, Seren?" he asked, as if he could see the trauma I hid deep inside.

I shrugged. "I don't think I'm meant to be happy, Antonio," I answered honestly.

"Even now that Deus is back?"

"He's ... he went through a lot. He's in the process of healing."

"And what about you?"

What was the point? I asked myself silently. I would be dead soon enough. "I'm fine, Tony."

"You forget," he said, moving a piece of hair from my face. "I know you better than you think."

I thought back to our time together.

"I think," I said softly. "I think the last time I was truly happy was right before I found out you were working with my mother. I was so oblivious then. I didn't know I was the vessel. Lucifer wasn't trying to kill me. The people around me were safe and happy. I was happy. I had a future I was looking forward to ... building towards."

"And now?"

"Now ... I'm just taking things day by day."

"I regret what happened between us each and every day. There isn't a day that goes by that I don't think 'what if'."

"I know," I said softly. "But even if you could go back, it wouldn't change anything. Deus would have eventually found me, and fate would have taken its course."

"I thought you didn't believe in fate?"

I shrugged. "I think we're all put on this earth for a reason. Regardless if we like the outcome or not, I'm learning that fate will always find a way to correct its course."

"What are you talking about, beautiful?" His brow furrowed.

"Nothing," I whispered, realizing I had admitted too much. "Forget what I said." I went to stand, but he caught my arm, pulling me back down beside him. He held me there, cupping my cheek with his hand.

"What is going on in that lovely head of yours?" he asked, searching my eyes for answers. "Let me help you. Let me in. I know after everything you don't trust me fully, but I am here for you, Seren. I want to help. I want to see you happy again."

"Tony," I whispered, heaviness settling deep inside of me. "There's nothing you can do. There's nothing anyone can do."

"I hate seeing you like this. I want ... I want you to smile. To truly smile and mean it."

I huffed. "I think I'm all out of smiles for this lifetime."

"Seren," he said, brushing his thumb against my cheek. Before he could say another word, a hand shot out and wrapped around Tony's wrist. His hand was pried away from my face with force. Deus stood behind the couch, looking at Tony murderously. Tony grimaced in pain.

"I suggest," growled Deus in a threatening tone, "you refrain from touching my mate." Deus's teeth flashed. A threatening rumble sounded deep inside of him. I stood and placed a hand on Deus's forearm, pulling him away.

"Stop," I demanded. Deus let go. Tony stood to his feet instantly. He looked at me for instruction, knowing better than to challenge a Prince of Hell. "I'll find you later, Tony."

"I meant what I said," Tony whispered, looking at me with compassion. I gave him a small smile and nodded. He left the room without another word.

Deus was fuming, his chest rising and falling dramatically. I didn't have the energy to defend myself. What was the point? I walked around the couch, heading for the door.

"Are we not going to discuss what I just walked in on?" he barked, his voice laced with rage.

"There's nothing to discuss. I have to go see Nonna. I'll be back in a moment." Without waiting for him to respond, I left.

When I opened Nonna's door, she and my mother were huddled together on the couch, discussing something in private. They turned to me as I approached.

"Everything okay, bambina?" asked Nonna.

"Yes," I replied. "I was coming to tell you that I'll be leaving for a bit. I know I just got here, and I didn't want to leave again without saying goodbye."

"Where are you going?" my mother asked with concern.

"Deus and I are going away for a bit. Just the two of us."

My mother stood and looked from Nonna to me. "Do you think that's wise right now with Lucifer's threat?" she asked.

"Our spies haven't reported any movement on his part," I answered. "Plus, Deus and I could use this time to heal."

Nonna nodded. "I agree. Have fun, bambina."

"Mamma," exclaimed Annalise.

Nonna turned her eyes towards her daughter. "Seren is a grown woman," Nonna said softly. "A very powerful woman, who happens to be mated to a very powerful Prince of Hell. She will be fine."

I smiled at both of them before turning to leave.

"Little bean," my mother called after me. "I ... I hope you and Deus have a nice time."

"Thank you," I replied, returning to my room.

When I arrived, Deus was standing on the balcony, leaning against the doorway. I felt his discontentment through the bond. He looked over his shoulder at me as I entered and approached him, leaning against the other side of the frame.

"Nothing was happening," I said softly.

"Could have fooled me," he replied, crossing his arms over his chest. "Is this because ... because I'm not ready to be with you physically? Is the lust you're experiencing because of my power that hard to resist?" It seemed an effort to get the question out.

"You really think that little of me and our relationship?" I was offended that the thought had even crossed his mind.

"You loved him once. He obviously still harbors hope for the two of you ... thus his *daily regret* as he put it."

"How long where you eavesdropping?"

"Long enough to know that the last time you remember truly being happy was with him." He looked down to his feet and smiled uncomfortably. "This world is cruel. I'm physically not designed to be monogamous, yet here I am, gifted with you, my mate, and I've already failed. Only mated for a few months, and you're already realizing you'd be better off without me."

"That's not it at all, Deus. I don't regret our bond, and I don't want anyone but you. That time with Tony that I spoke of … that was before everything. Before I knew I was the goddess and part demon. Before I knew about Lucifer and his deal with my mother. Of course that time was more peaceful. I was still in the dark."

He didn't look at me. "I should have stayed away. I should have never sought you out that day in the woods. Orion … even the Simonelli boy were better options."

"Well, there's no going back now," I said, losing control over my temper.

"Maybe. Maybe there's a way out of the bond."

A punch of disbelief hit me in the gut. "What?" I whispered.

"There has to be a spell or something that will free you from me."

I swallowed. "Is that what you want?"

His eyes finally met mine. "I love you, Seren. More than anything. I want you to be happy. Even if that means … even if I must walk away."

Fury built inside of me. I was done with the kid gloves. After everything I had gone through to get him back, the audacity of this man to even suggest what he just had. Before I could think twice, my hand flew through the air, making contact with his face.

Slap. His head jerked to the side from the impact. He slowly turned back to me, his jaw clenched. Something had shifted behind his eyes. I stood my ground, letting the rage overcome me.

"You are a selfish prick," I snarled. "A selfish, stupid, inconsiderate asshole."

"I know."

"Oh, shut the hell up," I snapped. "You are going to listen to me without saying a damn word and then, we are never going to have this conversation again." I took a breath. "I did love Tony once. Another version of me did, at least, but that girl ... that stupid, blind hopeless girl is gone. Since then, I have watched those around me die. I have killed, fought, bled, cried, and been tortured. Yet, through it all, I have grown. I am stronger, wiser, and braver. Much of that is thanks to you." He looked away, but I turned his face back to mine, forcing him to look at me.

"Everything in my life has led me to you, and I don't regret one damn moment of it." His brow furrowed as he closed his eyes. "You died for me, Deus. You sacrificed your life to save mine and I fought like hell to get you back, yet you stand here, allowing your own doubt and insecurities to rob us of this miracle that we made happen. I am done watching you beat yourself up for things that are in the past. I am done listening to you try and talk me out of loving you, and I am done watching you try and push me away.

"It's not going to happen. I am not walking away from you. Nothing you've done in your past scares me, nor does it make me love you any less. I am your mate. We were made from the same source that now flows through us. And even if I had a choice as to who my mate was ... I would still pick you. I'd always pick you. There has never and will never be another, better choice than you."

A tear fell from his eye.

"So no," I continued, "I do not want to find a way to release myself from you, because even if we did … I'd still fight like hell to be with you, and I'd still love you with my entire heart. But I won't stand here and watch you destroy yourself. I know you are healing, and I will be at your side every step of the way, but I want … no, I demand that my Deus be returned to me.

"The playful, confident, cocky, demon prince who risked everything to save me. The man who his brothers look up to with pride. Who rebelled against Lucifer. Who reigns over Hell and earth. Whose subjects serve him not out of force, but out of choice and honor. I want the man who … who wasn't afraid to love me. Who would sacrifice anything for that love.

"I'm begging you, Asmodeus, please … put what happened behind you. Allow yourself to heal. Focus on us and this gift we've been given … a second chance to live … to love. I need you, Asmodeus. I need you more than the air I breathe." Tears fell from my eyes as I trembled.

It seemed as if a layer of his pain melted away. Even though he was still buried in ice, it was progress. He ran his hand down the side of my face and smiled.

"Do you know what I did when the realization that you were my mate finally set in?" he asked.

I shook my head.

"I prayed," he whispered. "I got on my knees and prayed to my Father, thanking him for giving me you." He laughed, shaking his head. "A demon, praying to God the Father. No one would believe it, but that's what I did. I couldn't fathom why or how I had somehow been cut from the same cloth as you. Even knowing everything that I am, everything

I've done, you are still here, fighting for us ... for me."

"That will never change," I said, wrapping my arms around him.

"You are the most stubborn person I've ever met."

"So, you've told me," I said with a shrug.

"I think that might be what I love most about you. Your determination and vigor. Even though you have the innate ability to drive me completely insane."

"It's a family trait."

"Oh, I am fully aware. The others have a bet going as to which of us will go insane first; Levi or me." I laughed. He smiled, looking down at me. "Thank you."

"For what?"

"For telling me what I needed to hear. For calling me out and reminding me of everything I have to live for."

"It was selfish. I shouldn't have—"

"Don't," he said, placing his thumb over my lips. "Don't doubt yourself. I know everything you said came from a place of love. And you were right. Lucifer has stolen enough from us, and I refuse to allow him to come between us."

"Glad to hear it."

"Now, unless you had planned to meet up with another one of your ex's, may I suggest we be on our way?"

I hit him in the chest. He took me in his arms and we shifted between time and space, until I was greeted by the sweet scent of saltwater and sand.

Chapter Fourteen

The air was crisp and the moon shined brightly in the sky. It appeared so close; if I reached out, I swore I would have been able to touch it.

The ocean waves pattered against the shoreline in a soothing rhythm. We stood on the beach, looking out into the night sky that was filled with thousands of bright, burning stars. I smiled, the weight of the world releasing its hold on me.

Deus exhaled with relief. "I'm glad you like it," he said softly.

On the other side of the beach, a few yards away, was a beautiful white stone house. Large windows faced the ocean, and soft lighting illuminated the interior. Deus took my hand and led me up a path lit with candles. Bright and vibrant flowers met the sand, growing from the dry surface.

He led me up the white stone stairs until we arrived at two beautifully carved wooden doors. "Where are we?" I asked.

"Our own private Island. We're near New Zealand."

"Our?" I asked.

"Everything I own, you now have access and rights to."

"When did you have time to do all of that?"

He dropped his eyes. "When I was searching for you. When Lucifer took you, I had Mal draw up all the paperwork. Focusing on the future ... looking forward to sharing all of this with you gave me hope that I would find you again."

I stroked his arm, stepping nearer with a grin. "So, you mean to tell me that I own my own island?"

The sorrow left his eyes as they met mine. "Yes, mate. Along with fifty-seven other properties around the world. Over two thousand businesses, forty-three cars, two planes, two yachts and a few other smaller items."

My mouth gaped. "What?"

His smile grew. He wrapped his arm around my waist and pulled me into him. "You are disgustingly wealthy, my love. And I plan to serve this world up to you on a golden platter, however you prefer it." He leaned down and kissed me.

He pushed the doors open to a foyer with tall ceilings and an intricate abstract glass chandelier. The white walls were decorated with modern paintings of figures in the nude. The floors were laced with flecks of blue and gold that contrasted vibrantly against the white base. To the side, a large winding staircase led up to the second level.

Deus pulled me into the room to the left, a library. The colors were so much lighter than our home back in the mountains. An electric fireplace hummed in the wall and a painting hung above the fireplace of ... me.

I turned back to him with surprise. He shrugged.

"What can I say? I'm a collector of art and I find this specific subject to be quite captivating. Plus," he said, wrapping his arms around me from behind, "the lady of the house should be on display for everyone to see. Don't you think?"

I laughed. "Thankfully, I'm not nude in the picture like the rest of the paintings around here."

"Oh, that can most definitely be arranged."

Books adorned the shelves. Comfortable furniture of the highest quality was scattered throughout the house. The kitchen was modern and sleek, with the newest appliances and fixtures. The front of the house had a large porch that overlooked the wild and intricate jungle that made up the center of the island.

Upstairs, three bedrooms spaced widely apart were lavishly decorated with soft bedding and accessories. Deus pulled me up the stairs to the third floor where a large master suit awaited.

The entire room was made of glass, every wall and even the ceiling. From this point, we could see the entire oasis. A balcony with a firepit faced the ocean and wrapped around the suite. Dressers, a bathroom with a rainforest shower, and a deep soaking tub lined the room. In the center sat a large circular bed. The sheets were as white as snow with a few blue and teal decorative pillows.

"This place is ..." I said, losing my words.

"I hoped you'd like it," he replied. I took in the beauty of room and the island beyond. "There's a beautiful water fall not too far from here, along with a cave that leads to the most breathtaking view."

"I don't see any other houses."

"That's because there are none. We are the only ones on this island." I looked at him questioningly. "I promised it would be just the two of us, didn't I?"

"This is breathtaking, Deus. Truly."

"I'm glad you think so. What would you like to do first?"

I slid open the glass panel to the balcony, feeling the rush of the ocean breeze across my face. The firepit next to the seating area lit with a flick of my wrist.

"I think I'd just like to sit for a while. Will you join me?" I asked, extending my hand out to him.

He laced his fingers with mine. "Always." We sat in an oversized cushioned chair. He pulled me into his body, wrapping me up in his embrace as we sat in silence, lulled by the crashing waves of the ocean.

At some point I must have fallen asleep, for when I woke, I had been moved to the soft bed in the center of our room. I stretched out, feeling the ocean mist clinging to the sheets. I turned over and to my surprise, Deus was next to me. He smiled, brushing his fingers along the angle of my jaw.

"Good morning, my love," he said.

"Morning, demon," I replied, nuzzling into the soft pillow.

He laughed. "How did you sleep?"

"More soundly than I have in a long time."

"I'm glad to hear that."

"And you?"

"I woke a few times, but it seems you smacked most of the night terrors away."

I giggled, pulling the sheets over my mouth to hide my grin. He smiled, reaching for my hand. "Yes ... about that," I said.

"Would I be lesser of a man if I admitted that it actually stung?"

"What can I say? Demon strength and all."

"Oh, and did the demon force you to assault me?"

"No ... that was all my own doing."

"Is that so?" He pushed me to my back and began to tickle me. I laughed and thrashed, trying to fight him, but his strength was overbearing.

"Stop! Stop!" I pleaded, but he continued until I felt like I was going to die from the lack of oxygen.

"Say you're sorry," he said, still pinning me down to the bed.

"I don't want to lie to my mate," I replied.

He shook his head. "Stubborn little witch."

"Overbearing demon prince."

He grinned, still hovering over me. His hair was disheveled, and his face seemed softer. His eyes were no longer swollen from a lack of sleep. His skin retained a faint glow.

"You're beautiful," I said softly. "Do you honestly know how truly beautiful you are?"

He smirked. "Demon Prince of Lust, remember? I was designed to appear that way to everyone."

"I'm not talking about your physical beauty. I'm talking about you, Deus. I saw that part of you ... in the pit. The rawest parts. And every part of you is ... extraordinary."

He took a few moments before replying. "I think," he said hesitantly, "for the first time in my entire existence I am speechless."

"A new talent I can add to my ever-growing resume."

"Indeed. Now," he said, resting his head on his bent elbow, "what shall we do today?"

"I'm thinking a shower first, then food. After that, a quiet afternoon on the beach."

"Perfect."

I grinned, rising and heading towards the bathroom. I stopped by the closet, which was stocked with clothes just my size. I turned on the water in the large glass shower, allowing it to warm. I removed my leggings and went to pull my sweater over my head when I caught a glimpse of Deus in the mirror, standing in the doorway behind me. I froze, not knowing what to say or do.

"Would you mind some company?" he asked, gliding into the bathroom.

"I ..." I dropped my hands from my sweater, struggling to find the words. "Are you sure?"

He laughed, taking the ends of my top in his hands, sliding the fabric between his fingers. "I don't think a shower with you is going to break me, love."

"I'm not ... I don't want you to feel pressured."

"The Prince of Lust, pressured into having sex. How comical."

"Deus, this isn't a joke. I don't want—"

He pushed me into the glass door of the shower, pinning me with his body as his hands restrained my arms above my head. His eyes were full of heat and something else I couldn't pinpoint.

"You don't what, Seren? You don't want me? Is that it?" He trailed his fingers up my bare legs, stopping at the lace of my underwear. I closed my eyes, enjoying every moment of his skin on mine.

I felt the heat of his breath on my lips before I opened my eyes. His fingers lazily trailed the edge of the lace, taunting and teasing. Heat began to simmer deep inside of my core. My body warmed and my skin rose in response to his touch, now aware of every single place our bodies met.

"Just say the words," he said huskily, "and I'll stop. I'll stop touching you." He kissed the column of my neck softly. "Tasting you." He dragged his tongue up to my earlobe where he gently bit the sensitive skin. "And thinking of all the ways I want to make you scream my name."

I bit the bottom of my lip, fighting the urge to destroy every article of clothing on him. Even though every nerve screamed to have him, I hesitated. I didn't want to push him too fast. Just yesterday, he had told me he couldn't.

I pulled my hand from his restraint and wrapped it around his wrist, stopping him from explore me further. I drank in the sight of my exquisite mate.

"How about we start with a shower?" I replied.

His face filled with stark confusion. He pulled his hand out of my grasp, taking a step back. I closed the space between us, sliding my fingers into his pants gliding them to the floor gently. It took everything I had not to stare at his impressive length. The length that had made my mind explode in so many creative and delicious ways. The thought of how he would taste in my mouth was overwhelming, but I forced myself to look away.

I slid my sweater off my body to the floor, my underwear along with it. Deus stood deathly still, taking in every inch of me.

"How is it," he said, "that every time I look at you, I feel like I'm seeing you for the first time?"

I smiled, taking his hand in mine and leading him into the shower. In silence, we washed. He never once took his eyes off me. His gaze heated my skin. I took a rag and lathered it with soap, then gently brushed it over his firm and toned chest. He took a deep breath in, his fingers tightening into fists.

"Is ... this okay?" I asked.

His jaw tightened and heavy eyes looked down at me. "Why did you stop me before?"

I continued gliding the rag over his shoulders and down his arms. "The next time we make love, I want it to be because we both want it. I don't want you to feel pressured, or like you need to do it just to make me happy. I want you to want it ... as badly as I want you."

Placing his hands on my bare hips, he pushed me into the wall of the shower, pressing his body against me. His mouth slammed into mine. But this kiss ... it wasn't full of passion or desire. It was different. Forced. As if he was trying to prove something to himself.

I dropped the rag, hesitantly placing my hands on his arms. "Don't," he said, ripping his mouth from mine. "Don't hesitate when you touch me. I want you, Seren. I want every part of you. I need you. I need you so badly it hurts."

I ran my hands down his face. "I love you," I whispered, pressing a kiss to the side of his cheek. "We have time," I lied. "There's no need to rush this."

"Seren." He winced as if my words had scorched him. The truth—one that I would never speak out loud—was that I felt the fear that had rattled deep within him when I touched him. The bond between us was peculiar. I didn't understand it, not fully at least. But I had felt his hesitation when I placed the rag against his skin.

I wrapped my arms around him. His face buried in the crook of my neck. I ran my hands through his blue-black hair. His hands skimmed the sides of my body, tracing over every curve. "I love you," I whispered against his hair. "Every part of you, I love." He pulled back gently, looking at my face. I smiled. "Let me show you."

I opened my mind to him, reaching down the bridge of our bond until I felt his cool, soft presence. I pulled him into my memories like a lover's embrace.

The first time I had seen him in the woods; how beautiful and entranced I was by his mere presence. His flirting had driven me mad with frustration, yet lit a part of me back to life. How comfortable he made me feel in his castle the first time I arrived. How safe I always felt around him. The desire, the passion, the appreciation and love that consumed me as my affections for him grew. Memory after memory of our time together flashed down the bond. Every smile. Every laugh. Every moment of life I had been given, thanks to him.

I gently let his mind go. He was breathing heavily.

"See," I whispered. "You are not the devil in my story ... you're my restoration. My deliverance. You're *my* salvation, Deus."

"And you are my redemption, Seren De Salvo." He bent down and kissed me, more freely and passionately than since we had been in Hell. With every press of his lips against mine, I could feel him letting go of his trauma. We stayed in that shower for the next hour until our lips were bruised and our skin pruned. It was the most intimate memory we had created yet.

Weeks passed as we hid ourselves away on our own private haven. The world no longer mattered. The only thing that we cared about was each other. Our days were spent bathing in the sunlight on the beach, swimming freely in the ocean, and building new memories that seemed to strengthen the bond between us with each passing day.

As Deus allowed himself time to heal, he began to laugh and smile without hesitation. The darkness behind his eyes faded away layer by layer, and so did the memories and nightmare that haunted him.

We explored the island during the day and at night I cooked, exploring new spices and recipes. Deus attempted to assist, but I quickly learned cooking was not his strong suit. Instead, he played the piano. Each night as I prepared our meal, his fingers danced along the white and black keys, constructing the most beautiful compositions. A talent I didn't know he possessed.

We spent nights under the stars laughing, eating, and drinking. He told me about the famous historical figures he had met, along with firsthand experiences I had once only imagined from the Bible. Deus spoke of his brothers and the trouble they caused in their earlier years.

Though we weren't physically intimate, this connection that we were fostering seemed to be exactly what we needed. Here, I was just a woman, in love with a man. Nothing more. Nothing less. Hidden far away by the sea, our haven had become our renaissance—our rebirth.

I woke from an afternoon nap, still stretched across the lounge chair on our balcony. The sun was setting on the horizon, the colors so vibrant, warm and rich. I closed the book that lay on my chest and sat up. Deus stood in the doorway, leaning in his charming, casual manner.

"Were you watching me sleep again?" I asked.

"Yes," he replied shortly.

"Creep." I stood from the chair, making my way over to him. I wrapped my arms around his neck, kissing him softly on the cheek. "What would you like for dinner?"

"Actually," he said, brushing my hair away from my face, "I'll take care of dinner tonight."

I pulled away in surprise. "You ... cooking?"

"Don't look so surprised. I've been keenly watching you all these weeks. I think I've picked up on a few things."

"It's really no trouble."

He laughed. "Don't worry, my love. I won't kill you with my cooking. Now, I've drawn you a lovely lavender bath. Go relax, get dressed, and meet me downstairs in an hour." He kissed me and then headed to the kitchen. I sent a silent prayer up to his Father that he wouldn't burn our house to ground.

After the bath, I slid on a strappy satin cream dress that was open in the back and ended at my knees. My skin was now a deep rich tan and seemed to glow, thanks to the rest I had received these past few weeks. I had allowed my hair to dry naturally, revealing the loose curls and thick texture. Vacationing seemed to agree with me.

When I entered the dining room, I was met by soft classical music and a room littered with red roses and candlelight. Deus stood by the head of the table, hands behind his back, in black slacks and a fitted button-up black shirt. He was perfectly groomed with a bright smile adorning his face. My favorite part of him.

"Did you gather all the roses on the island?" I asked, overwhelmed by their sweet scent.

He shrugged. "I bought out an entire florist shop."

"You left the island?"

"Just had to collect a few items."

I approached him with a curious smile. On the table lay dishes of linguine with clam sauce, fresh salad, and an array of appetizers and breads. My mouth watered. "You cooked all of this?"

He crinkled his nose. "Not exactly. I shifted in a chef who gave me a few tips along the way."

"Again with the shifting."

He laughed. "Don't worry. He doesn't remember a thing and will be very happy when he discovers the fat envelope of cash I left as compensation. Now, sit," he said, pulling out my chair for me.

I obeyed. The scent of fresh lemon, basil, and seafood was magnificent. "What is the occasion?"

He bent down and kissed the side of my face. "Does a demon need a reason to spoil his mate?"

I laughed. "I suppose I should be used to the lot of you doing what you please."

"Quick study." He took a seat next to me, pouring sparkling white wine into our glasses.

Every bite was better than the next. The wine was flavorful yet intoxicating and our conversation flowed naturally. For dessert, Deus snapped his fingers and an arrangement of items appeared: crème brûlée, chocolate tart cake, lemon meringue pie, coffee cake, and an assortment of sorbets.

"Did you rob a bakery as well?" I asked while he placed a ramekin of crème brûlée in front of me.

"No need. Filthy rich, remember?"

I tried a bite of every sweet. By the time we had finished, I felt like I had consumed ten pounds of food. I sat back in the chair, laughing at a story Deus was sharing as we finished off our espressos.

Silence finally fell around us. The soft classical music filling the air. With the flames of the candles flickering, chasing the darkness away, the room was tranquil. I felt Deus's eyes on me.

"Can I help you?" I asked with an arched eyebrow.

"Just admiring how beautiful you look tonight. The beach seems to agree with you."

"I was thinking the same thing earlier." I reached across the table, taking his hand in mine. "I vote, we move here and forget about everything else."

He smirked, leaning down to kiss the back of my hand. "You will hear no argument from me." He pulled me from my chair, leading me out onto the beach. As we descended the stairs to the sand, my breath was taken away by what awaited.

For as far as my eyes could see, candles were scattered down each side of the beach, creating the most alluring scenery I had ever seen. In the ocean, blue shimmering specks of light glistened in the water almost like glitter. They were luminescent, glowing unnaturally. Magic.

The full moon sat on the horizon, so close I could see the craters that made up the surface. My toes buried in the warm sand as I stood captivated by the magical scene.

Deus who was watching me closely with a smile. "This is—"

"All for you," he interrupted, taking me into his arms. The sound of the music followed us outside as we began to sway in a slow and intimate dance.

"The demon Prince of Lust, a romantic, huh?" I said with a smile.

"Only for you," he replied, leaning down and kissing me. His grip on my waist tightened, his eyes scanning every inch of my face. "You are truly my reason for existing. Loving you ... has been the greatest pleasure and honor I have ever been gifted."

"Feeling a bit sentimental tonight?" I asked, my cheeks flushing with embarrassment.

He stopped moving. "I mean it, Seren. You have no idea how special you are to me. How much I truly love you. What you've done to me ... for me ... it's more than I thought I ever deserved. I still don't understand how I ended up being your mate but I promise you, every single day that I breathe, I will do my best to be worthy of you. To be a man you are proud to be with and to call your own.

"I've done so many dark things during my existence." He flinched. "I've hurt so many people. I'm not proud of my past or who I've been, but now, being here with you, I want to do better. To be better." His eyes met mine again. "I can't promise you a stainless future. I can't promise that there will always be peace or harmony. That I won't slip from time to time and make mistakes. But I can promise you this," he said, pulling away from me slightly.

"I can promise to be faithful to you. To never touch another. I can promise to love you, to protect you, to care for you for as long as I breathe." He slowly knelt to one knee. "I can promise to love you and cherish each moment I have with you. My heart, mind, and body desires no other but you. For me ... there is nothing but you."

He pulled a red velvet box from his pocket and cracked open the lid. Inside lay a massive red oval sapphire. The center seemed to burst as if a star had been caught inside. The stone was surrounded by diamonds attached to a gold band. He pulled the ring from the box as I stood speechless. He took my hand and rubbed it softly with his thumb.

"I know you didn't have a choice when it came to your fated mate," he said, pausing to take a breath. I smiled, realizing he was nervous. "But you do have a choice in the matter of choosing your husband." He grinned. "Seren Lucia De Salvo, would you do me the honor of becoming my wife? Become the person that I choose each day to love, to cherish, and to build a future with that we both can be proud of? Would you make me the happiest man"—he shrugged— "demon, and allow me the honor of devoting my heart and life to you?"

I fought to find my voice. He held up the ring, eagerly awaiting my answer. Finally, air filled my lungs as I whispered, "Yes. Yes, of course I will be your wife."

In the next breath, I was swept into his arms while he laughed with happiness, twirling me around and around in the air. I held onto him tightly, relishing in the pure joy. Nothing compared to this moment. Nothing had made me more happy, more excited, more alive than what this precious occasion had brought me.

He placed me back on the ground, kissing me passionately, still grinning from ear to ear. When he finally pulled away, he took my hand and slid the ring onto my finger. The weight of the stone was noticeable. I laughed. "Didn't spare any expense, did we?" I said playfully.

"We can go bigger if you'd like."

"Oh, no. This is perfect," I said. The moonlight bounce around the curves and edges of the ring. "It's beautiful," I whispered. I looked back up at him: my fiancé ... my best friend ... my mate. "I have never felt so complete as I do in this moment." Silent tears of joy fell from my eyes.

"This is only the beginning, my love," he said, taking me into his arms once more. I held onto him tightly, closing my eyes while the world around us seemed to melt away. Nothing mattered. Not the politics, not our families, not the impending war ... none of it. The only thing that mattered was the love of my life. The man who had healed every part of my broken mind and heart. Who loved me enough to choose me. To marry me. To want to spend the rest of our lives together.

CHAPTER FIFTEEN

When I finally opened my eyes, Deus had shifted us to our room. Candles and flowers scattered the surfaces. I looked into his sensual eyes. His smile revealed those perfect white teeth. He was truly the definition of lust; yet, he had become my definition of home.

"If you'd have me," he said softly, running his fingers through my hair. "I'd like to celebrate by spending the rest of this day, and most of tomorrow, and possibly the rest of this week, making love to you."

My stomach twisted with excitement and anticipation. I tried to conceal it, but a smile stretched as my cheeks flushed. "Are you sure?" I asked.

His fingers found the two strings that held my dress in the back. With one intensely slow tug, the laces loosened. His eyes darkened with desire.

"You tell me," he whispered into my ear, his voice low and sensual. He opened his mind to me. Through his dense walls of shadows and brimstone, I drifted deep into his thoughts. Where there once was torment and pain, I now found hope. The wounds that had plagued him were gone. I found his love and desire in full bloom.

I opened my eyes, pulling my conscious from his. His fingers traced small circles along the bare skin of my back.

"I told you I'd find my way back to you," he said. "Back to us."

I swallowed deeply, beginning to fill with need. Not from lust, but love. I needed to love him. To show him that word meant nothing in comparison to what I felt. Only when we were connected mind, body, and soul could he truly understand what he meant to me.

"This will be the first time," I said softly, "that we've been together since we've been mated."

He smiled, playing with the string of my dress that barely clung to my shoulder. "I'm aware," he replied, flicking the small strap to fall.

I ran my hand down his chest, tracing my fingers over the buttons.

"You take the lead," I said. "If, at any point, you feel un—"

He placed a finger of my lips, shaking his head slowly. "Nothing and no one will ever keep me from you again." He bent his head towards me, gently kissing my lips, brushing his fingers over the final strap of my dress, sending the smooth fabric to the floor. All that remained was soft, paper-thin underwear.

Deus kissed me passionately, taking his time with every brush of his lips and flick of his tongue. His hands slid across my body, not leaving one part of me untouched. My skin heated in response. I unfastened each button slowly until his bare chest was finally exposed. I pushed the shirt off his masculine torso and moved to his pants.

Once we were both unburdened of our clothing, he slowly backed me to the edge of the bed, his mouth never leaving mine. When I reached the mattress, I finally pulled back, searching his face for any hesitation or fear, but there was none—only happiness flickered behind the gateways to his soul. I ran my hand down the length of his neck to his chest.

He gently pushed me onto the bed and stood at the edge of the mattress, towering over me, displaying his perfectly sculpted body. His skin was richly tanned thanks to the hours we had spent in the sun. His shoulders were wide and his stomach tight, with shapely mounds of muscles. He was built like a god.

The heat deep in my core roared to life as my eyes locked on the thick, hard length between his strong legs. I licked my lips, wondering what he tasted like. There were still so many parts of him I had yet to explore, even though I had dreamt about each scenario multiple times.

My hungry gaze seemed to amuse him. His eyes roved over every inch of my body, admiring me like a piece of priceless art. As his eyes fell between my legs, his muscles jerked. I opened the door in between our minds that I had created just for him.

"See something you like?" I asked, trying my best to sound seductive.

"Everything I see, I like," he replied, his lips curving to one side in a sexy grin. *"Somehow, I forget how beautiful you are."*

I laughed softly. *"Nonsense. You tell me how beautiful I am every day."*

He bent down and drew his thumb against my lips, then trailed his fingers down my neck, my chest, and the center of my breasts. He continued across my abdomen and stopped once he got to my knee. He placed his other hand on the opposite knee, pulling my legs apart.

The breeze off the ocean swept through the room, sending goosebumps across my skin as the cold air met my already wet center. I gasped faintly. Deus's eyes darkened as he knelt at the edge of the bed.

"I may tell you how beautiful you are ..." he said, his voice becoming predatorial. "Now, let me show you."

His soft, warm lips met against the inside of my knee, and I almost came at the contact. I had wanted him like this for so long. A part of me had feared I would never experience this again. Yet, here we were, mated. Engaged. Happy.

His lips brushed down my inner thigh while his hands followed, gently stroking the sensitive skin. My head leaned back, relaxing underneath his care. One of his hands splayed across my stomach, trailing up until it found my perked breast. He kneaded the sensitive tissue softly, causing my insides to tighten with desire and need.

I bit my bottom lip, finally falling completely flat against the mattress. He pressed soft kisses around my sex, teasing me with each pass of his lips. My legs began to quiver while my mind began to lose patience.

"Deus," I whispered, trying to remain in control. I felt his warm breath laugh against the center of me.

"Someone is impatient," he replied, continuing to torture me.

"Please," I cried, running my fingers through his dark, thick hair. I opened my mind, body, and soul to him completely. I felt him tense before his desire and need followed me off the edge. His mouth slammed into my sex, consuming me, his tongue lashing desperately to taste me ... to please me. My legs clenched around his head, my moan of pleasure roaring from deep within my throat.

His hands gripped my ass as he brought my hips higher, allowing him to press his mouth deeper around my bundle of nerves. Everything inside of my fought to release. I ground my teeth, clutching his hair with one hand while the other tangled into the sheets.

As my own pleasure flashed through my body, another feeling—similar, but not entirely my own—began to bloom. As Deus sucked and kissed and flicked his tongue across me, taking away any self-control I had, that sensation began to grow. My hips moved in a rhythmic motion as my clit swelled, my insides throbbing.

The intensity.

The pleasure.

It was all too much. Deus pulled away from me, sliding his devilish tongue down my center, starting from the top and ending at my entrance, right before he pressed that same tongue inside of me. I shattered, feeling like the wind had been knocked out of my chest. I cried out, gripping at anything my fingers could find.

He held me there as my orgasm crashed into me, setting all my nerves on fire. His tongue moved in and out while night exploded around us, laced with trickles of moonlight and something else. Something new and dark, yet smooth and captivating. My body shook uncontrollably while his hands pinned me to the bed, forcing me to experience every moment of my own release.

Finally, I inhaled, filling my burning lungs with air. My throat was scratchy and sore from the frantic screams that had bellowed from deep inside. My hips fell to the bed in exhaustion. Even my limbs felt heavy and weak.

Deus continued to softly kiss the area, flicking his tongue against me every so often while his hands grazed across my glistening skin. I opened my eyes as he rose above my immobile body, a prideful smile adorning his beautiful face. He laughed softly, a dimple to appearing on either cheek.

At the mere sight of his happiness, something inside of me roared to life. Some need that I had never experienced before. An uncontrollable urge to consume ... to ravish ... to dominate.

I pushed up from the bed and slammed my lips into his frantically. My hands tore at his body, ripping at the smooth flesh. My powers flared to life. Deus tightened his grip around me, matching my hunger with his own. This frenzied need was too much. I couldn't think, couldn't process what was happening. All I knew was that I needed him inside of me—*now*.

Straddling him as he sat on the bed, I gripped his hard length, positioned myself above him and slammed my body down with force. I cried out, stars and fire blazing behind my eyes. Deus roared the moment our bodies united. His fingers dug deep into my hips, bruising the area in the most satisfying way.

From our union, a massive wave of power exploded from our bodies, shattering each window in the house. We didn't stop. I moved on top of him, desperation turning to greed with every thrust and stroke I took. He sank his teeth into the column of my neck, sucking and licking the soft skin. I did the same, riding harder and faster, now exhilarated, and full of life.

Sex with Deus had been amazing before we bonded, but this ... this was something unnatural. Inhuman, yet extraordinary. The small blossom I had felt brush against my own pleasure now exploded to life with vibrance. I could feel the bond between us strengthen, reinforcing itself each moment we spent inebriated by our passion.

Deus slammed me into the bed, pressing his full weight into me, forcing himself deeper until his angle rubbed his tip against that perfect spot deep inside of me only he could reach. I cried out again, giving myself over to be completely ravaged by him. All control was gone, and the walls I had built around my being crumbled away.

In that perfect moment, as my body succumbed to the pleasure of my mate, I took a deep breath and then was pulled from myself, my awareness bursting into a familiar yet foreign form.

Lust. Passion. Sex. Pleasure. Need. Desire. Love. All these emotions swept over me, yet they weren't my own.

Deus ... I was feeling him, what he experienced while we were together. Another breath and I was pulled back into my own body, invigorated by the revelation of his bliss while buried deep inside of me. He slowed for only a second, bringing his eyes to mine in surprise. We both laughed with joy. The bond allowed us to share in each other's pleasures, con-necting us completely—as one.

Without a word, he leaned down and pressed a calm kiss against my lips. I wrapped my arms around him, matching his slow and deep pace with my hips. This was the very definition of completion. To not want nor need for anything else.

My insides tightened around his length with each passing thrust. One of his hands wrapped around the headboard for support while the other held me close, as he filled me with his desire. The pressure building inside me was like nothing I had ever experienced. His pace quickened again. I could feel him losing the small amount of control he had mustered. He needed release.

I dragged my nails down his hard back. I tangled my fingers through his hair, pulling his neck down against my mouth, sinking my teeth into his skin for my own enjoyment. He groaned, ramming into me like a wild animal.

I came over and over again, soaking the sheets around us as he slid in and out, screaming against his skin while my body took every hard thrust he offered. I held onto him, utterly out of my mind as he thrust one final time, convulsing inside of me as we held each other tightly, neither willing to be separated. He roared, shaking the house around us.

Night. Shadows. Red sparks. White flames. All our power ruptured in that moment as some final piece of our bond clicked into place. I gasped with a feeling like a wave of adrenaline. Something heavy and powerful pressed into my chest.

All of him. His power, his strength, his dominance, the very essence of who Deus was flew across the bridge that connected us, wrapping itself around me like a sheet of darkness. My own power reached and raced towards the opposite side.

The rush of his strength hit me like a dangerous drug. The power was like nothing I could have ever imagined. I felt invincible. Deus shuddered against me. My skin blazed with fire while the bond finished snapping into place.

I gasped, fighting for air while our powers calmed—a power that was now shared between us. Deus was panting, his grip now softer and more relaxed. I held onto him and knew that I now had access to his power, and he to mine. The miracle that had been cleaved in two during our creation had now been reunited. We were truly one.

Deus lifted his head, leaving his body on top of mine. He ran the back of his knuckles down my face. A soft smile appeared on his face lazily.

"Well, that was …"

"… intense," I finished for him.

He laughed deeply. "I had no idea that would happen."

"Me either. I mean, I could feel your strength when we bonded, but not … not whatever this is."

He raised his hands above me, focusing on his fingers. A moment later, my white flames swirled around his fingers and upper arm, just like they appeared for me.

"Would you look at that," he said, alternating the flame over each finger in a serpentine manner.

"So … does this mean I can control lust now?" I asked.

He shrugged. "I would assume so. If I have access to your gifts, it would make sense that my arsenal is now at your disposable. And here I thought you couldn't get any more powerful."

"Thee of little faith," I said.

He chuckled uncomfortably. "Faith has nothing to do with this."

"No," I said, running my hand down his beautiful, sculpted face. "But fate does ... destiny."

His eyes filled with love. "My reason for existing," he whispered, placing his forehead against mine. I allowed a moment to pass, relishing our intimacy.

"How are you feeling?" I finally asked.

"Powerful."

"And ... about being ... together. Were you—"

He stopped me by pressing his lips firmly to mine.

"Nothing has ever been more perfect than the moments we share together like this. I'm perfect, my love. Truly."

"Good." I bit the bottom of my lip. "So ... how quickly can we do that again?"

Surprise flickered behind his eyes. "Apparently, I am a bit out of practice if you're already asking for seconds."

I laughed. "It has nothing to do with that. It's just—" I paused, feeling that all-consuming need burning inside of me. It was like an insatiable craving I would never satisfy, no matter how often I had him. I wanted him inside of me ... no, I needed him inside of me. I wanted it hard and rough and fast. I wanted him to fuck me like an animal until I couldn't move.

His eyebrows rose with understanding, followed by a sensual grin. "You feel it," he said; not a question, but a statement.

"Feel what?"

"The lust. The power it contains. The need to unleash it. To bury yourself inside of it. To feel every moment of it, because nothing will ever compare to the power and pleasure it holds over you."

"Can't it just be because I love you?"

He chuckled, tracing a finger down my chest to my stomach. "My love," he whispered. The very sound of his voice felt like his fingers had dove deep inside of me, twisting and stroking the spot only he had ever touched. I groaned.

"My power is intrinsic, yet, in all the thousands of years I've been alive, nothing has given me more pleasure than being buried inside of you. Feeling you clench against my cock. Watching those perfectly round breasts tighten at the sound of my voice. The way you bite your lip right before you scream from the pleasure I give you. Knowing ..."

He paused, sliding his fingers to the seam between my legs. I gasped as he slipped down my lips, tracing my entrance tauntingly.

"... that I can make your body wet. That I can make you find release time and time again." My hips rose in a silent command to go further. "Everything with you has become more. Better. Stronger. Power or no," he traced my brow tenderly, love and awe flashing across his face, "This desire is because of our love."

He bent down, kissing me softly on the head. "Nothing else." He kissed my cheek. "It is because our love is inimitable." Kiss. "Unparalleled." He hovered over my lips, barely grazing his against mine. A shiver went through my body. "Transcendent."

He shoved his fingers deep inside of me. I unleashed, releasing our darkness into the room. I gasped from the pleasure, succumbing to every need only my mate could sate. My fiancé. My world.

That night, we didn't sleep a single moment. Just as one adventure would finish, another would begin. We tasted every inch of each other, leaving no area unexplored. As the sun began to rise, Deus held me against him. I was safe. We both were. I pressed my ear against his chest, listening to the beating rhythm of his heart—the one that was fully and completely mine.

Some hours into the late afternoon, I stirred from my exhausted sleep needing to use the restroom. I pulled away from Deus, trying not to wake him as he slept peacefully. Stumbling to the sink, I washed my hands. Taking in my disheveled appearance, I laughed in astonishment. My skin was lightly bruised in random places thanks to my mate's fierce kisses. My hair was a hot mess, and I looked completely spent.

I dried my hands, taking care with the beautiful ring that now decorated my finger. I would wear this ring for the rest of my life ... which wasn't going to be long.

The knowledge of my impending doom came crashing around me. I clasped the porcelain sink, making it groan under my grip. I threw wall after wall around myself, trying to stop my panic from escaping down our very bright and flourishing mating bond.

My chest felt like it was going to collapse. I gasped for air, panicking. Everything that I had worked so hard for was going to be ripped from me. I stared at the ring, wondering if I would even get to share a wedding ceremony with my mate.

I splashed cold water onto my face, forcing deep breaths until my rapid heart finally calmed. This sacrifice was necessary for the people I loved to live a life without fear or pain. I closed my eyes tightly, fighting the pain that threatened to destroy me, and stroked my ring.

Was it wrong of me to want to be selfish? To leave everything else behind and walk away, so I could live a happy life? How much more did the universe expect me to sacrifice? I guess it wouldn't be happy until I forfeited my life.

My reflection fought the tears that burned my eyes. I focused and blinked. Behind me, a static black blur flickered in and out of sight. My heart pounded against my chest in fear as I swung around, readying for an attack.

Nothing.

I calmed, using all my senses to take in my surroundings. Was I dreaming again? I heard only the sound of my steady breathing. Then ... a darkness flashed in the corner of the bathroom near the shower, laced with bright ribbons of white light. A woman opened her long gaping mouth, unleashing a high-pitched, wailing scream, lashing her head from side to side, stretching her hand towards me as if fighting against being pulled from this existence. Her image vibrated in and out like static from a television.

I lit my flame, preparing for whatever or whoever she was, but she flashed out of sight again. I frantically looked around, waiting for her return, but the dark figure never appeared. After waiting ten minutes, I returned to our bed to find Deus sound asleep, as if there hadn't been a woman screeching at the top of her lungs twenty feet away. Which forced me to wonder ... could he hear her, or was her visit intended just for me?

I curled my body against his, replaying the image of her ghostly presence. I couldn't make out many details except that she was a woman. The darkness surrounding her felt tainted in a way I had never experienced before. And the flickering, that was unsettling. Even when I had seen spirits, such as Giana when she had been dead, they always remained whole. Not fragmented, like this one.

I closed my eyes, trying to push the thousands of questions down, but I couldn't ignore the impression I was now being watched. As if, during her visit, she had somehow latched onto me, using me as an anchor to this world. This was the third time I had been visited by this spirit. She obviously had a message for me. Yet, who was she? What new monster had come to leech the happiness I had found? What new horror awaited?

The next week was filled with love, passion, and sex. Troves and troves of sex. Deus had gladly introduced me to his world—*our* world—of lust. We couldn't keep our hands, mouths, or bodies off each other. We graced every surface, room, and wall of the house. On the beach. In the pool. In the jungle.

I never thought sex could be like this. So freeing and consuming. And just when I thought I had experienced the most astounding pleasure of my life, Deus introduced a new method, device, or position that sent me over the edge. His favorite addition was restraints. No matter where we were, he found a way to confine me, forcing me to endure whatever method of pleasure he chose to bestow upon me.

The nights passed with ease, yet I still had the notion that a presence lingered in between realms. The flickering spirit didn't appear again. I would have shrugged it off as a dream or an illusion, yet my intuition warned me otherwise. I didn't bring it up to Deus. He was finally happy after everything he had endured, and I didn't want to burden him with something I couldn't explain.

Sunday morning, I pulled myself from our bed. My body was pleasantly sore and relaxed, the scent of us lingering on my skin and clothing. I smiled, knowing I would never tire of this. I stalked through the halls down the stairs towards the kitchen, desperate for food. I wore one of Deus's black button-up shirts and nothing else. The tiled floor felt cold against my bare feet as I turned the corner and screamed.

I unleashed my darkness, which was laced with red ribbons of static, towards the figure that stood at the edge of the kitchen island. The intruder threw up a shield, forcing my shadows to bend around the sphere of protection. A second later, Deus was at my side.

The shadows dissipated, revealing Belz in a defensive stance, hands outstretched towards us, keeping the shield in place.

"For the love of Father," he mumbled, relaxing and standing up straight. "Was that really necessary?"

I shifted my feet, embarrassed. "Sorry," I whispered. His gaze trailed slowly over my barely covered body. A sensual grin rose on his face, his eyes darkening. I pulled at Deus's shirt, trying to force it to cover more of my body.

Deus growled at my side, stepping in front of me protectively. "I suggest," Deus growled, "that you force you attention elsewhere, *brother*, and rather quickly, before you lose your eyes."

"Oh, come now, Deus," Belz said tauntingly. "Now that she's your mate, don't you think it's only fair that you share with the rest of us? I've never been with a tribrid before. I bet it's one hell of a ride."

Bam. Deus's fist flew across the air, smashing into Belz's face. Before I could gasp, Deus and Belz were flying across the room, slamming into every surface, wall, and object that had the misfortune of getting in their way. Their powers seeped from them, zapping with electric energy while they pummeled each other like schoolboys.

Walls cracked. Tables broke. Glass shattered. Deus managed to take Belz down to the floor, pinning him underneath his own body. A deep laugh bellowed from Belz. At the sound, Deus seemed to relax a bit, hovering over him while trying to steady his breathing. Deus released his brother's arms.

Belz patted his face mockingly. "Good to have you back, brother," Belz said with a bright grin.

"You're an asshole," Deus growled, standing to his feet. He extended his hand to my mate.

"Aren't we all," Belz replied, dusting off his pale blue shirt and dark black jeans. He smirked at me. "Nice to see you again, dear Seren."

"You too, Belz," I replied.

Deus returned to my side. "What are you doing here?" he asked.

"Well, if the two of you hadn't turned off your phones, I wouldn't have needed to waste the last week of my life popping across this Father-forsaken planet searching for you."

If he had gone to this much trouble to find us, something must be terrible wrong. "What is going on?" I asked, panicked.

"Fun time is over, I'm afraid," Belz said, looking between the two of us. "Time to come home."

"Is everyone okay?" I asked.

"As of right now, yes. But Hashen and Mal have discovered what Lucy has been up to and why he's been so quiet since our little adventure into Hell." Belz paused, examining the tray of cinnamon rolls I had made the morning before. He pulled one from the plate, placing a piece in his mouth and moaned with satisfaction.

"Belz, focus," demanded Deus. "What did they find?"

"Right," Belz said, still chewing on the sticky bun. "Our brother appears to have discovered a spell to mute all magical abilities, including ours. This requires a rather extensive and priceless selection of ancient relics that have been imbued with Father's power. When the covens got a report about an Italian relic that had been stolen from an abbey in Montecassino, Frankie cross-referenced the relic to other reports around the world and discovered two other relics stolen."

My heart dropped at the mention of Montecassino. Deus felt it. He ran his hand down my back for comfort. "What did they ... what did he steal from Montecassino?" I asked, hesitantly.

Belz shrugged. "Your cousin has the specifics, but if I remember correctly, I think it was an urn full of some dead saint's remains."

"Saint Benedict?" I whispered.

Belz looked surprised. "Yes. That's it. How did you know?"

"Because I grew up in that abbey," I answered. I racked my brain trying to figure out why Lucifer would want Benedict's remains. Why was this saint so important? But then ... it all clicked into place. "I need to get to Frankie," I said, turning from the princes and heading back towards our room.

I fumbled through the closet full of unused clothing and pulled a dress over my head. Deus appeared behind me a moment later. "What did you remember?" he asked.

"St. Benedict ... he's the saint that protects against curses, evil, and vice. Evil ... meaning our magic, according to the Christians."

"Well, then, it makes sense why he chose to place you there," he said, buttoning his shirt slowly.

"What do you mean?"

"Placing you in that abbey prevented your powers from manifesting fully. It helped silence your magic. Though, once you hit the proper age, your magic was too strong. Even for the relic to work."

"Wait. So you're saying the relics actually contain power?"

"Why do you think the Catholics horde them so desperately? They do offer an amount of protection and healing. They work well as a repellent against lower demons. To us, they just deliver an annoying headache and bouts of dizziness depending on how strong they are and how close they came in contact to the Son."

"And the spell?"

"Unfortunately, I have never heard of such a spell."

I tied my hair back into a ponytail, rushing around the room to gather my belongings.

"He would need a witch powerful enough to create and cast a spell of that magnitude. Someone with unnatural gifts. My mother is no longer an option. Who else would be able to do that?"

Silence. I turned towards Deus; he stared at the floor, solemn-faced, hands in his pockets. Something like panic and guilt flickered down the bond. I walked over towards him. He didn't seem to notice me until I was standing right in front of him. I pressed my hand against his chest.

"Love," I whispered softly. "What is it?"

His eyes finally found mine, his brow furrowed. "Victoria," he answered.

At her name, my vision tunneled and a buzzing sounded in my ears as my skin heated. The last time I had seen her, she had been curled up in my mate's lap, her hands on his skin, her lips pressed against his, her tongue sliding along his neck. And God only knew what happened after I left. If she had ... if they had ...

I felt hands on my face, cool against my blazing fury and jealousy. I met Deus's eyes. He gave me a knowing smile.

"That wasn't ..." he began to say, but stumbled over his words. "That wasn't me. Not the real me at least. I chose you, remember. And I will choose you every day for the rest of eternity."

My heart calmed, muscles releasing the tension of the memory of them together.

"I know," I exhaled, surprised by my flames flicking up and around my arms. I absorbed the power and ran my hands over my face. I went back to gathering my personal items throughout the room. Deus just watched me.

I paused, turning my attention back to him. "What?"

He dropped his head. "I just don't want what we've built here to be ruined when we go back. When our pasts—my past—eventually catches up with us." He smirked. "Some part of me wishes we could stay here forever. Leave everything else behind."

"That we got this time is a blessing in itself," I replied. "But our responsibilities and families would have eventually caught up with us, no matter how hard we tried to outrun them."

Deus nodded, smiling as he looked around the room. "I think this might be my new favorite place."

I laughed, throwing the small bag over one shoulder. "Mine too." I walked towards him, wrapping my arms around his waist. He looked down at me and grinned, though worry still danced behind those icy eyes.

"We're stronger than ever," I said. "Nothing is going to change that."

"I know. I just hate what I put you through in Hell. That you saw Victoria and I—" he paused again, unable to finish his sentence.

"Oh, make no mistakes," I said, gathering our darkness around us. "I am going to kill that bitch, and I am going to enjoy every moment of it. And this time, she will stay dead." I smiled, pressing my lips against his as I shifted us back to Castle Salvo.

CHAPTER SIXTEEN

As soon as we arrived, I headed for Frankie's room. She wasn't there. I rushed to Nonna's, where I found my family with the addition of Levi, Giana, Gor, and Tony. Mammon was leaning up against the balcony doorway, appearing to be in a bad mood.

"Where in the hell have you been?" Frankie said, pulling me into her embrace. "We were worried sick."

"I told you guys we needed some time," I replied. "Sorry I didn't check in. We were ... occupied."

Aunt Thora smirked. She looked at my mother, who bore the same facial features. They shook their heads in unison, a perfect mirror image of one another.

"I'm never going to get use to that," I said.

"Tell me about it," replied Frankie.

"Fifty thousand dollars apiece, brothers," boasted Belz, trailing in behind us and looking at the other princes. "Pay up."

"Thanks a lot, Mammon," mumbled Gor, rolling his eyes.

Belz laughed. "When will you all learn?" he said with pride. "I'm gluttonous when it comes to victory."

"Oh, shut up already," growled Mammon. "You had an unfair advantage."

"How so?" spat Belz.

"You own an ungodly amount of property around that area," replied Mammon, pushing off the doorframe, storming towards his brother. "You also have been keeping tabs on Deus's property holdings for centuries now."

Deus straightened. "You've been doing what?" he asked.

Belz scoffed. "Oh, don't act so offended. We all saw your little journals with maps and information on our territories in Hell."

I felt Deus flicker with anger.

"For Father's sake," intervened Gor. "We're all paranoid, territorial assholes. No one should be surprised here. Now, if all of you would shut up already, maybe we can find a way to stop our brother from immobilizing our powers."

My mother and aunt were huddled together, covering their mouths, attempting to mute the laughter that was slipping through. Nonna rolled her eyes, making her way over towards me.

"They've been like this since they all arrived," Nonna said, throwing an arm around my shoulders lovingly. "Insufferable, the lot of them." She looked over her shoulder at the princes. They smiled, and Belz, being the smartass he was, gave her a playful and dramatic bow.

"I refuse to be clumped in the same category as those imbeciles," Levi said, stepping next to Frankie.

"Suck up," Nonna murmured.

"We're all cut from the same cloth, Envy," commented Mammon.

"Don't remind me," Levi replied, turning to Deus. "You're looking better, brother."

"I'm feeling better," Deus said with a thankful nod.

"Well, fucking can do that to you," said Belz. My cheeks flushed with embarrassment.

"Will you shut the hell up already?" yelled Gor.

"Apparently it doesn't improve *everyone's* mood," Mammon added, bumping his elbow into Belz. They both laughed.

Tendrils of brown smoke laced with electricity began to snap and swirl around Gor. His brothers were getting the best of him, as usual. Giana approached and ran a soothing down his chest. "Ignore them, bear," she said softly. "They're just jealous."

"That I can confirm," Levi added.

"Bear?" Deus asked.

"Oh yes," replied Belz. "Their relationship has progressed to the cutesy nickname stage." He made a puking face.

"Father, take me now," grumbled Mammon.

"All of you," demanded Nonna, "shut up. You are older than the rest of us combined, yet you all act like teenagers. And to think, I use to fear the lot of you when I was a bambina." She huffed a laugh of amusement.

No one dared say a word. I smiled up at Deus next to me.

"Told you she could be scary," I said playfully.

"Frightening," he replied, running his fingers down my spine. The contact made my core tighten and heat. I closed my eyes, trying to control myself.

"Mm, I feel you," I heard him say in my mind.

"Yes, and if you don't stop whatever it is your doing, we're going to be useless," I replied.

"It's just been so long," he said, his desire sliding sensually down the bond.

"It's been three hours."

"Exactly. Too long."

Belz stood by Aunt Thora. He arched an eyebrow and gave her a slight smile, then leaned down, whispering something I couldn't hear. She fought to hide the grin creeping along the edges of her lips. She shook her head, rolling her eyes before stepping out of his orbit. He smirked, clearly proud of himself for the reaction he gained from her.

I stepped out of Deus's touch, trying to focus.

"Belz said Lucifer took Saint Benedict's remains?" I asked Frankie.

"Yes," she answered. "Among other relics." I followed her to Nonna's large table. Books and scrolls scattered across the surface. "The first relic Hashen discovered while following Lucifer's trail. St. Paul's chains were stolen which made every news outlet across the world. I thought to myself, *'there was no way some average Joe would steal such a priceless relic'*. Then, three silver pieces given to Judas at the time of his betrayal went missing from a Catholic church in Germany."

"Frankie came to us immediately," said Aunt Thora.

"I contacted our coven near the church, and they confirmed that they had encountered demons in that area around the time of the theft," added Nonna.

"So, Lucifer has three powerful artifacts," I said. "What is his plan?"

"I'm thinking he needs to collect two more," said Frankie, "which need to be extremely powerful to nullify magic completely. We know relics weaken our powers, but I've never heard of one completely silencing them. Hashen is still tailing him as we speak. He also needs to find a powerful enough witch willing to conduct the spell."

I felt the ripple of hesitation trickle down the bound. "Victoria," said Deus.

"Victoria?" asked Nonna, confused. "You mean, Victoria Prather ... the former moon goddess vessel ... *your* former lover?"

"That would be the one," Deus replied.

I sent my essence down the bridge between us, wrapping around his. *"This isn't your fault,"* I said, mind to mind.

"Aradia, help us," Nonna whispered, leaning over the table.

"That just leaves the question of which two relics Lucifer will be aiming for," continued Frankie. "He needs two more to compete the pentagram."

"It would have to be something of immense power, right?" asked Giana.

"Shit," said Tony, faintly. I had almost forgotten he was in the same room.

"What is it?" asked Levi.

Tony stepped towards the table, running a hand through his dark hair. He looked at my mother and between the two, something clicked in recognition. "When I was working for Lucifer and Annalise," Tony began, "one of the tasks that I was assigned to was to track down and locate any artifact or relic that had been stained with the blood of Christ."

"The most powerful relics of them all," Annalise whispered. Shame fell over her.

"And how many did you find?" asked Nonna.

"Six," answered Tony. "The four nails, the crown of thorns, and the Shroud of Turin."

"The what?" asked G.

"The cloth that was laid over Christ and stained with his blood after he died," answered Gor.

"That's all that there is, right?" I asked.

"Not quite," said Mammon.

"There's the spear that pierced his side," explained Belz.

"And the cross," said Deus. "Which Lucifer would only need a shard of. Not even the entire structure."

"And where are they?" asked Giana.

"We don't know the location of the entire cross," answered Levi, "but Spain has the largest piece that we know of. Rome has a piece, along with Notre Dame. The spear head is being held at Hofburg Treasure House in Viena, so the humans think, but it isn't the true head that pierced the Messiah. At the time of His sacrifice, no one thought to gather the items that had been stained with his blood. Only in the past few millennia have the Christians found these items to be holy."

"This is going to be impossible," said Frankie, dropping her head.

"For now," said Nonna, "we will station coven members around the churches that hold the relics we know of. Tony, get with Thora and disclose any information you can about their locations. We need to be alerted if any other relics go missing." Nonna paused, her face scrunched together.

"What is it, Mamma?" asked Annalise.

Nonna's eyes rose to mine and then flickered to Deus. "Someone needs to kill that traitorous bitch, Victoria. One less piece of his puzzle to contend with," she said, her lips firmly pressed into a line.

"That won't be an issue," Deus said.

"Good," Nonna answered. "We also need to discover where Lucifer plans to conduct the spell."

"Holy ground," answered Frankie. "It has to be."

"We can take that assignment," offered Belz, elbowing Mammon.

"We'll get our forces on it and sniff out where big brother is setting up camp," added Mammon.

"Good," Nonna nodded. "Thora and Annalise, I need you to rally the covens. Everyone goes into training. If magic won't be accessible in this fight, then we all must prepare our other skill sets if we want to stand a chance at surviving."

"I can help with that," offered Levi.

"I will also assign Mal and Hashen to assist," added Deus. "You will not find two more revered warriors."

"I will continue to help Frankie with the research," noted Gor.

"Perfect," Nonna said. "Everyone has their assignments. I suppose it's time to get to work." Nonna clapped her hands, dismissing everyone from her room. "Seren, please stay."

Deus turned back, kissing me softly before nodding towards Nonna. Once the door was shut, I joined her at the couch in front of the fireplace. She poured herself a glass of wine and another for me.

She exhaled. "I'm getting too old for this shit," she said, taking a drink.

"Hopefully, this will all be over soon, and you will live out the rest of your life in peace," I said softly.

Her eyes filled pain and worry. "And what of your life, bambina?"

I swallowed hard. "You know the answer to that question already, Nonna."

"There has to be another way."

"There isn't. And we don't have time to search for one, either. Our to-do list grows by the hour."

A long moment passed.

"How was your time away?" she asked.

I smiled, remembering the moments I would carry with me from this life into the next. "Perfect. Exactly what we needed."

"Your prince seems to be in better spirits."

"What can I say? I am a Salvo woman after all." I smiled at her.

Laughter erupted from her fiercely as she hunched over. "Oh, dear girl. You are that."

I joined in her amusement, relishing in her humor. "But in all seriousness," I continued, "the bond ... it's ... it's unlike anything I've ever felt. I can feel him, hear him, sense him. And, I can access his power, and he mine. The closer we become, the stronger my gifts grow."

Nonna's eyes went wide. "You have access to another Prince of Hell's magic?"

I nodded. "It's addicting, in the most alluring way. It's not like Lucifer's ... it's something different all together. The darkness there, mixed with my light. I can't explain it, but it's powerful, dangerous, yet ... captivating."

"You've lived through a lot of darkness in your short life. I wish I could have kept it from you. But you must remember, the light will always guide you back to your heart. To your true self. But the darkness ... the darkness, child, will reveal your greatest strength. The darkness can be seductive and intoxicating, but give into it completely, and you will lose who you truly are. You must be careful. You have access to both Deus and Lucifer's magic. Two of the most powerful demons ever to walk this earth."

"What if losing myself is what I need to do in order to defeat Lucifer?"

Nonna stroked my cheek in a loving caress. "You losing yourself is what he is banking on, Seren. You've been able to defeat him thus far because you've been fighting for everyone you love and everything you care about. That is the light ... that is your light. Your heart, your convictions, your blood ... family." She took my hand firmly in hers. "This," she said, holding our hands in between us, "is the anchor you must never let go of."

I nodded, knowing she was right. I held onto her hand. "There's something else I wanted to discuss with you. Something that not even Deus knows."

"Go on."

"The night Deus and I spent together as a mated pair." I thought back to that haunting moment. "When he was asleep, I was visited by a presence or a spirit. I am not sure what it was. She didn't appear like Giana had, in a solid form. She wasn't … whole, if that makes sense. And this isn't the first time she has visited me"

Nonna's brow furrowed. "Explain everything. And don't leave a single detail out."

So, I explained the eerie presence, the female figure hidden in darkness. Her heart-wrenching scream and flickering form..

Nonna thought silently for a moment. "Have you tried to use your goddess gift to call it forth? A door to this … realm, like the other door you created to Hell?"

I nodded. "Yes, but I don't think it resides in Hell. And from what I saw, the spirit isn't in heaven either. Each time, she was surrounded in darkness that I couldn't see through. I could feel her fighting from somewhere foreign. Someplace I have never been before."

She nodded slowly. "Tonight then, we'll conduct a summoning spell and try to reach this spirit. But we will need the others: your aunt and cousin, even your mother. The more of us, the better chance we stand—just in case it is not a pleasant thing we are opening the door for."

"I don't want to put them in danger," I said hesitantly.

"Seren, we are your family. We are stronger—"

"—together," I finished with a soft smile.

She nodded, rubbing her thumb along the back of my hand in a comforting manner, stopping as her finger hit my engagement ring. Her eyes flashed down to the large red ruby. Her gaze rose to meet mine in a silent question.

I nodded. "I almost forgot," I said, smiling softly.

"Oh, Seren." Her eyes filled with tears as she pulled me into a firm embrace.

I pulled away, looking down at my hand. "I wonder if ..." Tears fell from my eyes. "I wonder if I'll live long enough to finally get to marry the man I truly love. The man I got to choose."

"You will, child," she said, taking my face in her hands. "If I must confine Lucifer myself, you will get the wedding you've always dreamt of. And the husband you've always deserved. I swear this to you."

I fell into her arms, letting out all my fear of leaving my mate, my family, and the life I now so desperately wanted. Destiny was a cruel and unpredictable thing. No matter how hard I fought it, or what I did to outrun it, it always found new ways to end my life.

Chapter Seventeen

"How long will you be gone tonight?" Deus asked, running a finger down the center of my bare chest and circling around my bellybutton. I tangled my bare legs with his.

"I'm not sure," I replied. "I haven't been able to spend much time with them since someone has been taking up most of my time."

He laughed softly, pulling me into his hard chest. "Are you complaining, fiancé? Based on the sounds you were making five minutes ago. I'd say you didn't mind any time I've been taking."

I nuzzled my nose into his neck, a sense of complete peace warming me.

As soon as I had walked through my bedroom door, Deus had been on me. We were like wild animals. Our clothes were torn to shreds and we had lost ourselves in each other's bodies, taking every moment of pleasure we could.

"You were making sounds too, mate," I whispered, pressing tender kisses to his neck. He moaned while I trailed my lips down the front of his chest.

His fingers entwined my long white hair, then he yanked my head back, claiming my mouth with his. He had been inside me moments ago, but I already craved more. I pulled away only to take a breath. A smile stretched across his face, revealing his beautiful dimples.

"How am I supposed to focus on anything else when all I can think about is you?" I asked while he pressed soft kisses on either of my cheeks.

"I'm the wrong person to ask, since all I can think about is how perfectly you take me." His fingers slid down the seam of my sex, forcing my hips to arch in response. "How perfect you clench around me." With a taunting caress over my bundle of nerves, a moan of pleasure escaped me. "How wet I can make you." His teeth crazed against my earlobe, nipping tenderly. "How delicious you taste."

I couldn't control myself. I shifted on top of him, forcing his body back against the mattress and positioned him at my entrance, sliding myself down around him with force. I screamed in ecstasy, moving in a desperate rhythm, needing to consume as much of him as possible.

His closed tightly while his hands held my hips firmly, grinding me harder against him. Within seconds, I was coming undone. Heat rose inside of me with each thrust. I was throbbing, everything inside of me screaming for a release until finally, with one more deep thrust, I came undone. Evidence of my pleasure slid down my legs, drenching his beautiful body and our bed.

Deus roared alongside me, forcing himself deeper inside, holding us there while my body convulsed and shivered around him. I collapsed on top of his chest, heaving in exhaustion. He caressed his fingers down my spine, sending gooseflesh erupting along my skin. He pressed a tender kiss to the side of my head, wrapping his other arm around me.

"I love you, Seren," he whispered.

I pulled back, gazing into his beautiful eyes. "I love you too, Asmodeus." I lazily pressed my lips against his. Deus tightened his arms around my body, pulling me closer against him as he deepened the kiss.

A knock came at the door, but I barely heard it. Deus traced my lips with his tongue while his hand cupped my aching breast. The knock came again.

"For Aradia's sake," I heard Frankie yell from the other side. "You two have been at it for hours. Come up for air already and give the rest of us some peace and quiet."

I laughed against Deus's lips, pushing myself off his perfect body. "Don't you have your own prince to entertain yourself with?" I yelled back.

"Oh, don't worry about us," she said. "We're perfectly satisfied, but we've learned how to balance our physical life with our duties. Do you need some pointers?"

"I need more," Deus whispered, flipping my body underneath his and sliding his tongue down my abdomen towards my sex. I gasped from the instant pleasure that overcame me.

"We're meeting in Nonna's room in ten minutes," Frankie called out.

"Got it," I replied in a breathy voice.

"Ten minutes," Deus said, trapping my thighs with his arms. "I can work with that."

I managed to shower, even after Deus had immobilized my body with his wicked talents. I walked down the halls of Castle Salvo, memorizing every small detail of the beautiful palace that had become my first true home. My family had been raised within these walls. I would have grown up here, alongside Frankie, if things had been different. If it weren't for Lucifer.

Inside Nonna's room, I found my family waiting near the seating area. Engagement ring balloons were scattered around the room along with flowers, hors d'oeuvres, and decorations. Aunt Thora popped a bottle of champagne. My family clapped, all grinning widely as they rushed me.

Frankie barreled into me, squeezing my ribs until I gasped for air.

"Oh, my gods!" she gasped. "I cannot believe you didn't call me as soon as it happened. I want all the details."

"Give her some air, Francesca," Aunt Thora said, taking me into her arms. "I am so happy for you, sweetheart. Truly."

My mother approached next. She reached for me slowly, testing if I would stop her, but I embraced her first. She pulled away with a smile on her face.

"I am happy you've found the one your heart truly loves, little bean."

"So am I," I replied.

"The Prince of Lust," Nonna laughed, hugging me tightly. "Only a—

"—Salvo woman could bag the Prince of Lust," Aunt Thora, Frankie, and my mother all said as one. We all laughed while we made our way back to the seating area.

"And have we forgotten, this is Seren's third engagement in the past year," added Frankie.

"Yea, thanks for the reminder," I said, rolling my eyes. The thought of Orion tugged at my heart.

"We're very desirable women," my mother said, in an unsure tone. This was the first time I had heard her try to joke. It sounded unnatural, but I was glad she was trying to regain the person she had been before Lucifer had taken her soul.

"The hell we are," Aunt Thora said, clinking her glass to Annalise's.

"If I recall," added Nonna, "you've caught the eye of the Prince of Gluttony."

"Oh, Mamma," Thora said, rolling her eyes.

"No," Frankie chimed in, "Nonna's right. He seems very taken with you."

Aunt Thora balked. "There is no way in hell," she said.

"I wouldn't count him out." I laughed. "They have their ways about them."

"I second that," Frankie added.

"Absolutely not," Thora huffed.

"Oh, stop being such a prude, Thora," Nonna spat. "Taking him for a test run wouldn't kill you."

Frankie and I looked at each other in shock. Mom choked on her champagne and then we all burst into laughter.

"What?" Nonna said. "I may be old, but I am not dead."

"Okay," Frankie said, grabbing my hand. "Tell us how he proposed. Every detail."

I smiled, taking myself back to that night. For the next half hour, I told them about our time on the island and how he asked me to spend eternity by his side. My family eagerly listened, laughter and *awws* coming at the right moments. I told them about the bond and what I experienced when we had connected, leaving the more personal bits out.

When I had finished, Nonna wiped tears I hadn't noticed before from her cheeks. She took a deep breath and smiled.

"I suppose tomorrow wedding planning shall begin," she said. We exchanged a painful glance—my marriage would be short-lived. "But tonight," she continued, "I have gathered you all here to conduct a summoning."

Aunt Thora and Mom's faces went blank.

"A séance? What are you talking about?" asked Aunt Thora.

"And what are we summoning?" asked Mom. "If my memory serves me, you banned Thora and me from ever doing a summoning again after that little incident back in the early '90s."

"Aradia, was that a shit show," mumbled Thora.

"And for good reason," snapped Nonna. "You two didn't know what the hell you were doing."

"What are we summoning?" asked Frankie.

"Something that visited me," I said, taking charge. I told them about my experience with the woman hidden in darkness. When I had finished, my mother looked panicked.

"Have you told Deus?" asked Frankie.

"No," I replied. "I want to figure out who she is first before I involve him in this. She visited me when I was alone. I need to know why. The timing also baffles me. After the mating bond was completed, she decides to show up? That can't be a coincidence."

"I agree," added Nonna, standing. We all joined her. "Time to find out what your new friend wants. Seren, shift us to a place hidden from sight. A place in nature, so we will be able to ground."

I closed my eyes, trying to imagine such a place. And then an image came to mind, a place full of beauty and peace. Orion's favorite place. I swallowed the tears, taking Nonna and Frankie's hand. Once we were linked, I shifted us to the beautiful landscape.

When I opened my eyes, all I could see was Orion. The time we spent here when he was helping me train. The bond we had forged. My heart tightened from the pain.

"Where are we?" asked Frankie.

"Ligurian Alps," I answered. "This was Orion's favorite place. We used to come here to train. It's safe." Aunt Thora stroked my arm gently.

"It's beautiful," added my mom softly.

"Everyone, gather in a circle," instructed Nonna. My aunt and mother helped her prepare, setting out the candles and appropriate herbs and crystals. Nonna lit the sage and then stood at the top of the pentagram. "Circle up, girls."

We did as she said, taking our places. I had never done a spell of this magnitude before, and I didn't know what we were calling forth. Too many unknowns, but if this woman had answers that would assist us in the upcoming war, we had to try.

Nonna took out a dagger, slicing two long slits down either of her palms. She passed it to Mom, who did the same, passing it to Thora. Frankie and I looked at each other and shrugged before following suit.

"Now," continued Nonna, "once we lock hands, recite the spell after me. Do not, by any means, let go of each other's hands. Our blood ties will keep us from harm and the circle will lock the spirit into place. If at any point the spirit becomes violent or we wish to end the link, we will recite the words, *et ita factum est*."

"And so, it is done," whispered Frankie.

"Exactly," replied Nonna. "Seren, since the spirit made contact with you, you will be the one to talk to it. It may respond better to you than a stranger."

"Understood," I replied.

"Everyone ready?" asked Nonna.

We nodded. One by one we clasped our hands together in a circle. I could feel the power of our blood as it passed through each of us. My family's eyes began to glow with a yellow light, just as the cool force of our power struck me, taking my breath away. This kernel of our magic connected us to one another—to our legacy.

The pentagram in the center of our circle lit on fire, streams of burning flames running across the lines of the star, blazing with heat and magic. I felt the ripples of magic, now that we had funneled our energy into one. It wasn't like the bond between Deus and I, or the magic I felt from my goddess or demon parts. This was natural, familiar. Something that had always been there, now magnified that I stood hand in hand with my bloodline.

Nonna began chanting slowly, letting us hear her pronunciation of each word. In unison, we repeated the spell, our magic flowing through us, joining together in the center of the pentagram. I closed my eyes, imagining the woman who had visited me a week ago: the sound of her voice, the pain in her eyes, the darkness that surrounded her. I focused, holding the image at the forefront of my mind.

The wind picked up around us, tossing the flames wildly. I tightened my grip on Nonna and Frankie, holding the image of the visitor in my mind. My hair lashed at my face as the wind violently tore through the trees. The branches whined and the leaves hissed. The ground shook under our feet, rattling the loose rocks against the surface.

Our chanting became louder, overpowering the noise of the rushing air. Power rose from the center of the star, tying itself to each of us with a beam of pure white light. My magic was tugged from within, like a hand reaching deep inside of my chest and latching onto my heart. In a flash, the breath from my lungs was ripped away. Our bodies extended, frozen in the air for a moment until the power let go, silencing the nature around us.

Still grasping Frankie and Nonna's hands, I drew my gaze from the ground to the figure that now stood in the center of our circle. A tall slender woman in a tattered black dress examined our faces until she landed upon mine. Her beautiful curly white hair drifted in the wind, falling the length of her back. Her tanned skin looked freshly kissed by the sun, though she was covered in dirt. Small brown freckles dusted the bridge of her nose and cheeks. Her eyes were dark as night.

"Goddess," she whispered, a sly smile adorning her face.

"Who are you?" I asked.

"My name is Talia Mizrahi," she said, taking a breath. "I am the first vessel of Aradia."

"Impossible," Nonna whispered.

Talia turned towards Nonna with surprise on her face, as if she had forgotten we weren't alone.

"What do you want?" I asked, regaining her focus.

"To help you defeat Lucifer Morningstar," she replied.

I glanced to Nonna, hoping Talia didn't give my plan away to the others. A flicker of darkness struck through Talia's body, causing her to gasp in pain. She fell to the ground, gasping for air.

"I don't have much time," she said, sitting back on her knees. "It's pulling me back."

"What is?" I asked. "Where are you?"

"Purgatory," she replied, and another ripple of darkness slashed into her, slicing her cheek wide open. "Find me. Use your doorway and find me. I will answer all your questions. I can help."

"In exchange for what?" I asked.

She gritted her teeth, whimpering a bit as the darkness seeped from the ground, encasing her form. Two invisible claws made slash marks on either side of her shoulders, as if digging into her. She cried out in pain.

"All I wish is to destroy Lucifer once and for all," she answered, and vanished.

A massive force slammed into the ground, tearing our grips from one another, sending us flying backwards. I hit the soft grass and lay there, breathing deeply and processing the revelation we had just uncovered.

"Too old. I am too old," Nonna said, shaking her head while wiping the dirt off her pants.

"Valeriana Ravenmore was the first vessel," snapped Thora. "Our records do not mention any before. This has to be a trap."

"Has Deus or Levi ever mentioned other vessels before the first?" asked Annalise.

"No," I replied, and stood, looking at Frankie. "Deus cared for Valeriana. She's the reason he was reunited with his soul. He wouldn't keep this from me."

"Levi also believes Valeriana was the first," added Frankie. "All the vessels have been in contact with the princes one way or another in the past. They would have known."

"Unless ..." I said slowly, thinking. "Unless something with Talia had gone very wrong."

"What are you thinking?" asked Nonna.

"There was magic in the world before Valeriana," I continued, "before Aradia. Aradia just strengthened our gifts. But even in religious texts, magic is mentioned."

"You're suggesting that our goddess lied to us?" said Thora.

"Look at Victoria," I said,. "She went against her own nature, what she was created for, just to have a chance to be with Deus. Now, she is working with the very evil we were designed to defeat. Free will is a choice. And then ... when I completed the rite," I paused, preparing to share more secrets I had hidden from my family.

"When Aradia bestowed her power into me, Deus was released from Hell and his power reached for me. Aradia panicked when she saw his magic. She reached inside of me and felt the darkness that waited there. She kept saying 'not again' and that she wouldn't allow it to happen again ... right before she tried to kill me."

They gasped.

"Seren," Nonna said, her face furrowing with disappointment. "Why have you kept this from us?"

"Too much was happening," I replied. "I didn't think much of it until now. Maybe Aradia was referring to Talia. Maybe there is an entire part of our history that has been kept from us."

"We still have too many unanswered questions to start speculating," said Nonna. "First, I suggest we ask the princes if they know of this Talia character. Then, Seren, the choice is up to you how you wish to proceed."

I nodded, gathering us all in a circle and shifting back to the castle. As soon as we landed, I sent a message down the bond, asking Deus to gather his brothers and meet us in Nonna's room. Within ten minutes, five Princes of Hell stalked through the doors, each more devastatingly handsome than the next, but none of them held a candle to the Prince of Lust. My heart skipped a beat just at the sight of him.

"Being summoned by witches," Mammon grumbled. "How low we've fallen."

"I don't mind," Levi said, heading straight for Frankie.

Deus slid his arms around my waist, kissing my head softly. I didn't miss the wink Belz gave Aunt Thora before taking his place next to Mammon.

"What's going on?" asked Gor. G following closely at his side.

I took a deep breath and said down the bond, *"don't be mad that I kept this from you."* Deus looked at me with confusion.

"A spirit began to visit me when I was in Hell. At first, I thought it was just a dream, but then she appeared to me a week ago when Deus and I were on the island. She was trapped in darkness and in pain. She flickered in and out of existence and screamed in agony, but was unable to speak. I asked my family to help me locate and speak with her. We called upon her tonight. She claims her name is Talia Mizrahi ... the first goddess vessel."

Gor's eyes went wide. Deus's mouth pressed into a thin line.

"Impossible," said Belz.

"She says she has a way to defeat Lucifer permanently," I continued. "She doesn't want anything in return."

"Have any of you heard of her?" asked Annalise.

They all shook their heads in silence.

"The first we knew of was Aradia," said Belz.

"Then Valeriana," added Deus. "She had no memories of other vessels. Only small parts of Aradia's life."

I paused, thinking things over. "When did Obsidian begin?" I asked, looking around the room.

"Their coven predates any text we have," answered Thora.

I looked to Deus and the others.

"There has always been evil in this world," explained Belz, "but mention of Obsidian began in the year, what ..." He paused, looking at his brothers for confirmation. "1500 BC-ish?"

"I believe so," said Levi. "It was near the time of Moses, if I recall correctly."

"I would have to agree," said Gor, looking as if he was deep in thought. "After Moses freed Father's chosen people, they were denied passage into the promised land because of their disobedience when told to invade—" Recognition flashed across his face, along with the rest of his brothers.

"Fuck," mumbled Mammon.

"How did we miss that?" asked Belz.

"Maybe because we were all soulless animals at that time," Levi suggested.

"Anyone care to enlighten the rest of us?" snapped Nonna.

"Canaan," Deus said, "was ordered to be destroyed by Father. Moses and his people were the first to be given the order, but they disobeyed, causing them to fall from Father's favor. When the mantel of leadership passed to Joshua, the order was given again and this time, his people obeyed."

"But between the shift in power," said Levi, "the Canaanites used that time to build forces of great strength."

"And dark power," added Gor. "Canaan was known for its wickedness. Their worship of satanic idols and false gods."

"The first mention of a group of people using magic," said Belz.

"A coven," Frankie whispered.

"So," said Nonna, "we think this Talia figure came from that time?"

"It's a theory," answered Gor, "but we can't know for sure without more information."

I exhaled. "Well, I guess that settles that," I said, looking to Nonna. "Off to Purgatory I go."

"Purgatory?" Deus blurted. "Absolutely not."

"This woman is in Purgatory, not Hell. You're sure?" asked Gor.

"That is what she says," I answered. "And I can't sense her in Hell."

"Seren," said Levi, taking a step forward. "We can't enter Purgatory. That realm is off limits to us."

"And if I can't go with you," said Deus, "you are not going."

"I will go," my mother said from behind me. We all turned towards her. "I'll go with Seren to find Talia."

"Annalise," Thora whispered, concern lacing her tone.

"It only makes sense," my mother explained. "The covens need Mother here to lead. You and Frankie are next in line. The princes can't go, which leaves Seren and I to track down this Talia character."

"I said no," Deus growled, shaking the castle. I turned towards him, stroking his face.

"My love," I whispered, trying to calm him. "You have to trust me. She is the key to your brother's undoing. Have you so quickly forgotten how formidable your mate is?"

"We don't know what to expect there," he said, his voice shaking a bit. "I won't risk you."

Another hand appeared on his forearm. My mother stood beside us. "I won't let anything happen to her," she said with a compassionate smile. "I know you have no reason to trust me, but I swear to you, I will gladly sacrifice my life ..." she paused, turning towards me, her eyes full of love and devotion, "... if it means that my daughter gets to live."

I reached up on my tiptoes, kissing Deus on the cheek. "It's settled then," I said. "Mom and I will retrieve Talia."

"And how are you exactly getting to Purgatory?" asked Mammon.

"I can create a doorway," I replied, looking at Gor. "Right?"

"Essentially, but ..." he paused, scrunching his face. "Cecilia never attempted to go anywhere but Hell."

"Infuse the doorway," G said next to him. Gor's head popped up, his eyes gleaming with pride.

"Brilliant," he said. "Beautiful and brilliant." He kissed her on the head and turned towards me. "We need Talia's bones."

Frankie flung her hands dramatically in the air. "Yeah," she said sarcastically. "No problem. Let's just hunt down the bones of some girl that lived over three thousand years ago. Why not? Oh, and have we all forgotten ... bones don't last that long!"

"I have a feeling these bones will be well preserved," I said, thinking back to the haunting image of the woman."

"We'll scry for them," said Aunt Thora. "So dramatic, Francesca."

"I can help," offered Giana. Thora nodded her thanks.

"Great," I said. "In the meantime, I'll begin infusing my magic into a new doorway until we have her bones."

"This is crazy," Mammon said.

"Most fun we've had in centuries I would say," Belz said, smacking Mammon on the back with a wide grin. "Leave it to the Salvo women to always show us a good time." His eyes landed on Thora, desire blazing behind them.

Chapter Eighteen

I followed Deus out of Nonna's room and down the hall without a word. His frustration and anger rippled through the bond. His pace made it difficult for me to match his speed as we weaved through the crowd of witches and warlocks. Deus headed for the front doors and threw them open in utter silence.

He spun on me, grabbed hold of my arms and shifted us away from the castle. I staggered backwards as the wind hit my face, sending my head spinning. I took in my surroundings, catching my breath and bearings. We were on the ledge of the belltower that stood at the highest point in Triora. From this high up, you were able to see the beauty and simplicity of my ancestral home.

Deus stood at the edge, looking across the landscape. His hands were firmly clasped behind his back and his eyes fixed on the horizon.

"A little warning would have been nice," I said, stepping next to him.

He didn't turn to me. "Why did you keep this from me? How—" He paused, furrowing his brow. "The bond. How can you still be hiding things from me, even with the bridge linking us?"

"Deus, I'm sorry. I didn't want to hide this from you, but I didn't want to worry you if it was nothing. You've already been through so much, and I—"

"So have you," he interrupted, finally turning to face me. "We all have, Seren. That doesn't give you the right to keep things from me. Especially of this magnitude. I am your mate. Your fiancé. The person you are supposed to trust above all else. The person who is supposed to protect you—"

"Exactly, Deus," I snapped. "And though I love you for wanting to protect me, that need to intervene, to put yourself at risk for me, sometimes gets in the way of me doing my job."

"And what is your job, exactly?" He faced me then, his expression stern and unyielding. "Have you not given enough? Your time of sacrifice has come to its end, and I'll be damned if I don't see to that personally. If this burden is anyone's to carry, it is that of my brothers and I, not yours."

I was approaching my limit. "Don't tell me what I can and can't do with my life. If I choose to sacrifice myself to save the people I love, then that is my choice and mine alone!"

His angry demeanor stilled. "What are you planning? What else are you keeping from me?"

"Nothing," I said, a little too quickly. I broke away from him. Before I could take another step, he grabbed me by the arm, forcefully turning me back to face him.

"Do you not understand what you mean to me?" he said, aggression masking the pain entangled in his words. "Do you understand what it would do to me if I lost you? How can you stand here and say that your decision to sacrifice your life is yours and yours alone?"

"Deus, I didn't mean anything by it. I was just frustrated by you telling me what I could and couldn't do. That's all."

He let me go, dropping his eyes to the floor. "You're keeping something from me," he whispered. "I don't need the bond to tell when you're lying. Your face is horrible at keeping secrets."

I reached my arms around him. "I'm sorry," I said again, softer. "I'm sorry for keeping Talia from you and I am sorry for contacting her without you knowing. You're right. We're a team, but you must understand … that same drive you have to protect me, I have for you. Thus, my little trip into the tormentor's pit." I smiled playfully.

He smirked, pulling me closer against him. "You're insane," he replied.

"Of course, I am," I said flatly. "I'd have to be. I mean, my mate's the Prince of Lust, my best friend is the Prince of Sloth, my cousin-in-law will most likely be the Prince of Envy, and Lucifer Morningstar is pretty much my father."

Deus grimaced at the last comment. "Father, please spare me," he said.

I laughed, pressing my face against his chest. I took a deep breath, the peace of his arms enveloping me. "I guess I should start working on the door."

"Mm," he hummed, running his hands down my back. "Or … we could take a little break from the whole saving humanity bit and grab a bite to eat."

I pulled away, shaking my head. "We don't have time. I need to—" His hands cupped either side of my face. He bent his neck so we were eye to eye.

"You have time to eat, my love. Everything will be as it was, even after you fill your belly."

I smiled, leaning into his touch. "Okay," I replied. "But it has to be quick."

He pulled me close and we shifted to a restaurant near the edge of the town. Deus led me to the back of the brick building, where a private dining room was separated from the public. Around a large rectangular table sat all our family and friends.

Levi and Frankie, Aunt Thora, Nonna, my mother. Giana, Gor, and Tony. Belz and Mammon. Everyone was laughing, wine poured freely and passed from person to person. It was the most beautiful sight I had ever seen.

"How did you do all this so quickly?" I asked Deus.

He shrugged. "I sent a mental message to my brothers to collect the others. Everyone agreed, a relaxing, apocalypse-free dinner was in order before the work began tomorrow."

I wrapped my arms around his waist. "You're amazing."

He smiled. "I know," he whispered, leaning down, and pressing a soft and suggestive kiss against my lips.

"Alright already," I heard Frankie say as she approached us with two glasses of wine. "Give it a break for all our sakes. Honestly cousin, I don't even know how you can manage to stand upright from all your ... dalliances."

"What can I say," I replied, taking the glass, and holding it up towards my nonna, aunt, and mother. "I'm a Salvo woman."

"Through and through," they answered back, holding their glasses up and then laughing in the most extraordinary melody I'd ever heard. Every woman in my family, every woman I loved, cared for, and looked up to, was sitting in this room, sharing in this joyous moment.

I took a seat between Nonna and my mother. Deus sat amongst his brothers, grabbing the bottle of whisky and pouring himself a glass. The food was brought out: every dish, appetizer, and fixing you could imagine. Stories were shared. Jokes were had. Memories were made.

By the time dessert came, Frankie and I were doubled over laughing from a story Mother and Thora had told us a story from their youth. Watching them together was like watching the night sky meet the horizon. It was seamless and fluid. My heart filled with happiness for the two of them.

Frankie squeezed my hand as if she could read my mind. She gave me a tender and understanding smile. I leaned into her, laying my head on her shoulder. Nonna sat amongst us, shaking her head in horror of the secrets her daughters had just divulged.

Down the table, my mate sat casually in between his brothers while they argued and yelled across the table at one another playfully. As usually, they were ganging up on Gor. Tony sat amongst them, observing their actions in disbelief. Deus arched a brow, revealing his perfect set of white teeth. My skin heated at the sight.

"What are you thinking, my love?" He whispered into my mind.

"I'm thinking that this ... this moment might be the most perfect moment of my life. I'm thinking that if you were to ask me to describe the word happiness ... it would be this moment."

"And if I were to paint the image of happiness," he replied, *"it would be the smile that has not left your angelic face this entire evening."*

I blushed, speechless. The only thing that could have made this night better would have been the promise of many more dinners like this to come. Where we all sat around a table, sharing stories and memories, knowing tomorrow held the promise of a better future. A future where we all walked out of this alive.

Chapter Nineteen

"Needless to say, I'm very impressed," said Gor, lounging lazily in a chair in the corner of my room.

My arms shook, beads of sweat sliding down my warm neck into my shirt, the fabric clinging to my skin. I released the power, staggering over to the couch across from him and slumped into the soft, velvet cushion. I closed my eyes, trying to steady my breath.

"Drink up," Gor demanded. I opened my eyes and gladly took the cup he offered me, consuming the cool water in one gulp. "You're already a third of the way finished."

"I don't understand," I gasped, still trying to calm my racing heart. "When Deus and I were in Hell, I was able to construct the gate back home almost instantly."

He shrugged. "Our powers are more potent when we are in Hell. We're directly connected to our fuel source. Maybe that contributed to your expeditiousness."

"I don't think I'll ever understand how magic works," I answered, wiping my brow with the back of my hand.

"It took you weeks to create your first gate. By the looks of it, this is going to be done in two days. That's impressive, little goddess."

"Thanks. Now, all we need is Talia's bones. No word from G or the others on the location of the body?"

"Nothing yet."

"And the artifacts?"

"Still no sign of Lucifer or his minions."

Knock, knock, knock.

"Come in," I called sitting up. Tony's head popped around the corner of the doorframe, traveling from me and then to Gor. His brow furrowed. Gor smirked slyly, lacing his fingers behind his head. I couldn't help but snicker.

"Sorry," Tony said. "I didn't realize you weren't alone."

"Were you trying to catch my brother's fiancé alone, little Simonelli?" asked Gor.

"And why would it matter to you?" Tony asked.

"Well, Giana seems to like you breathing, and I presume I don't have to remind you how territorial Asmodeus is. Especially when it comes to *his* mate." Gor sat up straight, leaning slowly forward, his posture turned intimidating. His tone shifted, no longer amused. "So, for all our sakes, turn around and get the fuck out."

"Gor," I interrupted before this visit got out of hand. "It's okay. Tony is just a friend."

"No, sweet Seren," he said lightly. "You don't fuck friends."

"Gor," I snapped, louder than before. "I appreciate the overprotective brother act, but I assure you, Deus trusts me. Nothing is going to happen."

Gor stood casually, as if he wasn't just about to burn the room to the floor, and brushed his long brown coat with his hands, releasing the wrinkles. He walked over to Tony, his hands folded behind his back just like Deus. Gor's face was a frightening calm that made my blood freeze.

He assessed Tony from head to toe.

"If you end up dead," Gor said softly, "and cause Giana any pain from your stupidity, I will personally make the rest of eternity a slow and painful hell for you once you arrive in my home." Gor leaned in to his ear. "And I assure you, Antonio Simonelli, that is where you are going." Gor exited, leaving Tony standing unnaturally still.

"Are they all that dramatic?" Tony asked, finally relaxing his shoulders.

"Yup," I answered, refilling my waterglass. "Go figure, the princes of Hell are all just a bunch of territorial, boasting teenagers."

"Isn't he supposed to be lazy?"

"He's more of a bookworm. His place in Egypt is filled with priceless treasures, but the entire place looks like an episode from one of those hoarding shows. He usually doesn't involve himself in politics, and he's not ambitious like his brothers. They all have their own afflictions of the sins they represent. Some are blindingly evident, while others require you to look closer at the specific prince."

"I'll never understand the appeal."

I laughed. "You don't prefer men ... you wouldn't. Did you need something?"

"Nonna asked me to inform you that the covens will be gathering here within the next few days. Training will begin."

"Will ... will the Soleil Coven be arriving as well?" I asked. I would always carry that burden with me.

"All covens, Seren."

I sat back onto the couch, thinking of Orion. Of his mother. And his groom-less bride.

Tony sat down next to me. "It wasn't your fault," he whispered.

I struggled to find the right words. "I ... I've gone over it time and time again," I replied. "There were so many different paths I could have chosen that wouldn't have resulted in our capture."

"You can't do that to yourself. Even with all the power you possess, foresight is not one of them. And yes, we can ponder 'what if', but that only deprives us of the joy around us. No matter how much we want to, we can't change the past."

"If there was a way to go back, I would have done it already." Tears fell down my cheeks.

"I know you would have. And so does he," Tony said, grasping my shoulder in a comforting gesture. "He loved you. The connection the two of you had will never be replaced. But Seren ... you lived. He wouldn't want you to waste that by constantly carrying this guilt around with you. Live, Seren. Be happy."

An uncontrollable laugh escaped me. I shrugged back against the couch. "If only I could," I whispered.

"I think after everything you've experienced, you're due a little happiness, wouldn't you say?"

I smirked at the irony of his statement, knowing what my future held. "I don't think the universe likes me very much."

"What's there not to like? Except your mate." Tony grinned playfully and I couldn't help but laugh.

"I didn't have a choice, you know."

"Maybe not in your power, but you did have a choice in loving him. You were in love with him before the mating bond clicked into place."

I replayed the journey Deus and I had gone through to find one another. I nodded softly. "I did ... You know ... I think he found me long before I met him."

Tony took my hand, squeezing it tightly. "You will have your happily ever after, Seren," he said. He sounded so sure, his voice absent of jealousy or pain. I truly believed his words. "I want you to be happy. And after all this ... you will be."

I swallowed back the lump of sadness in my throat. My heart felt heavy. "Do you believe in miracles, Tony?" I whispered.

His brow furrowed. "What do you mean?"

"A miracle. Something that transcends all understanding ... all logic ... all sense."

His eyes fell to our hands, still holding each other's. A soft smile spread across his face. "After everything I did, the woman I love is sitting next to me, allowing me in her life. Not only did she forgive me, but she saved my sister and made my family whole." His eyes lifted back to mine. "Yes, Seren De Salvo, I believe in miracles because you are mine."

I wrapped my arms around his neck, pulling him into me. I cried, releasing all the stress of what had occurred, and was yet to come. No matter how little time I had left, Tony was right. I needed to live it.

I pulled away, wiping my cheeks as we smiled at one another. "Thank you, Tony. I think I needed that."

"Anytime, beautiful," he said, pinching my chin between his thumb and finger. He stood from the couch. "Well, I better get going before your mate or one of your soon-to-be brothers-in-law shows up to end my life."

I laughed, following him to the door. "You know, if G and Gor work out, they'll be your brothers-in-law as well. And I guess that would make me your sister-in-law."

"Aradia, help me." We both laughed as I showed him out.

I showered and then curled underneath the covers, the cool breeze of the impending snowfall creeping into my room. I was exhausted by the magic it took to build the gate. Within moments, I drifted into a deep slumber, surrounded by shadows and starlight. In the distance, a figure, so familiar and serene, waited for me. His shadows swirled around him. His eyes, a deep red, flickered in the darkness like a flame dancing in the night.

Without hesitation, my unconscious self stepped towards the figure. He offered me his hand. My icy cold flesh slid across the warm, smooth shadows of his fingers and then his palm. Fire sparked, heating as he pulled me into him. I allowed our bodies to meld into one, my soul seeming to call to his.

I relaxed, my head falling against the shadow's broad chest. His arms, securing tightly around my waist. I closed my eyes, no longer wanting to think. An uncontrollable smile drew across my lips, parting them slightly, right before I heard myself whispered, "home."

CHAPTER TWENTY

The scent of fresh, crisp bacon filled my nostrils. My eyes opened slightly, sunlight trickling through my windows blinding me. I turned away from the bright light, groaning from how tender and heavy my body felt. Building the new gate had really depleted me.

The wafting scent of fried pork strengthened. I forced my eyes to focus as the haze of my deep slumber began to wear off. Deus's beautiful face came into view. His lips curled back into a smile, revealing his deep dimples. My gaze slid along his bare chest and the black ink markings outlining his wing scars.

He waved a strip of bacon under my nose again.

"I thought this might wake you up," he said in his deep and sensual voice. "Your adoration for this disgusting excuse for meat baffles me, but what my mate wants, my mate gets."

I snatched the piece of delicious fat from his fingers. He lunged over me, trying to retrieve the greasy bit, but I stuffed it into my mouth, relishing the taste. He laughed, pinning my body to the mattress.

"You slept hard last night," he commented, brushing loose strands of hair from my face. "I tried to wake you to eat, but you weren't having it."

I swallowed the last of the bacon piece, licking my lips. "The gate took a lot out of me. I thought with my demon powers and the bond in place

I would be able to blow through it, but that doesn't seem to be the case."

He pressed his lips to my forehead, trailing more kisses down the side of my head to my cheek, finally making his way to my lips. I let out a comforting moan of satisfaction. He pulled away with a smile.

"I dreamed of you last night," I whispered. "Well, sort of."

His brow arched. "Sort of?" he asked.

I laughed. "It was you, yet ... not all of you, if that makes sense. I was cold and surrounded by nothingness, yet there you were, in the foreground, waiting for me. You were cloaked in darkness, your shadows and power twirling around you, yet your eyes blazed the same shades of red they always do when you use your gift. You extended your hand out to me, and I took it."

"Hmm. And how can you be so sure this shadowed figure was me?"

I wrapped my arms around his neck, trailing my fingers through his thick hair. "Because when I was in your embrace, I only felt peace. The kind of peace only you can give me. I was home."

His eyes blazed with desire and passion at the words leaving my lips. Before I could continue, his mouth was on mine, devouring me wholly. His hands roamed my body, throwing the sheets back, needing to feel my flesh against his own. I giggled with happiness.

He paused, pulling back to look at me. "And what, my beautiful fiancé, is so funny?"

I shrugged. "Nothing. I am just ... happy."

"My purpose in life is complete, then," he said with a soft smile, running the back of his knuckles down my cheek.

"I was talking to Tony yesterday and I—"

"My love," he interrupted me. "I never want to hear another man's name leave your lips while you are in *our* bed."

I rolled my eyes. "Big demon baby." He laughed. "As I was saying, when I was talking to ... that individual ... I remembered something and I wanted to see if you had anything to do with."

"Go on."

"When I was still in the nunnery, there was a night where I had an episode, and the nuns over did it on the drugs. I lay in my bed, paralyzed from the neck down. A black shadow appeared in the corner. I wasn't scared of it. Even as I watched it morph from a bull to a ram, and then into a man with with red eyes. I was comforted by the strange presence. Was it you?"

"When did this happen?"

"About two days before I arrived here. So, May of last year."

"I ... I don't honestly know. At that time, I was still being held prisoner from the bargain I had made with Lucifer, but ... but there were these little moments during my imprisonment where I would allow my mind to drift. It usually happened after my brother had used my power or sin against me, making me do—" he paused, closing his eyes in discomfort.

I ran my hand along his face in a comforting manner. He leaned into my touch. "When I was forced to do things that were inhuman," he continued. "In those moments I would allow my mind and power to detach from my control, searching for memories that were pure and peaceful. Experiences, even if they weren't my own, that would allow me to hold onto my power, so I wouldn't forget that my chains were only temporary. In those moments, I suppose it is possible that your power called to mine, summoning me ... even from Hell."

"When I died before, Aradia confirmed that the experience she and I witnessed during the right was your magic, reaching out, searching for me." I laughed. "It appears your magic was in love with me long before you were."

"Only a week or so," he replied, smiling.

"Oh, so that day in the woods you were struck by Cupids' arrow, huh?"

He laughed. "You've obviously never met Cupid."

My eyes widened. "Cupid is real?"

"Very. And one of my worst creations."

I gasped. "You created Cupid? But I thought he was an angel."

"Farthest thing from it. He's a horny little shit who gets off on watching other people in the act. He even tends to join in at times. His arrows are laced with hormones that send you into a heated frenzy. He's impossible to catch and his appetite is never satisfied."

"Sounds like someone else I know," I said playfully, nipping at his ear.

"Do not compare me to that ... experiment."

"Hell is just full of surprises."

"You have no clue," he replied, his eyes filling again with a heaviness.

"I'm sorry for all the pain you've had to endure," I whispered, my heart breaking for my mate.

I felt him reach down the bridge between us, wrapping his essence around my own. "It was a necessary evil. Especially, if it led me to you."

"For heavens, sake," I said, leaning over the large wooden table in the library. Deus, and his brothers were spread around the room, along with my family, Tony, and Giana. "Why can't any of this ever be easy?"

"My question is," piped in Belz, "why has our brother held onto her bones? Especially for this long? If they aren't a heaping pile of dust by now, he must have casted a spell to preserve them. Why are *these* bones important to our brother?"

"They obviously knew each other," said Levi. "If Talia is determined to end Lucifer once and for all, he must have done something that really pissed her off."

"Whose idea was it to scry for the body in Hell?" asked Nonna.

"Mine," Mal said, pulling herself from the wall. "I watched for hours as your little band of misfits scried map after map. Then I thought to myself, 'what would Lucy do?'"

Mammon huffed. "Carefully, Mal," he said sarcastically. "That's blasphemy."

"Anyways," she continued, "he's been five steps ahead of us this entire time. The only time we even surprised him was when you and Deus mated and Deus sacrificed himself. So, I thought about the places he could be keeping her bones. The only place is his castle in Hell."

"But Seren can create a gate that leads right to his front door," stated Frankie.

"Yes," answered Mal, "but he would be alerted the moment any of you stepped foot onto his territory, including Seren. And if you were caught ... game over."

"So, Talia's bones are in Hell?" asked Aunt Thora.

Mal nodded. "In Hell ... inside of Lucifer's castle, most likely"

"Son of a ..." Nonna said, shaking her head.

"We need to come up with another plan," added Mammon. "Something that doesn't involve us having to go to Hell."

"What do you suggest?" Levi said, aggravation lacing his voice. "Asking him nicely?"

"No, you dumb twat," Mammon spat. "But I don't see you volunteering any alternatives."

"I swear to Father—" Levi growled.

"I have an idea," Mal intervened before the brothers began throwing blows. She looked down at her nails, as if she wasn't holding onto the thing that could save us all. "Ask Satan for his help."

There was a moment of silence in the room as the words landed on all our ears. Then all the princes, except Gor, burst out in laughter.

"You have lost your mind," said Belz. "You've had your fair share of interactions with that pompous, ill-tempered asshole. What makes you think he would ever side with us over big brother?"

"Out of all of us," added Levi, "even Lucy, Satan is the least trustworthy."

"He'll do it," Mal said flatly.

"And what makes you so certain?" asked Deus.

"You," she replied, looking firmly at my mate.

"Explain," I said, stepping closer to the table.

"We've all witnessed firsthand the hatred Satan has for Asmodeus. He is Lucifer's favorite brother, is he not?" She paused, looking around at the other princes. They all nodded their affirmation. "A position Satan covets. No matter how loyal Satan has been, as soon as Asmodeus was soulless, Satan become nothing more than a pincushion for Lucifer's insults and the butt of their jokes.

"The jealousy and wrath he possesses is unmatched by any of you. That wrath has begun to turn Satan against Lucifer. I witnessed a few conversations he had with some of his subjects. He wishes to overthrow Lucifer and take over his portion of Hell. He sees Lucifer's games and trickery as weaknesses. He no longer finds him fit to be the ruler of Hell."

"And how to you purpose we go about this?" asked Frankie. "Surely Satan will want something in return."

"We tell him parts of our plan," explained Mal. "Small portions of the truth mixed with lies ... just enough to make it believable. At the end, we tell him that Lucifer will be imprisoned. We don't tell him the specifics or even who Talia is, but we offer Lucifer's throne over to Satan as a bargaining chip."

There was a moment of silence while each of us thought the plan over.

"It's brilliant," Deus said first. "This could actually work."

"If we are wrong," added Levi, "we risk everything."

"It's our only shot," Mal said. "It will work. Trust me."

I looked to Nonna for the answer, but she shook her head with a soft smile. "This decision is yours, bambina," she said to me.

I took a deep breath, sifting through the details, searching for any pitfalls, but Mal was right. This was the best plan we had. "How do we make contact with Satan?" I asked.

"Leave that to us," said Mammon.

Belz stepped up beside him and nodded. "We'll get him to the table," he said. "Then you lot do the convincing."

"Okay," I said, still unsure of my decision. "Looks like we have a plan."

"More like a suicide mission," Gor said sarcastically.

"When Satan is ready to meet," said Nonna, "send word."

"We will find a safe location that is far from Castle Salvo," added Aunt Thora. "With all the covens gathering, I don't want to risk things going poorly and their members being caught in the crossfire."

"Good idea," Nonna said with a smile of approval.

"Training will continue until then," I said. "And I will work on the gate so once we have the bones, we will be ready to go."

Chapter Twenty-One

Mal and Hashen began to train our coven members. After a single day of training with the demons, members of every coven were limping and hobbling around the castle, sore from the regimen they were now expected to follow. I worked on the gate, using as much of my magic as I could without burning myself out. It was ready. All I needed was Talia's bones.

Three days had passed since Mammon and Belz reached out to Satan ... nothing. I trained with Deus, preparing to rely on my body and weaponry skills alone. Using magic had become second nature to me. The thought of Lucifer possessing a spell or object that would tear it away was unfathomable.

Winter had arrived and I was thankful for it. I stood on my balcony, allowing the small snowflakes to land on my skin, chilling my warm skin. Moments of silence like these were rare. I was always surrounded by Deus or my family. My opinion seemed to be needed when making all decisions. The weight of the responsibility was unbearable. I was happy I would never have to become an elder. It wasn't a job I coveted.

"Hello," I heard a small voice behind me.

I turned, startled by the sound. A young girl stood before me, dressed in a white nightgown. Her long blonde hair fell to her waist. Her eyes were a cold blue, wet like she had been crying. Her skin was pale as the snow.

"How did you get in here?" I asked, taking a step towards her.

"I ... I don't know. I'm ... lost," she said, holding her face as she sobbed. I reached out to comfort her, but my hands went straight through her. I pulled back, startled. She was a ghost.

"You're ..." I couldn't finish the sentence. The girl couldn't have been more than ten. Her little face was so beautiful and innocent.

"I don't know what happened. I was sick and then, I think ... I think I died."

"That's right," I said softly. She was the only other ghost that had ever sought me out, besides G. I didn't know what to do. "What happened next?"

"I saw a bright light. It looked like ... like a door, but I ran away from it. I didn't want to leave my mamma. I'm all she has."

My heart broke for the little girl. "I am so sorry you had to leave her so soon."

"I don't understand. Why? Why did I die? I just got sick. It was only a normal cold."

"I don't know, sweetie," I replied, wishing I could touch her. "I'm still trying to figure out why the universe is the way it is. But the good thing is, there's peace waiting for you on the other side."

She twirled a small ribbon from her nightgown around her finger. "Do you think my daddy is waiting for me there?"

"I sure hope so."

"And ... and maybe my nonna and nonno?"

I smiled. "That sounds beautiful," I said, feeling a single tear escape down my cheek.

"Okay ... I think I'd like to see them again."

"Sounds like a plan." I waited. The girl looked around the balcony. "Do you see the white light?"

Her little face scrunched with worry. "No. I don't see the light anywhere. Do you think ... do you think they won't let me go now?"

"I'm sure that's not the case," I said. I closed my eyes, focusing on the mental, color-coded filing system I had set up for each goddess vessel's memories. I pulled Celia's cabinet forward and sifted through the memories. There was one I had never been able to make sense of before. I pulled it out, allowing the sensations and images of her life to replace my own.

Cecilia glowed brightly as a white light shot from her center. Her features and clothes were no longer visible, as if her white flame had consumed her entirely. A person walked through her and disappeared into the light she had become. She faded, taking a deep breath, reaching for her heart. She breathed heavily, wiping the tears from her face before standing upright. Her hands were full of blood. She took a cloth from her pocket, wiping the blood from either palm.

I pulled my conscious forward. Cecilia was the gate ... but how? The little girl had watched me the entire time.

"Are you okay?" she asked.

I smiled, bending down towards her. "Yes. Just working on a way to get you to your family. What's your name?" I asked, realizing I didn't know.

"Kayla," she whispered.

"Nice to meet you, Kayla. I'm Seren. My friend, Gor, will know how to get you home. Do you mind if we go and visit him?"

She shook her head.

"Good. Let's go," I replied, leading the way.

We searched the castle for Gor. He wasn't with G, which was unusual. I finally found him buried in a pile of books at the back of our library. He didn't notice us as we approached. Before I could say hello, Kayla began to scream. I turned behind me, ready to attack. Her little face was wrecked with fear, eyes locked on Gor. She breathed heavily, beginning to shake.

"What?" I asked her. She didn't say a word.

"Seren?" I heard Gor say behind me.

I knelt in front of the little girl; her eyes still fixed on Gor. She pointed her finger out towards him, her little breaths gasping.

"That is my friend, Gor," I replied. "The one I was telling you about. He is going to help me reunite you with your family."

"Who are you talking to?" asked Gor, approaching my side. Kayla took a step back, shaking her head.

"Kayla," I replied, standing straight. "She died and needs to find her way back to the light."

"Ah," he replied, placing his hands in his pockets.

"He's a ... a ... a monster," Kayla bleated.

"She sees the demon roaming underneath my skin," explained Gor. "Once a spirit is separated from its physical body, they can see the realities of the spirit realm. Our masks no longer work."

"G never mentioned any of this," I said. "In fact, I specifically remembering her go on and on about how handsome you were."

He shrugged. "I still don't have an answer for that. I was just as surprised she took an interest in me as you are right now. Is the spirit still here?"

"Yes," I answered, kneeling in front of the little girl. "It's okay, sweetie.

Gor is my friend. I promise, he isn't going to harm you." Her eyes finally left Gor, flashing to me for only a moment before returning to him.

"You came to ask about the gate ... to heaven," Gor said.

"Yes. I saw Cecilia become it, but how?"

"Her grandmother. The blood and magic they shared acted as an anchor to the other side ... to heaven."

"Okay, so what am I supposed to use as an anchor? Everyone I know and love is here or will end up in He—" I stopped. Gor's face softened.

"Orion," I whispered. We were forever connected though the gods that had formed our vessels. I swallowed, looking back at the little girl. She was frightened and scared. I needed to help her cross over. I needed to put my own fears and guilt aside, so she could be safe. I turned back to Gor. "Teach me."

We went back to my room, where Gor walked me through the process. I sliced my palms, allowing the warm blood to spread across my skin. I quieted my mind, focusing on Orion, on that part of my soul that Cyrus and Aradia passed to us. The part of my heart that would always belong to him.

The blood from my hands began to run up my arms, swerving and roaming across my skin, covering me entirely until I was overtaken by my own life force. A bright flash of light blasted out of me, my white flame consuming me. I couldn't breathe for a moment, then cool, crisp air filled my lungs.

I opened my eyes, greeted by the sweet scent of summer. I stood in a radiant, lush field. The wind swayed the blades of green grass in a tranquil rhythm. The sky was clear, and the sun was bright. Birds flew overhead, singing their beautiful songs.

One of them landed on the tree stump in front of me, tilting its head back and forth without fear. My heart clenched. I walked slowly towards it, tears now falling from my eyes. I bent down in front of the beautiful white bird, trembling from the overwhelming emotions. "Orion," I whispered.

"Hello, little dove."

I shot up, turning see his beautiful face behind me. I rushed towards him, arms extended, until my grip was firmly secured around his neck. The tears tore through me. I could feel him. Smell him. Touch him.

He held me tightly, cradling my convulsing body against his as I bawled. He was okay. He was safe. He had truly made it.

I finally pulled away, still holding onto him in fear that he would disappear if I let go. He wiped the tears from my cheeks, smiling from ear to ear. God, he was so incredibly beautiful. His long, curly brown hair drifted in the wind. His skin glowed unnaturally and his face ... his face was so peaceful. He was dressed in his normal fashion, a pair of dark jeans and a tight black shirt, revealing all his glorious muscles. I laughed, feeling like that part of me that died alongside him had returned.

"I've missed you," I whispered, at a loss for words.

"I've missed you too, little dove," he replied. The sound of his voice soothed the aching inside of me. "I was wondering when you were going to figure out how to use this part of your gift."

"You knew?" I asked.

"I was informed once I crossed over. Been waiting for you to show up ever since."

I laughed, still doubting this was real.

"It's real, Seren. You're here, and so am I."

I looked around at the captivating landscape. "Is this heaven?" I asked.

He shook his head. "Not quite. This place is in between. It was created for the anchor and the goddess, to create the gate needed to help the lost souls cross over. That is why you're here, I presume? Helping a lost soul?"

I nodded. "A little girl. She's very frightened."

"I see. They don't start you off easy, do they?"

I laughed. "No. The universe has a real hard on for me it appeared." I paused, taking in the sight of him. "How are you?"

He smiled, exhaling. "Honestly ... wonderful. Here, there's no pain or worry. Nothing to be afraid of. I'm just ... peaceful and happy." He laughed. "If I would have known it was like this on the other side, I would have died a lot sooner."

I hit him in the arm. "That's not funny," I said. "We miss you back home."

His gazed fell. "How ... how's Delphine?"

"After you ... she and your mother cleared out your room and returned to their covens. I haven't really had a chance to speak or see her since then, but I should be seeing her soon. All of us are gathering at Castle Salvo to prepare."

"For Lucifer?"

"The one and only," I smiled sarcastically.

"I don't miss that feeling ... preparing for war."

"I just can't wait until it's over. And it will be soon enough, for me at least."

His brow furrowed. "Little dove, what are you talking about?"

I forced a smile on my face. "Got room for one more up here?"

There was a long pause before he spoke. "You're planning to die," he finally said.

"It's the only way to kill Lucifer. I've come to terms with it. Plus, if it's as cozy as you say it is up here, it can't be that bad."

His face remained stern. "Seren, your mate is a demon ... a Prince of Hell."

"And ...?"

"His power, his essence, is inside of you. Which means, when you die, you won't be heading here."

I froze; my head began to spin while a sick feeling in my stomach took hold. My ears were buzzing, and my vision began to tunnel. "Wh ... what?" I whispered.

"Your mate is a demon. Your magic comes from his source. A magic that powers Hell itself. A power that must be returned to its rightful place to keep the balance."

I shook my head in disbelief. "After I'll I've done ... sacrificed. After all I plan to sacrifice ... Hell is what has awaited me this entire time? Where is the fairness in that?"

Orion gently cupped my cheek with his large hand, bringing my eyes to his. "You forget, little dove; Hell is part of you. It always has been. When the day comes that you leave the earthly plane, you will rule over Hell."

I pulled back in shock. "What? What are you talking about? That's impossible."

He laughed, standing straight. "It seems that in Lucifer's desperation to become a god, he created the one thing that could take it all from him ... an heir. Between your natural power, the power of Aradia, Asmodeus, and now Lucifer, you are the most powerful being of all."

I shook my head. "No ... no. I don't want it. I don't want to be King of Hell."

"No Seren ... you are the *Queen* of Hell. When your earthly life has ended, you will not go to Hell to suffer. You will go to Hell to rule. His

Father has decided; Lucifer's time to play king of the underworld has come to an end."

"No ... no this can't be happening. That means I'll never see you, or my family. I will be separated from all of you ... for eternity."

"This plane will always exist. Our souls will always be tied, and the bloodline between your family is strong. There are loopholes to everything, so I've learned."

Panic, desperation, and fear all slammed into me. I had been approaching my limit on the amount of crazy one person was capable of handling, but this had hurtled me over that border and then some.

"The girl," I whispered, not knowing what else to say.

Orion's eyes were still full of love and kindness. "Do not be afraid, Seren De Salvo," he said in his deep, gentle voice. "Your destiny was decided long ago, before you ever were born. Conquer your fears. Claim your fate and take your rightful place. Once you accept your fate, you will find the peace you've always searched for. This, I promise." Orion pulled me into him. I allowed myself to be engulfed by his large form, relaxing at the familiar feeling and scent of my friend.

I closed my eyes, trying to let the devastation of it all go. I felt Orion kiss the top of my head and then, I felt a small tingle slither along my soul. The girl, Kayla. She was passing through me into the heavens. I felt her fear, her excitement, her wonder, and then ... her peace. I pulled away, looking up into his deep brown eyes.

"I'll be seeing you, little dove."

I smiled. "I love you, Orion."

"And I love you." He pressed his lips to my forehead.

I closed my eyes and then faded back to reality. The air rushed into my lungs. I felt like I hadn't breathed in minutes. I grabbed for my chest, willing the burning to stop. Gor was there instantly, supporting me with his arms.

"It's okay," I heard him say. "Everything is okay."

I shook my head, still trying to understand my newest title ... Queen of Hell. My head snapped up as I remembered the only other time I had heard that title ... Mal.

Chapter Twenty-Two

I shifted instantly, landing among the coven trainees Mal was currently torturing. Her eyes instantly flashed to mine. A sly smile grew.

"You knew," I whispered in disbelief. "After all this time … you knew."

She clapped her hands, dismissing the witches and warlocks in the room, leaving us alone as she slowly approached me.

"And what exactly are you accusing me of knowing?" she asked, walking forward until we stood eye to eye.

"That day when you agreed to help me find the pit in Lucifer's lands. You said, *'Hell had never had a* queen *before.'* You knew, even then. How?"

She laughed, looking away. "I've waited for you for a long time, sweetheart." The tone of her voice changed in that moment. Gone was the formal and uptight Malphasia I had grown to care for. In her place stood a woman with a fire blazing within her spirit.

"What are you?" I asked.

"Oh, I am a demon"— she cocked her head —"of sorts. In your history books, the name I go by is Lilith."

My heart dropped. "Impossible."

She smiled. "Now, of all people, you should know there is nothing that is impossible at this point." She nodded towards a room in the front of the training arena. I followed her, needing answers. Once the door was shut, I examined her closely.

"Lilith, as in the Lilith that was Adam's first wife?"

"Oh, no honey, I was never married to that buffoon. I was created during the same time as him, though. I wasn't taken from his rib, as was his dear, sweet Eve. I was like him: my own creation, perfect in every way."

My head was spinning. How many more twists and turns was my life going to take? "Does Deus know?"

She huffed with amusement. "No. He believes I'm his faithful assassin, which I am."

"What do you want?"

"The same as the rest of you. For Lucifer to suffer. To watch as he loses everything he risked so much for. I want to be there when he is banished from this precious earth once and for all, never allowed to return. I want to make him pay for his lies and empty promises. For his seductive manipulations and his corrupt schemes. I want to watch as everything he has fought for is taken from him."

Another woman who Lucifer had royally screwed, now ready to do whatever it took to see him pay. The list just kept growing and growing.

"I have waited for you for millennia," she said, stepping closer to me. "I didn't know what form you'd take or when you'd arrive, but I knew God would eventually send someone to uproot his bastard child for good." She laughed. "And he created it in the form of a woman. Poetic justice at its finest." She knelt before me, looking up with a large grin on her face.

"What are you doing?" I asked, taking a step back.

"I, Lilith," she said, her voice calm and steady, "first of her kind, first of her name, hereby swear my undying allegiance and fealty to thee, Seren Lucia De Salvo, Queen of Hell, first of her kind. My sword is your sword.

My power, your power. Your vengeance, my vengeance. I swear to protect your life with my own, stepping before any who mean to harm you. I am your faithful servant from this day forward. So help me God."

She stood, that fire still blazing behind her eyes. In that moment, I didn't know who I was more afraid of: Lucifer, or Lilith. I extended my hand to her. She latched her hand around my forearm, and I tightened my grip.

"I accept," I whispered.

She laughed, the sound more haunting than I could have imagined.

A smooth, loving tendril reached down the mating bond, politely waiting for a response. I stretched my magic towards his, wrapping the two together.

"Where are you?" I heard Deus ask in my mind.

"God, I have so much to tell you," I replied.

"Well, it's going to have to wait. Satan is on his way, and he is insistent on a location you are not going to like."

"Just tell me."

"Montecassino Abbey. Thora believes he is trying to throw you off, get under your skin. He knows you have an emotional connection to that place."

"Dammit," I said out loud.

"What is it?" asked Ma— Lilith.

"Satan has agreed to meet, but he insists the location be Montecassino Abbey. Thora believes it's a tactic."

Lilith nodded, thinking over the new information. "This smells of emotional manipulation. I am going to have to agree with your aunt on this one. She saw straight through his shit. I can see why Beelzebub is intrigued by her."

I laughed. "So, I'm not the only one who thinks so?"

"Oh, no, sweetheart. The brothers already have bets as to how long it will be until your aunt inevitably invites him to her bed."

"They obviously don't know my aunt very well, then. They'll be waiting a long time, if not for eternity," I said, walking out of the room towards Nonna's.

Lilith followed close behind. "You obviously don't know the Prince of Gluttony very well then. He is ... he is extraordinary in that department."

I side-eyed her. "You and Belz?"

"And Mammon." She shrugged. "What can I say, I was young and stupid once."

I laughed, waving at passing coven members. "Did you and Deus?"

"No. I swore my allegiance to him long ago. After Lucifer, I swore to never mix pleasure with business again."

"Why choose Deus over the other brothers?"

"His power and resilience to break from Lucifer. I knew that if any of them were going to aid in the Morningstar's demise, it would be Asmodeus. And I was right," she said, turning her eyes to me. "His power will be the key to what I have waited so long to witness."

Chapter Twenty-Three

Being back in the abbey was eerie. The smells, the silence, the color of the sun setting over the horizon were all the same; still, this place felt foreign. I had spent most of my life within these walls, yet Deus's home had become more of a haven than this place ever had been.

I stood in the empty courtyard, now dusted in a fresh coating of snow. The lights were dim and the doors to the entrance were shut. Much of the abbey had been repaired since the fire had eaten through the old bricks the night I had been taken, but signs of work were still evident.

A soft touch graced my back. I turned to see Deus looking down at me with a tender smile. "How are you doing, my love?"

I shrugged. "Better than I thought I'd be," I answered, leaning into his comfort.

He wrapped his arms around me, holding tight. "So, this is where the love of my life was raised?"

"You mean kept prisoner?"

"I suppose it's all about perspective."

"Are we ready?" asked Levi, approaching us.

"As always," answered Deus. I looked around at the other four princes, Lilith, and G. Everyone else had remained at Castle Salvo.

Lilith stayed close to my side like a faithful guard dog. Mammon kept his eyes on her, assessing her new position as my keeper. I had decided to wait until after our meeting with Satan to tell the group about Mal's true identity. I could only handle one catastrophe at a time.

I assessed the demon female, still unsure if I trusted her completely. She had been lying for thousands of years, hoping a time would come when she would enact her revenge. She was full of secrets ... I could feel it.

"Incoming," called Mammon to the rest of us. We all gathered in a group, watching as Satan appeared in a stormy haze of blue and red smoke. He came alone, as he promised, no minions in sight.

The fog finally dissipated, revealing the tall, broad demon prince built for war. His crimson hair was a deeper shade of red than the last time I had seen him. His facial hair was neatly trimmed, and his brown chocolate eyes swirled taking in the lot of us. He took a step forward, his thick black boots thudding against the stone of the courtyard. Snowflakes fell on his leather jacket, sizzling before they could stick.

He stopped in front of Deus, looking him up and down with disgust before his eyes turned to me. The left side of his mouth turned up in a half smile.

"You, little goddess, are impressive," he said, then turned back to Deus. "I thought for sure you were going to kill her." Ripples of rage trickled down the bond between me and Deus. "Especially after she outsmarted you and Lucy. In fact, I remember you saying specifically that you would enjoy having her hung naked from your bedroom ceiling while you fucked Victoria right in front of her. Yes, that was it, because you had that redhead down on her knees sucking your cock while you—"

Bam. Deus's fist flew faster through the air than I could process. Satan wiped the blood from his lip, laughing as he turned back to face Deus.

"And that," said Deus, stepping up to him without a hint of intimidation or fear, "is why you have always been the outcast. Unwanted by anyone who has ever known you. You are a pathetic stain on this existence that should have never been given the gift of life."

Wrath's eyes blazed with a mixture of red and blue turning to a deep, rich purple. His jaw clenched along with his fists.

"Brothers," said Belz, "though we have a long history together, this is not the time nor place to unpack that very large bag of sibling rivalry. May I suggest we get back to the actual purpose of this conversation?"

"Right," Satan said, turning his head towards Belz. "You mentioned you could offer me something I wanted. I'm curious, how is it you know what I want?"

"Because of me," Lilith said proudly, sauntering to my side.

Satan arched an eyebrow, taking a step towards Lilith, placing himself above her dominantly. To her credit, Lilith stood tall, unwavering. Gor laughed softly.

"And what, sweet Malphasia, do you presume to know?"

She smirked. "Oh, you and I both know exactly how capable I am, so I'll skip the dramatics and get to the point. You no longer find our boy Lucy fit to run Hell."

Satan tilted his head, narrowing his eyes on her. "And?"

"And we all agree with you, for once," she answered.

He paused before laughing. "My brother's lapdog, presuming to strike a deal on his behalf." He looked to Deus, then back at Lilith. "You've trained your demon scum well, brother. A little mouthy for my taste, but I can't deny that my cock seems to like your snarky little tone."

"Well, maybe I should be talking to your cock then," Lilith bit back, "as it appears to have more braincells than the current asshole I am looking at."

A haunting laugh rattled deep in his chest before he assessed the group of us. His attention caught on G who was standing next to Gor's side. Satan's smile widened. "What is it with this family and their obsession with witches. Now, who are you exactly?"

Giana stepped forward, still within reach of Gor. "Giana Simonelli for the Luna Coven.

"Ah, the spirit," he said, turning his eyes back to me. "You sneaky little bitch." He clicked his tongue and stepped in front of me. Deus moved closer, but I stood my ground. "Hasn't anyone told you, you're not supposed to steal souls from Hell? And now you've stolen two."

"Well," I said, "when you become King of Hell, you can stop me, but until then ..."

He froze, stiffening his posture. "What is she talking about?" he asked his brothers.

"She," I said, "is talking about a way to give you everything you've always wanted. A key to Lucifer's land. His power. His kingdom."

"And what about Lucifer?" Satan asked. "Do you just plan on asking him nicely to step down?"

"We've found someone that knows how to capture him," I answered.

Satan laughed, shaking his head. "There is nothing in this realm or the next that can hold Lucifer."

"Not according to the first goddess vessel," I let slip. Mixing some truth into the story.

Satan went absolutely still. "How do you know about Talia?" he asked.

"*Bingo*," I said through my mind to Deus.

"*We're not done yet. Keep playing the game, my love. You're doing brilliantly.*"

"I've been building a gate to where she's been hiding all these years," I answered. "She's somewhere safe only I know about, here on earth."

"Impossible. She died thousands of years ago. I was there."

I huffed. "You're a prince of Hell, and you think a body means someone is gone forever? As we've proven time and time again, death can be easily manipulated when a moon goddess is involved. It was Talia's plan to hide from Lucifer." I paused, making this up as I went. "She's been using a spell to keep herself alive all these years, until the time to enact her revenge had come. She knows how to restrain Lucifer and she's willing to help us."

"You're lying," he said, looking to his brothers. "Her remains have never left Lucifer's castle."

"And thus, why we need your help," I continued. "The remains Lucifer possesses aren't Talia's. They're her mother's, which she wants back in exchange for helping us capture Lucifer."

Satan laughed, not saying a word. I didn't know if I had mixed the lies and truth effectively enough. His silence was torturing me. I was done waiting.

"Look,' I said, walking into his personal space. I felt Deus go on alert through the bond. "You can either help us or not, it really doesn't matter either way. I personally would not like to go to war with Hell, but I know that's your thing, so I am sure you can't understand. This way, you get something you want, we get something we want. Mutually beneficial and all. But, if you don't want a chance to prove that you are just as good—if not better—than Lucy at ruling, who am I to question you?

"Instead, I'll make a doorway into Hell right on the front steps of pride's castle, and with the help of the other sins and their legions, I'll lay waste to what you desire most, take the bones for myself, and then make the bargain with Talia. And I'll make sure to tell her how much of a non-participant you were in helping retrieve her beloved mother's remains, so she locks your ass in the cage with your favorite brother for all eternity. Sound like a plan?"

I heard Deus yelling before I registered what was happening. One moment, I was in the abbey courtyard. The next, I teetered on top of a bridge, fighting to regain my balance so I wouldn't fall into the busy traffic far below.

Satan let go of me, walking a few paces away on the thin steel beam. The wind shoved against me, threatening to toss me off the high platform. Cars zoomed and honked below. It was night, wherever we were.

Satan paced back towards me. I readied myself, lighting my flames. He smiled.

"Don't worry," he said. "I'm not going to kill you. Not today, at least."

"Like you could," I answered.

"All juiced up on that mating bond. I see."

I shrugged arrogantly. "Among other things."

He laughed, placing his hands on his hips. "I like you, Seren. You're a hell of a lot better than that Victoria bitch. Always with the whining and the pouting day in and day—"

"Why did you bring me here?" I said, cutting him off. "What do you want?"

He walked over to me, stopping once we were face to face. "You're lying," he sneered.

"What?" I replied.

"About Talia's mother's bones," he said, turning back to pace in frustration. "Talia despised her parents, especially her mother. She burned her alive, if I recall correctly, bones and all. Nice try though."

Fuck! I yelled in my head. "The offer still stands," I said quickly, trying not to miss a beat. "You bring us the bones; you get the keys to Hell."

"How did you find out about Talia?"

"She found me," I answered.

"How?" he growled.

"I don't know. She just ... appeared."

"From where?"

"I am not saying another word," I answered firmly. "Agree to do as we've asked, or this conversation is over."

He chuckled, bending his neck back as he stretched. "This family is a pain in my ass." He assessed me, his eyes surprisingly soft. He growled in a ... sensual manner, wrapping his fingers in a piece of my hair. "I'd like to know," he moved his lips to my ear, "why Father chose Asmodeus as your mate, when you are clearly more suited for me." Before I could stop him, his teeth were buried in my neck, clamping down barbarically.

I yelped, stumbling back in shock. His hot tongue grazed across the sensitive part of my skin. I gritted my teeth. "What the hell is wrong with you?"

He laughed, his teeth red with my blood. He licked his lips and moaned. "I'll help you, little goddess, in exchange for the keys to Hell."

"How fast can you get them?" I asked, holding my bleeding neck. Before he could answer, a black mist appeared overhead. Lilith shot out of the shift before Deus appeared, her knives hurtling towards for Satan. He dodged one but wasn't fast enough to avoid the second. She buried the curved blade in his thigh, before nailing him in the stomach.

"Stop!" I yelled, just as Deus appeared. Lilith looked back at me. "He's agreed to help."

Deus rushed to me. I pulled the collar of my jacket over the bite mark on my neck so my mate didn't kill Satan before he was of use. Satisfied that I was alright, Deus turned back to Satan.

"Tomorrow," Satan said, and disappeared into the fog that lingered high above the bridge.

"Are you alright?" Deus asked, taking my face in his hands.

"Yes," I answered, nodding to Lilith with thanks. "Let's get back to the others." He nodded and we all shifted back to the abbey.

"Thank Aradia," G said, flinging herself into me as we landed.

"Is he dead?" asked Levi.

"He's apparently agreed to help," Deus informed, turning his eyes to me. "How did you do it?"

"He claims that Talia didn't give a shit about her mother and burned her to ash. I didn't tell him much, but it was enough to get him to agree."

Gor appeared at G's side, wiping a stain from her face. "Sweetheart," he said to her, "you appear to be bleeding."

G grabbed her face in shock. "It's not mine," she answered, turning towards me.

"Crap," I said, just before Deus pulled back my jacket, revealing Satan's teeth marks.

"What in the fuck is this?" Deus growled.

"Your psychotic brother bit me," I replied.

Mammon and Belz burst out laughing.

"And why, in Father's name, was he that close to you?" Deus asked.

"I don't know. We were talking one minute and then the next thing I knew, he was burying his teeth into of my neck."

"What where you two talking about?" he asked. I rolled my eyes, crossing my arms over my chest. "Seren!"

"He said that he didn't understand why your Father made you my mate and not him, since I am obviously better suited to be Wrath's mate. Wherever he got that crazy conclusion from."

"He said what?" growled Lilith with rage.

"Time to go, sweetheart," Gor said to G, shifting her out of the courtyard.

In the next second, a massive force of power unleashed from Deus, sending everything and everyone flying backwards. The others destroyed a stone column, a statue of Mary, and a bench. Before my body slammed into anything hard, Deus's arms were there, shifting me out of harm's way.

Once his shadows faded, I pushed off him, my own rage and anger taking hold.

"What in the hell was that for?" I said, fuming.

"You let another male bite you!"

"I didn't *let* him do anything, you demon baby! And I got him to agree to our terms. If the price was him taking a chunk out of my neck, so be it."

"You are *my* mate," Deus said, now face to face with me. "Mine!"

"Your point?"

He growled, the stone cracking beneath his feet from his power.

"Seren darling," intervened Belz, approaching with caution. "You must understand, we are all … jealous in nature, but none of us have ever had a mate before. I mean, we've watched plenty of poor saps go through the process, but my—oh for fucks sake, Deus. Just find Satan and beat the crap out of him already. I'm done being the mediator today." Belz ran a hand through his hair and shifted out of sight.

Levi laughed, looking from Deus to me. "Good luck," he said, shifting.

Mammon reached for Lilith, but she pulled away, looking as if she was going to cut his balls off. He grunted, his face furrowed in aggravation, then lunged, shifting and taking her with him.

My mate continued to fume, pacing across the courtyard. After a few minutes of the silent treatment, I finally approached, waiting until he graced me with his attention. He took a deep breath, hands on his hips, turning his eyes towards me.

"I didn't ask for this," I said, trying to remain soft.

"I know … I'm … sorry," he replied, as if it was killing him to apologize.

"Thank you. Now, can you please heal the thing on my neck?"

He grimaced, pushing my hair away from the wound. He hovered his hand over the bite, his magic erasing his brother's mark. He went to pull away, but I stopped him, wrapping my arms around his waist. I smiled, the weight of the situation lessening.

"Jealous much?" I asked playfully.

A corner of his mouth turned up into a smile even though I could tell he was fighting to keep it hidden. "If I recall, you did light a few women on fire while you were in Hell."

My eyebrow arched. "That was completely different. They deserved to die after—"

He pressed his forehead to mine. "And I will make Satan pay for even looking at you."

I smiled. "Can we please go home, my little demon baby?"

"Only if you promise to shift into the shower immediately so you can clean the foul stench of Wrath off you. And then …" he paused, looking down at me with heavy eyes, "allow me to mark you anywhere," he kissed the side of my cheek, "and everywhere," another kiss, "I please."

Chapter Twenty-Four

That night, I warred with myself over all the new information I had gathered in such a short time. I was going to be the Queen of Hell, yet I would have to die to make sure the ones I loved remained safe. I couldn't keep this from everyone. Not when so much was on the line. I knew what I had to do, but saying the words out loud would mean it was no longer my imagination, but the truth.

I called a meeting with everyone the next morning, knowing if I waited any longer, I would talk myself out of it. Lilith showed up at my door bright and earlier. I let her in, still preparing myself for what was to come next.

Deus came out of the bathroom, surprised to see his right-hand demon warrior casually lounging in a chair next to me.

"Mal," he greeted her with a forced smile. "Is there something I can help you with?"

She shrugged, twirling a dagger in her hands. "Nope," she replied, winking at me. "I'm here for her," she replied, pointing the knife at me.

Deus scanned his mate and his warrior. "Am I missing something here?" he asked. "When did the two of you become best friends?"

She pushed herself from the chair, making her way over to him. "Somewhere between you losing your soul and me kicking her ass on the mat day in and day out." She patted him on the shoulder. "Don't worry, she's in capable hands." Lilith turned to me. "Everyone is waiting in your nonna's quarters." She mouthed the words 'my queen'. Her lips pulled up to one side in a snarky grin.

I stood, shooting her a stern look. "Let's get this over with," I replied, heading for the door. Lilith followed.

"What are we getting over?" Deus asked. "I don't think I can handle any more surprises."

Lilith's laugh filled the air. "Oh, just you wait, princy," she replied.

"What did you just call me?" he asked firmly.

She looked back at him as we made our way down the hall. "Oh," she said, "I forgot to inform you, I resign. Got a better offer elsewhere." She chuckled and walked faster.

He looked at me and then ahead to his former right hand. "What in the hell is going on?"

I took his hand in mine. "I'll explain everything, I promise."

We were the last to enter Nonna's quarters. Our family and friends surrounded us. Lilith appeared at my side, assessing each one as if they were a threat.

"Malphasia," Mammon said, taking in the demon from head to toe. "I think you'd be more of use training the witchlings."

"I go where my queen goes," Lilith said, standing at attention by my side.

I rolled my eyes. The attention of the room snapped to me.

Belz huffed. "Queen?" He turned to Deus. "What did you become king of?"

"She does not need him to claim her rightful title," snapped Lilith. "That title is hers and hers alone."

"Enough," I said. "This is not going to turn into a shit show."

"Would anyone like to bet on that?" Mammon asked, looking from person to person.

"What is she talking about?" asked Belz, stepping forward. "Why do you have your mate's assassin calling you queen?"

I took a deep breath. "Because I am the heir to Hell," I admitted out loud for the first time. Nonna, Aunt Thora, and my mom looked like they were about to pass out. "And this isn't just any assassin." Lilith nodded, holding her head high. "Everyone, meet Lilith, the first woman ever created."

"Son of a—" Mammon.

"You've got to be shitting me?" Belz.

Laughing, Gor leaned over the table. "Father, this just keeps getting better."

"How?" asked Deus, stepping towards us, assessing his supposed friend.

"I aligned myself with you because of your strength, power, and conviction," she said. "I've wanted to destroy your brother ever since he lied to me and tempted me out of the garden. I knew in that moment I had made a mistake." She paused, looking around the room at the other princes. "Just like each of you knew the mistake you had made as soon as you fell from His grace. Lucifer has gone on unchecked long enough. I was confident that God would eventually tire of his games and rip everything from him." She looked at me with pride.

"Thus," she continued, "Seren. Created in the womb of a witch. Chosen by the goddess of the moon. Forged from the power of a prince. Saved by the greed of a demon. Once Lucifer is muzzled, she will sit upon his throne. Three in one. Witch. Goddess. Demon."

Deus looked at me in shock.

"It's true," I admitted. "Orion told me."

"Orion?" Frankie asked.

"Yes. I ... I was helping a soul to cross over. Turns out, I'm also a gate to heaven. Orion is my anchor because of our connection. He told me that when I die, I won't be going to heaven, because I was made from Hell thus Hell I must be returned to."

Nonna shook her head, taking a seat. "No. No. This is not happening," she said frantically. I had never seen her react this strongly before. She smacked the table with her hand. Everything around us began to shake and rumble. Nonna sat, trying to make sense of it all. I watched as she slowly lost control.

"No," she yelled, standing as the windows behind her shattered out over the mountainside. "No granddaughter of mine is spending eternity in Hell!"

I walked over to her, smiling softly. "Nonna," I whispered, rubbing her arms. "It's okay. This is all a part of a greater plan. Orion told me the sooner I make peace with this the faster I will obtain the very peace I've been searching my entire life for."

"It is Hell, bambina," she said, utter defeat in her voice. I looked around the room, taking in the faces of the princes that had become my brothers. My friends. My lover.

"Hell has a few things I don't mind being surrounded by for eternity," I said. The brothers smiled, nodding their thanks. Nonna's face fell in defeat. I could only imagine how devastated she felt.

"Any other secrets you'd like to share, Lilith?" asked Mammon.

"Not at the moment, thank you," she replied flatly.

The room laughed softly. "That's really *the* Lilith," asked Aunt Thora.

I nodded. "I didn't think things could get any more complicated," I said, turning to my mother and cousin.

Frankie arched an eyebrow. "Well, we haven't rescued the crazy vessel from Purgatory yet, so just hold that comment until then." My family and I laughed, pulling each other into a group hug.

"We'll figure this out," said Nonna, trying to sound reassuring. "We always do."

"Yes, Mamma," said my mother, looking at Nonna in a way that made me wonder if there were secrets between the two of them. "We always do."

Everyone exited the room, returning to their routines and duties while we waited for Satan to make his appearance with the bones. Deus pulled me onto one of the balconies without warning. Lilith made to follow, but he held out his hand.

"I go where she goes," Lilith growled.

"Yes, you made that revelation very clear," he replied, stepping into her face. "But she is my mate and if I want alone time with her, I get my alone time."

Lilith didn't move. She slid her eyes to me for orders. I nodded.

"Wait back in the hall," I instructed. "I'm perfectly safe."

Once she was stationed on the other side of the balcony doors, Deus turned to me for answers.

"I only just found out yesterday," I blurted.

"Then why not tell me then? I should have been the first person you told."

"I needed time to myself ... just to process it all. Plus, we were dealing with Satan and Talia's bones and—"

"We're always going to be dealing with some catastrophe, or demons, for that matter." He was getting heated. He took a moment to gather himself, slowing his breaths before he spoke again. "I am your mate. Soon to be your husband. I don't give a fuck what is happening around us. If something of this magnitude is discovered, we tell each other. Complete transparency."

I knew he was right. I wanted to tell him everything, but if I did, he would try to stop me from doing what had to be done. Deus loved me possessively, which meant, he would let the entire world burn down and everyone in it, if it meant I got to live. I could never live with myself if it came to that.

"I'm sorry," I whispered, holding back tears.

He stepped forward, wrapping me in his arms tightly. I stood there for a moment, relishing his warm embrace. He chuckled, kissing me softly on top of my hair. "My mate ... the Queen of Hell. Oh, Lucy is going to just love this."

I pulled away, forcing a smile. "What, you don't think I'll look good in a crown?"

He drew his thumb across my jaw line. "There isn't a thing I wouldn't find you ravishing in. Though, I prefer nothing at all."

I giggled, sliding my gaze toward Lilith, who stood on the other side of the glass.

"You don't trust her?" I heard Deus ask.

"Do you blame me?"

"No, but for whatever it's worth, she has never betrayed me. Not once."

"How does Lucifer not recognize her? They've been in the same room together multiple times."

"I expect she's been using a glamor all these years. I am not sure. That would be a question for her. Whatever she has done, Lucifer has never taken an interest in her ... not once. She's good at the façade."

"That's what I'm afraid of."

The rest of the day, I stayed out of everyone's way. I didn't want to discuss my new job title further and, with everything going on around me, the quiet was a welcome change. We waited for Satan to make contact about the bones, but he never did. I didn't trust him, nor did I like him much.

Early the next morning, I lay in bed next to my mate while he slept peacefully. I was thankful that the harder parts of his recovery were nearing an end, yet my own horrors were only beginning. I looked up at the ceiling, contemplating what I could expect when I got to Purgatory. Whatever was keeping Talia there seemed horrific, based on her screams during each encounter we'd had.

Finally, realizing I wasn't going to be falling asleep anytime soon, I slithered out of the bed and headed down to the kitchen. It was four in the morning. The castle and all its guests were sound asleep. I gathered the ingredients to make lemon bars, in honor of Orion. I began to sift and mix the ingredients when Annalise appeared in the doorway.

"Seems like I'm not the only one burdened by our impending vacation today," she said, moving over to the counter where I was worked.

"Honestly, after Hell, I'm hoping this one is a walk in the park," I replied.

She laughed, taking a seat on a stool. "Did you get any sleep?"

I shook my head. "I can't seem to shut off my mind. With all this new information, I'm just—" I paused, placing the whisk in the bowel. There it was. Finally. I had been waiting for it all day.

The realization of everything hit me like a pile of bricks. I began shaking, working through the emotions one by one. I took deep breaths, telling myself it would be okay. I had mastered everything thrown at me thus far. There was a reason for everything. I had found my purpose, even if I didn't like it.

I felt a hand on my shoulder, turning me around. Then I was pulled into my mother's embrace. I didn't cry; I didn't panic. I was overcome with the magnitude of my future, yet everything around me in that moment calmed, allowing me to think and process more clearly than I had before.

Annalise had never held me like this before. So ... intimate and familiar. She smelled of eucalyptus and mint. Her embrace was tender yet reassuring. I accepted comfort from this stranger I had longed for since I could remember—experiencing a mother's embrace for the first time in my life.

I pulled away, looking up at her. She smiled softly, running her hand through my hair. "You know," she began, "since the moment my soul was reunited with my body, I have been worrying about you. I felt so guilty about the bargain I struck with Lucifer to save you. The hand in life you had been dealt. Everything you had missed out on. Every horror you've experienced. Yet, when you told us yesterday you were to become the Queen of Hell ..." she stopped, softly laughing to herself. "All of that worry went away."

"That makes one of us," I replied.

She took my face in her hands. "Seren ... do you realize what that title means?" She searched my eyes. "It means that nothing and no one will ever have the power to harm you again. Think about it. You will be ruler over the realm responsible for everything in your life that has haunted you. As queen, you will be untouchable.

"I know this isn't the ending you expected or saw for yourself, but ... but maybe this future, this realm of impossibilities will allow you to write your own narrative for once. Where you will have the power to construct the life, the *eternity*, you want. Once you embrace this, the possibilities will be endless, little bean."

"Orion told me once I made peace with my future, I would find the peace I've always longed for," I admitted.

"I believe you will. There is no good without evil. Unfortunately, both will always exist. But ... I do believe it is also about perspective. One person may perceive something to be wicked, while another person sees that same thing as a blessing. Take your prince, for example."

The very thought of him made me smile. My mother grinned, pinching the side of my cheek. "There are no words to describe how happy that smile makes me," she said. "And to think, it's all thanks to a demon prince."

"A very handsome demon prince," I corrected.

She laughed. "There is no denying that."

"I don't know how to prepare myself for this new role."

She took my face again, pressing a firm kiss to my forehead before her face grew severe. "I promise you, little bean, I will do whatever it takes to make sure you have as much time on this earth as possible. Your happiness and safety are all that matters to me. I pray someday you get a chance to be a mother. Only then will you know how much I truly love you. Only then will you understand that there is nothing and no one that will keep me from protecting you."

I forced a smile, pulling her into a hug. How much time I had to prepare to become queen depended on when Lucifer planned to attack.

I would never know what it was like to be a mother, to hold my child for the first time, to see Deus as a father, to watch the child our love created grow and flourish. There was so much I would never experience, and there was nothing my mother, my family, or my mate could do to change that. My end had been written before I existed.

Mom sat with me while I finished making the lemon bars. We talked about our expectations of Purgatory. Neither of us had a clue what we were walking into. Once the lemon bars were done baking, they cooled while I filled her in on my childhood. She told me about when she had discovered she was pregnant and how excited she had been to become a mother.

Annalise relived her own childhood year by year. Through her stories, I felt the love and admiration she had for Nonna and her twin. She had prepared her entire life to stand next to her mother's side as Elder. To walk in her footsteps and serve our coven as our ancestors had done for generations. But now, that path no longer existed.

The realization of what Lucifer had done to her settle deep inside of me. I had been so focused on all he had taken from me, but I hadn't really stopped to think about how his actions, his obsession with me, had altered my mother's life in the process.

Around six in the morning, I made my way back up to my room, leaving the lemon bars uneaten on the counter ... in memory of Orion. As I turned the hall, I froze, coming face to face with Evaline Camerino ... Orion's mother.

Her small stature, to the untrained eye, looked that of an innocent, grumpy old woman. But I knew better. I could see the dragon roaming underneath her skin, begging to be released. Her eyes bore into me. Her thin lips—Orion's lips I now realized—remained taunt and expressionless.

"Seren," she said, nodding.

"Hello Mrs. Camerino," I replied. "How have you been?"

"Miserable," she replied, "and you?"

"Can't say it's been much different for me either." At that time, Delphine exited her room next to Evaline's, shutting the door softly before turning towards us.

Her tall and once curvaceous body was now thin and fragile. The shine of her blonde hair had dulled. Her skin, white as snow, exhibited bruises underneath her eyes and hollow cheeks. The entrancing light that had made her so stunning was gone.

She froze, looking from Evaline to me without revealing what she was feeling or thinking. There was an emptiness that I empathized with. Those weeks without Deus had almost destroyed me. If things had been different, if it weren't for my powers, that would be me: empty and dead inside. Even though my future was heading in a fiery direction, I couldn't admit I hated my gifts. Without them, my mate would still be dead.

"Good morning, Delphine," Evaline greeted, forcing a smile for her almost daughters-in-law's sake.

"Good morning, Mamma," she replied, kissing her on the cheek before turning her attention to me. "Seren."

"Delphine. It's nice to see you," I replied, my voice wavering.

She didn't respond. I debated telling her about Orion, how I had just seen him the day prior, but what good would that do? Knowing his ex-wife has access to him whenever she pleased, yet his mate did not.

"I see your castle is overrun with your in-laws," commented Evaline.

My brow furrowed in question.

"The demon princes," explained Delphine.

"Oh, yes ... them," I said.

"And we hear congratulations are in order as well," Evaline continued, her gaze flicking sharply to my left hand.

"Thank you," I replied, feeling a sense of shame.

"Three engagements in under a year," Evaline said. "You Salvo women sure know—"

"Mamma," Delphine interrupted, placing a loving hand on her shoulder. She turned back to me and forced a smile. "Congratulation, Seren. I'm happy everything worked out for you. After all you've been through, you deserve happiness." Evaline huffed, but Delphine kept her hand on her almost mother-in-law. "Now, if you'll excuse us, we were just heading to breakfast."

She took Evaline by the arm and moved past me. Without thought, my hand reached out, grabbing onto Delphine's arm as if it were my lifeline. Tears fell uncontrollably down my face. She turned back towards me, her blue eyes so dull and lifeless.

"If there was a way," I cried, looking into the eyes of my best friend's mate, "even if it meant sacrificing my life, I would have done it. Without a second thought, I would have done it. He deserves to be here. Out of everyone, he deserved to live."

Delphine turned fully towards me, taking my hands in hers. "So do you, Seren," she said. The kindness in her voice caused me to cry harder. "He loved you very much. Even though it bugged me for the longest time, I can see why. I know you two had a connection. I can feel it. I can feel him, standing here with you. I will never understand why he had to die, but I cherish the time we had together, in our youth and as mates. I wouldn't change that for the world."

"He was the best person I've ever known," I said.

"Yes, he was," she replied, returning to Evaline as they turned the corner.

I finally made it back to my room, crawling underneath the covers next to Deus's warm body. I looked at his beautiful face. His dark hair. Tan skin. Toned body. The memories of the feelings I had experienced during our time apart came rushing back.

I felt his arms wrap around me as my vision blurred from my tears of pain.

"What is it, my love?" I heard him say, pulling me into him.

I opened my mind to him, unable to speak, showing him all that had occurred this morning. I shared the memories of those weeks that I had lived on this earth without him. The pain, torture, and sadness I had experienced. His grip tightened around me, providing me with a place to be vulnerable and safe.

At some point, I ended up crying myself to sleep, my body, mind, and soul exhausted. Maybe being the Queen of Hell would have its perks. I could demand everyone to go and fuck off while I had some peace and quiet for once in my life.

When I woke up, Deus's body was still wrapped around me. He was awake, watching me sleep. I rolled over, stretching while I forced my eyes open.

"Creep," I said, yawning.

He laughed. "I enjoy watching you sleep," he replied, propping his head on his elbow. "Snoring and all."

I smacked him in the shoulder. "Rude. Why couldn't you say something sweet like, 'you're so beautiful when you sleep.' Or 'I love how peaceful you look'?"

"We're mated and you'll soon be my wife. You're stuck with me, so what's the point of lying?"

I smacked him harder, flipping on top of him. He laughed and smiled from ear to ear, holding my wrists so I couldn't abuse him further. Before I could get free, he flipped me underneath him, pinning me to the bed.

"Careful mate," I said sarcastically. "If you aren't careful, I know one brother in specific that would love to take another bite out of me."

His eyes darkened as he leaned down, nipping at my neck, his lips moving to my ear. "You and I both know there is no one on this plane or any other that is capable of satisfying you the way I do."

My toes curled at the promise of ecstasy that laced his tone.

Knock. Knock.

"Every. Single. Time." Deus said, dramatically rolling himself off me.

I laughed, moving to the door. Frankie came strolling in, not a care in the world. "Good morning, lovebirds," she greeted.

"Morning Frankie," I replied.

Deus got out of bed, making his way towards us, only sporting a pair of black pants. The sight of his rippled muscles and glistening hair set a fire inside of me. The desire to lick along every one of those muscles overcame me. Tasting his smooth skin all the way down until I was able to trail my tongue up that perfectly crafted cock of his. I smiled.

His eyebrow arched, knowing exactly what I had just thought. My walls around my mind were down. I smiled, feeling my cheeks blush.

Frankie took a deep breath in, going still. "For Aradia's sake," she gasped. "Will the both of you put a lid on that power of yours? I may need to find Levi if I stay in here for too long."

Deus chuckled, while he wrapped his arms around me from behind. "Good morning, Francesca," he said, kissing the nape of my neck. "What brings you by so early?"

"Early?" she gasped. "It's two in the afternoon."

"Sorry," I replied. "I didn't get much sleep last night with everything going on."

"I don't think any of us have gotten a good night's sleep in a long time," she commented. "Anyway, I was hoping we could focus on something fun until dear old Satan decides to grace us with his presence ... and Talia's bones, that is."

"Frankie, I don't think I can handle drinking right now."

"Not that, silly. Though, now that you mention it, drinks would be a great addition. I was hoping to get started on wedding preparations. It will be something we can all look forward to."

I paused, turning to Deus. He was smiling, wiggling his eyebrows in a playful way.

"I like that idea," he added.

"With everything going on," I said, trying to divert the conversation, "do you really think now is the best time?"

"Hey," Frankie shrugged, "this wasn't actually my idea. It was Nonna's. Go figure she'd be so excited for her granddaughter to marry a demon prince, but ... she is. She insisted I get the party started, so once you return from Purgatory, we can get you hitched. Hopefully for the last time."

I smacked her in the shoulder while she began to laugh. Deus smiled so brightly, my heart swelled at the sight. But that light was quickly shadowed by the knowledge our marriage, at least here on earth, would only be temporary. I swallowed those feelings down and forced a smile.

"Sounds like a plan," I replied.

"Well, don't I get a say in any preparations?" Deus asked.

Frankie arched an eyebrow, putting her hands on her hips. "You want to be involved in wedding preparations?"

"It is my one and only," he replied, pinching me in the butt. I jumped, smacking him in his rock-solid abs.

"How about I work with Seren today," suggested Frankie, "and you and I finish things off while she's gone?"

"Perfect," he said, bending down to kiss me.

"I'll meet you in your room after I shower," I said, heading for the bathroom.

"Sounds good," she replied with a wink before heading out of the room.

I looked back at Deus as we headed for the bathroom.

"What?" he asked.

"Mr. Party Planner, are we?"

"Oh, come now, you've seen the type of soirees I'm capable of throwing."

"So, I should expect naked acrobats and fire breathers with an after party consisting of a massive orgy?"

He laughed. "Well, there will be lots and lots of sex after our party, but I plan to keep it between the two of us. Hey, if you think I'm bad, just wait until Levi's wedding. Envy and all."

I grabbed Deus's arm. "Wait," I said, a smile creeping across my face. "Is he planning on asking Frankie?"

Deus smiled subtly, leaning down to my ear. "I'm not supposed to say."

I yelled, jumping up and down for joy. "Oh, my, God! When? Where? How? Why hasn't he asked for my help? He better ask for my help. You need to tell him I need to be in on this, after all she's done for me in the past. Plus, I've been thinking of all the places he could do it. Has he picked out a ring? He better not have without showing me first. She is going to be pissed if he gets her something she doesn't like."

Deus was now laughing. "My love, calm yourself. He only told me yesterday he has decided to go through with it. I am sure the preparations haven't begun just yet."

I bit the side of my lip. "Does it not matter to them that they're not mated?" I asked.

He shrugged. "I don't believe so. He loves her unconditionally. I recognize the look," he said, pinching my chin. "I don't think a mating bond would make much of a difference. To find what we have is a one in a million chance. Though, a mating bond shouldn't stop two people in love from being together. Wouldn't you agree?"

I nodded. "But what if he eventually does find his mate, or she finds hers? What happens then?"

"That is a very big if," he said, pulling the nightgown over my head. "And frankly, none of our business."

"How can you say that?" I replied, while he prepared the shower. "This is my cousin and your brother we're talking about here."

He slid his pants to the floor. "My love, I think you're missing the point here. Two people who love each other very much are about to commit their lives together. Stop focusing on the possible ways their relationship could end in demise. Instead, look at the happiness they've found in one another." He pulled me into the shower, pressing his body fully against mine. His eyes began to glow.

"You're right. I'm just being crazy."

"I won't contest that."

My mouth fell open in offense. I tried to pull away from him, but he continued to laugh, holding me tightly against his hard, bare body.

"I love how much you care about your family," he said, running his fingers threw my wet hair. "But can I ask something of you?"

"You can, but after you just agreed that I'm crazy and all, I can't say I'll grant your request."

He smiled, trailing his fingers down my wet sides. "After you return from Purgatory, and you will be returning from Purgatory, I would like the few days before and after our wedding to be solely about us. About you and me. Then, after our wedding bliss, we can go back to worrying about saving the world so it doesn't end in the nasty prophecies from Revelations. Is that something you're capable of?"

I shrugged, allowing a small smile. "I mean, I guess our wedding is kind of a big deal. I can spare a few hours here and there."

"Oh, love, I'm going to need far more than a few hours in order to accomplish all the delightful, indecent, and pleasurable things I am planning to do to this magnificent body of yours."

My cheeks flushed as my core began to heat. "I think we've done just about everything two people can do together ... physically that is."

A low, seductive laugh rattled in his throat. "Oh, sweet Seren. You forget, you're marrying the Prince of Lust. There is an entire world I've yet to indoctrinate you into." He paused, sliding his finger down the center of my abdomen, continuing until he slid across the bundle of nerves and then deep inside of me. I gasped. "And I plan on taking eternity to wring every last sound of pleasure from those sweet, supple lips of yours that I love having wrapped around my cock."

In the next breath, I came undone.

Chapter Twenty-Five

"Indoor or outdoor?" asked Frankie.

"Outdoor," I answered. "The snow is kind of our thing."

"You two are weird."

"We're weird? Are you kidding me? You and Levi fight more than cats and dogs."

"Yes, but the sex after is worth it. You should try it."

I smiled, still feeling the aching sensation between my legs from our shower escapade. "Don't worry cousin, sex is the least of our worries."

"Oh, right, Prince of *Lust* and all," she said, making a face.

"Is that envy I sense? Levi must be wearing off on you."

"Oh, shut up. Now, back to the dress—"

"Red. Tight. Lace. Dramatic. Long sleeves. Plunging neckline."

"Sure, with only a few days' notice that shouldn't be a problem at all." We both started laughing, sitting in the middle of her bed, surrounded by sweets and champagne.

"I don't know what I'd do without you," I said, taking her hand in mine.

"Well, after your long resume of engagements and weddings, I was thinking of starting my own event planning business."

I smacked her in the arm. "This is the last one, I promise."

Her face softened. "I have no doubt about that. Now, about your bridal party. I, of course, hold the reigning position of maid of honor, then next in line is G, and then ... Lilith?" she asked with uncertainty, dragging out the letters of my new demon protector's name.

"Sure, why the hell not? Speaking of, have you seen her around today?"

"No, not that I've been paying much attention."

An uneasy feeling turned in the pit of my stomach. She had guarded me relentlessly since I discovered her true identity, but today, she was noticeably absent. I slid off the bed, putting my shoes back on before heading to the door.

"Hunting for a demon, are we?" Frankie asked, following me.

"What's new?" I replied, heading into the hall.

The castle was packed. Witches and warlocks from all the covens had come to learn from the demon princes. Even Elder Torrian Astra had dared to show his face, only after Nonna made him grovel for her forgiveness. God, I loved that woman and her resilience. Torrian's betrayal and attempt to throw my family out of our home would never be forgotten.

I turned the corner of the residence hall where Lilith was staying and opened her door without bothering to knock. Lillith leaned against the frame of a window overlooking Triora. She turned quickly with a startled expression.

"What do you two want?" she snapped, moving towards us. She peered over her shoulder in a suspicious manner.

"I can't wait to see her face." Frankie laughed, nudging me with her elbow.

I furrowed my brow, assessing her body language. "Are you expecting someone?" I asked.

"I do have a life, you know," she replied. "Now, what do you need?"

Frankie clapped, smiling from ear to ear. "I'm thinking tulle," she said sarcastically. "What do you think, Seren?"

Lilith checked over her shoulder again. "Actually," she said, ushering us towards the door. "This really isn't the best time for me. I have an appointment I need to keep, but I will come find you after."

Lilith shoved us back towards the door aggressively. I pushed her arm away.

"Lilith, what are you—" I began to say, just as dark, purple smoke filled the area next to the window. The fog dissipated, revealing a massive form with red hair as radiant as fire and a face that promised death. Satan.

Before I could act, Frankie's starlight blasted from behind me, slamming him into the wall across the room. I sent a message down the bridge to Deus. Within seconds, he and Levi appeared.

"What in the hell is he doing here in your room?" I asked Lilith, approaching her with caution. She rolled her eyes, placing a hand on her hip before exhaling.

"He's not our enemy," she replied.

Levi laughed. "And where have you been these past few millennia?"

Lilith shook her head and offered Satan her hand. He accepted it, standing to his feet. He rubbed the back of his neck, smiling as he stretched.

"You Salvo women really know how to pack a punch."

"And you're just now realizing this?" asked Frankie.

"What in the fuck is going on, Lilith?" asked Deus, his voice carrying a violent edge.

She took a moment, looking to Satan as if asking permission to speak. I took another step forward.

"Lilith," I said. "Does the pledge you made to me only a few days ago mean nothing?"

"Of course it does," she replied. "I am bound to you. To protect you from any threat. That is why I am currently not pulverizing his smug face in. Even though he deserves nothing short of a slow, miserable death, after what he said about you being better suited for him."

"And what about yesterday?" asked Deus. "You attacked him then."

"He bit another female," she roared, glaring at Wrath. "Of course I wasn't going to let him get away with that."

In a waft of multicolor fog, Mammon, Belz, Gor, and G all appeared in Lilith's room. Lilith crossed her arms, her stare at Deus full of disappointment.

"Really?" she asked him. "After all these centuries, all I've done and proven to you, you really trust me that little?"

"I don't know what to believe right now," Deus answered.

"It's fine," Satan interrupted, putting a comforting hand on Lilith's back.

"Start talking," insisted Belz.

Satan took a step forward, facing his brothers. "As always, I am in this for myself. As sweet Lilith pointed out yesterday, I no longer find Lucifer worthy of his crown. So, if there is a chance for me to earn my rightful place as king, I will stop at nothing to achieve it. Even if that means working with the lot of you. There is a lot you don't know about me."

"Yeah, no shit," Mammon interrupted him.

"Do you want answers, or are you not finished listening to your arrogant, small-minded, narcissistic selves?"

A simmer of rage rippled down the bond. "Go on," Deus said.

"As I was saying," Satan continued, "there is a lot you all have missed since ... well, the beginning of time. As soon as we landed in the earthly realm, Deus broke from Lucifer, giving the lot of you the courage to do the same. But in doing so, you left the most powerful celestial being unchecked. I couldn't let that happen. Not knowing what he was planning, what resources he had up his sleeve, left all of us vulnerable. In the past, his antics have worked in my favor, but recently, his actions have become reckless."

"So, you made a deal with Lilith?" I asked, turning to my so-called friend. "And you betrayed us."

"I have never betrayed you," Lilith replying, rubbing her temples. "It is far more complicated than what you know."

"Then explain it to us," said Deus.

Lilith looked at Satan before replying. "I was human once, remember? If Lucifer is the being I hate the most, and the rest of your beloved demon princes knew nothing of my true identity, didn't you ever wonder how I became a demon?"

"She was the first I ever created," admitted Satan. Pride flickered through his tone. "Nailed it on the first try." He looked at Lilith with more endearment than I thought the demon of wrath could possess. He winked at her, and I could have sworn she blushed.

"Satan found me after Lucifer had ruined my mortal life," explained Lilith. "I had foolishly fallen in love with the prince of lies and deceptions, turning my back on Adam and God. I chose Lucifer over all else, blinded by my stupid, useless heart. Little did I know, I was just a tool in Lucifer's pissing contest with his Father. As soon as I chose the life Lucifer promised me, the gates to Eden were shut to me ... forever.

"Lucifer had succeeded in taking away one of his Father's most beloved creations. I was no longer any use to him. He left me stranded in the desert, alone and starving, to die."

"I had been watching Lilith for some time," continued Satan, looking at her with adoration. "She was fearless and truly a woman of her own mind. I knew my brother's affections were a farce, but playing the role I had committed to, I didn't interfere. Lucy was still running around without a soul. Any promise of love or admiration towards Lilith was all a part of his plan to stick it to Father.

"Then, when he left her in the desert to die, I made my move. I had been watching Lucifer dabble with the creation of his own brand of demons. The rest of you had begun creating creatures and figures of horror by using your darkness and life force while compressing it into physical beings. I wondered what would happen if I intertwined my life force with that of a living thing ... a human."

"Long story short," Lilith took over. "Satan found me knocking on death's door. He offered me a deal; one I accepted without hesitation. Then I experienced the most painful and torturous transition to date. When I woke after passing out, I was stronger, more powerful ... immortal. A demon made of wrath and rage. Exactly what I required to seek my revenge."

"What was the deal you made?" I asked.

Lilith looked up at Satan and smiled, taking his hand in hers. "That I would stop at nothing until Lucifer had suffered," she answered. "I vowed to wreak havoc on him, taking away anything and everything he holds dear. To destroy any hope he had of ever becoming a god. But to do this, Satan and I had to keep our relationship a secret from the world."

Satan turned to Deus. "I knew you were strong, and that to defeat our brother, we would eventually be left with no choice but to join forces."

"So, we concocted a plan," explained Lilith. "I would become your trusted right hand, making sure you remained safe and out of Lucifer's grasp."

"You've been spying on me," growled Deus, "this entire time?"

"No, I became your friend," Lilith countered aggressively. "I aided you while you built your forces and found your true self." Deus was fuming. "Satan and I agreed that we would only meet once a century, in private, so our bargain would not be discovered. Until ... until the key to our plan was discovered." She turned her eyes to me. "Until we found you."

"Hold on just a minute," barked Mammon, taking a step forward. "You mean to tell me you ... and my brother are ... together?"

Lilith smiled and so did Satan. "We're mated," she admitted.

"For fuck's sake," Belz blurted.

"You've got to be shitting me," said Gor.

"This just keeps getting better," added Levi.

"How long?" asked Deus. "How long have you two known you were mated?"

"A few months after I made her into a demon," answered Satan.

"But," Mammon said, looking very confused. "Lilith, Belz, and I—" he stopped, realizing he was approaching a very dangerous subject.

Wrath's eyes lit with flashes of red and blue, swirling into a brilliant shade of purple. His jaw clenched. "I am aware of what you and Beelzebub did to my mate," he growled.

Belz put his hands up in a defensive manner. "We had no knowledge of who or what she was to you, brother," Belz said. "If we would have, even hating you as we do, we would have never crossed that line. Some things are sacred, no matter the circumstances."

Lilith slid a comforting hand down Satan's arm. "We all had to play a part," she said, her tone full of regret. "No matter how much it killed me, I did what I had to do so we could all get to this point." She looked at the other princes. "We didn't know which of you we could trust. If my identity was revealed, any of you could have turned that information over to Lucy to further your own agendas, not knowing what it would have cost us all."

"How does Lucifer not recognize you?" asked Frankie.

"When I was made," answered Lilith, "Satan altered my appearance."

"Red hair, like mine," he said, twirling a finger through a curl. "White complexion to represent the innocence that he stole from her. But I kept the eyes the same. I couldn't bear to part with such beauty."

"I'm going to be sick," Mammon said, moving to the back of the group.

"So, you knew about Talia the entire time?" I asked.

Satan turned to me, his face now stern. "I know of Talia, but not enough to be of any use. That is one individual Lucy has gone to great lengths to erase from the world ... even from me."

I turned to Lilith. "So, scrying for the bones, suggesting we use Satan to retrieve the remains, it was all a plan to get us to work together?"

"To be clear," said Satan, "I have not decided what side I am on." Lilith elbowed him in the side.

"Then what are you doing here?" asked Deus.

"My mate asked me for a favor," he answered.

"Always the lapdog," Belz mumbled.

"Did you bring the bones?" I asked.

Satan nodded, snapping his fingers. A brown leather bag appeared in front of me. I bent down, opening the top, needing to see them for myself. I smiled, a sense of relief filling me as I looked upon the remains of the first vessel.

"Perfectly preserved," I whispered. "G, go get my mother ... it's time." She left without a word.

"Seren," Satan said, stepping in front of me. Deus went stiff in a defensive manner. Satan looked down at me and then the bag I now held in a death grip. "I don't know much about this witch you are trying to rescue, but I do remember the time from which she lived. A time that marked the beginning of an era of darkness and the magic you and your covens now fight. This can't be a coincidence, especially if Lucifer has gone to the lengths he has to keep her a secret."

"Thanks for the advice," I said sarcastically. "But as you just reminded everyone in the room, you are out only for yourself—which means, I think it's time for you to go."

"I am not trying to change your mind, goddess," Satan replied. "All I am suggesting is that you go into this with your eyes open."

"Message received," I replied.

"You got the bones," I heard Nonna say with excitement from the door. She, my aunt, and mother froze at the sight of Satan. Nonna's back went straight in a defensive stance. "What in Aradia's name are you doing standing in my home?"

"Wait for this story," Frankie mumbled. "More hidden secrets we've just uncovered. Turns out Satan here created the first human-demon hybrid, Lilith, who just happened to be his mate, and now we're all just one big happy family."

"What?" asked Aunt Thora, confusion stretched across her face.

"Now you know how I feel," Frankie added.

"Time to go, brother," Belz said, approaching Satan. Wrath turned to his mate one final time. He stroked her long, red hair before shifting out of sight.

I threw my hands up towards an empty part of the room, solidifying my magic into the new gate I had strained to create. Out of the black and gray fog, the bridge materialized brick by brick into a beautiful archway with ribbons of red and purple intertwining through the structure.

I took a deep breath, my hands falling to my sides in exhaustion. I looked back. "Gor," I said. He came to my side. "What do I do with the bones?"

"You need to compress them. Break them down. Pull the magic out of them and then infuse that into the existing bridge. It should, in theory, act as the anchor to get you to Talia."

I looked to my other side at Deus. He smiled. "What do you need, my love?" he asked.

"A little magical boost wouldn't hurt," I replied.

"Anything," he said, kissing me on the head. "Promise you'll come back to me in one piece."

"I promise," I replied, leaning into his body. "I wish you could come with me."

"As do I," he replied. I still didn't understand why the princes couldn't set foot in purgatory—another question I would likely never get an answer to.

I turned back to Annalise. "Mom, you ready?" I asked.

"Ready," she answered, coming to stand next to me.

Deus wrapped his arms around my waist, our shared power heightening. As I pressed my back into him, I focused on the bones. I hovered my hands over the bag, steadying myself as I began. The bones drifted up into the air until I contained them between my hands, concentrating my power and will. I closed my eyes, searching for the link that connected

Talia and me. The power of the goddess.

A darkness flashed behind my eyes. Pain, suffering, and fear all rushed in, consuming me with an overwhelming sense of panic and despair. I could hear cries of people, of children in the background. Fire cracked and the earth split, consuming villages, farms, and innocents along with it. Darkness devoured me. Power consumed me: a desire, a *need* for divine sovereignty.

A low, descending hum slammed through the room, silencing everything and everyone around us. A massive explosion of power and light ruptured through me, shattering the bone fragments into dust. My power latched onto hers instantly, pulling and drawing me in, but it wasn't the goddess I felt ... no, this power, this darkness, was demonic.

I moved my hands, forcing down the need to consume her essence, before thrusting my hands towards the gate, infusing her to the structure. A brilliant white light radiated through the arch, energizing the stones, stirring them to life. A blast erupted from the bridge, flinging the door to Purgatory wide open with a powerful gust of wind.

We all flew back, landing on our asses. Wind and light tore through the room. I felt Deus's hands on me, pulling me to my feet. I looked into my mate's eyes, feeling the love we shared. He caressed the side of my face before pressing a desperate kiss to my mouth.

"Promise me," he whispered, while the wind and fury of another plane whipped around us.

"I'm coming back," I replied, placing a hand to his heart. "I'm coming home."

I turned towards my mother. She took my hand and gave me a small, reassuring nod. We both faced the women we loved. Nonna nodded, Aunt Thora smiled, and Frankie blew a kiss. Annalise and I looked at each other one more time. Her grip around my hand tightened as we took a running leaping into the unknown.

CHAPTER TWENTY-SIX

Silence. An unbearable silence greeted us. I closed the portal the instant our feet hit solid ground, preventing anything that shouldn't from escaping into the realm of the living. There was no wind. No sun. Everything was masked in a veil of gray.

We were outdoors at the cusp of an entrance that led into a deep, decaying forest. Everything around us had been drained of life. The grass, the flowers, the trees; this land was completely barren.

"Well, this wasn't what I expected," whispered my mother, still holding onto my hand.

"Where is … everything?" I asked.

"Don't be fooled. I am sure there are things lurking out there that are already aware of our presence. I just don't know what they are or what they want."

I looked around, but the only path available to us was forward, into the dead forest.

"I don't even know where to begin," I admitted. I had been so focused on getting us here that I hadn't stopped to think about how to find Talia once we crossed over.

"You two share a link, just like you do with the vessels before you. Open yourself to that link. Allow your power to reach for her."

I nodded, taking a step towards the entrance of the hollow trees. I closed my eyes, reaching for the power Talia and I shared. I touched the magic of Aradia, allowing it to form into a single entity. I forced the power forward, taking what I knew of Talia and what I had felt when I had pulled the magic from her bones, creating a connection between the two of us. I opened my eyes, surprised to see a small purple orb now floating in front of me.

Annalise stepped to my side, smiling with pride. "See," she whispered. "Told you, you could do it."

"I feel like I learn something new every day," I laughed.

"And you will. Magic is ever changing, ever growing. The more you nurture it, the more it will give back to you. This is a gift that needs to be tamed and mended. Never forget that."

I nodded, focusing on the purple orb. "I guess we follow it?" I asked.

"I would assume so."

We moved forward and sure enough, the orb moved. It floated silently through the air, leading us into a forgotten forest, full of mystery. Annalise continuously scanned our surroundings, searching for any sign of life. I focused my energy on the orb, holding onto the connection that threaded Talia and me together.

An hour into walking and we still hadn't come across anything or anyone that was living. The only sound was our footsteps crunching the brittle roots and vines that littered the floor. Nothing in the sky moved or changed. There was no sign of clouds or any light whatsoever. Everything was just ... gray.

Despair began to settle deep inside of me. The hope I had clung to at the beginning of this journey was slowly beginning to fade. What was I doing, dragging my mother and myself into this situation? We didn't even know if Talia was the key to ending Lucifer. This whole plan was concocted on a series of unknowns.

And if I failed ... no, I couldn't fail again. No one else in my life was going to die because of me. I couldn't handle being responsible for the death of another person I loved. No matter the gain, it wasn't worth it. The only person that would be losing their life would be me. And Lucifer.

"Seren," my mother whispered.

I froze, realizing she was no longer beside me. Behind me, she went deathly still. I looked in the direction of her gaze, but couldn't see a thing in the haze of gray.

"What is it?" I asked, apparently too loudly. She whipped her finger to her mouth, signaling for me to be silent. I did, focusing on my surroundings. My adrenaline began to pump through my system, filling my ears with the sound of my panicking heart beating faster with each passing second. The small hairs on the back of my neck rose, signaling we were not alone.

Something lunged from the thick wall of tangled branches and vines, pummeling my mother to the ground. I shot off a tunnel of fire, blasting the creature off her. It shrieked and cried, rolling on the dry ground, attempting to extinguish the flames.

I rushed towards Mom, pulling her from the ground. A chorus of cries and clicking noises filled the air, coming from all around us. Annalise and I went back-to-back, trying to prepare, but we were quickly surrounded. The sounds grew into a crescendo as the horde of creatures closed in around us.

Out from the trees stepped a creature. It was male, worn and tattered clothing hanging loosely from his thin figure. There wasn't an ounce of fat on him. All his ribs and bones were visible underneath his pale, white skin. His eyes were hollow and bruised underneath. Patches of hair hung from his scalp in thin strands. His nails were jagged and uneven as his long fingers wrapped around the hilt of a makeshift knife. He growled, revealing the few yellow teeth that remained.

My mouth fell. "They're—" I began to say.

"—human," my mother finished.

Dozens of them poured from the tree lines, weapons aiming to attack. Annalise reared back and slammed her power into the ground, sending them hurtling back around us. I lit the edges of the perimeter with fire to act as a barrier.

"Run!" yelled my mother. Hand in hand we took off, following the purple orb of light. Ducking and diving through the rough terrain, we ran faster and faster through the gray landscape of death. The humans pursued us, running and leaping like a pack of wild animals. Some of them took to the treetops, jumping and swinging like monkeys.

I released my flame behind me, sending a massive wave of them back, burning their shriveled skin until there was nothing left but a pile of ash. Annalise latched onto my hand, siphoning my power to fuel her own. She released a massive surge of magical energy above us, just in time to repel the ones that had leaped from the treetops, aiming for a kill.

My lungs began to burn from exertion as my muscles screamed, but the adrenaline had taken over, pushing my body past its physical limit. Blast after blast of power erupted from us, but the humans just kept coming. It seemed that the more power we used, the more of them it attracted. Every time we seemed to kill one, three would take its place, falling in line behind the others in pursuit.

A clearing was ahead and we ran faster, desperate for a clear line of sight. I dodged a tree limb, following the purple orb out of the forest towards a rocky ledge. In seconds, the landscape changed from a dead forest to a dry, desert mountain scape. I looked back to see the dozens of humans had transformed into hundreds, just as my mother's arms wrapped around my shoulders, preventing me from moving forward.

I was jolted back with force. We were now standing at the lip of a cliff. I peered over, unable to see the bottom. The purple orb just floated over the edge, calmly. I turned around, trying to assess our escape routes, but there were none. We were trapped.

"What do we do now?" I asked.

"We fight," my mother said, with an exhilaration I hadn't seen since before she'd had her soul returned. She took another hit of my magic, my flames becoming her own. I paired my flame with my shadows, creating black tendrils of death. The creatures paused, only for a moment, smiling as if they were looking upon their next meal. Drool and blood seeped from their lips. There wasn't an ounce of humanity left behind their eyes.

Then they attacked. Fire, shadows, and power surged through the landscape, cracking the ground around us into pieces. I wrapped my darkness around the humans, flinging them off the cliff. My mother blazed through crowds of them, as if the flame had been her power all along. Massive ruptures of energy exploded from her, smashing into their frail bodies, shattering their bones as soon as it made contact.

I used my darkness as a weapon, slicing through their flesh, severing limbs, heads, and torsos. Kill after kill, and still they continued to emerge. The ravenous humans began to close in around us, inching closer until our footing danced along the ledge. One jumped towards my mother. With speed she turned, dodging its attack, sending it tumbling into the abyss. My mother fought with a skill I had never seen her display before now. She was truly her mother's daughter ... as was I.

One creature appeared suddenly, taking me off guard. It sank jagged teeth into my shoulder, ripping a chunk of flesh free. I slammed my fist straight through its head. Brains, blood, and tissue clung to my skin. I was going to be sick.

The creature fell as another appeared. I took the dagger from my side, slicing anything that got too close. I sent another forceful push of energy into the crowd, forcing them back, only for a second. My mother found her way to my side. Her brow was drenched with sweat and her breathing was heavy.

"I'm approaching burnout," she said.

"I know," I replied. The ball of purple light still floated over the edge of the cliff. There had to be another way. What was I missing?

And then, I felt it. A dark, slithering presence stretched along the mental wall of my mind. It felt cold ... dry. It prowled along my barriers, searching for a way in. It approached the door I had carved out for Deus. I could feel it examining the entrance with curiosity, then it began to drive its thin essence against it.

Desperate for a way out, I opened it ... just a little.

"Jump," the voice hissed inside of my mind.

"What?" I said out loud.

"Jump, you stupid girl!" it yelled.

Exhaustion was overtaking my mother. "Trust me," I said, extending my hand to her. Without hesitation, she took it. I turned us towards the edge of the cliff, and we leaped into the darkness that promised to swallow us whole.

The humans jumped after us, so desperate for something to eat that they were willing to risk their lives for a single bite. My mother and I clung to each other, the wind ripped from our lungs as we plunged to our deaths.

A enormous wave of power rammed me forward, freezing me in place. My grip tightened onto my mother as gravity continued to pull her into the darkness. I yelled, my shoulder popping out of place as I supported her weight.

"Hold on," I called down to her, still suspended in midair. The bodies of the human creatures continued to fall around us. Behind me, a bright white static power encased me. It was coming from the wall of the cliff, but I couldn't see who was its master.

I groaned, my sweaty palm slipping from Annalise's grip. I reached down with my other hand, locking my fingers around her wrist. The white magic began to pull us towards the rocky side of the cliff. As we approached a small cave opening carved into the jagged wall, I used the little strength I had left to swing my mother into the mouth of the opening, before the magic finally dropped me to the ground.

The impact rattled my bones, causing my shoulder to scream in pain. I cradled it with my hand, rolling to my back. Annalise was there in an instant, examining my injury.

"Where did it come from?" I whispered through my teeth.

"What?" replied Mom.

"The magic ... where did the magic come from? Someone is here. We're not alone."

Mom's eyes snapped back into the darkness of the cave as a figure stepped from the shadows into the faint light. Her frame was frail and lean, barely able to hold the tattered scraps of cloth that clung to her body. Her hair was a heap of tangled white curls, long and unkept. I couldn't make out the shade of her eyes, but her cheeks were sunken, revealing the sharp edges of her jaw and cheekbones.

Scratches and wounds marred her skin from her face all the way down to her bare feet. No weapons were visible, but I had a feeling she didn't need any to protect herself. A ring made of a thin gold band that bore a white stone sat on her left ring finger. I looked back into her empty eyes.

"Talia," I whispered, pulling myself to a sitting position. Her eyes flicked from Annalise to me, pausing when she focused on my shoulder.

"You're hurt," she replied in a dry and raspy voice.

"My shoulder," I replied. "I'm pretty sure I dislocated it."

She knelt in front of me, extending her hands. My mother lunged forward, placing herself in between Talia and me. Talia held Annalise's gaze, cold and unfeeling.

"Move," Talia demanded.

"What are you going to do?" Mom asked.

"Mend her shoulder," she replied. "If I wanted her dead, I would have let her fall."

Mom slowly moved to my side, still on alert. Talia placed her hands around my shoulder and, without warning, snapped it back into place. I yelped, feeling the bones grind against each other.

"I'm sorry, but I can't use anymore magic," she said. "It will attract the ammit."

"The what?" asked my mother.

"The ammit. The creatures above," answered Talia.

"What are they?" I asked. "They look human."

"They are ... but not. Their souls have been sent here to atone for sins that have kept them from heaven's gates, but not rendered them completely lost. But once you enter Purgatory, your humanity, your desire for life, is stripped from you slowly. This reveals what a soul's true intentions are. When a person is left only with their baser instincts, you will see the true morality of the being. As I am sure you've seen, this plane is dead. Nothing grows; nothing thrives. Every ounce of life is extracted, leaving something that was once beautiful and thriving little more than a husk."

"So … what do they eat?" I asked, fearing I already knew the answer.

"Each other," she replied coldly.

"And what do you eat?" mom asked.

"I use my magic to conjure food in small portions at a time," she explained. "Our magic, since it pulls from our life force, alerts the ammit of our presence, so I have to be careful about when and how much magic I use."

"Are you the only person with magic here?" I asked.

"Yes. Purgatory wasn't created to hold our kind. This plan is for the human souls only who are attempting to atone for the sins they committed on the earthly plane. Their last attempt at entering the gates of heaven."

"Then … how are you here?" I replied.

"That is a long story, and one I am willing to tell once we are free from this place," she said, returning to her feet. "I am surprised you came for me. I had my doubts."

Annalise pulled me up, keeping a secured hand on my back.

"Before I open the gate," I said, cradling my arm, "I need assurance that you are who you claim, and that you can do what you say."

Her eyes burrowed into me. Something like annoyance flickered behind them. "I am Talia Mizrahi. I was enslaved by Pharaoh, as were my people, from birth. Once freed from our chains by God's 'chosen one',

Moses, I met Lucifer along our journey."

"Okay, so you know Lucifer," I said. "That doesn't mean you know how to defeat him."

Her eyebrow arched as her jaw clenched. "I know how to stop him because I was the one that created the cage. My coven and I, that is."

"A cage?" I asked.

"Yes," she replied. "A cage that is powerful enough to hold even the most dangerous prince of Hell."

"And what coven do you belong to?" asked Annalise.

Talia's eyes shifted to my mother in a predatory fashion. "Obsidian," Talia answered. My heart dropped into my stomach. "I am the first coven elder of Obsidian."

"We're leaving," demanded my mother, pulling me back to the edge of the cave.

Talia began to laugh. "After that reaction, I expect the coven is still operational?"

"They are under the command of Lucifer," I admitted.

Talia's face went slack. "What?" she growled. "*He* has taken command of my legacy. My life's work!"

"How do you cage him?" I asked again, desperate for the answer that would end all of this.

She took a moment, gathering herself. "My coven and I created a magical device that would aid us with entrapping him. It is buried deep in the desert of Phut."

"Phut?" my mother whispered, trying to decipher the time gap. "Libya. The Libyan Desert."

"How does the cage work?" I asked.

"The cage is fully functioning," she answered. "All it needs is a power source. The life of a god."

I swallowed, realizing what she was saying. A small smile lifted in the right corner of her mouth.

"Don't worry, girl," she said, as if she could read my mind. "I plan on sacrificing myself to power the cage. I've waited long enough for this moment. No one else will get the honor of stripping him of his *beloved power* but me."

"So, you're still … alive in here?" I asked.

"Yes," she replied. "Even though my body was left on earth when I sacrificed myself, my soul remained here. When we return to your home plane, I will be able to use my magic to regenerate my physical form, thanks to the bones you used to create the gate."

"And how did you know your bones wouldn't be destroyed?" I asked.

She smiled. "I placed a preservation spell over my bones before I died."

And Lucifer had kept them in his castle—but why?

"How did you get here?" mom asked.

"That is a part of a longer story I will share once you free me from this plane."

I took a moment to consider the little parts of information she had willingly shared. There were so many gaps in her story and unanswered questions. On top of that, she was the founder of the Obsidian coven. How was I supposed to trust her?

"*You don't have to,*" Talia said, mind to mind. I checked all my walls around my mind for any holes, but the structure was sound. She smiled. "*Once you let me in, I no longer have to be invited,*" she explained. "*But you have nothing to worry about from me, little tribrid. I mean you no harm. My qualm is with Lucifer, no one else.*"

"You must swear to me," I said, taking a step forward, "that no harm will come to anyone except Lucifer and his demons or those who work for him. No one else ... including any other demon that was sired from the other six Princes of Hell."

She cocked her head, her eyes squinting into slits, assessing me from head to toe. Slowly, Talia extended her hand, drawing a finger along the side of my face. Her irises flashed to a soft purple like my own, before submerging into an inky blackness as mine did when I accessed the demonic power.

She pulled away, her eyes clearing back to a deep brown color that could have been mistaken for black. A devious smile stretched across her face. "So that was why I was able to make contact with you."

"What are you talking about?" I asked.

"Lust, huh?" she replied, standing uncomfortably close. "Never had the pleasure of meeting that one, but I can only assume he's quite the spectacle."

"How did you—"

"How long ago was the mating bond completed?" she interrupted. "Time works a little differently here, so I am not sure how much time has passed since I first arrived, but based on your attire, I assume it's been a few centuries."

"Try a few millennia," said my mother.

"Millennia?" Talia asked, despair laced in her tone. "What year is it?"

"2025 ADC," I answered, feeling sorry for her. She blinked in confusion. "It's been at least three thousand years since you lived."

"And how many vessels have been born before you?"

"Only four."

"No," she said, shaking her head. "That isn't right. It should have been every three hundred years. Di was very specific when she created the magical loophole."

"Di?" my mother asked.

"Aradia ... the goddess," Talia answered, looking at my mother with confusion.

"You knew her?" I exclaimed.

"She is ... was my best friend," Talia said, a hint of sorrow in her tone.

"Until a few weeks ago," I explained, "we didn't even know you existed. We thought another vessel named Valeriana was the first in the year 800."

"It appears I've been away longer than I had accounted for," she said, then looked directly into my eyes. "I swear to bring no harm to you or those who aid you in the fight against Lucifer. I promise, the only one I will destroy is Lucifer and his loathsome pride."

The walls of the cave began to tremble. Small pieces of rock shook loose, falling around us. Talia ran to the mouth of the cavern, looking towards the top. "They sensed my magic," she said, moving from the opening in a hurry. "We have mere seconds before we become their dinner."

I looked at my mom, still hesitant. She gave me a small smile and nodded. I turned back to Talia, taking a deep breath in. This decision would either be the catalyst of our entire effort to rid the world of Lucifer for good, or she would be our undoing.

"Let's go home," I said.

Talia's smile grew. Terror rattled through my bones at the sight. This woman possessed an evil only matched by the devil we were trying to slay. I sent up a small prayer to God that she wouldn't betray us. Perhaps to destroy one evil, we must embrace another.

"Good," she said. The sounds of the cannibals grew, screeches and screams desperate for their pound of flesh. "How fast can you get the portal up?"

"I just need a few moments," I said, focusing on the back wall of the cave.

"That maybe all we have," commented Mom, readying for a fight.

"What power do you possess, witch?" Talia asked my mother.

"I'm a siphon," Annalise answered.

Talia laughed and approached her. "Well, prepare yourself for one hell of a power rush," she said, placing her hands on either side of Annalise's face. Mom's body extended as Talia's power flooded her system. Annalise's face glowed a heavenly white as her body shook. Finally, Talia released her.

Annalise took a deep breath. Her eyes flashed from Talia, then to me. "You're a—" started Mom.

"Ah, ah, ah," interrupted Talia, winking at her. "Story time begins when we are back in the world of the living." She turned back to me, lighting her flame. "Anytime would be nice, tribrid."

I nodded, forcing my magic into my center and forming it into the gate that would lead us home. That would lead me back to Deus. The gate began to appear, brick by brick, as the hordes of creatures ascended into the mouth of the cave. The sound of magic boomed all around me, but I focused on my task. The creatures shrieked as blood splattered all around us.

Finally, as the last brick clicked into place at the top of the arch, I pushed the last ounce of power needed to fuel the gate, causing it to glow with power.

"It's done," I yelled, turning to see the mouth of the cave completely engulfed with the bodies of the tormented.

"Get ready to run, witch," Talia said to my mother. The door to the gate opened. I watched in awe while Talia gathered all her power into a mass in front of her. The power glowed as her body began to tremble from the exertion. Demonic power seeped from her, filling the cavern around us. The walls trembled as if they, too, feared what she was.

Annalise let go of her own power, dashing towards me in a dead sprint. Talia began to scream, still holding the power between her hands as it grew. Finally, she thrust her arms towards the creatures. A blinding white light unleashed.

I felt it then: the familiar calling her power sang, as if it was a part of me. The way ... the way Lucifer's power called to my own.

The magic slammed into the creatures, incinerating them all into mist. Blood sprayed around us, the only remains left of the souls trapped in this plane. The walls around us broke apart, sending boulders tumbling down around us. Talia turned towards the gate; her face soaked in the blood of her victims. A warm, sticky residue slid down my cheeks, soaking my clothing. I looked down; I was completely covered in blood.

"Now," Talia yelled, running towards us. Annalise took my hand, hurtling us through the gate. I hit the floor, the impact rattling every one of my bones. A third thump hit the ground near us. At that sound, I forced my good arm forward, absorbing the power of the gate before any other creature followed us through.

CHAPTER TWENTY-SEVEN

Once the gate had disappeared, I collapsed to the ground, spent. To my right, my mother's familiar face smiled at me, smeared in red. She placed her hand on my shoulder and squeezed. I turned to my left, and there lay Talia, panting with exhaustion.

Her wicked smile appeared once again. She began to laugh, pushing herself from the floor and observing her surroundings. I watched as her white magic began to knit her new physical form together, creating a fresh body for her soul to inhabit. We had teleported straight back to where we had started ... Lilith's room.

A moment later, Deus appeared in a black and red cloud of smoke in front of me. His hands were on me before the shift had finished, wrapping me in his familiar embrace. I wrapped my arms around him, desperately needing his warmth.

"Father, I was so worried," he said, finally pulling away to look down at me. His face tensed. "Why are you covered in blood? Are you hurt?"

"No, I'm fine. It isn't mine," I answered. "We had to fight our way home ... per usual."

He smiled, wiping something from my cheek. "I can't wait until our days don't consist of killing or getting splattered in something else's liquids."

I laughed, feeling Talia's eyes on us. I turned to her as she studied Deus and me. Deus pulled me from the floor and then helped my mom stand to her feet. A moment later, the door flew open and Nonna, Thora, and Frankie rushed inside.

"Oh, thank Aradia," Nonna exclaimed, pulling Mom and me into a hug. Thora and Frankie joined in.

"Could you have taken any longer?" Frankie exclaimed, hugging me so tightly I thought my ribs were going to crack.

"What are you talking about?" I asked. "We were only gone a few hours."

"No, sweetheart," answered Aunt Thora. "You two were gone for over a week."

"What?" Annalise replied in disbelief.

"Has anything happened?" I asked, concerned about the time we had lost.

"No," answered Nonna. "Everything is still silent."

Lilith, G, and the other princes appeared from the doorway. Lilith went deathly still as she locked her gaze onto Talia. Talia's eyebrow arched and she smirked.

"Hello Lilith," Talia said in an alluring tone. Somehow, entering into this realm had changed her physical appearance. In Purgatory, Talia had been attractive even with the lack of food and sunlight the realm had offered. But now ... now she was exquisite. The silver highlights in her hair caught the light, flowing through the most beautiful curls that framed her flawless face.

And her eyes ... oh, those eyes glowed unnaturally, as if peering into golden honey swirling into a dark abyss. Her voice was seductive and soothing. I wanted to trust her. I wanted to please her.

I snapped myself out of the trance, pulling my eyes away from the blood-splattered witch. The others stood around the perimeter of the room, trying to assess the threat I had just released into the world.

"I know you," Lilith said, looking at Talia with confusion. "How do I know you?"

Talia walked gracefully towards her. All eyes were on the newest member of our little gang, yet no one made a move. With a slow, elegant motion, Talia placed her middle finger onto Lilith's head. The demon gasped as white light flared. Satan suddenly reappeared, launching towards his mate. Talia held up a hand, freezing him in place, rendering the demon prince powerless.

"Calm yourself, Wrath," Talia said. "Your mate remains unharmed." She released them both from her power. Satan's hands were on Lilith in a second, checking her for injuries.

Lilith looked shocked, her eyes wide and her breathing heavy. Slowly, her gaze rose to Talia. Her shock turned to rage. In an instant, Lilith's fist flew straight into Talia's face.

Talia soared backwards, knocking into a table ten feet behind her. No one moved.

The strange woman stood, wiping the blood from her busted lip. A laugh slithered out of her as she refocused on Lilith. "Good to see you too, friend."

"You psychotic bitch," Lilith growled, coming face to face with her. "I am not your friend. You used me for your own means."

Talia shrugged. "I had to assess the competition. Though, I've had many years to ponder my choices, and I am sorry for any pain I caused you. I recognize the errors I made and now stand ready to rectify the situation."

"You stole my memories!" Lilith yelled.

"I ensured that you remained safe," said Talia. "Lucifer never discovered your true identity or that of your mate, just as you asked. Plus, I had to make sure my plan was secure, and that you wouldn't run back to your lover and ruin everything I had worked so hard to build."

Lilith stared at nothing, seeming trapped in a memory. "Shit," she whispered.

Talia smiled. "See, I wasn't all bad."

Lilith flashed her teeth. "There is nothing good in you. How can there be when you're Lucifer's mate?"

The words dropped onto me like a ton of bricks. Lucifer's mate? I had freed Lucifer's mate? That was why my power had recognized hers. When I had used her bones to finish the gate, that was what my power had called to: not Aradia's magic, but Lucifers.

Deus placed himself in front of me, acting as a barricade. Levi did the same with Frankie. And, to my surprise, Belz stepped in front of Thora.

"What are you talking about?" Satan asked Lilith, coming to her side.

"Talia," replied Lilith, "is Lucifer's mate. She's also the one who began the Obsidian coven. In the beginning, there was only one coven. They practice good magic—white magic. But then, once Talia completed the mating bond with Lucy, she turned on her own coven, converting half of them to Lucifer's cause."

Talia tilted her head. "Now, little demon, that's not exactly how that story goes."

"Bullshit," Lilith snapped back. "I've lived a long time in multiple realms, and you are as crazy as they come. Lucifer's equal in every way."

"I would say superior in some things," Talia replied.

"Apparently the pride transferred over," mumbled Mammon.

"Shut up," whispered Gor, elbowing him in the side. Talia smiled, examining the princes one by one.

"You are just as he described," she said, with something like endearment in her voice.

"What are you talking about?" asked Belz.

"Lucifer told me about you," she answered. "Each of you. I wanted to meet you, but he wouldn't hear of it. That didn't stop him from sharing stories, though." She paused, studying Belz for a moment in silence. "Gluttony. The peacemaker in the family. Dashing and dapper while shifting into the sly fox when needed, able to talk anyone into anything."

She turned her attention to Mammon. "The greedy one. More playful and sarcastic than the rest. Luc warned me never to bet against you or play you in a game of cards. You like to use that brilliant smile to distract you opponents when you take them for all they're worth."

She focused on Levi. "The jealous brother, always coveting what others, have yet loyal to a fault. Never feeling like he was enough, like he could make a difference. Yet out of all of them, you are the most honorable. Then, there is Satan, Lucifer's most loyal pet. Little did he know you were playing the long game. You have a mind for games and strategic planning. You may appear to be a brute on the outside, but inside, you have the biggest heart." She smiled, looking at Lilith. "I saw that firsthand when it came to his love for you.

"Then, there's the little brother, Gor. Though you carry the mantal of sloth, you are not inattentive. I actually found you all those years ago, roaming the deserts of Egypt. Lucifer never saw you as a threat, but I saw his error in that assessment very quickly. You, little brother, are the most calculative and conniving of them all. Without the need to be hasty, time allotted you the gift of knowledge. I watched as you sat back and studied all that was around you, including your brothers. Silence, sometimes, is the most dangerous weapon of them all."

Finally, she turned to Deus. "The beloved one," she said sarcastically. "Oh, how Luc, adored you. He spoke of you as a father speaks of his first born. How strong and powerful you are. How entrancing and captivating it was to be in your presence, to sit at the same table and listen to you spin tales of your travels and your ... exhibitions. Out of everyone, your betrayal cut him the deepest. You broke his heart."

"Lucifer never had a heart," replied Deus.

"Oh, but he did," she said, looking to the floor. "For a time, at least."

"You said you would tell your story once you were freed," I reminded her. "You're free, so start talking."

There was heaviness in her eyes. "As promised, I will tell my tale. But first, is there a stream nearby where I may bathe?"

Mammon huffed. "Stream?"

"Yes," she replied, head held high. "I presume water is still accessible, since it is a necessity to life?"

"We have showers now," said Frankie.

Talia walked over to my family, taking notice of each of them. She looked back at me and smiled. "You have strong roots to our magic, little tribrid," she said. She approached Gor and Giana, stopping in front of G. She leaned in, seeming to sniff her. She pulled her head back instantly. "You wreck of death, child."

"Well, dying will do that to you," G replied.

Talia looked back to me. "You brought her back from Hell?"

"I did," I replied.

Talia laughed. "That's breaking the rules. I am surprised Di didn't strike you dead on the spot."

"Di?" whispered Deus.

"Aradia," I explained. "They were supposedly friends."

Talia looked back at G and then Gor. "You owe your brother's mate quiet a handsome price," she said to Gor.

"What are you talking about?" snarled Gor.

"You don't know?" She paused, seeming to enjoy the suspense. "Didn't you ever ask why you ended up in Hell instead of heaven?" she said to G. Giana didn't respond. Talia leaned into her ear. "Those who are mated to princes of Hell don't get to walk through the pearly gates. Our souls are created from the darkest parts of Hell, destined to return there once our earthly lives cease to exist."

Giana and Gor stared at each other, Talia's revelation still sinking in. "My ... mate?" Gor said softly.

"Hold on just a second," interjected Belz, taking a step forward. "How, in the matter of a month, have we gone from no mated princes of Hell, to now four of us miraculously finding our other halves?"

"Have you not been paying attention?" Talia replied, seeming annoyed. "Satan and Lilith were first, which occurred thousands of years ago. Then, Luc and me. Now, Asmodeus and Belphegor. Though, Sloth was never supposed to know his mate. Princess Lust took it upon herself to play God. I am sure your Father is thrilled by that new development."

"What do you mean?" asked G.

"You were never meant to find your mate," explained Talia. "Just because you are mated, doesn't guarantee you will end up together. Father needed vessels to split the magic in two, creating a balance. The two halves won't always be reunited. You outsmarted fate, little witch. Now, can someone please direct me to a location where I can bathe?"

"I will," G said eagerly.

"We will," Gor corrected her, still staring at Giana as if seeing her for the first time. A part of my heart swelled at their love.

"It's called a shower now," Giana explained. "I think you'll prefer it to a stream or lake."

"Thank you, sister," Talia said, nodding to her with a small smile.

"When you have bathed and eaten," Nonna said, "Gor and Giana will direct you to my rooms, where you will tell us your story."

Talia looked at Nonna with heavy eyes. "As you wish, elder," she replied, and followed G out the door.

Chapter Twenty-Eight

Deus and I shifted back to our room. Before the blood was completely washed from my skin, he was inside of me, leveraging my body between his and the wall of the shower. There was no talking, no discussion. The only thing that mattered the next hour was our bodies, minds, and souls, intertwining with one another, taking in the comfort of being reunited ... being whole and complete.

At some point we left the warm mist of our shower and tumbled into our sheets, taking each other over and over again. There were no restraints, no toys, no teasing: just the raw, animalistic need to connect, to possess one another entirely.

As I lay in the arms of my mate, I relaxed into the peace my mind and soul only knew in his presence. He trailed his fingers through my hair, kissing my face every so often. I looked up into his beautiful icy blue eyes, memorizing every detail.

"I was so worried," he finally said, his smile falling from his lips. "When two days had passed, and I couldn't sense you, couldn't hear you, I began to lose my mind."

"It really only felt like hours there," I replied, brushing my fingers along the column of his neck.

"Promise me you won't be going through any new gateways anytime soon, unless I can come with you."

"Believe me, you couldn't pay me to go back to Purgatory."

"Were the demons that brutal?" he asked.

The memories, sounds, and smells of that place would be added to my arsenal of trauma. "They weren't demons, Asmodeus ... they were humans. Savage, barbaric humans who fed on the flesh of others. All life, all humanity had been drained from them. Honestly, I don't know how Talia survived there. I prefer Hell over that place any day."

"That's saying a lot," he whispered.

"Exactly. Even with Annalise at my side, I had never felt more alone, more empty, than I did in that place."

"Well, hopefully we'll be getting some answers from Lucy's *mate* soon." He huffed a laugh, shaking his head. "I can't believe it ... Lucifer has a mate. And what in Father's name was she doing in Purgatory? Why hasn't he been searching for a way to set her free?"

"Add those to the list of ever-growing questions," I said, stretching across the bed. "Can't we just ... sleep for a few days?"

He smiled, running his fingers down my side. "Well, since you were gone for so long, Frankie and I finished all the wedding preparations."

I snapped my eyes to his. "What are you saying?"

"I'm saying, I don't want to wait another minute to make you my wife. How does tomorrow sound?"

I bit my lip, trying to tame the smile that fought to erupt. I wrapped my arms around his tanned, muscular torso.

"I think tomorrow sounds perfect," I whispered against his lips. We made love again, until we were forced to pry our bodies from one another.

"Listen," said Mammon, leaning against Nonna's couch. "I say we have Seren reopen the doorway to Purgatory, and we push the crazy bitch back through. Hell, I'll volunteer to do the pushing."

"We haven't even heard her story," said Gor.

"What is there to hear?" replied Mammon. "She is Lucy's mate. Lucy. For Father's sake, why in the universe did He give him a mate?"

"Where is G?" I asked, realizing she wasn't in the room with us.

"She insisted on staying with Talia," Gor answered.

"You left your mate alone with that thing?" Deus snapped.

"Just because Giana is my mate doesn't mean I have the right to tell her what to do," Gor said. "Plus, she assured me she doesn't feel any ill will from Talia. She feels ... sorry for her."

The others in the room began a heated debate about all the things they wanted to do to Talia to get back at Lucifer, and what would happen if she betrayed us. I made my way to Gor's side. I knew my friend well, and I could tell he was off.

"You okay?" I asked, bumping his shoulder gently.

"This is all just a lot," he admitted.

"You're telling me," I said with a smile.

"I have a mate," he said, sounded astonished. "Me ... the Prince of Sloth ... a mate. And she is ... Father she is perfect. Beautiful, brilliant, playful, strong, and kind. She is so understanding of everyone and everything. And she's mine. She was meant for me. Created from me. How?"

"Gor," I said, turning to him fully. "When are you going to stop and see how truly wonderful you are? I was able to see it from day one of our meeting. Heck, even Lucifer sees it. Why can't you?"

He smiled hesitantly. "In comparison to the others—"

"There is no comparison. You are each extraordinary in your own unique way. While also being difficult, territorial, and horribly narcissistic."

He laughed. "Glad to see we've made a good impression."

I shrugged. "Most of you have." I took my friend's hand in mine, holding it tight. "Giana is beyond lucky to have you as her mate."

"I hope I don't disappoint her."

"You won't. I know you won't."

He pulled me into his embrace, holding me close. "Thank you, Seren. Truly."

"Of course," I said, pulling away from him, "Now, I have a favor."

"I knew you were being too complimentary. Out with it."

"Deus and I are getting married tomorrow. I was ... I was wondering if you would do us the honor of officiating the wedding."

Gor shook his head, startled. "Deus has agreed to this?"

"Well, I haven't told him yet, but I am sure he will go along with whatever I ask. Yah know, being the blushing bride to be and all."

Gor smiled, his dark brown eyes seeming to glisten with happiness. "I'd be honored to join you and your mate in matrimony," he said, placing a hand on either of my shoulders. "And I am honored to have the privilege of calling you my sister."

My eyes filled with tears at the title. I was overwhelmed with happiness. I lunged, wrapping my arms around him, squeezing tightly. We both laughed as he returned my affections.

"Alright, what is going on over here?" Deus's voice came from behind me. "There's a lot of touching and it's not directed towards me, so naturally I am feeling a bit neglected."

I pulled away from Gor, elbowing Deus in the ribs.

"Demon baby," I said playfully.

"Don't worry, brother," said Gor. "Though I adore your mate, I seem to have been blessed with my own, whom I am quite found of."

"Blessed," Deus repeated the word, with a raw expression on his face. "Father has blessed us," he said, looking at me. "After all this time ... a blessing."

"I would have to agree," Gor said with a soft smile.

"Well," I smirked, "I have just found our officiant for tomorrow."

"Oh, you have?" asked Deus.

"Yup. Gor has agreed to do the honors."

Deus smiled, looking at Gor with surprise.

"If you're in agreement, of course," added Gor.

"It would be an honor to have you lead us in the ceremony," replied Deus with a grin. He extended his hand to Gor. Sloth took it, pulling Deus into an embrace. The brothers laughed with happiness. My heart was full.

The door to Nonna's room opened, revealing Talia with G at her side. Giana scanned the room. Once her eyes found Gor, her face lit, her spirit along with it. She walked straight for him, wrapping her arms around his tapered torso, beaming up at him.

He pressed a kiss to her head, a tenderness I knew well, thanks to my own mate's affections. "You're alright," he whispered.

She nodded. "I actually kind of like her," she admitted.

"Sweetheart, please don't get attached to Lucy's mate," groaned Gor.

She laughed. "Isn't she kind of like my sister?" G asked.

Gor looked at Deus. After a moment of silence, they both began laughing.

"Father, I think she's right," said Deus.

"Which means, Lilith is also our sister," I added.

"What are the lot of you yapping about back here?" Came Lilith's voice from behind us.

"Oh, nothing much," I said, wrapping my arm around her shoulder. "Just how the three of us are sisters."

Lilith's body stiffened as if I had insulted her. "Excuse me?" she replied.

"Well," G explained. "You're a part of Satan, and we're a part of our mates. They're brothers, which makes us—"

"Sisters," I interrupted. "Speaking of, Deus and I have decided to get married tomorrow, and both of you are in the wedding. Congratulations."

"I decline," snapped Lilith.

"I am currently not accepting declinations. So, suck it up and wear the dress Frankie picked for you."

G jumped up and down, clapping and grinning from ear to ear. "It is an honor," she said, pulling me into a hug. "I am so excited. My first wedding as a bridesmaid."

"Congratulations are in order, I suppose," came Talia's voice from the doorway. Every eye in the room snapped towards her. She didn't seem to mind, appearing use to the attention. She strolled into Nonna's room as graceful and elegant as Lucifer himself. Her deep black strapless dress trailed to the floor, hugging every inch of her desirable body. Her hair was pulled away from her face, flowing in loose curls down her back. Her hair was more vibrant than I had seen, but her eyes … her eyes were entrancing. They pulled one in and refused to let go.

She walked straight through the crowd, stopping in front of Deus and me, flickering her eyes between us. She forced a small smile across her lips.

"I wish you two nothing but happiness," she said. At the same time, her presence slithered across the walls inside my mind.

"Your mate doesn't know, does he?" she said mentally.

"What are you talking about?" I replied, annoyed she could come and go inside my head as she pleased.

"About the sacrifice you will have to make to save them all. You discovered how to kill Lucifer, removing him permanently from this plane. You cracked their brotherly *code."*

"You know how to kill one of them?" I said, fear now flickering through me. If she tried to kill any of them, I'd end her.

Her laugh vibrated inside my head. It was unsettling. *"How many times must I assure you I mean you and yours no harm. I am only here for Lucifer. Both of our sacrifices are necessary to rid this world of the plague we have entertained for far too long."*

"Don't tell the others," I pleaded. *"Only my Nonna knows what I must do."*

"Your secrets are your own. They will not leave my lips."

"Thank you."

"I believe I promised you all a story," she said, scanning the room.

"You sure did," said Mammon, crashing into the couch. "Let's get on with it then."

Talia nodded, sitting in a high wingback chair near the fireplace. My family gathered around, eager to hear of her and Lucifer.

She sat straight with perfect posture, like a queen. With her hands folded in her lap, she took a deep breath and began.

"I was born into slavery under a cruel pharaoh, raised to follow the Jewish laws and customs. But I always had a rebellious spirit. Due to our poverty, as soon as my bleeding began, my parents tried to pawn me off on the first man that showed interest, but I made that very difficult.

"Any suitor that my parents brought before me, I made sure to ... discourage their interests. This enraged my family, and they eventually threw me out into the streets to fend for myself. About that time, the great Moses entered the picture and freed my people from our overlords. Thus, our journey to the promised land began.

"It was horrific. After escaping the Egyptians, we found ourselves traveling through the desert with little food or water. Children were starving, the elderly were dying, and there was nothing any of us could do. We held onto the promise of a utopia for as long as we could, until people started getting desperate. With no end in sight, some began to defect, going against Moses and his commandments.

"A year into traveling, I met Aradia in a town we passed. I had never seen or heard of magic before. Little did I know, my family possessed the gift but had chosen not to embrace it due to our religion. Aradia informed me of the power that coursed through my blood and then took me under her wing.

"She and her coven chose to travel with us through the desert, towards a hope that began to fade with each passing day. I watched Di and her coven do miraculous things with their gifts as I began to develop my own power. I became obsessed, hungering for more power. Aradia tried to teach me about the cycle of life and how sensitive this system of balance was, but I refused to listen. I practiced day and night, until I became just as talented as any other witch in her coven.

"Aradia and I were like sisters. My family had disowned me, so I found a new one. Back then, there was only one coven, but it wasn't a coven ... not really. It was a family. A community of amazing people with amazing talents and gifts.

"When Di met Cyrus, everything began to change. Their love—their bond—came before everything and everyone else. I was jealous of their connection. The other coven members felt neglected and unheard. Strife began to stir within the group, and some questioned Aradia's loyalty to the community she had created.

"Though, through their bond, our powers grew, the members feared for the future generations of witches and warlocks. How would they remain safe? Would the power eventually fade? How would our way of life continue? That was when Aradia and Cyrus developed the three-hundred-year cycle, to preserve the magic gifted to the community."

Talia paused for a moment, rubbing the white stone ring on her finger.

"Aradia loved me," she said softly, "like a sister. As I did her. She and Cyrus planned to run away together to live out their lives in peace. She began to prepare me to become the first vessel. By encasing her power in me, I would be a beacon of hope for our coven. Since I wasn't infused with Aradia's soul in the womb, the process I endured was ... painful, to say the least.

"It changed the very makeup of who I was ... what I am. Cyrus did the same, finding a man named Jonah who he thought to be worthy. Once the process was complete, Di and Cyrus thought Jonah and I would share in their bonded love, but I was not interested in the weak male

Cyrus had chosen. I was imbued with Aradia's power, finally possessing the thing I had always wanted. I wasn't going to waste it by succumbing to love and falling under the hand of a man. Then, I met him. Lucifer.

"During this time, Moses had received a command from God to invade and destroy Canaan. We started towards the sinful territory when, along the way, we inherited a new group of travelers. Luc was among them. He went by the name Samael, at first. As soon as I laid eyes on him, I knew something was different. I had never been interested in men nor what they could offer me, but he felt familiar. As if I had lost something that was now found.

"But, there was something missing behind his eyes. How could I have known it was his soul? He took interest in me right away, knowing I carried the power of a goddess. He passed as a common warlock. He would do small bouts of magic to impress those around him. He was a born leader, someone others naturally gravitated towards.

"Aradia never cared for him. She didn't trust him. But I on the other hand ... I trusted him completely. We began to spend one on one time together, slipping away from the others unnoticed. The more of ourselves we shared with each other, the brighter the light behind his eyes became. Little by little, his soul was returning to him because of the love that began to grow between us. We became inseparable.

"Aradia discouraged me from seeing him, but I would hear nothing of it. Three months in and I was desperately in love with him. By the time he finally told me his true identity, I didn't care. There was nothing in this world or any other that could make me not love him. My acceptance snapped the bond into place. We both felt it and knew instantly what it was. So, one night in the middle of summer, we slipped away from camp and were officially bound together as husband and wife." Her eyes briefly drifted to her left hand.

"As time progressed, he shared about his brothers and the falling out. He told me his plans and how he was aiming to become like God. I shared those aspirations, wanting him to get everything he desired in this life. Then, we began to build our own army here on earth. I was the one that came up with Obsidian, that concocted the plan to betray Aradia and convert half the coven to our side.

"But … something uneasy grew inside of me as we moved forward with our vision. I had this feeling of uncertainty and eventually, paranoia. So, I formed a plan to insure I would remain safe. The new coven members I converted to our side signed a blood contract, pledging their loyalty to me and me alone. Luc didn't know about the pact, but I made sure the coven would obey me above anyone or anything else.

"Aradia was heartbroken, deeply betrayed. She and the coven members that remained loyal to her attempted to stop us before we reached Canaan, but I was too strong. As I was the first to command witch, goddess, and demonic powers, she didn't stand a chance. And with Lucifer by my side and our coven of hybrids, we slaughtered them." Her eyes dropped to her hands as she twirled her ring around her finger. "I was the one that killed Cyrus. After that, Aradia no longer felt she had a purpose in this world.

"Once their gods were gone, the remaining coven members fled, fleeing across the continent to hide from us. We began hunting them down one by one, absorbing their powers to fuel our mission. The ones that escaped us apparently developed the seven covens you now descend from.

"We resided in Canaan, making it impossible for Moses to enact his lord's plans of destruction. That city was where we first developed blood magic. Dark magic, mixed from my own talents and the demonic power Luc and I possessed. We were happy there, for a time, surrounded by others who were fearless and determined. But it wasn't enough … I wasn't enough.

"After a few months of exploration and conquering nearby villages, I could feel Luc getting restless. He still wanted more. He wanted to be like his Father. Omniscient. Omnipotent. He started pulling away from me emotionally and physically. He began to keep things from me. The bond between us was thinning. I could no longer feel him down the line that had connected our minds and souls. I was heartbroken, but I knew my mate. I knew how his mind worked and what he was capable of. So, I began to prepare.

"That was when I ordered Obsidian to create the cage that would hold him once he was trapped in Hell. They told me what the gate needed to power it and contain him. I was more than happy to oblige, but a part of me never thought it would come to that—that I would be forced to use the cage to contain my mate and all his glory. He was the love of my life. We would find our way back to one another.

"Then, one night I could feel that something had changed in him. He shifted us away from the camp into a nearby cave. He could barely look at me. He wouldn't even touch me." She took a deep breath and straightened. Her perfect poise fell, revealing her pain and heartache only for a moment.

"He told me that the key to him obtaining his power had been right in front of him all along. The way to become like his Father was to absorb my power, possessing all three gifts in one vessel. But in doing so … I would have to die the ultimate death. Merging our two souls together would be the end of me.

"It was his Father's morbid way of punishing him for break His heart. For choosing his greed and pride over the love of God.

"God had created a mate for Lucifer that possessed the power he so desperately craved, to force him to choose his lust for divinity over his own heart. I remember his face like it was yesterday. He was wrecked. I had never seen Luc cry before that moment, but he did. He was on his knees before me, begging for forgiveness for what he would have to do. Telling me how much I meant to him. How happy I made him. How much he loved me.

"I couldn't believe what I was hearing. My one and only mate, my reason for being, was willing to sacrifice me. He would end my life to possess power that he didn't even need. Together, we could have ruled the world, conquered anyone who stood in our way ... but that wasn't enough for him.

"I begged him to reconsider. He struggled with the decision, crying in my arms as we held onto each other like our lives depended on it, but I knew my mate. We were together one last time inside of that cave, our coupling more intimate and passionate than anything I had ever experienced.

"I thought that our love would somehow change his mind. That the happiness he found when we were together would be worth sacrificing all else for." She paused and laughed at herself softly. "I was such a stupid girl, so blinded by emotions." Her eyes flickered to mine. "I see so much of who I was in you. I hope, for your sake, your path takes a different route."

"I would never do anything to hurt her," growled Deus.

Talia smiled. "Not willingly." She looked around at the six princes. "But all of you have the capability of hurting those you love the most. All it takes is for someone to remove those precious souls of yours." Her eyes fell to me once more. "Something I know you've already experienced, sweet Seren."

"Back to the story," I snapped.

She nodded. "Where was I? Oh, yes. After we made love, we fell asleep in each other's arms. I woke to a snap in my chest, more painful and devastating than anything I had ever encountered. It felt like a part of my soul had been ripped out of me with a clawed hand. I looked around for Lucifer, but he was no longer beside me. When I moved deeper into the cave, I stumbled upon him leaning against the stone wall, panting and covered in blood.

"I rushed to him, worried he had been attacked. But when he turned his eyes to mine, the light that had once been there, that had been so full of love, was gone. He smiled at me, wiping the blood from his mouth. I knew in that moment what he had done ... he had removed his own soul, so he would be able to kill me."

"Fuck," grumbled Belz.

"He lunged for me," she continued, "but I was too fast. I shifted to my coven and then together, we shifted to an isolated location that I had arranged just in case something like this were to happen. My coven began to build the cage, but there wasn't enough time. Before it could be completed, Luc and his followers found us.

"I shifted and cloaked a few members along with the cage to another location where he would never think to look. I stayed behind to buy them time, knowing what came next. Even if I died, he would still have access to me, since he was the King of Hell, and my soul would return to the realm from which I was forged. So, I cast a spell to send my soul into Purgatory instead— somewhere he, nor any of his brothers, would be able to access. Thanks to the human part of my soul that remained, I was able to enter that plane. Then I slit my own throat, making sure I took my powers with me."

The room was uncomfortably silent while we processed her story. Her mate had tried to kill her, the very person she was made for. It was horrifying to think of Deus willingly parting with his soul to kill me.

"I would never..." his voice abruptly said in my mind. *"I love you more than anything. Including myself. Please do not ever doubt that."*

The memory of him sacrificing himself to save me flashed before my eyes. I looked at him and smiled, taking his hand in mine.

"I know," I replied. I looked back at Talia, my heart swelling with empathy. I reached for her in my mind, feeling for her slithering cold presence.

"I am so sorry you had to endure that," I said softly. *"Regardless of who your mate is ... I couldn't imagine."*

"Thank you," was the only thing she said.

"Where is the cage?" asked Satan, his tone getting to the point.

"In the mountain of Jebel Musa," she answered.

"The mountain Moses received the commandments?" asked Frankie.

Talia nodded. "I can feel it call to me. It's still there. I will need volunteers to transport the prison to Hell."

"So, we retrieve this cage," said Mammon, "somehow without alerting Lucy, transport the thing to Hell, again, somehow without alerting Hell's master ... then what? You just willingly sacrifice yourself to power it?"

"That is correct," she answered.

"What do you want in returned?" asked Deus.

"To take away the thing he loves the most ... so he knows how I felt in that moment he chose his power over me."

I heard a sniffle behind me and turned to see G crying profusely. She was in Gor's arms. I didn't draw attention to her.

"She can feel it," Gor said softly.

"Feel what?" asked Frankie.

"Talia's pain," G answered. "The truth ... she's telling the truth."

"Well," said Belz in a cheerfully sarcastic tone as he stood, fixing the cuffs of his sleeves. "Looks like we're going spelunking then."

CHAPTER TWENTY-NINE

Talia agreed to give Belz and Mammon the exact location of the cage. After which, she excused herself, claiming to need rest. Giana was still crying, unable to gather herself. She explained the feelings she could read off Talia. The pain, the longing, the betrayal—it was more powerful and more devastating than she could have imagined. There were no words to describe what she had endured.

I commended Talia for her poise. Without G, you wouldn't have been able to guess that Talia had any love or care left for Lucifer. Gor took his mate back to their room. Levi and Deus followed them out, leaving the Salvo women alone.

Nonna sat in her normal chair by the large window, resting her chin on her fist. We joined her in silence, still reeling from all we had discovered in the past twenty-four hours. Finally, Nonna ran her hands over her face, turning to face us. She looked between Frankie and me.

"Why couldn't you two have picked nice warlock boys?" Nonna said, her face worried.

"Mamma," said Annalise, "Deus has already proven he would rather die than live without Seren."

"Levi has done the same with Frankie," added Thora.

Nonna shook her head. "Bah, they're demons."

"So am I," I said softly. "At least a part of me is."

"And speaking from personal experience," Annalise said, "you don't know what you're capable of until you are soulless. It could happen to any of us."

"The question is," intervened Aunt Thora, "do we trust Talia or not?"

"I do," I said, still trying to process how she went through all of that and survived. "G doesn't sense any plot or ill feelings towards any of us either."

"Gods, that poor girl," Nonna said.

"Poor girl," snapped Thora. "She sided with Lucifer and killed Cyrus and most of her coven. There is nothing poor about her. She got what she deserved."

"When you're bonded," I said, picking my words carefully, "the need to please your mate, to protect them and everything they hold dear, is overwhelming. I understand how she could be blinded by the bond."

"And let's not forget who her mate is," added Frankie. "Mr. Persuasion himself."

"I would do almost anything for Deus," I admitted. "Sacrifice anything and anyone to guarantee his safety. The bond is ... it's animalistic. Untamable. I can't describe it, but it's all consuming. And don't forget I've met Aradia ... she's a bitch."

My family began laughing, their moods lightening.

"Our lives are never dull, that's for sure," said Thora.

"But tomorrow," Frankie said, wrapping her arms around me. "We celebrate something very special."

I laughed. "It's small, right?"

"Deus has thought of everything," my mother assured me, coming to my side. She moved a loose piece of hair behind my ear. "Can I just say,

I am so happy to get to witness you marry the love of your life."

I leaned into her. "I am too, Mom. Speaking of," I said, pulling back to look at her. "I was wondering if you would do the honor of giving me away?"

Her eyes widened, her mouth slackening as if she couldn't find the words.

"Really?" she whispered, tears beginning to well in her eyes. "You wouldn't prefer Nonna or Thora?"

Nonna came over to us, taking each of our hands in her own. "The bond between a mother and her daughter," she said with a loving smile, "is untouchable. Incomparable." She focused her gaze on Annalise. "I should know."

Mom turned her eyes back to me. "If that is what you wish, I would be honored." She pulled me into a hug as we both allowed our silent tears to fall.

"Well then," Aunt Thora said, approaching us with Frankie at her side. "Onto the bachelorette party."

"Oh no," I said, shaking my head. "I am exhausted. There is no way—"

"Oh, stop your babbling," snapped Nonna.

"Exactly," nodded Frankie.

"You are going," Aunt Thora demanded. "This was my one job, and I have excelled, if I do say so myself."

Frankie scoffed. "You mean besides being Belz's plus one to the wedding?"

Mom glared at her sister. "Not you too?" she begged.

"I have agreed to no such thing," Aunt Thora replied, trying to hide her smile. "Even though, he did ask."

"What is it with these demon princes and my girls?" gasped Nonna.

"I'm sure Mammon would be open to being your date," I said, bumping my elbow into Mom's.

"Oh, no," she replied. "No more demons for me. Regardless of how devastatingly beautiful they might be."

"Alright," Thora said, taking Frankie and Nonna's hand in hers. "Seren, sweetheart, I need you to shift us to Vegas."

"Vegas!" I gasped.

"Yes," she replied. "We have a high-stakes poker game in ten minutes that we can't be late for."

"What makes you think I know how to play poker?" I asked. Thora looked to my mom. Annalise bit the side of her lip and shrugged.

"I'm a bit of a card shark," she admitted.

Frankie and I looked at each other and laughed. A moment later, the door opened, revealing G and Lilith.

"Glad we're not late," said G.

"Time for the ultimate male destruction," Lilith said in a vengeful tone, squeezing in between my mother and Nonna. We all looked at her. "What? There's nothing more precious than taking money from an unsuspecting male. They get so hostile and bent out of shape. I love the way their embarrassment smells as I strip away all they've acquired."

A moment of silence passed before we laughed. "You are nothing like I had expected," admitted Nonna.

"I am going to take that as a compliment," she replied.

Before I shifted, I slid down the bridge into Deus's mind, his soothing darkness enveloping me. *"Off to a bachelorette party, it seems,"* I said in our heads.

"My brothers appear to have the same idea for our evening," he replied.

"Is it wrong that I would rather spend the entire night in your arms

instead?"

A soft caress slid down my spine. *"We will have eternity for that. Though, I can't help but agree I'd prefer your naked body instead of the company of my brothers."* He sent a flash of a memory he had of me, riding on top of him back at the beach house. My core warmed and my toes curled. It was as if I could feel the sensation of him buried deep inside of me. God how he fit so perfectly.

"Devil," I whispered.

He laughed. *"When it comes to you, always. Have fun, my love. I will see you tomorrow at the altar."*

I smiled at the thought of becoming his wife. I turned back to the others; they stared at me intently.

"Checking in with your fiancé?" asked Frankie playfully.

"And if I were?" I replied.

She laughed. "Tonight, dear cousin, is your last night of freedom. Whatever happens in Vegas stays between the seven of us, never to be spoken of again. Are we all clear?"

"Fuck yeah," replied Lilith.

"Absolutely," G said.

Thora and my mother laughed in unison while Nonna rolled her eyes.

"Alright, bride-to-be," said Frankie, "take us away to Sin City."

"I am never drinking again," G said, then hurled for the fourth time inside the bowl of the toilet. Lilith held her hair back, clearly annoyed.

"The hell you aren't," Lilith said. "We need to work on that tolerance of yours. Especially if we're all going to be stuck together for eternity."

"Aradia, help me," Nonna said, stumbling out of the back bedroom of the hotel suite.

Frankie groaned on the couch next to me. Somehow, we both hadn't made it to our room. "Mmgrfoooo," she mumbled.

"What?" I barely got out.

"Food. Coffee," she said, drooling on the couch cushion. Mom came from the other room in the back of the suit.

"Where's Thora?" asked Nonna. About that time, a man I didn't remember or recognize passed by my mother, heading for the door. He looked at all of us, smiled and nodded, and left without a single word. Frankie and I exchanged shocked looks.

"Where in blasted hell did he come from?" she asked.

My mother shrugged. "I don't remember bringing him home," she admitted.

Thora came up behind her, lacing her arm through hers. "I do," she said, wiggling her eyebrows. "Kept my ass up all night with that racket."

I smiled, biting back the laugh that wanted to escape.

"Under the same roof as your mother," Nonna snapped.

"Mamma," said Aunt Thora. "It wouldn't be the first time, and I am sure it isn't going to be the last."

Nonna began speaking Latin as she headed for the kitchen.

Mom joined us on the large sectional couch, brushing my hair out of my face. "Ready for today?"

"Do I look ready?" I asked, feeling dizzy, sick, swollen, bloated ... all the above.

"Beautiful as ever," commented Thora.

Mom chuckled. "Nothing a little espresso and makeup can't fix."

"How are you two still standing?" asked Frankie, rolling to her back. "You both drank us under the table last night."

"We've had a bit more experience than you younglings," replied Mom.

"You two are nothing compared to the trouble your aunt and I use to be," Thora said, pulling Frankie up to a seated position.

"And everyone thinks I'm the bad influence," Annalise said, rolling her eyes.

"Oh, please," replied Aunt Thora. "Don't sit there and play the innocent lamb. No one will believe that for a single second. Any bad habits I've formed, I've learned from you."

"Water," gasped Giana, sitting across from us. "I need water."

"Big baby," mumbled Lilith.

"Can demons not get drunk?" asked Mom.

"Oh, we can," she replied. "But someone out of this bunch needed to stay alert."

"Mother Lilith," I said mockingly. Frankie laughed, then grabbed her head in pain.

"Don't you start with that shit," Lilith snapped. "I don't care if it is your wedding or not, I will kick your ass from here all the way to the altar if I have to. And we both know I can without even breaking a sweat."

"Down girl, down," I said, raising my hands to a defensive position.

"Espresso, water, and ibuprofen for all," Nonna announced, carrying a tray. "I also toasted some bread to help soak up all the liquor."

"Thank Aradia," G grumbled, blindly reaching for the bread. Lilith rolled her eyes, snatching a piece from the tray and handing it to her so she wouldn't knock everything over.

"Thanks Mamma," Thora and Mom said in unison. Nonna smiled at her girls. I handed Frankie hers before taking my espresso and pills.

"Ugh, shut up," G whined while she lay on the couch across from us.

"Uh, excuse me, but no one was talking," Lilith said with attitude.

"I'm not talking to you," she replied. "I'm talking to Gor. He's yapping away in my head, demanding I tell him where we are."

"You've already learned to block him out?" I asked, surprised.

"Frankie helped me, but yes. He started sneaking into my head right when you left for Purgatory. I thought it was just a demon prince thing. I didn't know it was linked to the bond. And since we've officially accepted the bond, things have gotten ... intense."

"My link with Deus started with the deal we made when he saved Frankie. I didn't know it had anything to do with the mating bond."

"Two parts of a whole, becoming one," said Lilith sarcastically. "You get to hear and feel all of them, and vice-versa."

"That's," whispered G, "unnerving."

"Welcome to the club," Lilith said, sipping her espresso. "The stronger the bond grows and your power along with it, the deeper the connection becomes rooted."

"Seren, for the love of whatever god is listening, will you please drop your shields and let Deus know you're alright? He's berating Gor for updates." She popped her head up, staring at Lilith. "Is Satan not bugging you?"

"Oh, he knows exactly where we are, though he knows better than to cross me," she replied with a proud smile. "He's keeping his mouth shut."

"Uho," Nonna said, piercing her lips together. "Sounds like you've got some explaining to do."

Frankie started laughing. "He's not going to like the whole stripper part of last night, is he?"

"Gee," I replied sarcastically. "I don't know. Let's ask Prince Envy how he feels about it, shall we?"

"You wouldn't," she snapped, lunging forward.

"I'm not going to say a damn word about any of it," I replied. "Do you really think I want Deus to burn this entire city to the ground?"

Frankie turned towards Lilith and G. "You two keep your mouths shut," she barked.

Lilith huffed. "Sweetheart, I've been involved with a demon prince long before you were even thought of. Do you really think I would be so stupid as to let him know every detail of what goes on in my life?"

"I'm newly bonded," said G innocently. "I don't want to piss him off just yet."

"Good," nodded Frankie. "We're all in agreement. Nothing about last night, or this morning, leaves Vegas."

In my mind, Deus's presence swarmed outside my wall like a storm. I had snapped his door shut as soon as I realized we were headed into an all-male strip show. Mom was right, Aunt Thora was crazier than I knew.

The night had started off well behaved. Mom and Nonna had wiped a table of blackjack, winning over $500,000 apiece. We proceeded to dinner, then gambled on the floor. A party bus picked us up, taking us through the city as we drank until none of us could stand up straight. We ended up at the strip show where I honestly can't remember what happened. From there, we attended a show at three in the morning hosted by some DJ I had never heard of.

Champagne, glitter, and confetti still clung to my skin. To top the night off, we had ended up in the middle of the desert, dancing naked around a bonfire. *How witchy of us*, I thought. Thus, the question remained ... where had Mother picked up the man who scurried from our room this morning?

"The driver," Frankie exclaimed, snapping her fingers. "You slept with our driver?"

My mom shrugged. "What?" she answered. "He was young and agile. You can't blame a girl, can you?"

Thora, Frankie, and I began to laugh. Nonna rolled her eyes.

"I'm starting to see why the Salvo women have a reputation," commented G.

Frankie threw a pillow at her face. "You shut your mouth. You're just as bad as any of us. You were trying to get in Gor's pants before you were even breathing again."

"I couldn't help it," she replied. "The bond and all."

"Oh, right," I said playfully. "The fact that he's gorgeous with a side of mysterious had nothing to do with it. If I recall, you used to sneak into his room and spy on him when he was getting out of the shower."

"That was private," she said, her eyes going wide.

We all began laughing. "Nothing in this circle is private, child," commented Nonna. "Now, if everyone can manage to stand upright, I think we have quite the day ahead of us."

"Our girl's getting married," Aunt Thora said with a smile.

"For the last and final time," Frankie added.

"Ha, ha," I replied. "You just love to remind me of that."

"Alright you two," said Mom, "enough squabbling. Time to get going." She stood, pulling my limp body along with her. We gathered in a circle, clasping hands as I shifted us back to Castle Salvo.

CHAPTER THIRTY

We landed in Nonna's room. The shift was not an easy one. G slammed into the floor upon arrival, taking Lilith with her. I stumbled back, but Mom caught me before I hit the ground. Nonna, Aunt Thora, and Frankie weren't so lucky as they fell back, all landed next to one another in a fit of laughter.

"I'm too old for this shit," Nonna gasped, still laughing.

"Oh, shut it Mamma," replied Thora. "Knowing you, you'll outlive us all."

"Aradia, save me," Nonna answered.

Mom turned to me, brushing my tangled hair away from my face. "You smell like a brothel," she whispered.

"Because we were basically in one," I answered with a smile.

She laughed. "Go shower and take a nap. I'll wake you when it's time to get ready for your big night." She pressed a kiss to my head. "I love you, little bean."

I smiled, pulling her into a hug. "I love you too, Mamma."

I stepped into the hall, staying close to the wall while my head spun. Once I got to my room, I closed the door, but before I could turn around, a hard body slammed into me, pinning me to the surface. My body instantly lit to life, recognizing the presence. I smiled; my face pressed against the cold wood of the door.

A finger traced up the curve of my side, grazing over my breast until his fingers wrapped around my neck. He flipped me around so we were face to face and brushed his nose against mine. His grip tightened, pinning me to the door by my throat. I bit my lip in response. He nuzzled his face against mine, sniffing. His eyes glowed a vibrant shade of red.

"Why, in the fuck, dear fiancé, do I smell other men on you?" he growled.

I bit back the grin that threatened to give me away. "I'm not sure what you mean?"

He slammed his free hand against the door, sending a crack through the wood. "You blocked me out."

"I did."

"Why?"

"Because I wanted a moment of privacy," I admitted.

Before he could respond, I unleashed my own power on him, freeing me from his grasp and sending us both across the room. Now I was the one that pinned him to the wall by his throat. I laced my shadows around his arms, binding them to the wall while I trailed my free hand down his chest until I reached his hips and then ... my favorite part.

"Do you really think," I said in a heavy and sensual voice, "that I would ever take another after having this," I said, tightening my grip on the hardness that fought to escape the restraints of his pants.

He smiled. "Did you use our power while you were in Vegas?"

I shrugged. "A little. It enticed quite the show. I never realized how horny humans were until now. Until I could feel their lust, their ... animalistic instincts, fighting to be free."

"No one touch you?"

"No one, my love," I answered.

He broke free from my restraints, crushing me against him, pressing his lips to mine. The kiss was needy. Desperate. I clawed my nails into his back, wanting, needing more.

He shifted us to the bathroom, ripping my clothes off my body. The shower started as he pulled me against his naked body. He hoisted me up by my bare ass, wrapping my legs around his waist before diving his cock deep inside of me. There was nothing passionate or loving about this fuck. It was raw and full of hunger. I yelled out, biting down on his shoulder as he slammed me into the tile of the shower. The room filled with steam while he thrusted in and out of me at a pace that sent my entire body into a quivering mess.

He sucked and nipped and clawed at my skin, devouring every inch of me he could possess. I tangled my fingers through his dark hair, pulling his mouth from my neck before taking it with my own. Our tongues thrusted in and out of each other's mouths, tasting and savoring every moment. His body lit with gooseflesh as I dragged my fingers down his smooth, silken skin. He pressed me harder up against the wall just before he released, sending himself over the edge, taking me with along for the ride.

I screamed, fireworks exploding behind my eyes. The walls around us shook. Darkness and constellations exploded from our magic. The mirrors in the bathroom shattered and the lights flickered. He gasped, continuing to thrust inside of me until he filled me completely with his ecstasy. My legs shook from the pleasure, still locked around his waist.

He held onto my body, slowly lowering me back to the ground. He pressed soft kisses to my face as his fingers stroked my sensitive skin. Without a word, he washed me from head to toe, taking time to savor the sensation and sight of me. I looked upon the man that would soon become my husband. There was truly no word to describe what he meant to me.

After, he wrapped me in a towel, shifting us to the bed and then tucked me in. He pressed a tender kiss to my lips, brushing the back of his knuckles down my cheek. "Get some sleep, my love," he whispered. "The next time I see you, you will solely belong to me."

I smiled at him, kissing the top of his hand. "I was yours long before I ever met you, Deus. And I am proud of that."

He went still. In that moment, he looked so vulnerable and exposed. My fearless, brave, demon prince ...

"You are truly the greatest gift I have ever received. I will cherish each moment of this life with you, and the next. I love you, Seren."

"And I, you, Asmodeus." I closed my eyes, letting my tired mind fall into the darkness that was now my home.

"It's time," a voice whispered. A tickling sensation fluttered over my cheek. I pried my eyes open to see my mother's beautiful face staring back at me, bearing a soft and loving smile. "How are you feeling?"

I stretched out across the cool sheets. An image of my devastatingly handsome fiancé flashed into my mind and I smiled. "Excited," I said, the emotions hitting me in that moment. Tears filled my eyes. I was too tired and raw to try and fight them.

Annalise wiped them away from my cheek as they fell. "What is it, little bean?"

I took a moment, sitting up against the headboard as she took my hand in hers. "I'm just … I'm just so happy. I know we have a lot to still handle, but … is it selfish of me to feel like this? To be this happy when hundreds, possibly thousands will die?"

"Hey, hey," mom said, taking my face in her hands. She wiped away the remaining tears. "You deserve *every* moment of happiness this day brings you, and more after. You have sacrificed so much to get to this point—to find the kind of love many will never know. And you've literally gone to the ends of the earth to protect that love. This day is about you and him. Nothing else. Today is yours, my daughter." She pulled me into her arms as I laughed with happiness.

"I love him so much, Mamma."

"I know, my bambina. I know."

Nonna, Frankie, Aunt Thora, and Gianna took over my room as the preparations began. Makeup littered every surface. Hairspray wafted through the air. Laughter bounced from one wall to another. I smiled so much my cheeks hurt. Jokes were made, stories were told, and memories were created. The perfect beginning to a perfect fairytale wedding. My mother was right, today was about Deus and me. Nothing else. No one else. The world could wait.

I stood in front of the floor-length mirror surrounded by my family. "Oh, bambina," gasped Nonna with tears in her eyes. "You are breathtaking."

I smiled, nerves beginning to creep along my spine.

"Truly a vision," added Aunt Thora.

"Elegant, with a hint of lust," Frankie winked.

"A queen," added G.

"You're perfect," my mother whispered, kissing me on the head.

"Thank you all," I replied. "I couldn't have made this day happen without you."

The door banged against the wall as Lilith barged into the room. Her hair was fashioned into tight curls, pinned away from her face. The black satin dress hung on her curvaceous body, her well-endowed chest spilling from the top. Though she was the vision of beauty, her face was firm and fierce.

"Wow," commented Frankie, looking her up and down.

G stepped forward. "You look—"

"Ridiculous," Lilith interrupted. "How is one supposed to fight in this thing?" she asked, pulling at the sides of her dress.

"I was going to say gorgeous," finished G.

"And tonight is not about fighting," added Thora, making her way over to Lilith.

"It's about celebrating and having fun," finished Mom.

"You look magnificent," I said, approaching her. "Satan won't be able to take his eyes off you."

"Speaking of," added Frankie, "has he agreed to come? Ya know, since he's made it oh so clear that he's unaligned and all."

Lilith rolled her eyes and stomped over to the mirror, pulling at the bust of her dress in aggravation. "He declined the invitation ... at first. But then, I threatened to cut off his balls and feed them to him piece by piece. That seemed to change his mind, though, I am not sure if it was fear, or the thought of me fondling his most precious member that got him to reconsider. Either way, he will be there."

We all remained still, unsure of how to respond.

"And here I thought Levi and I were kinky," Frankie muttered.

"Looks like we have about thirty minutes to spare," said Nonna, looking at her watch.

I turned back to the mirror, taking myself in. "Would you all mind if I have a few moments alone?" I asked, needing some air.

"Are you okay?" asked Frankie, searching my face.

"Yes, of course. I'm just ... I just need a moment is all."

"Of course, sweetheart," said Thora, wrapping her arms around Frankie's shoulders.

"Our escort will be here in fifteen minutes," said Gianna.

"Great," I replied. "I'll meet you all downstairs in the foyer."

After everyone filed out of my room, I turned back to the mirror. The dress was perfect. Just as I had envisioned. Made entirely of red lace, it hugged my body sensually, plunging low in the front towards my bellybutton. The sleeves began at the very edges of my shoulders and trailed down to points in the center of the top of my hands. The back was completely exposed to the curve of my bum. The train was long and magnificent, catching every ray of light in the room as it sparkled and glistened.

My hair was left down and flowed naturally. It was curled in large waves, heavier on one side with a beautiful gold comb tucked in the other. My makeup was dramatic with a long cat eye and a deep wine red lip. Diamonds hung low from my ears, strung together with gold. I wasn't the vision of a typical bride, that was for sure ... but I was the vision of his bride. The bride of Lust.

I smiled, the overwhelming flutter of nerves stirring again deep in my stomach. I sat at my vanity, trying to calm myself. My attention caught on the small wooden drawer. I pulled it open and removed the black box that contained the two lives I had once thought to be my destiny. I opened the lid, revealing the engagement rings given to me by Tony and Orion.

I pulled out Tony's first. I thought what we had was true love. Even with his lack of judgment, Tony was a good warlock. He deserved to be happy and to find someone who loved him, but it could never have been me. I realized that now.

Then, I pulled out Orion's ring. The black diamond was beautifully set within the silver band. How happy and hopeful he had been when he'd given it to me. A tear fell from my eye. I slid the ring on. The paper that accompanied the ring had read:

Little dove, place the ring on your finger and repeat these words. "Septamor avalous".

"Septamor avalous," I whispered.

Flashed of his memories began: the first time we met, the first time we touched, our day at the festival, our training sessions—the hope and excitement. The love that began to grow inside of him, along with desire.

I pulled the ring from my finger, unable to continue. This band represented a future where he and I would have led the covens into our Renaissance: a future that would never happen. He died so I could have this chance: a future full of love and completion. Regardless of how short that future might be, I wasn't going to waste it.

"I love you, Orion."

I put the rings back into the box and placed them inside the drawer. I examined the ring Deus had gifted me, almost identical to his own, except bigger, somehow. Our love was incomparable. I hadn't known love until he came into my life.

That first day we met in the woods, he had made me so enraged and frustrated; but at the same time, I couldn't look away. He was captivating … even then.

I stood from the chair, blotting my face before shifting down to meet the others in the foyer. It was time. Time for me to take hold of my future. To pledge my life to the man that was perfectly created … just for me.

When the fog dissipated around me, my family stood by the door, joined by Gor. He took one look at me and beamed from ear to ear. I couldn't help but blush as he approached. He placed a hand on either side of my shoulders, looking down at me with endearment.

"You look absolutely divine, little goddess," he said softly. "My brother isn't going to be able to control himself."

I laughed. "That's the idea," I replied. "And thank you for the compliment."

He nodded, turning back to the group. "Are we ready to attend a demonic wedding?" he asked playfully. Everyone smiled.

"The faster we get this over with, the fast I get out of this dress," barked Lilith,.

We gathered in a circle, and Gor shifted us to the hidden location of my wedding, which only a few others knew about. When I opened my eyes, we were in a small hunting lodge filled with luxurious furniture and artwork. The log walls reached high into the air. I turned around to see a floor-to-ceiling window displaying the perfect image of a winter wonderland.

Snow-covered mountains stretched as far as the eye could see, sprinkled with patches of evergreen trees. The sky sparkled with every shade of blue, purple, and green. Stars shot across the night sky, creating paths of lingering light. It was the most breathtaking thing I'd ever seen.

"Aurora Borealis," I whispered.

"Deus thought you might like this as the backdrop for your wedding," said Frankie, approaching my side.

"Where are we?" I asked.

"Swedish Lapland," answered Gor. "Now, I believe the ceremony is about to begin. Everyone, take your places." He pressed a soft kiss to my head. "I'll see you out there, sis." He winked and left the cabin.

Nonna and Thora took the lead in the procession. Lilith lined up behind them, followed by Giana, and then Frankie. My mother joined me at the back. She handed me a bouquet made of aster, lavender, and sage.

"The purple reminded me of the shade your eyes turn when you access your goddess," she explained.

"They're beautiful. Thank you." I looped my arm through hers and took a breath, focusing on the door ahead that would lead me to my future.

One after another, each of the girls stepped through the door and allowed it to shut behind them. Frankie turned to me right before her turn and blew me a kiss, then strutted down the aisle like she was the showstopper.

My mom's grip on me tightened, her eyes filling with tears. "Are you ready?" she whispered.

"Absolutely," I answered, more confident about this decision than any that had come before. As I gazed into the face of my beautiful mother, the doors opened. I turned, taking in the magical world Deus and Frankie had composed.

Soft snow covered the ground and fell in large flakes around us, but there was no bite from the winter breeze. Pillars of perfectly contained cylinders of fire shot from the ground into the air, red and black flames lapping and twirling around one another in a beautifully orchestrated dance. The sound of a full orchestra strummed to life. I recognized the music instantly: the performance he and I attended during our first and only real date in Austria.

Red rose peddles were scattered across the snow, mixed with green pine needles. Every few feet, arches of bright white and yellow light stretched high above, releasing sparks of yellow light that gave the illusion it was raining starlight. It was truly the most beautiful thing I had ever seen.

Wooden chairs lined either side of the aisle, filled with only the closest people to us. On one side, I noted the faces of Roric, Adrianna, Loriana, Tyler, Joseph, Gabby, Bella, and Antonio. All Deus's brothers sat on the other side, along with Talia. Nonna and Aunt Thora were in the first row.

Then, at the front, stood the most devastatingly handsome version of Asmodeus I had ever laid eyes on. My heart skipped and a smile erupted from my lips. A silk edged lining adorned his perfectly tailored tux, threaded with red stitching. A red pocket square with gold details popped from the black background. His pants hugged every inch of his muscular legs. His hands were crossed in front of him. His hair shined, brushed to one side as usual. But that smile ...

His face was the definition of perfection. His bright white teeth flashed as I stepped into the snow. Two deep dimples highlighted the sides of his cheeks. His icy blue eyes flashed from red to blue as he drank me in. I noted that adorable little beauty mark on his upper cheek. He was breathtaking.

My mom pulled me alongside her as we began our descent to the small platform which had a beautiful arch filled with greenery for Deus and me to stand underneath while we exchanged our vows.

My smile never once left my face. No one mattered but him. I felt the warm tears of happiness slide down my cheeks with every step that brought me closer to my destiny. Finally, I stood at the bottom of the platform, unable to take my eyes off him. Without warning, he was in front of me, slamming his mouth into mine with a kiss of desperation.

The crowd around us begin to laugh before he pulled back, his eyes glowing red. I giggled with surprise, as did he.

"Should I just skip all the hard work I put into these vows then?" Gor asked sarcastically, looking down at us.

"On with the formalities, brother," Deus replied, never taking his eyes from me. "*I'm going to take my time peeling that dress from your delicious body tonight, my love,*" he whispered into my mind. "*I hope that nap energized you for what I have prepared.*"

I laughed again, feeling the heat rush to my cheeks.

"Who gives this woman to this man?" asked Gor.

Nonna, Aunt Thora, and Frankie joined my mother's side. "We do," they said in unison. I smiled at each of them, one more beautiful than the next.

"I am so proud to be a part of this family," I whispered, allowing the tears to fall. "Of this legacy."

"We are the ones who have been blessed, bambina," said Nonna, kissing each of my cheeks.

"You were the missing piece that our family needed," said Aunt Thora. "Our bright light." She kissed me.

"My soulmate," whispered Frankie, her face full of tears. "The piece of myself I didn't know I was missing." *Kiss.*

"You are my world, little bean," said my mother. "You are my everything." She kissed me and then turned her attention to Deus. "I am giving you the greatest gift you will ever receive. Never forget how fortunate you are. Never forget how much she is worth."

"You have my word," he said, kissing my mother on the cheek before she took her seat next to Nonna.

I handed Frankie my flowers and then joined Deus and Gor on the platform. Gor smiled at the two of us. He opened his mouth to speak—

"Whose bright idea was it to ask sloth to conduct the ceremony?" I heard Mammon say playfully.

"Father, we're going to be here well into the next decade," added Satan, grumbled, his face stern and emotionless.

Our guests erupted into laughter. Gor's face went taut with anger. I gave him a reassuring smile. He took a breath and began.

As Gor spoke, everything around me faded away while I lost myself in the eyes of my mate. All I could think about was touching him. Holding him. Tasting him. God, I wanted to taste him. I would never get enough of his glorious body or talents.

My heart swelled as I thought back to every selfless thing he had ever done for me. The shameless taunting and teasing. The time he gave me as my mind and heart healed. The training. A place to call home. A reason to look towards the future. A reason to hope.

Our story replayed in my head, the story that led me to this beautiful moment, where I would officially become his in every way that mattered. Life meant nothing if Deus wasn't in my a part of it. He was truly my definition of love.

Gor got to the part where we exchanged rings. Deus slid two gold bands around the large red oval incasing the stone. The bands were lined with diamonds, catching the light from the flickering flames that surrounded us. I slid a gold band onto his left hand that contained a strip of red in the center, matching my own.

Gor tied our hands with a piece of fabric, reciting a beautiful poem. Deus rubbed the back of my hand with his thumb, a soft smile never leaving his lips. Once Gor had finished, Deus reached out his hand, gently caressing the side of my face. "Tell me every terrible thing you ever did and let me love you anyways," he whispered.

I smiled back at him. "And I would ask you to show me your flaws, but I fear it would make me love you ... more than I already do." We exchanged our I do's, promising to love and cherish one another for eternity.

"And finally," Gor said, slamming his book shut, taking a breath. "By the power vested in me by—well, Hell— I now pronounce you husband and wife. You may kiss your bride."

Deus didn't wait another second. I was in his arms, his fingers digging into me as we kissed. Darkness, stars, and red light all flashed above us while our friends and family cheered and clapped with excitement and happiness. I allowed myself to melt into him.

And then two became one.

He pulled away slowly, his eyes heavy with love and joy. He laughed.

"The Prince of Lust," he said, "a husband. Who would have ever thought?"

"Not me, that's for sure," grumbled Lilith as she passed, headed for Satan.

"Thanks for the vote of confidence," he called after her. She didn't even turn around as she flipped him the bird. "I don't know what I'm supposed to do with that."

I laughed. "Let's allow that to be Satan's problem for now," I suggested, looking into his beautiful blue eyes. "Now, it's time to celebrate."

Chapter Thirty-One

The rest of the evening was spent laughing, dancing, and celebrating. A five-course meal was followed by the traditional cake cutting, toasts, and then our first dance as husband and wife. After that, things began to get a little fuzzy. Glass after glass of champagne was passed around, loosening everyone's spirits, and tongues, for that matter.

Everyone got along, teasing, and taunting one another in a playful manner. There was no mention of Lucifer or the upcoming battle we would all soon face on the front lines. Adrianna and Loriana let loose on the dance floor, accompanied by Tyler and Roric. Joseph and Antonio sat at a table most of the night, stewing, yet seemed to behave themselves.

Frankie and I were in the center of the action as the music blared over the speakers. We danced and twirled each other, laughing as we let ourselves be free. Aunt Thora and Mom eventually joined us. The joy in this moment was nothing like I had ever experienced.

Deus came up behind me, wrapping his arms around my waist, kissing the curve of my neck.

"Are you happy, my love," he whispered against my ear.

"The happiest," I answered, leaning back into him.

"Good. Now, you wouldn't mind sharing a bit of that happiness with your cousin, would you?"

I stared at him, taken aback by the question. He smiled softly and shrugged as Levi approached the center circle of the dance floor. Frankie saw him and lunged into his arms, clueless. She beamed and planted kiss after kiss on his face.

Levi steadied her, brushing his hand across her face. He spoke to her softly, and a moment later dropped to one knee, pulling a green velvet box from his pocket.

She covered her mouth as she began to cry. Unable to get the words out, she nodded over and over with acceptance. Levi gathered her in his arms, swinging her around. Aunt Thora began to cry tears of joy while my mom gathered her twin.

"You're sneaky, husband," I whispered to him.

"Let's just say, I'm not confident in your secret keeping skills when it comes to Frankie," he replied.

I laughed, hitting him in the chest. "That is so rude ... though I see your point."

Once Levi and Frankie were done kissing, I rushed to her, wrapping my arms around my best friend while she screamed and laughed with joy.

"Let me see, let me see," I insisted. Her ring was magnificent. The green emerald was cut into a large pear shape, outlined with small diamonds and held together with a gold band. "It's beautiful, Frankie."

"Isn't it!?" she replied. "He did so good. I can't believe it, Seren. I'm actually getting married." She grabbed onto me, bursting with happiness. "You will be my matron of honor, right? Say you will."

In an instant, my joy vanished as it hit me ... I most likely wouldn't be alive to fulfill that honor. I felt a pair of eyes on me. Behind Frankie, Talia stood ... watching. I forced a smile at my beautiful cousin.

"Like anyone else is more equipped for the job."

"Oh!" she squealed, jumping up and down before barreling into me. "Thank you, thank you!"

I grinned, holding onto her tightly. "Anything for you," I whispered, the sadness crushing me. I caught Deus's eyes. His face filled with concern and confusion. *Shit.* My walls had been down. He was feeling what I was through our bond. I slowly fortified my barrier, trying not to appear suspicious.

"Okay, enough about me," Frankie said. "This is your wedding after all."

"I hope you don't mind," said Levi, appearing at her side.

"Not at all," I replied. "This was the perfect ending to a perfect day." I watched as he looked at my cousin, his expression full of love and tenderness. Deus was right. Though the mating bond set the whole emotional experience over the edge, it wasn't necessary when it came to matters of the heart. I knew, without a shadow of a doubt, Levi would do anything to make Frankie happy and keep her safe. That was all that mattered to me.

"It looks like we're planning another wedding," Nonna said. Thora pulled Frankie into her, kissing her profusely. Mom stood on the other side of me.

"Yes," Frankie said. "But mine will be somewhere warm and tropical. Honestly, I don't know what Seren's obsession with the cold and snow is."

"It's breathtaking," Deus said, wrapping his arm around my waist. "Just like she is." He smiled down at me. *Everything alright? I felt you just a moment ago,* he said into my mind.

"Of course. Happiest day of my life," I replied. He looked at me curiously. I gave him a tight squeeze before needing some air. "I'm going to go freshen up," I announced and turned back to the lodge.

Our guests were enjoying themselves as laughter filled the air. I tried to focus on the celebration that surrounded me, but it had become a glaring reminder that this joy was temporary, as I wouldn't be at Frankie's wedding.

I entered the quiet lodge, closing the doors behind me and heading to a room in the far back, away from everyone and everything. I locked myself inside, taking a seat on the edge of the bed, trying to calm myself. In that silent moment, everything hit me. The nightmares from Hell that replayed in my mind every time I closed my eyes. Deus without a soul. The fear of losing him completely. The torture I had endured at Lucifer's hands. The loss of Orion. All of it overwhelmed me in that dark room.

I grabbed at my head, focusing on my breathing while I tried to make it all stop. I wouldn't let it ruin this day for me. Not this beautiful day.

Two cold hands gently touched mine on either side of my face. My eyes opened, met by two stunning deep brown irises. Talia. She smiled softly and tilted her head, silently asking permission to enter my memories. I nodded as a tear rolled down my cheek. She closed her eyes and breathed out. I let the walls fall, allowing her to see ... to feel it all.

Pain. Torment. Fear. Loss. Devastation. Depression. Guilt. All of it slammed into her slithering presence. I didn't hold back. Let her see—no, *feel*—what her mate had put me through. The evil I had been subjected to because of his obsession with power. The very thing he would have killed his mate to obtain.

Her eyes snapped open, her coldness softening into empathy. "I am so sorry, my child," she whispered. "How could I know you were haunted by such torments?"

"And there's still more to come," I replied.

She rose from in front of me, taking a seat on the bed. "Power leads to corruption. I've never known it to end any other way."

"I didn't choose this. I don't care about the power, or the keys to Hell. I don't care about any of it. All I want is to live with Deus in our castle, secluded and happy."

"From what I've learned and lived through, it doesn't appear the vessels have ever had their version of a 'happily ever after', as your culture refers to it. The universe seems to enjoy torturing us in the most inhuman ways, and I don't know why. What did we do to deserve all of this?"

"I don't want to die," I whispered, finally admitting it out loud. "I don't want to leave him ... my family ... this life I've built. It isn't fair."

"No, it's not," she said harshly. "But it's what we must do. It's what we were designed to do. I survived in Purgatory, looking death in the face every moment, protecting my life so someday I could sacrifice it again to stop him ... the person I love most in this world. None if it makes sense. None of it's fair. But we all have a role to play."

"Has anyone ever told you you're not one for pep talks?"

"What is this pep talk?" she asked, looking at me confused.

I laughed, thinking back to my husband. "How am I going to get away from him long enough to kill Lucifer?" I asked. "Deus isn't going to leave my side when the war finally happens. He's already proven he wouldn't hesitate to die for me. I can't let him do that again. I won't."

"Lilith," she answered without pause. "She will do as you ask. She is pledged to you. When the time is right, she can distract him to separate you from your mate."

"It's going to take a miracle to get him to leave my side."

"A barrier," she said. "We will have to create a magical barrier so you can do what you need to. Once you are locked inside, I will open my gate to Hell, where the cage will be waiting. I will infuse my lifeforce with it, becoming the thing that keeps him bound. When you kill him on the earthly plane, his spirit will be drawn to mine. To the cage, where he will spend the rest of eternity, watching time pass while he contemplates his mistakes."

"You've thought this out."

"You have no idea." There was a moment of silence between us before she finally turned to face me.

"May I ask you something?" I whispered. She nodded. "Why did you not contact me sooner? I could have come for you earlier and saved you from that place."

"We are connected, not only by our demons, but by Aradia's soul. Purgatory, as you saw, is without magic, or life, for that matter. Before the bond, you were not strong enough to feel me ... to find me. But when you and Asmodeus nurtured your bond, your powers grew and so did your reach across realms. I was able to sense you then ... latch onto your power and send you a message."

"I see," I replied, turning my attention back to my new wedding rings.

"If I were you," she said, seeming to sense my feelings, "I'd forget about the future and the past, and just focus on the present. You have no idea how lucky you are to have a mate who truly loves you. Every moment you two have together is precious. I have nothing left to live for in this life. But you do. Don't waste a second of it, Seren. Not a single second."

I smiled, knowing that her words came from a place of pain and regret. "I will," I whispered, taking her hand in mine. She looked down, appearing shocked at the affection. "I think I would have enjoyed getting to know you. You know, before you became the leader of a dark, psychotic coven and all."

A genuine smile appeared on her face. My mouth fell open in response. She arched an eyebrow arched at me. "What?"

"You're so beautiful. Smiling suits you, truly. You should allow yourself to do that more often."

We exited the lodge together, returning to my wedding reception. My husband was laughing amongst his brothers with a glass of blood wine in his hand. His eyes drifted to me the moment I stepped foot into the snow.

"There you are," he said, his smile beaming. "Seren Resnov."

"Uh, excuse me," Frankie interrupted. "She is a De Salvo, now and always."

"Does that mean you won't be taking my last name?" Levi asked.

"Damn straight," she replied. "And any daughters we have will also be De Salvo."

"Any heirs we sire will bear their father's name, as it is custom," replied Levi.

"Whose custom are you referring to?" asked Frankie, standing toe to toe with her fiancé. "Some, sexist, barbaric, rule create by men who believe us to be their property? Ha, not happening."

I approached Deus, unsure if I should interfere. He gave me an exasperated look.

"I," said Levi, "am a Prince of Hell. Our children will be heirs to *my* kingdom."

"And I," rebutted Frankie, "am a descendant of a long line of powerful witches who have changed the very course of history and mankind as we know it. Any children we have will be raised topside, if that hasn't been clear for you."

"Alright, alright," Nonna intervened.

"Thank Father," Deus whispered.

"This is a celebration," continued Nonna. "Put your personal issues aside and let's all focus on what matters." She looked around the open area at each person. "We're family," she said softly. "No matter what coven we're from, no matter what blood we may or may not share," She took Deus's and Levi's hands in her own. "No matter what realm we're sired from. Each of us have fought for one another. Have bled for one another. We are blessed to be surrounded with such strength and wisdom. No matter where we go from here, this is what matters. We mustn't forget."

Deus smiled at her, then kissed the back of her hand. "You are very wise, Elder Salvo. It is an honor to stand by your side." He paused, turning his eyes to me. "To join your family."

"To the two little love birds," bellowed Mammon, raising his glass in the air.

"To a match made in Hell," echoed Belz, the crowd laughing in response.

"To two halves of a whole," said Frankie, stepping towards us, "after millennia, finally finding their way back to one another. To my soulmate Seren and to my new brother, Asmodeus. May your reign be one of peace and order."

"Here, here," yelled Gor before the crowd erupted with cheers and rounds of applause.

Deus kissed me on the lips, pulling away only to look down at me with the deepest love and admiration. "Thank you for making me whole," he whispered. "For showing me what true love really is. For giving me something to fight for."

"You are worth everything to me," I said in return.

"You *are* my everything, my love." We remained entranced in each other's eyes while our guests resumed dancing and laughing. The servers began to make their rounds once again, refilling empty glasses. All I could think about, all I wanted, was him.

"Would it be rude if we slipped away?" I whispered, drawing my hands up his firm arms. He smiled, flashing those sharp canine teeth I couldn't wait to have scraping against my skin.

"It's our wedding," he replied. "I think they'll understand."

I bit the side of my bottom lip, the anticipation beginning to grow. I quickly made my rounds, kissing and thanking people for coming, as did Deus. Just before we shifted away, the multicolored sky lit with blasts of fireworks. I grinned from ear to ear while our guests cheered. Deus's and my eyes met and then we drifted between time and space.

CHAPTER THIRTY-TWO

I looked around the familiar room, feeling a sense of peace. Rose petals littered every surface. Candles made seductive shadows as the moon shined above us through the open glass ceiling. It was snowing here too, which I was thankful for. A buffet of cheeses, fruits, and delicacies was set out on the table along with an assortment of wine. I was home.

"Is this okay?" asked Deus, sliding an arm around me.

"Of course it is," I replied, leaning into him. "Why wouldn't it be?"

"I didn't know if you'd prefer something a bit more ... fancy."

I laughed. "You mean, a secluded castle in Romania doesn't cut it?" I wrapped my arms around his waist.

"I just ... I wanted our first moments as husband and wife to be spent here ... in our home. The place where it all began."

"It's perfect, Deus ... just like you." I pressed a kiss to his Adam's apple, feeling a shiver go through his body. "Now ... if I recall, you promised you'd show me a thing or two, did you not?"

The demon inside of him growled with delight. His desire surged down our mental bridge, only to be met with my own. His eyes lit to life.

"My wife gets what my wife wants," he said in a deep and sensual voice.

I pushed him back into a large high-backed chair near the fireplace, then stepped away. He tried to follow, but I used my power to keep him restrained. His eyebrow arched. A wicked smile followed. He unbuttoned his jacket, tossing it to the floor. His shoulders relaxed as he leaned back into the chair, draping his forearms on the armrests.

"No touching until I say," I said tauntingly.

"We'll see about that," he replied, licking his lips.

I reached behind myself, tugging the zipper of my dress down until I felt it snag. Slowly, I slipped the sleeves down each arm, paused, then, peeled the fabric away from my midsection, revealing the lingerie Frankie had custom made for the dress.

It was red, strapless, with a neckline that plunged to where my lips parted between my legs. The wiring of the lingerie pushed my breasts up and over the top. The sheer fabric left nothing to the imagination.

I stepped out of my wedding dress, my gold high heels sparkling. The revealing outfit cut high over my hips, my legs on full display. I turned around, moving my hair. The piece covered nothing from behind, the small strings that hugged my butt cheeks barely visible, allowing my back end to be the main attraction.

Deus's breathing deepened. His eyes glowed a bright red. One of his hands flexed into a fist as he took me in from head to toe. I sauntered to the couch in front of him, facing the fire. Crawling into the corner farthest away from him, I turned and placed one leg up on the cushion. The other fell away as I opened myself to him, ensuring he had the perfect view.

He growled, lunging for me, but before he could move from the chair, I slammed my magic forward, restraining him again.

"Am I going to have to handcuff you?" I asked.

He laughed. "I'm up for restraints if you are."

I smiled. "Sit back." Another rumble of frustration rattled deep inside of his chest, but he reluctantly did as I commanded.

I arched my back, my head falling on the arm of couch. My hand slowly traced my mouth, before I wet my fingers with my tongue. I traced a line from my lips down my neck towards my navel. The other hand teased my swollen, aching breasts, paying extra attention to my hardened nipples that pressed against the sheer red fabric.

I could feel his desire, his lust, raking against mine. The control I had over him set every nerve ending inside of me on fire. He tried to pull away from my magic, but I held firm, wanting him to lose all sense of control before I unleashed my demon prince.

I slid my fingers lower, moving the fabric between my legs to one side, letting him see how wet I already was for him. I brushed the bundle of nerves with a single finger, sending an electric shock through my system. A small moan slipped from me as I circled the area, imagining his fingers instead of my own.

Tracing the outline of my entrance, slightly opening myself to him, seemed to be his undoing. A cracking noise snapped me out of my bliss. I lifted my head to see the arms of the chair crushed underneath his grip. He was panting, face tense, his eyes flickering through different shades of red.

I smiled, slowly closing my legs and standing to move in front of him. He tracked me like a predator watching his prey. I knelt in front of him, trailing my hands up his firm, toned legs. My fingers brushed across his fully hardened length. My sex throbbed at the touch, remembering how it felt having him buried deep inside of me. I massaged the area over his pants, causing a groan to escape his lips.

"My love," he whispered, his voice deep and desperate. I drew my eyes up to his. "If you like our home in its current state, I suggest you release your hold on me before I bring this entire mountain crumbling to the ground."

I laughed, leaning my face into his, stopping just before our lips touched. I traced my tongue around his mouth softly and tightened my grip on his throbbing cock. He tried to press his lips to mine, but I froze him in place, pulling back, revealing my own devilish smile.

"I love how you think you're in charge," I whispered, trailing my tongue up the column of his neck. "Just so we're clear," I paused, pulling the button of his pants free. "You are mine." I unzipped his pants. "To do whatever I see fit with." With one forceful tug, his pants pulled away from his hips to his knees. "If I choose to subject you to torture—" I pulled his pants free of his legs, leaving him bare from the waist down. "—then that is what you must endure."

A vibration shook the floor underneath my feet as I knelt before him. "Seren," he growled, his face anguished. "I am serious," he said between his teeth. Without acknowledging his plea, I wrapped one hand around the base of his thick cock, then circling his tip with my tongue.

"Fuck!" he roared. The taste of him set my core on fire. I slid my free hand down my body until my fingers found my entrance, plunging two inside, needing to sate the raging desire that was seeping from me. I inhaled deeply and took as much of him in my mouth as I could handle. My own control was slipping.

My fingers pumped while my head bobbed up and down on his perfect cock, the fist around his base, mimicking the motion. My tongue flickered across the underside of his dick, tracing that sensitive vein. I whimpered, trying to keep myself from coming. I wanted him to come first. I needed him to experience the passion he ignited inside of me, but before I could, my control slipped, along with the power I had on him.

In a flash, my back was against the floor in front of the fire. My fingers were replaced with his, while his mouth smashed into mine. His tongue thrashed in my mouth, desperate for any taste of me he could get. His hand pinned my arms above my head, restraining me. My legs quivered from the motion of his fingers. I cried out, the intensity overwhelming me, sending my head spinning.

He slowed his motion before pulling out of me completely. I whimpered, missing the feeling instantly. His blue eyes gazed down at me and he smiled, pressing a kiss to each corner of my mouth.

"That, my sweet little wife, was not very nice."

"Don't act like you didn't enjoy it," I replied, my voice already horse from moaning.

I felt him chuckle against my neck as he continued to kiss any exposed skin he came across. He pulled away, looking down at the revealing lingerie that still clung to my body. His hand trailed my side, brushing across every curve.

"Have I ever told you how sinful you look in red?" he asked, tracing a finger around my left nipple. I arched my back, wanting him to grip the aching mounds instead.

"I think it's my new favorite color," I replied, wiggling underneath him, searching for his hardness I so desperately wanted pressed against my wet core.

"Glad to hear that," he whispered against my lips, brushing his mouth across mine. He grazed the side of his face along my cheek. His teeth nipped at my earlobe softly before he said, "my turn."

When I opened my eyes, I stood, restrained to a large three-dimensional metal frame that created an open cube. I tried to bring my legs together, but I was trapped, unable to move. My body was extended in the form of an X. I went to use my power to free myself, but the well inside of me was blocked.

Deus appeared in front of me, now shirtless, wearing a pair of black, leather pants, unzipped just enough for me to see the top of his sex. He walked over to a table littered with sex toys and objects of pleasure.

"My powers," I said.

"Don't worry, my love, it's only temporary. I couldn't have you freeing yourself and ruining all my fun, now, could I?"

"How?"

He looked over his shoulder, nodding to the base of the platform. Small white crystals were evenly distributed around the base. "Astrolite crystals," he explained. "They absorb any magic used within the circle. Once you leave the circle, all powers will be restored." He turned towards me, stepping up onto the platform with a devious smile. "But not until I'm satisfied by your screams of pleasure."

He slid a red blindfold over my eyes softly.

"Deus," I whispered, slightly nervous about this new adventure we were about to embark upon. The blindfold slipped up. He held either side of my face, his beautiful eyes, only inches from mine.

"At any time, if you feel uncomfortable, we will stop," he said sincerely. I nodded. "Do you trust me?" I nodded again. "Say it."

"I trust you."

He pressed a loving kiss to my lips before placing the blindfold over my eyes. A firm hand remained on my body as he circled me slowly. I felt a snap as he broke one of the strings of the lingerie, the front loosening.

He snapped the last piece of fabric on my body, leaving me completely bare and helpless.

A shiver skidded across my skin as the cold breeze caused gooseflesh. His fingers trailed from my jaw down the length of my neck, tracing over each breast before moving to my hips and then my legs. A kiss pressed against my ankle. He worked his mouth up the length of my legs, alternating between the two while his hands covered the skin his mouth missed.

His lips moved to the center of my sex, causing my breath to catch. I needed this. I needed him. I needed to feel release. He kissed around the area, avoiding the place I needed his mouth the most.

"Please," I whimpered, done playing games.

He paused. "Hmm," he said, stroking his fingers lightly over my skin. "How I love to hear you beg." Too quickly, his tongue slid up the slit of my wet, aching sex, his soft lips sucking one, hard time on my bundle of nerves before pulling away. I gasped, gripping my leather restraints, feeling like I was going to lose my balance.

A moment passed, then I sensed his presence on the platform, and my body began to shift in the air. I went from upright to flat on my back, suspended in the air, still held by the cuffs on my ankles and wrists. A cold, hard object rolled across my abdomen, moving towards my center. It slid down my lips, opening me, sending shivers down my spine from the cool material.

Deus traced the object around my entrance, placing his thumb on top of my slit, making small circles. I took a breath and then the object was pressed inside of me. I gasped as he thrust the object into me entirely. He turned it slowly, allowing me to feel every carving and groove that was designed for my pleasure. His tongue lapped at my swollen clit slowly, as if savoring the taste. He began to move the object in and out, moaning as he kissed and sucked.

I moaned with pleasure, my body completely overtaken by the feelings. His pace quickened, the pressure inside of me building. Faster and faster he pumped, turning the object in circles as my insides clenched around it. No longer in control of myself, I held my breath, shaking in release as I came all over the object.

Before I could finish, the object was removed, replaced by his mouth as he ate me into another uncontrollable orgasm. He was ravenous, taking me entirely in his mouth while his tongue thrashed from my clit to inside of my hole, tasting every moan and release of pleasure. Somehow he freed my legs, placing them over his shoulders, pulling me into his mouth deeper while his fingers dug into my skin.

I screamed his name as my body began to seize and shake uncontrollably, but he didn't stop. His tongue and lips made love to me so desperately, it sent a massive push of need down the bond. I ripped and strained at the cuffs, trying to get to him.

I needed to touch him. To feel him inside of me, finally complete.

"Please," I cried, rattling the cuffs against the metal frame. "Deus, please. I need you. I need you, baby. Please."

Finally, my wish was granted. He removed his mouth long enough to unlatch the cuffs from the metal frame, leaving them secured around my wrists. He picked me up by the ass, wrapping my legs around his waist as I took his mouth with my own, running my hands through his jet-black hair. My nails scraped down his back, tearing into him with the animalistic need he had unleashed inside of me. He slammed me into the bed, tearing his pants from his hips. I parted my legs, pulling his torso to mine, and then—

Stars erupted in a haze of black and red light. I screamed as he filled me completely. There was nothing tender or calm about our movements. We were desperate for one another, with a need that would never be satisfied. He rammed into me like a wild animal, tangling his fingers in my white hair, pulling my head back as he sank his teeth into my neck.

My nails buried into his back, holding on as I felt my soul being ripped from my body, consumed by his own. Faster and faster, we crashed against the mattress. Release erupted from my body and I held onto him, afraid I was going to lose myself. A moment later, his followed, his body tensing while his skin flared in gooseflesh from the sensation.

His body pressed against mine as our breathing calmed. I could feel his heart hammering against his chest. He lifted his head, hovering above me and smiled lazily. His fingers brushed my sweaty temple, moving the damp hair from my skin.

He licked his lips. "That was ..."

"... incredible," I finished.

"It amazes me. In all my years, I have never experienced this kind of passion with another. And here I thought I had already lived a full life."

I laughed. "Surprise."

"Yes ... you are just that. A surprise." He pressed a soft kiss to my lips before rolling to my side, pulling me into the curve of his body, wrapping his arms firmly around me. "How are you feeling?"

"Amazing," I replied with a smile, nuzzling my nose into his neck.

His fingers trailed down the length of my spine. "Is there anything else I could do to satisfy the needs of my wife?"

"Mm, your wife is completely and utterly satisfied. But I wouldn't mind being held for a bit, if you don't mind."

"It would be my pleasure," he replied, pressing a kiss to my head.

"Today was the happiest moment of my life," I whispered, the emotions of the day tightening around my heart. "Everything was perfect."

"It truly was. And you were exquisite. I've never seen something more beautiful. Not in all my years."

"I find that hard to believe. I mean, you've been looking at that sexy reflection for eternity. How could I possibly beat that?"

He laughed. "Don't be fooled. You outshine me in every way. Now, I suggest you close your eyes and get some rest, because that little contraption over there is just the beginning."

CHAPTER THIRTY-THREE

The next two days were a blur. I didn't know what time it was, nor did I care. We slept when our bodies demanded it and ate when we needed energy, but the rest of the time ... oh, the rest of the time was spent exploring. I didn't know the world contained so many contraptions, toys, and devices designed solely for physical pleasure. Tables, benches, seats, walls: all designed for restraint, but also to maneuver the body into flexible positions, creating mind blowing sensations.

Deus took his time, allowing me to fully experience everything he subjected my body to. I thought our time on the island had been educational. I was wrong.

My body was tender and sore from our "expressions of love". I wore each mark with pride, knowing my mate had put them there while he worshiped me. I wondered if it would still be like this once I died. When I was bound to Hell. Would the experience change? Would he still love me in the same manner?

The end of day two came too quickly. We showered and made arrangements to head back to Castle Salvo to join the others in preparations for Lucifer's impending attack. I took my time, absorbing as many details of our room as I could. This was likely the last time I would ever set foot in here: the space that had helped heal my soul. In this home, I learned I had a life worth living and fighting for ... even if that life was about to be cut short.

Deus came up from behind me, brushing my hair to the side while pressing soft, suggestive kisses down my neck and to my shoulder. I leaned into him, never wanting this to end.

"Is it wrong of me not to want to go back?" I whispered, feeling selfish for even allowing the words to escape.

"Not at all. I was just thinking the same thing."

"I think I've had enough adventure for one lifetime. I just ... I just want to be left alone."

He took my hand and led me up the stairs to the third floor where the balcony doors were frosted over with ice. He pushed them open and pulled me to the railing overlooking the beautiful mountain landscape of Romania.

"This, my love, is what we're fighting for. This will be waiting for us when we have finished what we've set out to do. Our peace. Our sanctuary. And when that day comes, I promise I will do whatever it takes to ensure you live out your long life in completely and utter happiness."

I looked up at him, my heart swelling with love. "Thank you for sharing your home with me."

"Baby ... it wasn't a home until you landed in a blazing funnel of fire on that very floor," he replied gesturing back inside. "I should be the one thanking you. Now, I have one more thing to show you before we return to Triora." He extended his hand to me.

I took it, following him back into the castle. The halls were unusually quiet. Only goldaburgs and a few meek female servants busied themselves with housework. There were no sounds of parties, no laughter or sensual music, no sounds of sex.

"Where is everyone?" I asked.

"What do you mean?"

"The parties. The orgies. The scantily-clothed women."

He laughed. "There's no need for all that anymore."

I pulled back, stopping us in the middle of the hallway. "What are you talking about? You're the Prince of Lust. There's always going to be need for *that*."

He smiled. "Seren, you provide every bit of what I need. Truly. My power, my body, has never felt more satisfied in my entire existence. I am complete ... because of you."

A sick feeling filled me. That feeling of completion would be short lived. The women, the parties, the sex would all have to return, sooner rather than later, because I would be stuck in Hell, never able to step foot in this world again. Since my human body would no longer exist, Deus would need to take others to maintain his power. Lust needed to be unleashed on earth to balance the needs of Hell. I needed to prepare myself and somehow figure out how to accept it.

Disgust enveloped me at the thought of my mate sharing a bed with someone else. I turned away from him, trying to hide my emotions.

"What is it?" he asked, his face full of concern. "Why are you feeling this way?"

"Nothing," I replied, trying to shake the feeling. "I'm just upset we have to leave our home so soon."

His face softened as he pressed his forehead against mine, tangling his fingers through my hair.

"You know," he said softly. "I was also thinking ... maybe after everything settles down, you'd consider blessing me with a son or daughter. We could fill these halls with small giggles and children laughing and playing."

I pulled back in shock, as if someone had reached into my lungs and ripped the air out completely. I knew my face was hiding none of it.

Deus's smile fell, replaced with an expression of worry. "I'm sorry," he said. "I didn't mean to pressure you. I was just thinking—"

"—I can't have children," I blurted out. "I'm the vessel. None of the vessels have ever produced children."

"None of them have lived long enough to really try. There's no proof that you can't have offspring."

"I ... I ..." I couldn't find my voice. Deus's faced shifted again. I could feel the embarrassment, the shame and worry flicker down the bond.

"I know I'm not perfect, and I am fully aware of my shortcomings, but I promise you Seren, I would do my best to be a good father. Regardless of what I am."

I shook my head, still trying to comprehend that he actually desired children—something I would never be able to give him. I grabbed his face, pulling it into mine.

"You would be an amazing father, Asmodeus. I don't doubt that for a minute. I love everything about you and so would our children." I pulled away, looking into his blue eyes. "You just threw me off guard. I didn't know a Prince of Hell desired children."

"The thought has never really crossed my mind. Not until I found you," he admitted.

My heart crumbled into pieces, tears pricking my eyes. I smiled, swallowing my pain. "Nothing would bring me more happiness than to start a family with you. Nothing." I pressed a kiss to his lips, hoping my performance would hold. "Now ... you had something to show me?"

Deus led us to the throne room. Behind the massive double doors, an empty ballroom sat quietly, undisturbed. He shut the doors behind us before leading me to the platform where a new throne had been placed. The gold metalwork around the frame was extraordinary, the phases of the moon carved into the metal.

Among the gilding I noted the Salvo crest, along with that of Asmodeus's coat of arms representing Romania. Mountains and suns scattered throughout the collage of symbols, pentagrams and arches representing my gate. A black metal intertwined the intricate details of the throne. On the face of the left armrest, Deus's initials were carved into the surface. On the right, my own. The cushions were covered in red velvet, not a thread out of place. The entire piece of art was magnificent and created with such care and detail.

I turned back to my husband and smiled. "Our story," I whispered. "You had our story carved into the throne."

He stepped up next to me and smiled. "A wedding gift. Something that represents our past and our future."

"It's perfect," I said, throwing my arms around him, passionately kissing his lips. His arms locked around my waist while I pressed my body into his, craving every ounce of physical contact.

I trailed my fingers through his hair, gliding my tongue along the seam of his mouth, committing every moment to memory. My hands slid down his chest as the desire inside of me began to take over. The unquenchable thirst I couldn't control.

My fingers fumbled with the button of his pants, desperately pulling at the fabric. Deus pulled away, in a calmer state than I appeared to be. His eyes searched my own.

"I need you," I said desperately, freeing the button from the loop. "Please. I need you now." I flung myself back into him, ravenously kissing the column of his neck, biting and scratching my way across his skin before I pulled his pants from his perfect body.

His desire erupted just before he flung me around. I braced on the arm of our throne while he lifted my dress up, ripping my underwear clean off and plunging himself deep inside of me. I screamed, grasping the soft velvety fabric. He pulled me upright, kissing and nipping at my neck while his hands roaming my body, finally freeing me from the last article of clothing.

With one arm, he held me steady around my waist as he took me slowly, savoring the feeling of our bodies connected. He cupped my breast with his other hand, kneading it softly. I leaned back into him, steadying myself as I focused on the feeling of him pushing in and out of me.

"You are so beautiful," he whispered in my ear, pressing a line of kisses down my neck. "And the way you taste ..." he growled, sending a shiver down my spine. "Fuck, don't get me started on the way you feel. The little moans that I can draw from you. How wet and perfectly tight you fit around my cock. How smooth and soft your skin is."

His hand traced up my body until his fingers tangled in my hair, pulling my head back. "And this hair ... mm, you have no idea how much I love to see it splayed out on the bed as your body is laid out below me like a feast." He bent me forward, positioning his hands on either of my hips, holding me tightly while he slammed into me.

I closed my eyes, feeling like I was going to come undone. Right before I found my release, he pulled from inside of me, turning me towards him and hauling me up, placing my legs around his waist. He carried me to the wall behind the throne, pressing my back into the cold stone, pinning my hands above me and taking my mouth with his.

He pressed back inside of me, my body shivering, a groan of pleasure erupting from my lips. Our bodies moved in one unified motion, his mouth never leaving mine. This intimacy, this connection, could never be matched.

As my pleasure grew, the connection between us seemed to strengthen. I danced from his perspective to my own, sharing in our love and ecstasy. He was gentle, making love to me while sating every one of my needs. He buried his head into my neck, tightening his grip on me as he found his release. I wrapped my arms around him, holding his beautiful body close, taking him in.

He chuckled and allowed my body to slide down the wall. He kissed me again, touching the ring on my left hand.

"You're mine," he said, his gaze loving. "You're really mine."

"Forever and always." I stroked my hands down his arms. "I've seen the darkest side of you and somehow, I love you more for it."

"Sometimes, I think this is a dream I'll wake from ... and realize I am still back in Lucifer's dungeons, being tortured," he admitted, his face falling in shame.

I cupped his cheek with my hand. "I'm real," I said with a small smile. "And you're free and will remain that way. I promise."

He smiled. "Though I am still sometimes haunted from what I've experienced and the things I've done, I would do it a thousand times over to end up here with you."

"Me too," I whispered. "You're worth everything to me."

He shook his head in disbelief. "Father, I am so happy."

"That means I'm doing my job then."

"I love you, wife."

"I love you too, husband."

As we dressed, I tried not to ponder how I would never see my home again. The next time Deus returned to Romania, he would be a widower, haunted by the happy memories we had just created. *It will be worth it*, I told myself. I had promised that he would remain free, and so he would.

We shifted to my room in Castle Salvo. When we opened the door to the hallway, witches and warlocks from every coven yelled, clapped, and hollered. Poppers sounded, spraying red and black confetti into the air as Deus and I walked hand in hand through the tunnel of people.

Despite my impending demise looming closer, I couldn't help it ... I smiled. I had lived such a full life. I had created memories with my family that would transcend time and space. I had found my strength and the power I had always possessed. I got to experience loss, heartbreak, and a love many will never know. My life may be short, but it was full ... so beautifully full.

People congratulated us, shaking Deus's hand and hugging me. I spotted Delphine in the crowd. She smiled softly and nodded her congratulations. I nodded back, thinking of Orion.

We finally got to the end of the hall where our family and close friends waited for us. Mammon and Belz spoke in a heated conversation to the side. Levi and Gor stood next to Frankie and G. Nonna's face beamed with happiness as she opened her arms to me, Aunt Thora and Mother flanking either side.

"Oh, bambinas," Nonna said, pulling both Deus and I into her. I found it funny she referred to Deus as a baby, even though he was older than the world itself. "How was it?"

Frankie snickered behind her. I pressed my lips together, hiding the devious smile that threatened to tell our secrets.

"It was perfect," Deus answered with grace, as if we hadn't just been fucking each other brainless all over the castle. God, if they only knew the things he had done to me. *"They will never,"* he said mind to mind.

"I'm so glad to hear that," replied Nonna.

Frankie careened into me next, squeezing the breath out of me. My tired body moaned in protest.

"I can't wait to hear all about it," she whispered.

"The things I've learned in just two days," I whispered back. She chuckled, winking at me. Deus shook his head as if he knew I was going to tell her every detail. He shook Levi's hand, pulling his brother into an embrace before moving onto Gor. My mother and Thora embraced me into a twin sandwich.

"You look so in love," Aunt Thora commented.

My mother moved my hair back and arched her eyebrow, her face going stern. "Did you two not have enough food wherever you were?" she asked. Thora hit her arm, hiding her laughter with her hand.

I pulled my hair back over my neck, blood rushing to my cheeks. "We ate," I answered.

"Yes," Mom said, "I can see that."

"Any developments?" I asked, desperate to change the subject.

"Unfortunately, yes," a deep, elegant female voice answered behind me. I turned to see Talia a few feet away in a deep blue, floor-length dress. I gave her a small smile.

"What has happened?" Deus asked while the witches and warlocks filtered out of the hall, returning to their normal routines.

"I believe he has found the ingredients needed to enact the barrier spell," she answered. "I can feel his power growing. He is preparing for war. The spell is going to drain all magic from anyone who is caught in its net. It will be permanent until the vessels he ties them to are killed."

"How do you know this?" asked Deus.

Her jaw tightened. "Because he is using a spell I wrote," she answered with vengeance lacing her tone.

"And why would you ever need a spell like that?" asked Frankie.

Talia's eyes turned to my cousin, emotionless. "I created it for Lucifer, to trap the remaining witches loyal to Aradia so he could absorb their magic with less ... resistance."

"Fuck," said Belz, running his hand through his hair.

"And what about these vessels?" asked Gor.

"Knowing Luc," said Talia, "he will choose supernatural beings that are hard to kill. Thick hides to act as armor. Tremendous strength. Lethal blows. Something that is going to take more than one of us to take down."

"Okay," Frankie said. "So, we set up five teams. Their sole purpose: destroying their assigned relic vessel."

"It's a good plan," commented Talia, "but he will be expecting that."

"It's the only plan that we have," said Levi, as we filed into Nonna's room.

"Then, how is our plan going to even stand a chance?" asked G.

Talia turned to me, and I swore I could see something dark and demented creeping behind her glassy eyes. "Me," she said plainly.

"We're planning our entire strategy around your assumption of his plans. What certainties can you actually give us?" asked Gor.

Talia's eyes slid to him. "I shared a mind with that sadistic bastard for centuries," she said, flashing her teeth. "I know how he thinks. How he operates. I would have taken the same steps to ensure my plan succeeded. We are one and the same."

"Father, help us," Belz mumbled, taking a step away.

"Do you know where he is going to be?" asked Thora.

"It has to be somewhere he is able to harness enough magic from the earth," my mother stated. "Somewhere open, vast, and yet a place of great destruction and war."

Gor went rigid, his eyes locking with Deus's. "Egypt," Gor whispered.

"The holy land," Deus finished.

Talia smiled, shaking her head. "Back to the beginning we go," she said, pouring herself a glass of hard liquor and throwing it back.

"Well, help yourself, why don't you," Nonna said.

Talia frowned at her. "May I?" She gestured dramatically to the canter.

"Ah," Nonna scoffed, tossing her hands in the air.

"That desert is massive," said Gor. "How are we going to know where to shift the covens in?"

Talia raised her hand, tilting her head with a little smirk. "Me again," she answered. "I can sense him."

"If you can sense him, doesn't that mean he can sense you?" asked G.

"No," I answered, remembering my time in Hell. "Talia can find him because she has a soul. The bond is still alive in her, pulling her towards her mate." I turned to Deus. "Just like our bond pulled me to you in the pit." He gave me a small smile filled with pain from those memories.

"Luc is soulless," agreed Talia, "thus, he can't feel the bond between us."

"Dammit, you are useful," commented Mammon.

"Too useful," Belz said, stepping towards her. "Our entire plan is based on our trust in Lucy's mate." He paused, looking around at the group. "Does anyone else not see the problem here? She will lead us to him. She knows his plan and just happens to be the key to his undoing.

How is no one else questioning this right now?"

"You can question my intent all you wish," Talia fired back. "I don't give a damn if you trust me or not. I will end Lucifer with or without your help. You need me ... I don't need you. Now, if you will all excuse me, I've had just about enough of this insufferable banter." She brushed through the group and left.

"Great plan," said Gor. "Let's just piss off our greatest asset."

"She is telling the truth," added Giana. "I can feel her intent. She is in pain, but her resolve is unwavering. She will kill Lucifer, regardless of the cost."

"That's what I'm afraid of," Belz said.

Chapter Thirty-Four

After theorizing with the others for hours, my mind was a muddled mess. There were still too many uncertainties that prevented us from coming up with a solid plan. Mammon, Hashen, and Gor would travel to Egypt to assess the situation, while the others stayed back to help prepare the covens.

That night, I was plagued by nightmares. I was back in Hell, haunted by the smells, the sounds, the visuals that I would never fully wash from my memory. I awoke in a panic, drenched in sweat. As I steadied my breathing, I checked my mental walls, satisfied they were still standing strong, keeping even my mate out.

He slept peacefully next to me. I got out of bed, grabbing my robe on the way towards the door. I walked slowly down the quiet halls of Castle Salvo, pausing at the open arched windows that held one of the most beautiful views from my ancestral home. The first time I had seen this view was the day Aunt Thora had given me a tour of our family home.

That seemed like another lifetime ago. I barely remembered that naive girl who believed this world was only black and white. Little did I know there was a hefty amount of gray, and that happened to be the category I fell into.

I headed for Nonna's room, making sure I wasn't too loud just in case she was asleep. What was I thinking? She had to be asleep. It was three in the morning. I cracked open the door but froze when I heard voices coming from the other side.

"Absolutely not, Annalise," yelled Nonna.

"Why else would you have told me if this was not an option?" Mom replied.

"Because you needed to be aware so you could prepare for what came next."

"You are not capable of possessing that much power. As great as you are, it isn't possible."

"You don't know that."

"And if you're wrong, what then? You put us all at risk," Mom said, her usual calm giving way to firm resolve.

"You know," Talia's voice came from behind me, "back in my day, if you were caught listening to a private conversation, you were held underwater. Or, if it was someone of importance, they could cut your ears off. That one was always fun to watch."

I closed the door quietly. "I didn't mean to listen in," I replied, moving back into the hall. Talia fell in step beside me. "Why are you awake?"

"I don't really sleep. Sleeping indicates a sense of peace. Peace is something I have been without for a long, long time now."

We walked out to one of the balconies on the side of the castle. I lit the outdoor firepit while Talia took in the view. I joined her at the railing, the cold breeze easing the warm, sticky sweat that clung to my skin.

"Nightmares?" she asked. I nodded. "Dreaming is overrated anyways." She attempted to playfully smile.

"Finding our sense of humor?"

She shrugged. "I try to find moments I can enjoy from time to time.

Also, I haven't had anyone but myself to talk to in years. It's nice to hear another voice besides my own."

"Can I ask you something?" I said.

She arched her brow in a devilish manner. "Sure ... why not."

I swallowed, gathering my courage. "Before Purgatory ... how evil were you?"

"Define evil," she said dryly.

"You know what I mean."

She gazed back to the hills of Triora, taking in a deep breath. "I've murdered, stolen, lied, indulged, gambled, lusted ... all of it. I've committed every sin ten times over again. I've butchered families. Burned villages. Lured men from their wives. Left children orphans. Killed ... children. I've done it all. So, if you're asking if I am evil ... the answer is yes, Seren. I am just as bad as he."

"Why?" I whispered.

"Why not? In my time, I was the most powerful thing ever to exist. A phenomenon that should have never been. Nothing could rival me, besides my mate. Even the other princes wouldn't have stood a chance. I was invincible. Why should I abide by the laws of man?"

"They were innocent."

She huffed. "Nothing I witnessed in my mortal life was truly innocent. I watched men take and rape whomever, whenever they pleased. I witnessed mothers killing their children because they were too poor to feed them. Oppressors using other humans as slaves, treating their pets with more humanity than their 'property'. Especially the women. Our only purpose back then was to breed. Love was an abstraction, a lie women chose to believe to endure laying with old, disease-infested men who only cared about their own pleasure."

She paused, her face falling into sorrow—the first raw emotion I had seen her express. "My parents sold my twelve-year-old sister to the highest bidder, who was older than our father. He was a violent man. My sister didn't last a year."

My heart constricted. "I'm so sorry."

"Don't be. I was powerless then, unaware of the magic I possessed, but that didn't prevent me from invoking my wrath upon that bastard." She lifted her head with pride. "He didn't know Evie had an older sister. I plied him with shekar, our liquor, and let him lure me back to his home. Then I tied him to the bed, gagged him, and made him watch as I carved his small cock off with a rusted knife. I shoved it in his mouth so he bled out while gagging on his own foreskin."

"My God," I said in shock.

She smiled. "I still replay that night in my head often." Her fingers clenched around the railing. "Evie deserved better. She was only a child. If I had known what we were, what we could do, she would have lived. Yet, my mother hid our ancestry from us, and Evie was brutally murdered."

"Did your mother even know about your witch heritage?"

"She did but hid it in fear of what others would think. She only confessed it once I had murdered my father in front of her, and then turned my power on her."

"You killed your parents?"

"I did, and I have never regretted it ... not once. They deserved what they got. You're lucky you have a family who truly cares for one another. That kind of devotion was something I only ever felt towards Evie."

"I am lucky," I replied, grateful for the women I had come to adore .

"Does that answer your question?"

"Yes. But there's one more thing I need to know before I decide to follow you into the desert."

"I'm listening."

I chewed on my bottom lip. I knew I would do almost anything for Deus.

"Lucifer," I began slowly, "if he were to regain his soul and attempt to make things right between the two of you ... professed his love and desire to be with you again ... would you side with him? Would you betray us?"

She became deathly still. I was unsure if she even breathed.

"The difference, little tribrid, between your mate and mine, is that somewhere deep inside, Asmodeus retained the angelic part that made him good ... that made him worthy of you. When he met you, that ember reignited, softening his heart, allowing him to love you completely. I can see that with Belphegor and Giana, Satan and Lilith, even Levi and your cousin, though they are not mated.

"Lucifer destroyed that part of himself long before he fell. I was foolish to think our love would be strong enough to awaken it. Regardless, he is the love of my life, and even after everything, I would never change that. The good moments that we shared together were still worth all of this. Even if, in the end, our love isn't everlasting.

"He made his choice, and I have made mine. I know him better than I know myself. He will never change. Nothing he can say or do will change the course of what is to come. But don't be fooled, Seren. I am not doing this to save the world, or to protect your friends and family. I am going to destroy him as my revenge for destroying me first."

"Thank you for being honest," I replied.

Talia's gaze fell while she turned slowly towards me. "Speaking of honesty, there is something you need to know." Talia paused. "The sacrifice you will need to make in order to defeat Lucifer will require more than just your earthly body."

I paused. "What is the cost?" I whispered, unsure if I truly wanted to know.

"Everything. Your entire existence."

"What do you mean?"

"In order for you to overpower Lucifer, you will have to flood your life force into him, forfeiting the part of you that he gave to save you ... forfeiting your life in the process."

My heart fell. "The ultimate death?"

She nodded. "He is the strongest thing that has ever been created besides you and me. It will take everything you have ... everything you are, to put him down for good. I would willingly make the sacrifice, but the gate only activates with my life force. I wanted to make sure that no one would be able to contain my mate except me."

"So ... what happens to Hell?"

"It will remain. Lucifer's essence will live within Hell, so the natural order of that realm will be balanced. The brothers, I assume, will have to manage Pride's territories since it will no longer have a leader."

"And ... Deus ... what becomes of him?"

"That, I am afraid, I cannot answer."

Everything inside of me went silent. I would never be able to see Deus again. Nor my family, or any of the brothers. I would cease to exist. There would be no afterlife for me. I would just be ... gone.

In that moment, being the queen of Hell sounded a lot better than this alternative. Yet, an existence without pain or suffering ... what would that even be? The thought of no longer existing was unfathomable to me.

"I am sorry," she said, breaking the silence. "I wanted to tell you earlier, but with your wedding ... I didn't think it was the appropriate time."

I shook my head, trying to wrap my mind around this. "No, you were right to wait. Thank you for at least allowing me that small moment of happiness."

She nodded uncomfortably.

"But Deus will remain alive," I whispered, trying to make sense of it all. "He will have to go on living and acting out his sin, to make sure the balance remains." My veins filled with fire at the thought of him falling in love with another. The notion made me want to burn the entire world to the ground. I would make the ultimate sacrifice, only to have my mate forced to take others because I no longer existed. Because I sacrificed our happiness ... my life, so everyone else can live.

"Love is a curse, Seren, is it not?"

"I'm beginning to think so."

We stood on the edge of that balcony for what seemed like forever, until the sun rose over the horizon, signaling a new day. I allowed myself to go through the emotions of what I would feel. Of what was to come. I had to stop suppressing it and come to terms with my destiny.

"Beautiful," complimented Lilith, "now, do it again."

I moved my feet back into the offensive stance and swung the sword through the air, nailing the target perfectly at every contact point. I slammed the sword into the dummy with all my might, exerting my emotions and pent-up energy. I roared with anger and the metal blade went flying. My vision blurred and I screamed, the burden I carried overcoming me. The sword sang through the air, shattering into pieces as it sliced deep into the target.

The vibrations from the impact rattled up my arms. I released the hilt and the pieces sprinkled to the floor. I looked at what I had done, breathing heavily from the anger and darkness that was enveloping me. I wanted to destroy Lucifer. I wanted it to be slow and agonizing, so he would feel even an ounce of what he had caused me ... of what he would cost me.

My head was fuzzy. My heart pounded in my chest, sending my blood rushing. My fists clenched, forcing the veins in my arms to protrude. I gritted my teeth, willing this darkness to fade, but it was intoxicating.

"Seren," Lilith said, softer than her usual assertive tone. I snapped my eyes to her, still breathing heavily. "Your eyes."

I took in my reflection in the mirrored wall to my left. My eyes were black as night. Small blue veins stretched from my sockets, traveling through the veins on my face like the roots of a tree. The blackish streams continued down my neck to my chest and arms. My sun- kissed skin had turned white as snow, a stark contrast to the black.

I grabbed my head, trying to force the darkness to subside, but focusing on it only seemed to make it grow. The well of power began to overflow, my body trembling from the force. The dark, inky substance inside of me slithered through my limbs, taunting me to play.

Needing it to stop, I gave in, the power reaching the surface. With one massive push, I thrust my hands towards the wall of mirrors. Tendrils of dark, silky magic exploded from my hands, shattering the wall into dust, straight through the foundation, blasting an opening in the side of the mountain.

But it wasn't enough. The power surged through me, more alive now that I had opened the box and let it out. The stone floor cracked, sending spiderweb fractures through the room and up the walls. Everything faded into the darkness as it took control.

I took a breath, a real breath, for the first time in a long time. My fears, worries, and stress faded. I heard myself laughing as I stretched my body, taken by the chaos. I was weightless. Powerful. Invincible.

I began to levitate. This room, this castle, this world was too small. Another loud boom ruptured through the air and then ... I was free.

I continued to rise, the smooth caress of this forbidden magic dancing around my body, slithering across my skin like a lover's caress. God, this felt incredible. Then, something tightened around me, compressing my magic, preventing me from unleashing it again. I fought against it, but the force was strong, and familiar.

I opened my eyes and the darkness cleared from my vision to reveal Talia floating in front of me. Her skin was pale and opaque, bluish-black ink spreading through her veins. Her eyes were black like mine, except a faded white fog swirled within them.

She opened her arms wide, then slammed her hands together, constricting the barrier around me. I couldn't move, my hands, legs, and head frozen by her magical force. I groaned, my power fighting to be free as she pulled me back to the ground.

As soon as my feet touched the stone, two arms wrapped around my body while Talia's magic continued to hold me captive. I thrashed, trying to fight my way back to my euphoric state. I heard myself screaming in an unnatural pitch. My head spun as I shook, trying to free myself.

The arms tightened, holding my head firmly against my captor. The magic inside of me burned like fire. At first, it asked nicely to be released. When I couldn't free it, the magic began to beg, scratching inside of my soul. Soon the scratching turned into thrashing and tearing within me, as it ripped its way through my veins like a ravaged animal trying to escape.

I screamed from the pain of it all. My skin was drenched in sweat. Streams of tears fell from my eyes while my head spun and my stomach heaved. I felt like I was dying. The magical barrier finally let go, allowing me to move. My hands clawed desperately at my arms, trying to dig the substance out so the pain would stop. The arms around me tightened just as warm blood began to trickle from my skin.

"Breathe," I heard a muffled female voice above me. "You are in control. It obeys you. Do not let it take control."

I took a few staggered breaths, trembling from head to toe.

"That's it," the voice said again. "Now, create a box in your mind and call the darkness into it."

I did as the voice said, imagining a large metal prison, fused together with magic. I stood next to it while the dark magic thrashed and fought not to be contained. All around me, the magic dug in its nails, resisting the trap. Finally, after the last of the poison entered the box, I slammed the lid shut. The cube rattled and screamed, the power fighting to be free once again.

I took a deep breath, the burning in my veins ceasing. My vision cleared as my body flung forward, gasping for air. The arms released me just before I hurtled over on all fours and retched my guts onto the floor. I sat back on my knees, taking in the destruction I had caused.

Two out of the four exterior walls were completely gone. The roof on the training facility was blown apart, snow from outside sprinkling around us. The floor was cracked and broken apart, no longer level or usable. All the glass in the area was shattered. The training equipment was destroyed and every blade in the room now protruded from the eastern wall.

The princes along with Lilith and Talia stood around me. Their faces twisted with confusion and fear. I turned behind me and found Deus's expression full of concern and worry. I didn't know what to say. Talia stood above me, her skin and eyes reverted back to their natural coloring.

"I ..." I tried to speak, but couldn't find the words.

"His power requires a very specific amount of control," she said, arching an eyebrow, assessing me.

"Did ... did anyone get hurt?" I asked.

"Lilith was able to get everyone out," answered Deus, running a hand down my back. "We shifted people out of the castle just in case."

"Oh, my God," I whispered, covering my face in shame.

"What in the fuck was that?" asked Mammon.

"That is what happens when Luc's power goes unchecked," answered Talia. "It took me years to master it, even with his help."

"Fantastic," exclaimed Belz. "We have a ticking time bomb on our hands."

"Something must have provoked it," Gor said. "What were you doing beforehand?"

"Just training," Lilith answered. "She was practicing her sword positions. She got a little overzealous and shattered the blade on a dummy ... then, the change started."

Talia's eyes never left me. *"Please,"* I whispered into her mind, *"get me out of here. I don't want to be interrogated ... not now."*

"Your mate isn't going to leave your side," she replied, glancing behind

me to Deus.

"Just make something up," I begged. I felt Talia's eyes on me, but I didn't meet them again.

A violent tug on my arm hoisted me into the air, but Deus grabbed my other side, preventing me from standing.

"What do you think you're doing?" he demanded.

"I'm removing a potential threat," Talia answered, pulling on my arm again.

"You aren't taking her anywhere," he growled, pulling me into his chest.

"She is obviously unstable," Talia said. "She could go off again at any moment. Let me take her somewhere safe until she can stabilize herself. I can teach her how to maintain control."

"Deus," I whispered, looking up at him with desperation. "I don't want to hurt anyone. Let me go ... please."

"Then I'm coming with you," he answered.

I shook my head. "No. I won't be able to focus. Please. I will be okay."

He examined me for a moment with confusion and hurt. "You're not going with her alone," he said firmly.

"We'll take Lilith," said Talia. Lilith nodded, accepting the invitation silently.

Deus's hands tightened on me. *"I don't understand why you're pushing me away,"* he said into my mind.

"I'm not, my love. I just need to figure this part of myself out on my own. Talia is the best chance I have to control this wilderness inside of me."

"How long will you be gone?"

"I'll be back by morning, I promise," I said, kissing him softly on the lips. The pain I was causing him flickered down the bridge. "I love you."

"I love you. Hurry home."

Talia, Lilith and I joined hands, and Talia shifted us out of the rubble. Her magic tore around us, more aggressive than any of the princes. It was violent and agitated like a beast caged, trying to escape.

Chapter Thirty-Five

I felt the heat of the sun first. When my vision cleared, dull beige sand surrounded me. The sounds of a bustling city could be heard off in the distance. Towering buildings with glistening rooftops radiated sunlight like a beacon.

"Seriously?" Lilith commented, dusting off her leather fighting clothes, clearly annoyed with the abundance of sand.

"Where would you have chosen?" asked Talia, seeming unimpressed. "A mystical garden?"

"Ha, ha," Lilith replied, rolling her eyes.

"Anyone want to clue me in on where we are?" I asked.

Talia's eyes narrowed on me. "Mizraim."

"It's Cairo now," Lilith corrected.

"Cairo?" Talia spat, turning to look at the city. "What a peculiar name. Regardless, this was my home long ago."

"Yes, well, thankfully we won't have to stay in a stable for the night," Lilith taunted.

"Why would we stay in a stable?" asked Talia.

"Stable ... manger ..."

Talia gave no indication she knew what Lilith was talking about.

"Oh, for heaven's sake," the demon sighed. "Just follow me. Hopefully we can get some rooms for the night." Lilith stormed towards the city, leaving Talia clueless behind.

We traveled on foot for an hour until we reached a hotel within the city limits. I felt like I was going to die. The fighting leather I wore clung to my body like a torture device, making it impossible for my skin to breathe. I was a drenched mess by the time we got to our rooms. All three of us went different directions, needing our moments of peace.

I showered, changing into a thin white cotton dress. My hair curled and frizzed from the heat. My skin seemed to glow, enjoying the drink of sunlight. After a moment to clear my head, I went down to the café on the first floor and was surprised to see Talia and Lilith already sitting at a table, ignoring one another as they sipped on their drinks.

"Starting without me, are you?" I said, trying to break the ice.

"What is going on?" asked Lilith. "Someone better start talking, or I am out of here." Always to the point, that one. The waiter came over, placing a glass of something cold in front of me. I thanked him and took a sip.

"I thought you pledged your services to the little tribrid," mocked Talia.

"I did," replied Lilith, anger brightening her eyes. When she got like this, I could see how she and Satan were perfect for each other.

"I vowed to protect her," Lilith replied, "I'm not interested in playing games. Obviously, she trusts you. Stupid decision on her part, but I'm not one for telling people how to live their lives."

"You trusted me once," Talia said nonchalantly.

"And look where that got me," Lilith snapped with aggravation. "What in the hell is going on?"

"We need your help," I said. "But everything you learn here tonight stays between the three of us. Nothing can be repeated. That includes to Satan ... and Deus."

Her eyes bored into me like lasers. "I don't like this," Lilith said.

"Neither do I," I agreed, "believe me."

"Start talking," she ordered.

I told her everything. What I had learned, the plan to kill Lucifer, the sacrifice Talia and I were willing to make—everything. If I had any chance of getting the space required from Deus when the time came, I needed Lilith to know the entire plan. Plus, she deserved the truth. If I was going to trust her with this, I had to trust her fully. This was my way of showing her I did.

"Why are you telling me this?" Lilith said, showing no reaction to my admission that I was going to sacrifice myself.

"Because I need your help," I answered. "When I go to make the final blow, Deus will try to stop me. He will figure out what I am about to do, and he will intervene. I need you to activate a barrier spell, locking me and Lucifer inside, making sure no one can get in or out."

Her eyes widened. "You want me to act against Asmodeus, trapping his mate inside a magical barrier so she can kill herself?" She paused, processing the words. "If you want me dead, Seren, just do it now."

"He will understand," I replied. "It will be hard, but afterward, when the world continues to live and those who we love are happy ... safe, he will understand. He must."

"Why can't Talia do it?"

"Once I am in range, Talia will use her gate to get to Hell, where the cage will be waiting. As soon as Lucifer is dead, leaving the earthly plane and returning to Hell, he will be sucked inside. To lock him in, she needs to feed her lifeforce into the cage. She won't have time to do both."

"Why me?" asked Lilith.

"Because, next to Talia and me, you are the strongest. Deus's brothers won't act against him. I can't trust them. But you ... you I can trust. You can understand the need to do anything to save your mate and the ones you love."

She looked down for a long time, not saying a word. "Asmodeus will never forgive me," she whispered.

I reached across the table, taking her hand in mine. "Maybe not, but at least he will be able to live a happy life on earth. He won't have to return to Hell."

"You really think he is going to find any type of happiness once you're gone?" she said. "Have you learned nothing about the effect of the mating bond and what losing one does to the other?"

"He will need to—" I stopped, swallowing down the pain that enveloped me. "He will need to continue on ... even after I am gone. Hell depends on it. The world depends on it." She wouldn't look at me. "Lilith ... think of Satan, of the years apart, of all you've sacrificed. After Lucifer is dead, you have the rest of eternity to make up that time. To live happily ... together."

She pulled her hand from mine, her face absent of emotion. "I'll do it," she finally whispered.

"Oh, thank the Father," mumbled Talia, calling the waiter over. "Now, we can begin drinking."

I reached back, squeezing Lilith's hand. "Thank you," I said, a tear running down my face.

"This will destroy him," she replied. "Utterly destroy him. You know that, don't you?"

I nodded. "But the others will live. The world will continue to live.

This is what I was designed for. My destiny was written long ago. I've tried to fight it. I've tried to change it, but my fate was decided before I even existed."

"What can I get you?" the waiter said in Arabic.

"Three glasses of your strongest liquor," Talia requested.

"Just bring the bottle," corrected Lilith. "We're going to need it."

That night, the three most deadly and powerful women in the entire existence of mankind sat around a small wooden table drinking, arguing, and debating until the sun set and then rose again. Three women, mated to the three strongest Princes of Hell, finding similarities between each other even though we came from different time periods.

I managed to get a few hours of rest. It was hard to sleep in an empty bed, but the distance was necessary. I had completed the last part of the puzzle ... getting Lilith on board to make sure Deus remained alive.

Talia appeared at my door the next morning. I stepped aside, allowing a deadly predator to enter my room. Her beautiful, silvery white hair was pinned away from her face, allowing her elegant features to shine brightly.

"Are you ready to return?" she asked, going to the window overlooking the vast desert.

"I don't really have a choice," I replied, "but I do miss Deus."

"Naturally." A moment of silence passed before I joined her.

"Do you miss your time?" I asked, noticing how her eyes scanned the horizon.

"Not particularly. This time ... this era has an easiness to it. Yet, at times, I do miss the stillness of my millennia. Here, everything is so loud and fast. Mankind overlooks and takes for granted the beauty and quiet that surrounds them. What is the point of living, if you never take time to enjoy it?"

I grinned. "That's why I enjoy my home with Deus. There's just ... silence. Everything stills and comes to a halt. Especially in the winter."

She tilted her head towards me, seeming to assess my being. "I find it curious how such a passive creature such as yourself is not only mated to a demon prince, but contains a part of the most evil creation ever to exist."

I laughed, shaking my head. "Imagine the inner conflict I deal with on an hourly basis."

"That's the problem," she said, turning fully towards me. "In order to overcome this instability, you must stop fighting yourself and allow the darkness in. This—our—power is not innately evil, but it is all consuming. Luc and I chose to use our magic for evil, but that was our choice ... our free will. You can choose a different path, but you need to embrace it. Like it or not, it is a part of you.

"You can allow the gift to consume you, or become one with it. Either way, the choice is yours on how you wield it. To defeat him, you will have to use every single ounce of power you have. You can't afford to fight the devil and yourself at the same time. If you reject this part of yourself ... he wins."

I mulled over her words, trying to make sense of it all. "It just feels ... wrong."

"And what were your feelings at first about Asmodeus, when you discovered his true identity?"

I thought back to the first time I heard the words 'demon prince' slip through Nonna's lips after our encounter in the woods. "Scared ... unsure ... dangerous."

"And now?"

"Peace," I said without thinking.

"Exactly. You embraced him entirely, something others fear. Someone others don't understand or even attempt to get to know. Once you opened yourself to the possibility that he was not evil, that you could trust him, you found your destiny. This will be the same revelation once you embrace all of yourself and stop fighting what has always been there."

I nodded, feeling I understood at least a bit more. "You're a good teacher."

Her eyebrow arched. "I prefer the title dictator, oppressor, tyrant even; but teacher, I am not."

"Well, I beg to differ."

She smirked for a quick moment before her stoic, fearless mask resumed.

A knock came at the door. I opened it, allowing Lilith to barge in with a greeting.

"Time to go," she barked harshly. "I refuse to stay another minute in this god forsaken land out of my own free will."

I smiled, making my way to her side. "Ya know," I said while we circled up. "Mal was a lot more joyful to be around than Lilith."

She narrowed her eyes at me. "Yes, I am aware of how spectacular my acting skills are. It just shows I am capable of anything."

Talia huffed in amusement. "Except preventing your memories from being erased."

Lilith glared at her as we completed the circle. White fog overcame us as the shift home began. "Bitch," Lilith said with a sneer, then we shifted home.

I thanked both of them and headed to my room. I opened the doorway to my connection with Deus, searching for his comforting presence, when I saw Nonna perched at one of the windows, watching the snow fall.

I approached her silently. Without turning around, she said, "Good morning, bambina. How was your retreat?"

"Nonna, I am so sorry about the castle," I said, the guilt of what I had done settling in my chest. "I will rebuild it myself if I must. Whatever it takes."

"Rebuilding has already begun, so there's no need for that. Your attention needs to be focused on more pressing matters." Her eyes finally turned to me. "I've been thinking about your little suicide mission."

I stepped closer to her, looking around to make sure no one was listening. "Lower your voice," I whispered.

"I am not daft, child. Do you think I would really be speaking with you about this if I thought someone of importance would overhear? Now, as I was saying … I've been thinking about Lucifer and his powers. It seems that even his mate is unaware of how deep his well of magic stretches."

"What are you getting at?"

"You will need all of us," she answered directly. "All the Salvo women to harness his power without burning out prematurely."

"Have you found a way to pull that off without telling them what I am really doing?"

"I will tell them that I've come up with a teleportation spell that needs the blood ties of our ancestry. I will write some bogus words for them to chant to help with the illusion. Your mother and I will be at the end of either line, keeping Frankie and Thora closest to you. When it is time, the power will transfer from our siphoning power, through the girls, and then into you."

"That's brilliant," I whispered.

"Yes, well, it will need to be a slow process to make sure you have time to absorb what you need. Thus, the blood tie providing a stable conduit."

I took her hands, rubbing the tops of her soft hands. "Thank you, Nonna. Truly."

She forced a smile across her tired face, reaching out to caress my cheek. "You are my heart, Seren. I would do anything for you."

"Love," Deus's voice called from behind me. I turned to see his beautiful figure a few feet away down the hall. My heart leaped and a smile erupted on my face.

I turned back to Nonna. She was still smiling, a small tear running down her chin. "Go to your husband, bambina. Cherish each other ... always." She kissed me on the cheek.

I resisted the urge to run into Deus's arms. As soon as I was in reach, his hands were on me, one latching around my waist while the other tangled in my hair, bringing my mouth to his. A rush of passion, comfort, and excitement filled me. God, the things this demon did to me.

He laughed, pulling away. "So, you like the things *this demon* does to you then?" he said with an arched eyebrow.

"Like there was ever a doubt in your mind," I replied.

His face fell in a more serious expression. "Did you get what you needed?"

"I did. I feel much more in control." I ran my hand down his smooth face. "Thank you for understanding that I needed time. I know it wasn't easy."

"I just want you to be okay," he whispered, pressing his forehead to mine. "I just want you to be happy and safe."

"I know," I said, running my hands through his hair while I basked in his presence.

Mammon and Belz appeared beside us in a storming rage of dust and wind, slamming into the stone floor. They were out of breath. Mammon bent over, his hands on either knee, trying to calm himself.

"What is it? What happened?" asked Deus. Nonna coming to his other side.

"It's not good, brother," Belz said, shaking the sand off his clothing.

"The bitch was right," said Mammon. "Lucy is in the Negev desert."

"But as usually," Belz added, "we are three steps behind."

"What are you two talking about," snapped Nonna. "What did you find?"

"He's raising his armies from the earthly plane—" Mammon gasped.

"And from Hell," finished Belz.

"Impossible," Deus whispered, his grip tightening on me.

"It's true," Belz continued. "He somehow has evaded our spies. We only found out because Hashen was finally able to locate Victoria."

"And where is my least favorite vessel?" I asked, trying to remain in control of my temper.

"Currently," Mammon answered, "teleporting Lucy's legions from Hell into Earth."

"Little bitch," Nonna spat, pursing her lips together.

"We can do that?" I asked with surprise.

"I am pretty sure they got the idea from you," answered Belz. "You were able to transport Deus and Giana out of Hell using your gate, remember?"

"Crap," I whispered.

"And from the looks of it," added Mammon, "that is what he's been up to all these months while we've been sitting on our asses doing nothing."

"There are thousands of them, Asmodeus," said Belz, already sounding defeated. "Possibly more."

"Aradia, help us," whispered Nonna.

"If Victoria can use her portal to bring demons from Hell," I said, "then why can't Talia and I do the same?"

"It's possible," answered Belz, "but it would take months to transport even a portion of his forces. Even with two of you."

"We'll start right away," I suggested.

Mammon shook his head. "We have days, at best, before he strikes."

The war had finally come.

CHAPTER THIRTY-SIX

Talia and I immediately began opening gateways to Hell, transporting dozens of demons in at a time. The amount of energy it took to maintain the stability of the gate was exhausting. I had never held it for more than a few seconds before. I was able to open my gate ten minutes at a time, while Talia's stabilized without faltering for over an hour. Her power was remarkable. I jumped back in as soon as I felt up to it, forcing everything I had into the portals, trying to hold them while Deus's legions made their way from Hell to earth.

These creatures were terrifying. They came in all shapes and sizes, monsters of myth and lore. I was thankful I wouldn't be fighting any of them—though, I had no clue what creations Lucifer had concocted for the occasion.

We informed the covens of our new alliances, making sure they were aware what they would be fighting against. Deus and Belz felt it was best to keep our new visitors secured within the confines of the princes' properties until it was time for battle. None of us challenged that decision.

The castle was buzzing with apprehensiveness. Everyone was restless, waiting for the trumpet to sound that would lead most of us to our deaths. Deus and his brothers were busy, making sure the covens were as equipped as possible. Everyone had been trained in the basics of sword fighting, just in case they ran out of bullets and our magic was still unusable. We had backup plans for our backup plans, but I knew it still wouldn't be enough.

Nonna had sent word to the other groups of witches and warlocks who were not at the castle, making sure they were ready and prepared when called upon. We had large groups of members all over the world gathering in one place so when it was time, one princes would be able to shift them to Negev. Our numbers tapped out at somewhere around three thousand, not including the children that we had already secured safe placement for.

After making the final travel arrangements, deciding which brother would go where, I found myself at Talia's door. I knocked twice before her monotone voice echoed, "Come in."

She stood in front of a mirror, her white hair braided back away from her face. She wore a pair of fitted leather fighting pants and a thin top that left her arms exposed, crossing in front of her to flow down to her midthigh in sections. She assessed herself, turning her head from one side to the other, moving uncomfortable.

"Why the women of this age prefer pants over dresses is beyond me," she said, finally bringing her eyes to mine.

"Depends on the event, I guess," I replied.

"What can I do for you, little tribrid?"

I shut the door behind me, walking towards her. "How are you doing?" I asked.

She held my gaze for a moment before speaking. "Fantastic," she said, returning her attention to the thin sweeping fabric of her shirt as she smoothed it against her body.

"Are you nervous to see him again?"

She froze, then turned to face me. "Am I nervous to see the love of my life who betrayed me ... who tried to kill me ... after three thousand years? Not at all."

I knew her sarcasm was an act; I could only imagine the turmoil her heart was experiencing. "If you want to talk about it," I said hesitantly, "I'm here. Just in case."

"Thank you, but that won't be necessary. As I've told you before, I am fully prepared for what must be done."

"He's your mate, Talia," I said, more assertively than I expected. "I don't know what the two of you went through, and I can't pretend to understand your unfathomable attraction to one another, but regardless of what he has done, I know that love hasn't gone away. Somewhere inside of you, there's a piece of you that is screaming to become one with him. To forget everything and start again, no matter the cost."

"And how do you know what my heart feels?"

"Because ... in Hell, when I saw Asmodeus at his worst, no matter what he did, who he killed or fucked, something inside of me tried to find the golden lining to every horrible thing he did. Just so I'd be able to touch him, one more time. I know that pull ... and I know how intoxicating it can be. For what it's worth, your resilience is honorable."

She laughed. "There is nothing honorable about me, Seren."

"Maybe not in your time, but I wouldn't say that about the Talia in mine. All the brothers have committed unforgiveable offenses, but it doesn't mean they're not worth saving. You're capable of love ... of laughter ... of compassion. As hard as you've tried to hide it, I can see the humanity still clinging to your soul." I paused to let my words settled in. "I think I would have liked to know you back in your time."

She scoffed, arching a brow as her devilish smile spread across her angelic face. "I would have killed you on the spot," she replied. "I don't like competition."

I laughed. "Regardless, I can't help but respect the woman who avenged her sister without a single shred of power. That Talia Mizrahi is a badass. That is the woman I would have stood by ... without question."

Her smile softened, face twisting with discomfort while she played with the fabric of her top. "I don't like the way you make me feel."

Without thought, I threw my arms around her lean body, hugging her tightly. Though she didn't return the gesture, I still held on, hoping someone would do the same for me if I were in her position.

I pulled away, looking into the broken soul that flickered behind her eyes. Eyes that had seen so much.

"I have nothing but respect for you, Talia," I said softly. "You are brave and strong. Stronger than you give yourself credit for." She stared at me with an emptiness I wouldn't wish on my worst enemy. Knowing I wouldn't get a word out of her after my little display of affection, I left her to her own reflection, needing to find my mate.

"Where are you?" I asked in my mind, following the tug on my heart.

"Training in the half-destroyed gym someone decided to blow to pieces," he replied a moment later. *"Everything alright?"*

My legs weren't fast enough. Before I could think better of it, I shifted, landing directly next to him. The scent of him put me over the edge. I barreled into his firm body, not caring who was there or what they were doing. My hands were on him, our mouths pressed against one another while I ripped his clothing from his body, needing to feel his skin pressed against mine.

He returned my silent request, unbuckling my pants first and then pulling my top over my head. Whoever had the misfortune of being in the room quickly escaped, shutting the doors behind them, leaving us to our passion.

Before his pants were completely off, I jumped into his arms, wrapping my legs around him, reaching for his hard cock, positioning it just where I needed. I groaned, pulling away from his mouth while I arched my back, enjoying every glorious inch of him. He drove his teeth into my neck, pulling another whimper from my lips before slamming me into the training mat as he thrust in and out. I held on, savoring every feeling, every sound, every memory of this perfect moment together.

I flipped him on his back, forcing his cock to hit the very top of me. I cried out, taking a moment to adjust. I slowly moved, quickening my pace as the slight pain was replaced with pleasure. He kneaded my breasts, sliding his thumb across my lips just before I bit down on it, moaning from the feeling of him.

He pulled my head down to his, taking my mouth with passion while his hands skimmed my skin, leaving gooseflesh in his wake. I felt the pressure build, the unexplainable feeling that arose inside of me every time he touched me. My core tensed while I approached my edge, and he slammed his hips faster inside, bringing me to climax.

I closed my eyes and yelled, my body going immobile while he moved, tightening his fingers into my hips until he found his release. He held me there, enjoying the sensation. Finally, his grip on me relaxed, and my body collapsed onto his, completely breathless.

My body was damp, causing my hair to stick to my face. His fingers gently moved the strands while he lovingly caressed my skin. He kissed me on my head as I lay on his chest, listening to his beautiful heartbeat.

"You know," he said, lifting my chin up so he could see my face. "All you had to say was meet me in the bedroom, and I would have been there in a heartbeat."

I smiled, pressing a kiss to the beauty mark on his upper cheek. "It would have cost me too many seconds I couldn't afford," I replied.

He chuckled, brushing the hair behind my ear. "If you wanted an audience, we could have thrown a party back home."

"Oh, God ... who was all in here?"

"Some young coven members and my brothers, minus Gor." I bit my lip, the embarrassment of my impulsiveness heating my cheeks. "Don't worry. I told all my brothers to get everyone the fuck out or I would remove their favorite parts. Seems I still have a way with words."

I covered my face, laughing into his chest. He rolled me over, pulling my body into his, holding me. "I guess I am living up to my new title. The wife of lust and all."

"I thought your title was Queen of Hell?"

I rolled my eyes. "I don't like that one," I answered.

He smiled. "Well, in my opinion, out of all your titles, mate of Asmodeus Rasnov is my favorite."

I grinned, relaxing in his arms. "There, we agree."

"And who ever said women couldn't be agreeable?"

I smacked him, a bout of laughter spilling from deep in his chest.

"I am very agreeable, thank you," I said.

"An argumentative pain in the ass at times, but I like that ass," he said, pinching my butt, causing me to jerk.

"Now, about round two," I said, pulling him on top of me.

Chapter Thirty-Seven

"How many does that make?" I gasped, my arms falling like wet noodles to my side.

"Just under a thousand," answered Gor, pushing a chair towards me before I collapsed.

"Dammit," I said, running the back of my hand over my sweaty brow.

"It's only been five days," he replied. "You and Talia have been working endlessly. It's more than we had to begin with."

"Lucifer has thousands," I pointed out. "They've had months to prepare."

"Yes, but we also have competent witches and six Princes of Hell. We are going to give them one hell of a fight."

I looked at my friend: the brother I'd never had, the reclusive prince I now loved with my entire heart. "Promise me, if things go bad, you and G will get out," I said, needing to know they'd be safe.

He looked at me, startled. "We're *all* walking out of this, Seren."

I scoffed, leaning over my knees. "Come on Belphagor, be serious for a damn moment. This isn't the first war you've been a part of. It's unrealistic to believe that. Especially with the odds we're facing."

He smirked. "I know I'm in trouble now ... you used my whole name."

"When in the hell did you get all playful on me?" I snapped. "You're supposed to be the serious one here, remember?"

"I'm tired of always looking at the glass half empty. For the first time in my entire existence, I have a future worth looking forward to. I'm choosing to focus on that and not on the other things I can't control."

"Exactly! You have a future with G. Now, promise me ... promise me that if the tides turn against us, you will take her and leave. Go somewhere he will never find you and live that beautiful life you've been waiting for."

His eyes narrowed, brow furrowing. He remained silent for longer than I liked, while I watched the gears in his brilliant mind begin to crank. "What aren't you telling me?" he said in a flat and stern tone.

"What?"

"You're hiding something. I know you well enough to see that. Now, what is it? What are you planning?"

I retained my solemn expression, controlling my face not to give anything away. "I'm not hiding anything. I just ... I love you Gor. You and G. I need to know you'll be safe, no matter what that cost might be."

He stood from his chair, kneeling in front of me. His beautiful porcelain face was calm, with a strong jaw and thin, slightly curved lips. His black hair was disheveled as usual. His deep eyes, seeming to pull you in as if they were black holes.

He kissed the top of my hand and rubbed his thumb across my knuckles. "I am your friend, first and foremost. I am your brother secondly; a title I wear with pride. But I am also your humble servant, Seren De Salvo. I will stand by your side in the midst of what is to come." Tears began to well in my eyes. "I will fight next to you ... for you. I would lay down my life to see that you live."

"No, Gor—"

"Seren," he interrupted, holding my face in his hand, wiping the tears away. "Your life means more to me than my own. You are the most honorable person I have ever known. A born leader with a heart that I cherish deeply. Father made no mistakes when he chose you for this task. You will be victorious. I have no doubt."

I fell into him, wrapping my arms tightly around his neck. "I love you, Gor."

"And I love you, little goddess."

Keeping the portals open had drained me. I returned to our room, looking forward to a warm bath and my favorite pair of sweats. I opened the door and found nothing but darkness inside. Moonlight trickled through the glass doors to my balcony as the snow fell softly. I smiled at the beautiful landscape.

I felt the bite of the cold, metal handles as I pulled the panes of glass open, allowing the cool breeze to ease my heated flesh. Soft snow fluttered against my skin, tickling my nose. I closed my eyes, basking in the stillness of the wintery haven.

The sound of flapping caught my attention. I opened my eyes just in time to see a small white figure flying through the snow towards me. I squinted, trying to clear my vision. As the object approached, I realized it was a dove ... a little dove. I swallowed, taking a step back. The bird was headed straight towards me.

Its beautiful white wings fought against the strong gusts of wind as it beelined for my face. Before it made contact, the bird flung out its wings, hovered above me, and combusted into flames. The bird shrieked and whined in pain as its small body burned.

The blazing force that consumed the little dove sent me stumbling back to the floor. It flapped and flailed until its body turned to ash, falling into a pile in front of me. The remains shifted and swirled, gathering into the shape of a rectangle, no ... an envelope. A black envelope, addressed to me.

Hesitantly, I reached out, taking it from the floor, ash sprinkling from the surface. I turned it over, breaking the seal and pulling out the paper within. It read:

Life.

An ever changing, ever escaping facet of this world we long to possess.

Possession.

An all-consuming obsession we all desire.

Desire.

That which we long to experience.

Experience.

The memories that build a life.

Life.

Unimportant until it no longer exists.

Something you will understand very soon, little Seren De Salvo.

...It is time.

~L

"Everyone, get your shit and get to your damn stations, now!" barked Nonna to no one specifically. The halls were filled with witches and warlocks scurrying from place to place, gathering weapons and telling their loved ones goodbye. Nonna had assigned each person a group location so it would be easy for those who could shift to move large numbers to the desert.

After I finished having a small panic attack reading Lucifer's morbid excuse for a poem, I informed the others. Everyone snapped into action, readying to leave at a moment's notice. With all the moving pieces now activated, I still couldn't process that we were now stepping into a war, even though we had been preparing for months.

Frankie rounded one a corner, dressed in black fighting gear with green stripes decorating the sides of her arms and at her waist. She bee-lined straight for me, wrapping me up in her embrace as her loose strands of hair tickled the side of my face. I pulled her into me as tightly as I could, not knowing if this would be the last time.

She pulled away, forcing a smile. "You look good in black and red," she said, touching the red leather swirls that extended from my shoulders down the length of my arms.

"I was thinking the same thing about you, except for the green," I replied with a soft smile.

"House representation and all," she said jokingly. I huffed a laugh, trying to hold myself together. "Hey," she whispered, pressing her forehead against mine. "We're all coming out of this alive. There is no alternative. Not after everything we've been through. There can't be."

"God, I hope you're right," I strained to get out, squeezing her arms.

"You're powerful. You're strong. You've got this. I believe in you."

I took a moment, blocking out all the commotion in the busy hall. "Promise me you'll be careful," I said.

"Have you met me?" she replied.

I laughed. "That's why I am making you promise. No unnecessary risks. Promise me."

"I promise," she replied, holding my hands tightly. "And when the time comes to send that sadistic bastard into his cage, I will be there, standing at your side."

"Nonna told you about the plan?" I asked.

She nodded. "We know where we need to be and we'll all be there, standing by your side." She took a dagger that was strapped to her side and sliced her hand before grabbing mine and doing the same. She placed her wound over mine, squeezing my hand tightly. "Tied by blood," she said softly. "Bonded by ancestry. Chosen by fate." A tear silently rolled down her cheek. "We will always be connected to each other. You are my sister. My soulmate. My best friend."

"I love you so much," I replied, pulling her back into me.

"I love you too, Seren."

"Move your asses," Nonna yelled at a couple of young warlocks who looked like lost sheep in the halls. Frankie looked at me and we both smiled. Nonna headed towards us, dressed similarly minus the pop of color. "Are you both ready?" she asked, touching each of our faces while she assessed the weapons we had strapped to our bodies.

"Ready to battle a legion of demons from Hell?" asked Frankie sarcastically. "Sure as hell am."

Nonna scoffed. "Smart ass." She winked at Frankie, then turned to me, her face softening. "And you?"

"I know what has to be done," I replied.

"As do I, bambina ... as do I," she said, rubbing the side of my face with her thumb. "Alright then, stop chitchatting and get your asses to your groups. We will meet again on the battlefield." She pulled us both in for a hug. I relished the stolen moment of peace.

Deus appeared behind her, waiting respectfully until our moment was over. Frankie and Nonna headed in one direction and I in the other. Deus took my hand, kissing the back of it tenderly. "Is your mind clear?" he asked.

"I'm doing okay," I replied. "And you?"

"Just ready for this to be over."

"Me too."

We approached the fork in the hall which would separate us into our designated groups. He stopped, pulling me into him and passionately kissing me. Pulling away, he pressed smaller kisses to my lips and face. I held on, breathing in his scent deeply.

"I won't ever be far," he whispered. "Keep that doorway of yours open to me, okay? If you get in over your head, I will be there in a second."

"I know," I replied. My heart broke knowing what I would soon put him through. "Don't do anything stupid this time ... like sacrificing your life to save anyone."

He laughed, looking down into my eyes while holding my face tenderly. "A sacrifice I would make a thousand times over again just to see those beautiful eyes of your smiling back at me."

"I love you so much, Asmodeus. I wish you knew how much."

He kissed me on the head, pulling me against his chest. "I do know how much, my love, but it doesn't compare to the love I have for you."

"Deus," Mammon's voice come from behind us. "They're ready."

Deus nodded at his brother, before kissing me one more time. "Send those fuckers back to Hell, baby," he said, smiling hesitantly at me.

"With pleasure," I replied, releasing him slowly.

I turned, forcing myself not to look back; because I knew if I looked into my mate's loving eyes a moment longer, I would reveal my suicidal plan, hoping he would talk me out of it. Hoping there was a way out, but I knew there was nothing that could be done. Nothing would change my course or my fate. I had fought this path long enough. I was created for this very purpose, and now it was time to bring balance back to our worlds.

I entered the dining hall, greeted by the two neatly organized groups I had been assigned to shift to the desert. A presence that was becoming familiar slithered in my head.

"I will be close," Talia's voice scratched against my mind. *"When it is time, call on me and I will be ready. Until then, don't let your guard down. Be aware at all times."*

"Thank you, Talia ... for everything."

"Thank you, Seren De Salvo. I wish our destinies had been written differently, but I am grateful that our paths crossed. Knowing you has been an honor."

"The honor is mine."

"Have you seen G?" asked Tony, approaching from the first group.

"No, but I am sure Gor has her glued to his side," I replied. His brow furrowed. "That's the safest place she could be ... I promise." I said, trying to ease his worry.

"I know," he said, running his hands over his face.

"Be careful out there, okay," I whispered, placing a hand on his shoulder.

"I will. You too, beautiful." He leaned in slowly, kissing me softly on the cheek. "The world would be a very dull place without you." He placed his arm around my shoulder, and I placed mine around his waist as he escorted me to the first group. I looked at my fellow coven members, armed from head to toe with guns, swords, bullets, and knives. Some looked ready to shred some demons apart, while others fought against the fear, their hands shaking slightly.

I tried to think of something inspiring or passionate to say to them, but my tongue was tied. Some looked so young, while others looked too old to fight. Many might not survive this war, and though it was out of my control, I would still feel their deaths on my conscious.

"We are honored to fight by your side, goddess," an older warlock said, breaking the moment of silence.

"We know what we must do and the sacrifices we must make," said a witch beside him.

"And we are ready to make them pay," said a familiar female voice from the back. The crowd parted. Delphine stepped forward, dressed in black from head to toe. Her blonde hair was pulled back in a braid, two sword hilts poking over each of her shoulders. She approached me with a smile, her eyes still empty. She stopped in front of me, taking my hand in hers. "For all they've taken from us."

I nodded, feeling the sting in my heart. "I wish he was here fighting with us," I whispered.

She placed her hand over my heart and then moved it to hers. "He has always been with us," she replied. "He always will be."

I nodded, knowing her words were true. I took a deep breath while the crowd made a circle, locking their hands together in unison. Delphine took one of my hands and Tony took the other. I looked at both of them for a moment and then shifted us to The Negev Desert.

Chapter Thirty-Eight

Groups of witches and warlocks were scattered throughout an open flat valley that Lilith had strategically chosen. Even though Satan had yet to show up, I was thankful that Lilith shared his knowledge and strategy when it came to war. Lilith was confident Satan would make the right choice, but I wasn't, and neither were the brothers. If I was being honest, we needed him and his forces to stand a chance.

A few scouts were positioned on higher altitudes to assess any incoming threat. The land behind our position allowed us to see for miles, but also served as an escape route if the worst should occur.

I shifted back to Castle Salvo, gathering my last group and escorting them to our rendezvous point. The desert was so beautiful. The sky above us was a bright, clear shade of blue ... it reminded me of Deus's eyes. The beautiful hues of brown that made up the sand and rock formations glistened at the touch of the sun. Everything here was quiet in the most tranquil way. Even the wind seemed to sing as it billowed through the mounds of sand and stone, brushing the hair from my face in a loving caress.

Every few moments, a group of warlocks and witches would shift to our location. Most, I had never seen before. I realized then how little I knew about our family's legacy. Nonna, I was sure, knew most of these members by name and coven. I had only ever been exposed to the members who had visited the castle.

I studied the coven members closely. A man and women stood close to one another, holding each other's hands while the female cried. They looked down at her phone in silence before the woman brought it to her lips and kissed the screen. I knew they must have been looking at a picture of their child or children, overwhelmed by the fear of leaving them orphaned—a fate I would never wish on another. My heart stung from their pain and worry.

"Seren," my mother's voice came from behind me. I didn't move. I just stared at the couple while they held each other. I felt my mom's hand trail down the side of my arm. "How are you holding up?"

Without looking away from the heartbroken parents, I answered, "As well as can be expected." Cloud after cloud of colored smoke puffed across the valley as the princes, Talia, and Lilith continued to transport the groups in. "When will everyone be here?" I asked.

"Your nonna calculated another ten minutes or so," she answered. "Castle Salvo is clear. The princes are now traveling to other countries and continents gather the others." A young boy, who looked no more than fifteen, walked through the crowd of people, handing out waters to those who waited.

I turned to study my mom. Her curly brown hair was pulled away from her face, the sun illuminating the freckles we shared across the bridge of her nose. Her tan skin glistened from the light kissing her softly. Her brown eyes sparkled, as the color seemed to dance within her irises. She was stunning, and her heart made her that much more beautiful.

"I wish we had more time," I whispered, taking her hand. "I wish could have known you before all of this. I wondered about you for so many years, if you were dead or if ... if you just didn't want me."

Her hands were on my cheeks in an instant, her face an inch away. "I wanted nothing more than to bring you into this world," she said, her voice breaking. "I couldn't wait to hold you, to see you laugh with your cousin, to watch you grow and learn. I've never wanted anything in this world more than I wanted you.

"From the moment I discovered I was pregnant, I fell in love with you—a love I never knew could exist. I hope you one day may experience that love for yourself. I knew there was no boundary or law that would prevent me from protecting you. I would defy nature itself to keep you safe ... and I did.

"I hate that I missed so much of your life." She began to cry. "But we can't change the past. All we can do now is look towards the future and be grateful for the time we did have together. Even though that time was short, I couldn't imagine loving you more than I do right now. You are everything I ever dreamed you'd be, and so much more. You are the best of us, Seren. You will continue the Salvo name and do us all proud."

I held onto my mother, sobbing, wishing I could tell her everything. There were no words to express how much I had come to love her. Clinging to her arms, I shook my head, trying to find the right way to give her a proper goodbye. "Mom ... I—"

"No," she interrupted, pressing her forehead against mine. "Don't say a thing. Just know I love you, little bean. I love you more than anything in this world and I will love you even in the next. There is nothing I wouldn't do for you," she said, looking into my eyes sternly, "nothing ... you hear me."

I nodded, unable to speak. She kissed me on the cheek, pulled me into her and held me for a moment I wished would stretch forever.

Sometime later, still wrapped in my mother's embrace, I heard Nonna's voice behind us. "We're all here," she said, approaching Mom and me. Aunt Thora and Frankie accompanied her, looking already spent.

"Where are the demons?" I asked.

"Levi says they will arrive once Lucifer's legions show themselves," answer Frankie.

"How are the princes' magic reserves holding up?" asked Mom.

"They're taking a breather, but they seem to be fine," answered Thora. "Talia and Lilith as well."

"Any sign of Lucifer?" I asked, the anxiety building the longer we were stuck doing nothing. Frankie shook her head.

"I've instructed everyone to get some rest," said Nonna. "We have tents going up as we speak. Might as well relax so everyone is at their best once things begin."

"I don't think anyone will be getting much rest, Mamma," said Aunt Thora.

"Well, at least there will be some calm before the storm," Nonna replied. "Once the fireworks begin, we need to stay close to one another, so when Seren is ready, we will be there."

Everyone nodded, understanding the parts they needed to play. "Why don't you go find Deus, little bean," Mamma suggested. I nodded, emptiness in my heart echoing through my soul at the thought of leaving the ones I loved.

I left without a word, aimlessly searching through the small camp the covens had constructed. My head was fuzzy, and my emotions seemed to go silent. Numbness overtook me while I tried to focus. As the sun began to set and one face seemed to blur into the next, I opened the bridge between us, reaching down the bond for my mate.

"Where are you," I whispered between our minds with a hint of desperation.

"Top ridge to your left," he replied instantly. *"I've been watching you for the past twenty minutes."*

"Then why didn't you say something?"

"I like watching when you're not aware."

"Creep," I replied, rolling my eyes before I shifted to him. I appeared on the ridge, standing over him while he sat casually on the rocky surface. He drew his eyes up to me and smiled. My heart almost stopped at the sight. "Why can't you just be a normal man and aim to make your wife's life a little easier?"

He laughed, pulling me down until I sat comfortably in between his legs. He wrapped his arms around me while I leaned back into his strength. He pressed kisses down the side of my face and then my neck. "Because, little wife," he said, turning my face so he could look into my eyes. "I am neither normal, nor a man. And I do love it when you get all flustered. Your little outbursts entertain me so."

"You're evil."

"And you love it."

I laughed, nuzzling into the side of his face. "I do ... I love absolutely everything about you."

"Yes, after this, we should probably get your head checked."

I pulled back, my mouth gaping. "And here I am, trying to be sweet, and you go and call me mental."

He shrugged. "I do prefer my women a little crazy. Makes bedtime that much more adventurous."

I smacked him in the arm, and he only grinned with amusement. He tightened his embrace while we settled into one another, turning our eyes to the horizon. After a few moments of silence, I felt myself relaxing, experiencing the peace only my mate could provide.

"It's so beautiful here," I whispered. "It's hard to believe this scenery will soon be covered in blood and the bodies of dead coven members and demons. It's a shame."

"Don't think like that," he replied, brushing his thumb down my arm. "You need to stay focused. If you worry about everyone else around you, you will get distracted. Distractions get you killed."

I nodded, knowing what he said was true. "Can I ask you something?"

"Anything."

"If you come face to face with Victoria," I paused, allowing the name of my mate's former lover to settle inside of me before continuing. "Will you be able to kill her?"

He exhaled deeply. "She's made her choice. The Victoria I once knew is gone."

"Do you still feel for her? I only asked because I remember how I felt about Antonio, even after I learned of his betrayal and lies."

"And do you still love the young Simonelli?" he asked, one eyebrow arched.

I smiled, rolling my eyes. "Really?"

"Inquiring minds would like to know."

"I love him as a friend. He is a good man, but ... but the love he and I shared has no comparison to our love. Nothing compares to this. I thought I knew what love was. I remember feeling the joy, even the heartbreak. But now, knowing what it's like to find my missing half ... nothing has nor will ever compare."

"I couldn't have said it better myself," he whispered, leaning down to kiss me softly. "It is unfortunate the Victoria has chosen to align herself with our enemy, but even if she hadn't ... even if she was fighting on our side, there is nothing she could say or do that would cause me to second-guess the blessing I've been given. You are the only one I will ever want or need, for the rest of my existence."

I smiled, completely confident in our love. I turned back to the silent valley. The temperature of the desert was dropping quickly. Small fires began to spring to life around the camp. There were no sounds of laughter or revelry. The camp was utterly silent while everyone waited for their impending deaths.

"What is he waiting for?" I asked, the heaviness of this war settling.

"My brother likes to make a dramatic entrance," he replied, still holding me against his body. "He's trying to get us to let our guard down, so when he attacks, our forces will be scattered and disoriented. I know Nonna wants the covens to rest, but it's probably for the best they don't. Everyone needs to be on guard."

Across the camp, a member of Luna coven gestured and a violin appeared in his hands. Music filled the silent air around us, a sad and haunting rhythm that danced from note to note, seeming to voice my inner emotions. Deus and I sat holding one another while the song consumed us. My eyes shifted from one side of the horizon to the other; one part of me wished the war would begin, while the other hoped we could stay like this ... forever.

CHAPTER
THIRTY-NINE

Hours had passed, yet there was no sign of our enemy. Deus allowed me into his mind to listen while his brothers bantered their theories about what Lucifer was planning. Satan was still radio silent.

The coven members remained quiet. The violin continued to strum from one tune to the next, remaining the only voice that could be heard for miles. The sound of the haunting music led us into the early hours of the morning. The stars out here were so bright and vibrant, creating an exquisite blanket across the sky. I tried to keep my mind clear, taking pleasure in what time I had to silently sit under the stars, safely cradled in the arms of my husband.

Something deep within me began to stir. The power ... the slithering darkness, small yet dangerous, danced with glee.

I flung forward, breaking away from Deus, trying to catch my breath. The flash of magic began to swirl in my chest, trying to escape the cage I had created around it. I would have to tap into that forbidden power to have any chance of winning this fight; but the thought of letting it out of its prison scared the shit out of me.

"What is it," Deus asked.

"It ... I think it's—"A puff of white smoke appeared in front of us.

Deus jumped to his feet in a defensive stance, but I could feel her before she finished materializing.

"Did you feel it?" Talia asked, her calm voice laced with panic. "Did you feel him too?"

Deus relaxed, offering his hand and pulling me to my feet. I nodded, gripping him tightly. "Yes," I whispered. "He's coming."

We alerted Nonna and the elders causing everyone sprang into action, seeming relieved the waiting had finally ended. The faces of our coven members, once filled with pain and sorrow, were now replaced with the masks of warriors.

The princes took their places, strategically spread around the ground we had chosen as our battlefield based off their magic and combat strengths. There was so much we still didn't know. How many demons had Lucifer and Victoria brought to this plane? When would he use the relics to disarm our magic? And would he attempt to separate me from the others to take my power?

I had to remain alert. I knew what he was planning, I just didn't know when he would use it. Plus, we had something that would certainly push him over the edge ... Talia. We had agreed to keep her existence hidden until the last minute. He might turn and go after her to obtain the power he wanted from me, so it was best that we not reveal her presence too soon—not until I had him where I needed him.

I joined my family on the front line. The elders were spread throughout the group, stationed within different units of the coven to distribute their power evenly. Deus and Levi took their places behind Frankie and me. Out of the corner of my eye, I saw Lilith, keeping her distance but staying close enough that when it was time, she would be there to cleave Deus away from me.

The plans were in place. The covens were ready. The princes were prepared. I took a deep breath, quieting the voice inside of me that begged to save myself ... that wanted to live. There was no going back. I knew what needed to be done and even though I was terrified, I was ready to play my part.

A hand slid into mine. I looked over at the face of my beautiful cousin, the first person I had truly loved. My soulmate. She smiled and nodded. We didn't need words. I knew her heart as she knew mine. No matter how my story would end, this ... them ... they were all worth it.

"Time to call your little pets, boys," Nonna said, her face stern and focused while she prepared herself mentally for the battle ahead.

Deus nodded, closing his eyes while he called on the legions we had managed to transport in the short time we were allotted. I felt him reach for our magic, then the memories of my time in Hell came flashing back in bright and vivid colors. The sounds of the demons: the chattering of teeth and the hissing that rattled from their lungs plunged me back into the pit.

I pushed my trauma aside, not allowing it to take me under. Creatures of all shapes and sizes appeared on the higher cliffs that surrounded us. Some shifted to the outer edges of the covens, becoming our first lines of defense. The princes had handpicked their best fighters and most powerful races of demons from each of their territories.

Scales, claws, spikes, and mouths filled with razor-sharp teeth appeared from the smoke, ready to tear their enemies to pieces. We had prepared the coven members early in the week, introducing each type of demon that would be fighting at their sides so the shock of wouldn't be so drastic; but seeing them gathered around us in full form and power set every one of my nerve endings on fire.

I could feel him ... Lucifer. The closer he got, the more desperate his power inside of me became. It was as if the magic I carried called to him, fighting to become whole. How was I going to control it? How would I use it to kill him?

"Because it is your *power,"* I heard Talia's voice inside my head. *"He may have given it to you, but it is the reason you are alive. It has grown inside of you, lacing itself within every fiber of your being. It is yours, Seren. It will do as you command. Harness it. Use it."*

I shook off the self-doubt, trying to calm my mind before the slaughtering began. No matter how hard I looked, I still couldn't see him or his legions. It was some kind of trick ... it had to be. He was clever and calculative. Even with the other princes aligned together, Lucifer was still a rival to fear.

"I love you," Deus's voice said from my side.

I pulled my focus from the horizon and looked into my mate's beautiful blue eyes. I could see the worry and fear spiraling behind them, though he fought to hide it. He brushed his thumb across my cheek, his mouth forming into a soft smile.

"You are powerful, my love," he whispered. "I don't think you've even begun to grasp just how much." He seemed to study every detail of my face. "Use it ... use it all. Reach as deep as that pit inside of you goes and incinerate anything and everything that comes against you. Promise me ... promise me you won't hesitate."

I tilted my head into his touch, savoring the feeling of his warm skin. "I promise," I replied, closing my eyes to stop the tears from falling. "I love you, Deus. Thank you for giving me a life worth living ... worth fighting for."

"You are my salvation, Seren. I will move Heaven and Hell to protect our love and our life together. I made you a promise once that nothing would ever come between us again. I fully intend to keep that promise." He pulled me into his chest, wrapping his strong arms around me. I buried my nose into him, breathing deeply in his scent. He pressed a kiss to the top of my head just as the ground underneath our feet began to rumble. A powerful vibration grew, the small grains of sand popping and dancing into the air.

I pulled away, trying to find the source of the quaking, but the horizon remained empty. The tremors grew, and some of the coven members lost their balance. Our demon forces growled and barked as if they too could feel his presence approaching. Talia stepped next to me, her face cold as stone.

"The gate is in place. This is where I leave you," she said, looking straight ahead.

"How will you stay hidden from him?" asked Deus.

"I know his blind spots," she replied. "Don't worry about me. I will be ready when the time comes." Her eyes shifted slowly to mine. "You have what it takes, little tribrid. Don't doubt yourself. Let the power inside of you become the monster you fear most." Before I could reply, she dissipated in before our eyes.

A loud *crack* invoked yelling from the coven members as the ground began to split, mounds of sand and rock tearing from each other. Veins zigzagged into various roads, dividing our strategic battleground. Large pits appeared from the cracks, revealing red hot, molten lava. The coven members were split by the flows into separated plots of land.

Steam and fog filled the air around us as the wind began to pick up, tossing the sand into the air, preventing a clear line of sight. I guarded my face, the specks scratching against my exposed skin. Rolling waves of sand blasted against us. Deus positioned his body in front of mine, taking the brunt of the impact.

High-pitched screeches rose in the distance in a slow crescendo. As if perfectly controlled by a maestro, the sound grew with an eerie calm and precision. Another loud *crack* slammed into the ground, blasting us off our feet. Then the roars of war erupted clear as day.

A blinding white light shot past my face, accompanied by a humming noise that muted every sound in the valley. The hum deepened and mellowed, and my skin prickled into gooseflesh just as the low tone erupted, blasting through our forces.

The white light faded, revealing hordes of demons. Powers and weapons unleashed, funneling through the air towards the ungodly creatures. Swarms of leathery, black-skinned monsters crawled on top of one another, desperate to sink their teeth and claws into anything that got too close. The creatures descended on our forces, tearing coven members limb from limb before feasting on their flesh.

Our demon forces appeared, launching into their opponents, giving our members time to regroup. Terror rippled through each of them. It was more horrific than I had prepared for.

I dodged a demon hurtling towards me with teeth bared and claws elongated. It screeched, tumbling into the lava pit behind me. Deus appeared in the next breath, bracing my body against his while I regained my balance.

"I've never seen these demons before," he said, blasting his black tendrils towards a group that had gotten too close. One of the demons raced across the sandy terrain on all fours, as fast as a cheetah, dodging every bullet and blast of magic that attempted to take it down. Thick claws dug into the shifting ground, giving it leverage to propel itself forward.

Its long, lean body and powerful legs and arms seemed aerodynamically designed for this climate. A yellow, sticky substance dripped down the creature's teeth, staining its lips. Memories of my time in Hell flashed before my eyes. I turned back to the coven members.

"Don't let them bite you!" I yelled as loudly as I could manage over the sounds of their screams and roars. "Their teeth contain a paralytic." I turned back around, blasting my white flame into another group. Their squeals and screams filled the air while their skin burned to ash.

"He designed them specifically for this battle," I said to Deus. We stood back-to-back, firing our powers into our enemies.

"Doesn't surprise me," he replied, flinging his arms out, sending his power hurtling forward in a wave of black and red static. "Lucy was always talented with arts and crafts."

My shadows became spears, slicing through the demons with little effort. Tunnels of white flames cleared the hordes that attempted to attack my divided coven members.

"Why don't they have magic?" I asked.

"My guess is, Lucy plans to remove our source of power soon. They don't need it if they can't use it."

I scanned the battlefield. Mounds of human body parts and pools of blood splattered across the sand. I pinpointed my family, noting they were safe. Each of them proved a force to be reckoned with. A high-pitched yell caught my attention. As I turned towards it, one of the demons jump through the air, claws and teeth aimed for me. Before I could move, Deus's hand slammed into the air above me, burying in the creature's throat, severing its head from its body with one powerful squeeze.

"Focus!" he yelled, firing a wave of white flames forward. "You can't worry about anyone else during battle—only what is right in front of you."

I listened, tuning my senses to my surroundings. Demon after demon fell around us. My tendrils of darkness slashed through the air, dismembering creatures before they could sink their teeth into our allies.

Three of the monsters crashed into the ground in front of me, causing sand to blast into my eyes. On instinct I turned away, dropping my guard long enough for one of them to slash its claws across my abdomen.

I felt the burn first, then the warm, wet feeling of my blood spilling from the wound. I forced my hand forward, blasting one demon off the edge into the pit. The other two catapulted into the air. Deus caught the first, but the second slammed me to the ground, snapping its teeth at my neck.

The creature sank its claws into my shoulder while I fought to keep the poisonous teeth from my flesh. I let out a scream of pain and gritted my teeth, feeling the dangerous power inside of me thrash, fighting to be released. My arm began to shake, the grip keeping the creature from my neck weakening. A white light appeared from my palm, intensifying with each passing second.

I could feel it then. The creature's skin underneath my own began to soften, melting around my hand. The thing screeched in pain, fighting to free itself from my grasp, but I only tightened my fingers around its neck until the white flame from my palm grew so hot that with one final grasp, my hand severed the creature's neck.

The head fell to the ground as a deep red blood poured from the opening. Its body fell on top of mine. I pushed the foul thing away, scurrying to my feet just in time to see Deus overtaken by demons. I blasted my flame and whipped my shadows forward, wrapping around the legs of the demons and flinging them into the pits. Deus released his own power, sending the rest of them flying backwards and disintegrating into thin air.

"Are you alright?" I asked, noting the deep wounds and scratches that he now bore.

He nodded. "You?"

I looked down at myself, covered in blood and pieces of charred demon flesh. A sick feeling turned in my stomach. I pushed it down and nodded, wiping my sticky hands on the sides of my pants.

Around the battlefield, our enemy's numbers were thinning. More of our own remained standing amongst the piles of dead and dismembered creatures. Slowly but surely, the sounds of battle faded as the last demon was slain.

CHAPTER FORTY

I turned to Deus. "What are we missing?" I asked, inhaling deeply. "There has to be more … this can't be it." His face showed no sign of relief or excitement. He stepped into the field, assessing our surroundings. Our remaining allies began to laugh and cheer. Members of every coven hugged each other while cries of relief filled the air. My family and the princes made their way towards us. Deus remained unnervingly quiet.

"What is it?" I asked, just as Frankie and my mother approached my sides.

"This was too easy," Deus whispered, his brow furrowed.

"Easy?" Frankie laughed. "That was anything but easy. By the looks of it, we've lost half of our coven members to those things."

Deus turned to me. "Can you feel him?" he asked. "Lucifer … can you still feel him?"

I paused, opening the door in my mind only a crack, allowing the part of me I kept under lock and key to see the light of day. Instantly the power rattled to life, screaming to be let free. A shiver ran up my spine and I slammed the door shut. I nodded at Deus. "He's still here," I answered.

"Why hasn't he shown himself?" asked Levi.

"Strategy," said Lilith, stepping forward. "He's bidding his time. Allowing his creatures to thin the herd and tire us out, while he remains rested and at full power."

"And where are the relics?" asked Aunt Thora. "I didn't see anything on the field."

"I don't like this," said Nonna, looking back at her coven members, still celebrating a battle that seemed far from over.

The ground underneath our feet began to rumble, but this time in a rhythmic pace, perfectly spaced apart. *Thud ... thud ... thud ... thud.* The laughter faded back to silence as the realization that more was yet to come settled into the spirits of our people. The loose rocks on the ground jumped with each passing boom. My eyes were drawn to the horizon, focusing on the large figures that slowly approached. I circled around; more of the giants closed in on us, creating a barrier, making it impossible for us to escape.

Each stood at least twenty feet tall, two curved horns adorning either side of their heads. Their bodies were covered in a deep reddish-brown hair. Eyes the color of fire blazed, revealing the wild animal inside. A wide, gaping mouth of sharp teeth growled and sneered. Long and muscular arms ending in clawed fingers dangled from either side of the creature as their hooved feet stomped into the dirt, quickening in pace as they spied their targets.

"What are they?" Frankie asked in awe.

"Goristro," answered Mammon. "Beasts that guard Lucifer's borders, making sure anything unwelcomed gets torn to shreds."

"They're strong," added Gor, "fast, and lethal. They can heal quickly, making them the perfect guard dog to keep the creatures of Hell I'm sure you remember from slipping onto our lands."

"Stout fuckers," added Mammon.

I examined the nearest beast as the Goristro drew nearer. Something around his neck caught a ray of light and shined. The object was thick and clunky, bouncing against the beast's chest as he picked up his pace and began to run.

The breath was ripped from my lungs. I turned; another Goristro had small pieces of silver strung onto a chain hanging from its neck. Yet another carried a large rectangular box on its back. Brown leather pouches hung from the necks of the final two.

"The relics," I blurted, just as a beam of white light shot from the sky, slamming into the center of the covens. The witches and warlocks stumbled back. Our demons formed up, readying to attack. The light faded, revealing a beautiful woman with white hair. Victoria. Her eyes were closed. Her hands folded together like she was praying, while holding some type of orb between her palms.

Her mouth moved quickly while she recited the spell. The Goristro took off into a full-on sprint, closing in the boundary around us. The orb between her hands began to glow with a bright yellow light.

"Kill her," Nonna said, too quiet for anyone but us to hear. "Kill her!" she yelled to the coven members.

Before anyone could move, the light shot from the orb, blasting into the chest of Elder Angela Ferrara. Then, Elder Torrian Astra. Elder Victoria Cavelleer. Elder Lilith Bloodborne.

Delphine shot from the crowd, running faster than light, and crashed into her mother before the light exploded into her chest, sending them both to the ground.

Time slowed. I watched as a yellow whip of light extended from the orb, heading straight for Nonna. Without thinking, I took a play from Delphine's book, racing forward as fast I could, praying my legs wouldn't fail me.

I could hear it, the static zap and snap of electric power, aimed to bury into my Nonna's chest. Out of the corner of my eye, the light raced faster, jumping from particle to particle, reaching for its target. I jumped, throwing my body forward into Nonna, using myself as a shield. We fell to the ground, slamming into the rocky surface. I pinned her down with my body until the zapping sounds dissipated above us.

The elders latched by the white light hovered around Victoria, their bodies paralyzed. A white dome surrounded them, preventing any other member from attempting a rescue mission. Their bodies pulsed forward, convulsing and flailing as if being fed on.

The Goristro came to a halt, taking their places evenly distributed in a circle surrounding us. I focused on Elder Ferrara as her veins filled with a black substance. Her skin paled to a deathly white, the black magic consuming her muscle, fat, and any water that remained. Her cheeks hollowed as her eyes sunk into her skull. Her face was strained with pain, her mouth open as if trying to scream, yet no sound could be heard.

Her body stopped moving, still suspended in the air above the ground. Her skin wrinkled and sagged as the nutrients were sucked from her veins. Her deep, dark eyes filled with agony, a silent plea for help sending a tear down her cheek before the last ounce of life was drained from her entirely.

The arms of yellow light snapped back into the orb, releasing the dead bodies of our elders, sending their empty husks to the ground. The white dome fell and yellow lights blasted out again, sending the power it had stolen from the elders into the Goristro. The creatures roared as the relics they wore activated.

"She used the magic of the elders to power the spell," Nonna whispered, devastated.

And then I felt it. A powerful grip latched inside of my chest, holding firm as it pulled every ounce of life from my body. I gasped, trying to breathe, but there was no point. I was helpless. I reached for my chest, falling to my knees in pain. Cries of anguish filled the air from those around us while our powers were expunged from our DNA, just as the spell had been designed.

Finally, it let go. Gasps for air rang through our forces. Deus was hunched over, fighting to breathe alongside the rest of us. I reached for my magic, but it was no longer there. The witch ... the demon ... the goddess inside of me ... all gone. The emptiness was unnerving. Something that made up so much of my being was now gone.

Victoria had disappeared from the center of our forces. I stood and reached for the guns at my hips, cocking the chambers, readying myself for phase two. Our allies did the same. Our demons readied for attack.

The princes, my family, and our friends lined up next to one another. Belz tilted his head down at me, one eyebrow arched with a devious grin. "Together we stand," he said with a nod.

Mammon stepped up next to him. "Together we fight."

Frankie's beautiful face appeared last. "Together ... we survive."

"We have trained for this," yelled Nonna. "Prepared for this. Everyone knows their places and what must be done. Now, groups—"

The ground around us rumbled. Legions of Lucifer's poisonous black demons appeared, filling in the sections around the Goristro. My heart sank. Our forces didn't stand a chance.

"Focus," Deus said. "Push the doubt out of your mind. Focus on the kill, and then the next." I nodded, while our group moved in closer toward the other coven members.

A figure appeared at the top of the nearest rock mound. The sun shone behind him, creating a halo. He wore a white suit, his hands folded behind his back casually as his blonde hair fluttered in the wind.

"Lucifer," I growled. His eyes found me instantly. His beautiful, wicked smile stretched across his flawless face.

"Once all of your friends are dead," he said, "I am going to make you watch as I gut each of your precious Salvo witches. Then, I am going to force you to watch me remove your mate's soul, setting his true nature free. And this time, little witch, there will be no hope of saving him, because I intend to destroy it completely ... just before I destroy you."

"You really like to hear yourself talk, don't you?" I replied, rage fueling my desire to kill.

He chuckled. "See you soon, Seren De Salvo."

The creatures around us snapped and growled, impatient to sink their teeth and claws into anything that moved. I held out my gun, steadying myself. Deus drew his sword, taking a defensive stance at my side.

"Are we ready?" asked Aunt Thora, as we tightened our perimeter.

"Ready to die, you mean?" asked G.

"You're not dying," snapped Gor.

"I call the big one with Paul's chains," Lilith said, a smile of pure evil stretching across her face.

Lightning above us struck, reaching across the sky, revealing the white clouds twisting with fury. Strike after strike snapped above us, the sunlight fading. Puffs of purple smoke filled the air, rotating violently. The funnel of purple fog widened and lightning struck through it just as four cylinders smashed into the ground around us.

The cylinders spun wildly, forcing us to cover our faces until they calmed, pulling away from the ground and back into the sky. As the sand settled and the fog cleared, light returned to the valley. I opened my eyes, trying to clear my vision. Around us, four women stood in the place of each tornado. Their white hair, some curly, some straight, fluttered in the wind. Their faces were stern and their attention focused, ready for battle.

"Cecilia," I heard Gor say.

"Josephine," Frankie said, pointing to the woman who stood to the right.

"Valeriana," Deus nodded to the one to the left.

I focused on the one directly in front of me. Her back was towards me while she assessed the threat that surrounded us, but I knew who she was without having to see her face. The power she possessed radiated from within; her dominance and stature said it all.

"Aradia."

CHAPTER FORTY-ONE

"Well, this just got interesting," commented Belz.

"How?" asked Nonna.

"Who cares?" answered Frankie. "Now we have six goddesses on our side along with six Princes of Hell. The odds just turned in our favor."

"Now!" screamed Aradia. Cecilia, Josephine, and Valeriana blast their white flames into the crowds of Lucifer's armies. The creatures attacked, hurtling into the air while the Goristro held their positions. The goddesses still had their magic. It was as if Aradia had planned this perfectly, waiting until after Victoria had initiated the spell, to guarantee that her and the other previous vessels still had access to their magic.

Bullets began to fly. Fists, legs, and swords slashed through the air. I moved through the battlefield, keeping my senses honed while I searched for Lucifer. I pointed the gun forward, nailing a demon in the head with a bullet as it attempted to sink its teeth into a young witch. I swung the barrel to the left, firing off two more bullets. I raised my second gun and spun to the right, taking down two more creatures.

A mass slammed into me from behind, causing me to stumble forward. Claws ripped at my fighting leathers while it fought to get its teeth into my neck. I struck back with my elbow and aimed my right Glock over my left shoulder, firing off two rounds into its head. The creature fell to the ground while my ears rang ferociously from the blast. My head spun, pounding with pain, and I lost my balance.

I took a few deep breaths while I prayed for the ringing to stop. I needed all my senses if I was going to survive. Before I could regain my balance, another demon barreled into me from the right, sending us both to the ground. I lost hold of my guns and reached for the creature's neck to prevent it from dosing me with its paralytic poison.

I punched the side of its face, avoiding its sharp dagger teeth. It flailed wildly, tearing into my arms and sides. I gripped the hilt of a dagger at my hip, but before I could plunge it into the creature's head, one of Deus's demons hurtled into it, driving the thing off me. The two animals slashed and tore into each other.

With its long, powerful fingers, the demon of lust pinned Lucifer's pet by the neck, locking its teeth around the black, inky flesh, ripping out its jugular. Lucifer's demon ceased to move, its arms slacking to the ground. Our demon arched its head into the sky and howled victoriously. Two more of Lucifer's demons appeared, jumping for ours as the three beasts fought to the death.

I refocused, picking up my guns and snapping two fully loaded clips into them. I cocked each gun and began firing. Mayhem surrounded us. White fire from the vessels torched the field, causing my skin to bead with sweat. The sound of metal sung through the air as the princes drove their bloodthirsty swords through our enemies.

I kept firing, sending demon after demon back to Hell, but no matter how many I took down, dozens continued to appear. It was impossible to determine if there was an ending in sight. I moved to the side, reaching for another clip to reload when a searing pain flared behind my left shoulder. I yelled, quickly ducking low to the ground.

I swung my guns towards the source of pain and began to fire blindly. Victoria stood ten feet from me, white flames flickering around each hand. I pulled the triggers as fast as I could, fighting the blistering sensation coming from my shoulder. She shifted out of the way, reappearing on a rocky mound a few feet from me and slammed her hands forward, sending funnels of fire in my direction.

I forced myself to run, faster than I ever had, trying to outrace my own magic. I dove behind a rock formation, reaching for another clip, but I was out. I tossed the guns and pulled out the slender sword that was strapped to my back. My stomach turned as the smell of my own burning flesh clung to my nostrils. I reached back, gently touching the wound. Instant pain shot through my nerve system as my fingers met my sticky, melted flesh.

My head was still pounding from the shots I had fired a few moments earlier, and my body stung from the dozens of claw marks. I was soaked in blood; some was my own, but most came from the demons I had slain. My hands were now shaking. I took a few deep breaths, closing my eyes while I tried to focus.

"Come out, come out, wherever you are, you little slut," Victoria taunted as she approached.

I pressed my back to the rock, my nerves settling as my grip around the hilt of the sword tightened. Even though I no longer had my magic, there was another power that would give me the strength I needed to kill this bitch.

I allowed myself to remember the sight of her on Deus's lap. The way they touched one another, caressed and kissed each other while I watched, helplessly. I imagined them together intimately, her lying next to him instead of me. Rage began to numb my physical pain as my mind tormented itself, jealousy becoming my weapon.

I held the sword vertically, quieting my senses until I pinpointed her soft, delicate footsteps, mere feet from my locations. I kept my eyes closed, waiting until the perfect moment to unleash my fury upon her.

She may have been a goddess, possessing power I currently couldn't, but she wasn't trained, at least not like I had been. I was thankful for the endless, painful hours I had spent in the training facility with Lilith while she kicked my ass from one end of the room to the other. After all Victoria had done, I wasn't going to allow her to walk off this battlefield alive.

The rocks softly shifted underneath her feet, and her steps halted just on the other side of the rock formation.

"You really think you will be enough for him?" she said, trying to taunt me into coming out. "He is the Prince of Lust. Mate or not, he will eventually need to lay with others. I love him enough that I made peace with that fact, accepting him for who he truly is. You, on the other hand, hinder his power by keeping him shackled at your side." She laughed. "You ... a weak, pathetic, orphaned nun ... the mate of the second most powerful demon in history. The universe is wrong!" I could hear the betrayal in her voice, the heartbreak of losing something she had loved.

"I belong with him," she growled. "I have fought for the past three hundred years to return to his side. I am what he needs and what he truly desires. You will destroy him. Once you are dead, he will realize the error of his ways, and when he does, I will be there. I will make sure that you are erased from his memory ... permanently."

My eyes snapped open, my body now calm and in control. With the sword still held before my face, I moved swiftly, like the shadow of death. I stepped up onto one of the rocky ledges, then took another step, and another, until I held the higher ground. I flung into the air, leaping off the formation, sword above my head and aimed for Victoria's neck.

I let out a scream of rage as I plummeted through the air. She turned towards me, her eyes widening, and brought her hands up. Fire sparked between her fingers, but she was too slow. I brought the sword down with all the strength I possessed. She took a single step, dodging out of my direct path just at the blade hit the flesh between her shoulder and neck, splitting her perfect skin wide open.

She cried out, reaching for the wound that gushed blood. She extended her arm out, sending shadowed tendrils towards me. I moved instinctually, climbing another rock mound, outrunning her pathetic attempt to attack. I pulled a dagger from my boot and tossed it towards her as I leapt from the rock, landing on my feet. The dagger sung as it tumbled through the air until it slid into her abdomen, just as I had intended.

She lurched forward, reaching for the hilt. Her whimpering cries were pathetic and weak. She pulled the blade from her flesh, crying and shaking. I ran straight for her, my sword leveled to kill, when she slammed her hands into the ground, a force of power sending me tumbling to the ground at least twenty feet from her.

The hard landing tore the sword from my grip while the wind lashed at my face, sending sand into the air. I covered my eyes, fighting the wind and dust, but there was no use. I was blind.

Bam. A fist smashed into my face, and then another, and another, until I could taste my own blood pooling in my mouth. The sand settled and I saw Victoria standing over me, smashing the left side of my jaw with her fist. Her face enraged, her simple white dress now saturated with her own blood.

I tried to throw my own punch, but her shadows latched around my wrists and then my ankles, pinning me to the ground while she continued to punch my face with her delicate fist. She straddled my torso, pulling my bloodied dagger from her belt.

A vicious, hungry smile spread across her angelic face. Madness consumed her. She forcefully gripped the top of my scalp, pulled my head back and laughed, holding the knife to my throat.

"You have no idea how much I am going to enjoy this," she said, pressing the wet metal against my skin.

Just as the cold blade broke through the first layer of my skin, a black figure slammed into her, forcing her shadows to release me. I scurried upright, diving for my sword and rolling to my feet. Victoria blasted Deus away from her and he landed a few feet from me. I moved to his side, helping him stand while he pulled his own sword from the sheath.

Victoria stood, jealousy written on her sneer. Deus scanned me, noting every wound I had endured. His face twisted with worry.

"I'm okay," I assured him. He wrapped his free arm around my waist, pulling me into him, resting his forehead against mine.

"Get away from her!" Victoria demanded, darkness and flickers of fire seeping from her. The ground around the former goddess shook, splintering as her eyes filled with rage and tears fell. Her breathing became rapid, her teeth gritting together as darkness and power consumed her.

"It's over, Victoria," Deus said, without an ounce of pity in his voice. "There is nothing you could do that would ever make me love you ... nothing."

The wind around her began to spin, her hair lashing at her face. Her eyes were now pits of darkness.

"No!" she yelled. "No! This isn't right. Everything I did ... everything

I sacrificed to get back to you. It can't all be for nothing. We belong together, Deus. I am your destiny ... not her... not some pathetic, weak, naïve bitch—"

A hand slid through her white, curly hair, gripping the strands by their roots, yanking her head back. A knife appeared at her neck just as Nonna's face came into focus over her left shoulder.

"That naïve bitch is a Salvo," Nonna said, her teeth inches from Victoria's ear. "And no one fucks with a Salvo and lives." Nonna slid the blade across her throat in one deep stroke. Blood spilled from the wound like a thick curtain of death. Nonna released her grip, tossing the body forward.

The wind settled around us. The shadows faded and the fire dissipated as Victoria's body fell into the sand. Her white curls splayed around her head, her eyes still open as the last ounce of life faded from them. Her beautiful face, now stained with her blood.

I looked back at Nonna still in shock. She arched an eyebrow and tilted her head.

"What?" she said without an ounce of empathy. "You expect me to stand by and let her talk to my granddaughter like that?" she huffed, shaking her head. "I don't think so."

"See," Deus whispered at my side. "Terrifying." He kissed me on the head, just as a massive thud sounded behind us. I looked back just in time to see the sand cloud fade, reveling a dead Goristro. Our forces moved to the next, continuing to execute the plan that we had created.

"Get your asses out there," ordered Nonna. "They need your help."

Deus took off towards the closest Goristro. I studied my nonna carefully, still in awe of her strength. She smiled at me softly. "You're welcome, bambina," she said with a nod.

"I love you," I replied.

"I love you. Stay close to your husband. Now go."

I nodded, taking off after him. With each pump of my arms, my blistered flesh and the wounds slashed into my skin yelled in protest, but I forced the pain down, remembering all Lilith had taught me.

Coven members sliced and stabbed the Goristro, but the damn thing shook off every attack. The wounds our weapons made quickly healed before my eyes, but to their credit, the coven members didn't give up. They clamored over the creature, stabbing their swords and daggers into it over and over, hoping to weaken the beast enough to get a killing blow.

The black demons continued to appear from thin air. The vessels and Aradia blasted them apart, creating coverage for us while we tried to take down the Goristro. A thud sounded across the battlefield, signaling the destruction of the another Goristro, meaning two relics had been deactivated. The remaining three Goristro swiped their long arms across the field, knocking witches, warlocks, and demons into the air with little effort. The one closest to us bent its head down low, aimed its horns forward and took off into a dead sprint ... straight for Aradia.

The creature was too fast as it came at Aradia from behind. She was unaware as she fought off the demons before her. The Goristro let out a deep groan, picking up its pace with each long stride.

"Aradia!" I yelled. There was no way to reach her before it impaled her with its horns. Aradia turned just as a figure shot through the air. The sun bounced off their sword as they swung it high above their head, then drove it straight into the Goristro's skull. The creature dropped instantly, crashing into the ground, sliding through the sand until it came to a stop at Aradia's feet.

The figure twisted the sword twice before pulling it free from the beast's brain. Talia stood triumphantly on top of the Goristro carcass, her deep eyes assessing the moon goddess, expressionless. She jumped down from the beast, walking slowly towards Aradia until they were face to face.

Aradia's own expression didn't reveal an ounce of emotion. The two women locked eyes, as if daring the other to speak first. Talia had told me the two of them used to be best friends— sisters, even. Aradia had taught Talia all she had learned about magic and had entrusted her with her own power.

A sly grin appeared on Talia's face as a corner of her mouth tugged upward. "Aradia," she said, seeming to pause for dramatic effect. "It's been a few years."

Before Talia could say another word, Aradia's fist flew through the air, cracking Talia in the side of the face. Talia froze, licking the corner of her lip.

"You fucking traitor," snarled Aradia. "After everything I gave you ... I trusted you more than anyone. Even Cyrus."

"I never betrayed you, Di," answered Talia. "You meant everything to me."

"Not more than him ... not more than your precious prince."

"He was my mate. You know the pull, the power that bond possesses. Regardless, I never betrayed you ... not for a moment."

"Bullshit. You went against everything our coven stood for. The coven *we* created together." In the next breath, a demon hurtled across the terrain towards them. With one fluid swipe, Talia cut the creature in half with her sword.

"Unfortunately," Aradia said, "this conversation will have to wait." She turned away, but Talia grabbed her by the wrist. Aradia pulled away instantly, lighting her flame defensively.

Talia looked at her with something like regret staining her expression. "There won't be time later," she said.

"What are you talking about?" snapped Aradia. She studied Talia closely. "What are you planning?"

"Just know that if I could go back," replied Talia, "if I could change what I did to you ... to us, I would. I never took what you gave me for granted. You were my best friend. My family. I loved you. That never changed."

"What is it?" asked Aradia, her brow now furrowing with concern. "What are you going to do, Talia?"

"Something I should have done long ago," Talia answered. "I'm sorry, sister." She shifted from the battlefield just as the fourth Goristro crashed into the ground, defeated with the help of Cecilia and Valeriana.

"One more to go," yelled Frankie, racing across the battlefield, slicing her sword into anything that moved.

Aradia turned to me, her face still confused and concerned. Her eyes went wide. "The cage," she whispered. "She plans to use herself to power the cage."

I nodded. A thick white mist swarmed the area. Everyone who inhaled began coughing, fighting to breath. Aradia and the vessels began to chant, clearing the poisonous gas. Out of the white mist stepped the Lightbringer, God's favorite archangel, the Prince of Pride: Lucifer Morningstar.

Each of his steps fell more elegantly than the one before. His perfectly pressed white suit showed no signs of the war that had been in progress for the past few hours. Every inch of him was perfect and untouched. His flawless face and stunning smirk oozed with arrogance. He stopped a few feet from Aradia and me, looking between us.

"Well, this was unexpected," he said with an arched eyebrow. "I pride myself in being prepared for anything, and this I did not foresee."

"Is your pride bruised, Lucy?" Aradia said. "Finally realizing that you're just a fucked up little boy with daddy issues and a god complex?"

Anger flickered, only for a moment, across Lucifer's face before he bottled it, resuming his cool demeanor. He smiled, tilting his head to the side.

"Oh, Di," he said softly. "How I wish I had severed that pretty little head from your shoulders years ago. Would have made so many things easier."

She huffed with amusement. "Like you ever stood a chance," she replied.

"You know," he said, "come to think of it, nothing would bring me more pleasure than to permanently silence you for good." Lucifer's eyes turned to me. "I think that will be the first thing I do, once I rip little Seren's soul from her fragile vessel."

A shimmer of sunlight blinded me before I saw the blade flying towards Lucifer's neck. Without hesitation, Lucifer put his hand up, blocking the attack. As the sword touched the Prince of Pride's hand, the metal shattered into thousands of pieces, not leaving a single scratch on the archangel's flawless skin.

Deus dropped the hilt of the sword before the splintered metal finished falling to the ground and sent his fist directly into his brother's jaw. Lucifer's head flung to the opposite side while his body remained stationary. A large drop of blood fell from his lip.

"You will not touch her!" yelled Deus.

Lucy laughed, removing a pressed handkerchief from his pocket to dab at the small cut in the corner of his lip.

"Oh, brother," he said, smoothing the fabric of his jacket with his hands. "How weak love has made you. A pity, really. You were a formidable opponent before this plague stepped into your life," he said, gesturing to me.

"She is the best part of me," Deus replied. "A happiness you will never know."

Lucifer laughed, shaking his head. "You know nothing of what you speak, Asmodeus." Was he thinking of Talia? Of the love he had sacrificed in hopes of gaining ultimate power?

"You'd be surprised," Deus replied in an arrogant tone.

"Speaking of love," Lucifer said, looking around the battlefield, "where is sweet little Victoria?"

"Dead," I replied too quickly.

Lucifer's face didn't show a sign of remorse. He shrugged, throwing his arms forward to shake out his cuffs. He adjusted each sleeve individually. "Doesn't surprise me. You always had horrible taste in women, little brother. Always going for the weak, unstable type." He finished adjusting his cufflink. "Some things never change. Either way, she served her purpose."

A loud thud rattled the ground around us, signaling that the final Goristro had been taken down. A massive force slammed into my back, my body stretched forward, paralyzed. I couldn't breathe, couldn't move, while the cold, familiar substance slithered through every pore, every cell of my being, using my veins as its pathway throughout my system. I felt it then—the witch ... the goddess ... Asmodeus ... Lucifer—all my powers swirling together as one, igniting the magic deep within me that had changed the course of my life.

I took a deep breath, every nerve jolting to life. White flames flickered and swirled around my fingers. Dark tendrils of power crawled from beneath my feet. Lust and desire overcame me, and then the darkness ... oh, how sweet and supple the power tasted, now freed from its cage, roaming through my system, saturating every corner of my soul. I couldn't help it. A sly smile spread across my face as I looked upon my enemy. I lowered my head, power welling in the palm of my hands before I blasted everything I had towards Lucifer.

His body flew back, landing in the sand, his perfectly pressed suit now stained and torn. Around me, our allies had regained access to their gifts, whoops of joy accompanying the hiss of magic.

"Don't fool yourself," Aradia said at my side. "This thing is far from over."

Lucifer levitated upright from the ground, dusting the sand from his suit. When he looked up, darkness consumed his eyes. Small black veins slithered from his eyelids down his cheeks and neck. He tilted his head like a predator, his tongue lashing out.

"Now, now, little witch," he said in a demonic growl. "That wasn't very nice." He extended his arms slowly out to his sides, his palms facing the sky. He focused his power and the ground trembled. His arms began to shake as he pulled his magic from the depths of Hell and with it, legions of demons.

My heart sank into my chest while they formed from the grains of sand beneath our feet, growing and shifting into creatures of nightmare. The sounds of these hell beasts echoed through the air, sending shivers of fear down my spine.

My family regrouped alongside the vessels and the Princes of Hell.

"We've faced worse," I heard Belz say, trying to sound optimistic.

"The final stand," Nonna whispered, turning to me. She nodded. "It's time."

I gave her a small smile and nodded, then turned back to Deus, sliding my hand into his. He pulled me in, taking my face between his hands.

"Stay close to me," he whispered, pressing his head firmly to my own. "We're almost there … we're almost free."

A small tear ran down my cheek. "I love you so much," I replied. "No matter what … you were worth it … you were worth all of it."

"Don't talk like that," he said firmly. "We're so close. Keep fighting. Don't give up."

I nodded, pulling away from him. He kissed me firmly and we faced Lucifer together. My mother approached, running her hand down my back.

"I am so proud of you, little bean," she said, her face full of dirt and blood. "You are truly the best parts of me and none of the bad. What every mother prays for in a child."

I took her hand and squeezed it. "I'm proud to be the daughter of Annalise De Salvo," I whispered. Her face fill with pride, and then sorrow. Her eyes were so heavy and tormented by the past twenty years.

"Everyone know their places?" asked Nonna. We all nodded, trying to fend off the fear that surely gripped us all at the sight of the masses we now faced. "Good, then stop standing around and get to your positions."

Our family and friends fanned out, creating a perimeter. I caught Lilith's eyes in a silent plea. She nodded, assuring me our plan was still in motion. Before I could take another breath, the demons descended. Dozens shot into the sky, attacking from above while others ran, jumped, leaped, and rolled on the ground towards us.

Power erupted from our side, slamming into the hordes, holding them back as long as we could until they overpowered our barriers, forcing us to engage in hand-to-hand combat. Everything became a blur of blood, rage, and fire. I kept my eyes on Lucifer while cutting down any demon that stepped into my path. Ducking and dodging, I set my flames free, clearing a way for myself.

Lucifer just stood there, hands beside his back, unfazed by the carnage that surrounded him. I couldn't wait to erase the crooked smile that stretched across his face. I unleashed my shadows, dozens of solid arrows streaking towards him. With a wave of a hand, they disappeared before they could even touch him.

Frustration began to build inside of me. I let it become fuel, unleashing my power in a tunnel of fire and fury. Lucy put up his hands, blocking it with an invisible shield, the white flames bending and folding around the protective barrier. I released the stream of magic just as he slammed his own power forward, knocking me to the ground. White sparks of electricity danced over my skin, stinging and burning.

I forced myself to my feet, throwing everything I had into him. I called on the power of my coven, whipping the wind around him, preventing him from focusing his magic. As the funnel entrapped him, I began reciting a spell. His mouth gaped open, paralyzed. Small droplets of water drew from his pores. I drained him of life, though I could feel him beginning to regain control.

Lucifer slammed his hands into the ground, breaking the restraint I had on him. He whirled his hands, gathering his power into a solid form and shot it towards me. I dove out of the way, rolling into a standing position and flinging another wave of fire in his direction. Blast after blast we fired at one another. He was quick and able to predict my next attack, but I didn't give up. The lives of the people I loved were on the line, and I wasn't going to fail them.

His power brushed against my skin, opening wound after wound, my blood pouring from my veins. I nailed him a few times, but the damage I dealt was nothing compared to what he did to me. I dove behind some rocks as a line of fire blazed past, barely missing my leg. I breathed deeply, trying to calm myself. I was spent and my body was tired and beat to hell.

"You need to tap into his power," Talia's voice said in my mind. *"You won't stand a chance if you don't. Fight fire with fire."*

I nodded to no one, too tired to speak. I closed my eyes and allowed myself to reach for his magic. This magic had terrified me, destroyed my home ... and it had saved me before I even took my first breath.

No longer would my fear overcome me. I would embrace my destiny. I would honor those who had fallen in the name of love ... of family ... of good. I had experienced heartbreak, loss, and a love that transcended time. I had a family who was worth sacrificing everything for, and friends who had blindly followed me into this battle to face death head on.

Talia was right; this power was not something to fear, but something to revere. It was mine. It had made me strong, the perfect weapon—everything I had become. A witch ... a goddess ... a queen.

"Seren!" A female voice screamed from far away. I opened my eyes slowly, my body encountering a strange sense of transformation as the demonic magic swelled. I turned my head toward the sound, my vision clearing. "Move!" the voice screamed, the figure now barreling towards me.

The woman threw out her hand, slamming her magic out towards the threat. My eyes focused to revealing Delphine's tall, lean body running at full speed towards me. I heard the crack from the release of magic before

I saw it. Delphine threw herself in its path, bringing her hands out in front of her just in time to block the attack from Lucifer.

I jumped up, the dark magic still crawling through my blood. I sent out a wave of fire. Lucifer shifted unscathed, appearing a few feet away. He picked up a sword from the ground and hurtled it towards me. Before I could shift to safety, Delphine stepped in its path, her body jolting back as the metal buried itself in her sternum.

Her face fell. Blood began to drip from her mouth as she staggered and fell to her knees.

"No!" I screamed, looking down at Orion's mate. "No! No!" I reached for her as she slouched to the ground, choking on the blood that filled her lungs.

Deus appeared in front of Lucifer, along with his brothers. Massive waves of power rippled from the princes, shaking the ground around us as they commenced an epic battle.

I held Delphine's head in my lap, brushing her beautiful golden hair from her face. Her eyes, so full of pain and suffering, looked up at me and in that moment, I felt him ... Orion. The connection that we had also connected Delphine and me.

Tears streamed down my cheeks. I bent down and kissed her sweaty forehead, her breath now wet from the blood in her lungs. "I'll shift you back to the castle," I whispered, pulling her body into mine. "They can fix you there. It's not too late."

She shook her head, grabbing onto me before I could move her. "No," she gasped, her eyes filling with tears. "No more."

"Delphine, please," I whispered. "I promised him I would take care of you. I can't let you die."

"I—I died ... the moment he did," she cried. "I did what ... what he would have. Protected ... you."

I cried harder, shaking my head as the weight of her sacrifice now lay on my shoulders.

"I am—I am ready ... to see him again," she said, pulling the sword from her chest. I reached for the fountain of blood that pooled from her wound, attempting to make it stop. She grabbed my hand, clenching it tightly.

"Promise me—" She coughed on the blood, splattering it onto her beautiful white face.

"Anything, Delphine."

"Promise me, you will make him suffer ... for all he stole from us."

I nodded, feeling her grip lighten. "I promise. I promise you."

She nodded, turning her eyes to the sky. Her breathing quickened and then ... she was gone. I fell on top of her, pressing my head to hers as I cried, feeling like another part of my soul had been stripped away, leaving this emptiness nothing would ever be able to fill. I looked down at my hand, seeing her blood covering my skin and then I felt it. I felt the magic reaching its peak.

Black veins appeared at my fingertips, running up the back of my hands to my forearms and then my shoulders. The darkness was cool and crisp, inviting me to play in the most alluring way. I laid my friend's body down gently on the ground and stood, ready to end this once and for all. My metamorphosis was now complete.

CHAPTER
FORTY-TWO

In the distance, a wounded Giana held Gor while he tried to stand. Belz was pulling an unconscious Mammon from the battlefield while fighting off the demons who tried to feed on their flesh. Levi and Deus flanked Lucifer, hammering him with everything they had, but it still wasn't enough.

Lucifer blasted Levi back into a rock wall, cracking his head into the hard surface, leaving him unconscious. The force caused Deus to lose his footing, sending him sprawling. Deus unleashed his rage, a red gust of magic brushing past Lucifer, burning the side of his leg. Lucy let out a scream of pain, slamming his hands towards his brother. Before the attack could nail Deus, Lilith appeared in front of her friend, using her magic to shield him.

Lucifer began to laugh, looking between the two of them with disgust. "Always such a pathetic excuse for a warrior," Lucifer said to Lilith. "And now look at you ... mated to a demon while fucking your way through his brothers. How pathetic."

"Shut your fucking mouth," Lilith growled. "You, of all beings, are the least qualified to pass judgment when it comes to defining a pathetic excuse for an angel."

Lucy arched his eyebrow. "You are a demon, you whore," Lucifer spat.

"I own you. Mate or not, I could have you in a second if I wished. I am your king."

Lilith held her head high. "You may have fooled me in the garden all those years ago, but make no mistake; you are not my king, Samael. You never were and never will be."

Lucifer took a moment to examine the woman who spoke as if she knew him from a former life. He huffed in amusement and then shook his head, smiling. He looked to Deus. "Harboring Lilith of Samaria, all these years. Did you know?" he asked. My mate did not reply as he stood to his feet. Lucifer turned his eyes back to her. "Clever, clever little bitch."

Red and purple thunder clouds began to form overhead. Lightening snapped and flashed high above, causing the earth to shake. The storm erupted violently, heavy rain falling from the sky as the sound of clashing metal rattled in the near distance.

I turned towards the far-off echoes to see a horde of muscular demons twice the size of any man lining the upper ridges of the territory. Each bristled with at least a dozen weapons. These creatures were built for war.

My heart sank as hundreds of new demons approached the battlefield. We were already outnumbered, but this new addition tipped the scales in Lucifer's favor. I watched, unable to look away while the creatures began to pick up their pace. They remained eerily calm as they entered the battle and then ... to my surprise, the demons rushed the field, passing our legions to deliver fatal, strategic blows to Lucifer's forces.

A massive force tore through the air accompanied by a purple haze of fog. Before the smoke faded, a massive hammer swung forward, smashing straight into Lucifer's beautiful face.

"Do not speak to my mate," Satan roared, taking a protective stance in front of Lilith. Tears fought to fall from my eyes, relief filling me as I allowed myself a moment to breathe.

Lucy lifted his bloody head to Satan. An unsettling laugh escaped from his lips. "I underestimated you it seems, brother. Creating the first demon born of a human, who just happened to end up as your mate. Father does have a wicked sense of humor, doesn't he?"

Enough. I was done hearing him boast about himself. He had just murdered Orion's mate, and he was going to pay. The power inside of me roared to life. I let the streams of his magic free. My fire, once white and pure, now raced across the terrain in a thick ooze like tar, melting and eating anything it touched. Lucifer tried to dodge, but was too late. The substance leaped at him like a wolf springing on its prey. Lucifer screamed as the flames lapped at his face, melting and searing his skin.

Deus and Satan used his moment of weakness to attack. Both brothers rushed him from either side, slamming their power into him over and over. Lucifer took some of the hits, but was able to regain his footing. Lilith focused her magic on the demons that rushed to Lucifer's aid, incinerating any that got too close.

I snapped my shadows forward, slashing into Lucifer's skin, taking chunks out of his perfectly sculpted body. Then a deafening hum triggered, starting high and then dropping to a low tone before a blast of pure demonic power struck us, knocking us to the ground. Sand and dust wafted in the air as my ears rang from the blast.

I felt hands on me; the four women of my family stood above, hauling me to my feet. We were together. Lucifer had been weakened. It was time for the final step in our plan. His final demise ... and mine along with it.

I nodded to my family, stealing four seconds to study each of their faces and committing them to memory. Deus still struggled to get up, his power exhausted from battle. I took in every detail of the man who had brought me back to life. Who had shown me a love worth fighting for.

Deus's body stiffened as he slowly turned over his shoulder towards me. In that moment, I let my walls fall. I let him feel and see all that I had so carefully hidden from him for all these months. I let him into the deepest parts of my heart, so he could see just how completely I loved him. I would move Heaven and Hell to save him, so he would never suffer at the hands of his brother again.

Deus's mouth dropped open, his head shaking from side to side. His eyes filled with tears as he dragged himself towards me, shock and horror filling his expression.

"I love you," I mouthed, unable to find my voice. *"Forever,"* I said in our minds, *"no matter what plane or time ... I will love you. No matter who else you take or where you go ... I will always be yours."*

"Seren, no!" he screamed, fighting his tired and broken body to get to me. "No! You can't! Seren!" I turned to Lilith, unable to look at him a moment longer.

"Do it," I told her. Lilith nodded, shifting from corner to corner, placing stones around the perimeter. She recited a spell and a dome of raw, natural magic encased me, my family, and Lucifer inside, leaving everyone else out, including my mate.

"Don't leave me," he cried in my mind. *"Please, my love ... please. Not again. I can't live without you."*

"You will live. You will live a beautiful life, free from the leash of this monster." I turned towards him as he banged on the barrier, fighting to get inside. *"Everything I do... I do for you."* And then, I shut the door to our bond, detaching myself so I could focus. The painful sting in my

heart radiated throughout my body, but it had to be done. I had to do this without him. I had to do this for him.

"Well, well," Lucifer's voice echoed in the dome. "I didn't see this coming. You sacrificing yourself to me on a golden platter. Though, I must say, I do like the dramatic exit. Providing your poor mate a front row seat to witness your death ... how very wicked you are, little Seren. Seems we're more alike than I had anticipated."

"Does he ever shut up?" spat Frankie.

"Doesn't seem like it," answered Aunt Thora.

"How about we shut him up then," Nonna said, beginning to cast a spell.

My mother pulled me in, kissing me one more time quickly before the five of us dispersed around the circle just as we had planned. Powers flared and lashed while we dodged and dove around Lucifer's attacks. My shadows lashed out with barbs, slicing and tearing into him. His blood coated the ground around us. I fought against my own injured body, feeling the burns and wounds I had endured these past hours.

Lucifer flung his hand out, knocking Frankie and Thora against the shield. He sent a tunnel of wind towards my mother, but she ducked just before it could touch her. I flung another wave of my black flames in his direction. Fear flashed across his face. He dove out of the way, crashing into the ground. My mother placed a hand on my shoulder, siphoned some of my magic and twisted her hand, snapping and breaking bone after bone in his body.

Lucifer let out a roar of anger while his body broke and healed and broke again. Before he could stand, Nonna appeared, placing the restraints we had created from the rope Judas had hung himself with on either of Lucifer's wrists to bind his powers. We had weaponized our own relics for this very purpose.

Lucifer sat up on his knees, laughing in amusement as he looked at the restraints. My family flanked my sides, looking down at the devil who had destroyed so much of what we had loved.

"You really think these can hold me?" he said boastfully. "You do not have the means nor knowledge to stop me you, foolish witches."

"No," a female voice said from behind us. Talia stepped around Nonna, locking eyes with her mate. "But I do."

Lucifer's face fell. Talia smiled, reveling in the moment.

"Impossible," he whispered in disbelief. "I searched every corner of Hell for you."

Talia knelt in front of him, fearless. "Well," she whispered, "here's a little secret, Ahuvi. I was never in Hell. I sent myself to Purgatory, biding my time until your Father had finally had enough of your little temper tantrum." She paused, turning her attention to me. "And then he sent her ... the final piece of your demise."

Lucifer looked from Talia and then to me, then at the cuffs. He pulled at them, trying to free himself. Talia stood, walking back towards us.

"Don't bother, Luc," Talia said, standing at my side. "They're infused with your daddy's blood, along with our magic. There's no getting out of them."

"No," he said, looking down at his wrists in disbelief. "No!"

Talia looked me in the eye and nodded. "It's time," she said softly.

I nodded back and my family got into position. I faced Lucifer directly. Aunt Thora and Frankie stood next to me, and then my mother and Nonna at the ends, forming a V.

We cut our palms, clasping hands for the last time. Nonna and Mamma looked at one another and nodded before placing their hands on either of his shoulders. He fought, but Talia used her power to hold him in place. The magic swam through each of us like the midnight waves of the ocean. My power laced and danced with his, filling my body with a heat and desire that craved more.

I breathed deeply, trying to control myself until it was time. Lucifer weakened, no longer putting up a fight while we siphoned his life force. Talia nodded at me one last time and then disappeared, heading to Hell for the final step in the plan. I focused, my body boiling as I approached my limit. Frankie and Aunt Thora began to shake, but we held firmly to one another; we knew this wasn't going to be easy. My head felt heavy, and my scorching blood felt like it would melt layers off my skin, if only to escape the agony of my body. It was almost time.

I turned to Deus, needing any comfort his presence could provide. The shield in front of him was covered in blood as he slammed his hands and body into it over and over again. His eyes were full of anger and desperation, his face saturated with tears.

The last bit of magic that I needed slithered into my body from the blood ties of my family. I felt it ripping every inch of me apart, fighting to escape. The power ... the force ... it was all too much ... I was ready. I let go of my aunt and cousin's hands, the energy gathering in my center as I tried to force it into a single stream of power.

"Now," I managed to say, dazed and sick. "Get back!" I ordered. I closed my eyes, willing the force inside of me to obey. I fought to command it, just as Talia had instructed. A white light appeared at the center of my chest while the wind lashed around us. I focused, knowing what needed to be done. I took a final breath and then—

Hands latched onto my own. The power I had worked so hard to gather and focus began to drain from my body. I opened my eyes, trying to rip my hands away, but there was no use; I was trapped.

At my sides, my nonna and mamma siphoned the magic from me with a speed I had never known possible. The white light in my chest faded, the heat in my blood cooled and my mind became steady as I tried to process what was happening.

Both Nonna and Mamma began to shake ferociously. Knowing what the power would do to them, I fought to break the link between us, but with the stolen power, they were too strong.

I felt them expunge the last of Lucifer's lifeforce out of my system. They let go of my hands in unison and then joined hands with one another, facing Lucifer. I fell to my knees, completely drained. Then ... everything made sense.

"No," I whispered, trying to crawl towards them, but I was too weak. They had taken everything. "No! No!" I screamed.

Two white lights blasted from their chests into Lucifer as my mother and nonna stood firmly hand in hand. Their bodies extended towards their target while the power billowed from within their souls, burning through their lifeforces and the magic they had siphoned from me. I reached for them but was restrained by Aunt Thora as she wrapped her arms around me.

A massive explosion knocked us back. The white light expanded, blinding everyone. Silence; a pure, peaceful moment where all existence seemed to cease. As the white light faded, one last loud *bang* sounded. The earth shook, the sky cracked and then....

My ears rang and head swam from the impact. I fought to push myself up from the ground, but failed. Hands were instantly on me, moving my hair away from my face in a firm yet loving manner. I opened my eyes, my tears clearing my sight. Deus knelt in front of me, his face wrecked with fear and worry.

His bright smile flashed before he pulled me into him, pressing my head against his chest. I folded my arms around his strong frame, taking in this moment I thought I would never experience here on earth again. As the dust settled, I pulled away from him, looking back where Lucifer had been shackled. His body was gone, but on the ground in front of us lay two motionless forms.

Thora was up and moving faster than I could process. Her sobs echoed through the quiet desert as she took in the bodies of her mother and twin sister. I crawled over to them, still dazed and weak. Frankie knelt in front of Nonna, hesitant to touch her. Thora cradled my mother against her chest, rocking her forcefully as she sobbed, screaming and crying from the pain her heart felt. She had lost her sister. Her best friend. Her soulmate.

I looked at Nonna, tears welling behind my eyelids. I reached out, touching her soft skin, now stiff and cold. Her eyes were closed, and her face was at peace.

"What ... what went wrong?" asked Frankie, still in shock.

"It was supposed to be me," I whispered.

"What are you talking about?" she replied.

I struggled to find my words. "I found out how to kill a Prince of Hell. But to do so, I had to sacrifice myself in the process. I told Nonna of my plans, knowing I would need all of us to absorb Lucifer's power so I wouldn't prematurely burn out but ... but they siphoned the power from me instead, at the last second. They struck the final blow ... saving me in the process."

I looked between the two dead women who I loved entirely. My emotions welled as the thought of a life without them became my new reality. Tears fell uninhibited and I buried myself in Nonna's chest, trying to think of a way to bring them back, to save them, but none came. I turned to my mother, still wrapped in the arms of her sister.

Aunt Thora murmured randomly while she wept and mourned. Her eyes turned to me as I stared helplessly at my mother: a woman I had only just begun to know. I reached out, brushing the back of my knuckles against the bridge of her nose that bore the freckles we all shared. And then I fell to pieces.

Everything inside of me let go. I was alive, but for that to be so, they had to die.

I don't know how much time passed or when it was that I came back to reality, but once the last tear had fallen and my body was exhausted from the violent cries of sorrow, Deus scooped me into his arms and shifted us back to Castle Salvo.

Chapter Forty-Three

Hell

Bam! Lucifer slammed into the hard brimstone floor, surrounded in darkness. The realm smelled of earthly minerals. A faint dampness thickened the air, the humidity uncomfortable.

The shackles around his wrists rattled with each movement as fury overcame him. A deep, vicious roar tore from him as he swung his arms into the thick metal bars of the cage. Over and over, he beat at the bars and yanked on the ropes of Judas, but they held him firm.

How could he have been outwitted by Asmodeus, of all beings, and his little bitch of a mate? Asmodeus was dead to him. Any affection or attachment he once had for his brother would never again blind Lucifer. Deus would need to be put down. As soon as he got out of this cage, his brother would be his first target, and then his whore of a mate. Father, how he would make Deus pay for choosing a woman over his own flesh and blood.

From the corner of the cage, veiled in the darkness, a feminine laugh trilled through the thick air. Lucifer spun towards the sound, squinting his eyes at the darkness. Though his sight failed, he knew who lingered in the cage with him. No matter how much time passed, he could never forget the sound of his mate's laugh. Soul or no soul, she would forever be branded into his genetic makeup.

The female figure snapped her fingers and small balls of yellow light filled the obscurity of the cell. Lucifer looked around at the twelve-by-twelve-foot cage he was trapped in. The outside terrain was barren. Black brimstone covered every surface. The darkness extended to the sky where clouds of shadow and smoke prevented any light from reaching his prison.

Talia stood from the stool she had been sitting on in the corner. The light bounced off her curly white hair. Her tan skin, so smooth and flawless, glistened as his gaze lingered on the small batch of freckles that dusted her cheeks.

Memories flashed behind his eyes. The tender moments between the two of them as they lay under the stars and moon, their bodies exhausted from their dalliances. He remembered watching her sleep, brushing the small strands of hair from her face, revealing all those small, delicate freckles. Fifty-one ... fifty-one freckles adorned her face, twenty-seven on her right arm, seventeen on her left. And then all those little freckles that led to the most delicious center he had ever—

"You're not as angry as I thought you'd be." Her voice pulled him from those seductive memories, snapping him back into reality.

He brought his eyes to hers, feeling a stirring deep inside of him. A need to touch her, to have her ... to bury himself inside of her. He shrugged, forcing those thoughts and needs down deep.

"I've waited this long to gain the power I am owed," he said. "What's another thousand years? I am nothing if not persistent."

She laughed; not just any laugh, but a genuine one. She shook her head in amusement. "That you are, Luc ... that you are."

"Your involvement did tip the scales for the little witch and my brother. I would have succeeded, if it weren't for you."

Talia took a moment, seeming to study the details of his face. Lucifer recognized something familiar and soft behind those dark and haunting eyes. As if in response to his recollection, she shifted her face, hiding what truly plagued her.

"Surprise," she said softly, taking a step away from him.

"Yes," he said, formulating a plan to manipulate her into helping him out of this prison. "You're the only one who has ever bested me at my own game. Doesn't surprise me, with you being my equal and all. My ... mate."

Her face flared with rage and disgust. "Do not call me that," she growled. "You lost the right of that title the day you decided to end my life in exchange for your *precious* power." She huffed. "And how daft do you think I am, if you truly believe I would fall for your manipulations now? There is no chance in any realm that I would help free you from this prison you built of your own accord."

She paused, her eyebrow raised, then approached him slowly. "But you are right about one thing ... I've always been able to beat you at your own game."

Before Lucifer could respond, Talia drove her hand straight through his chest. A wave of cool, chilling matter seeped through his body as a white, cloudy substance raced from Talia into Lucifer. He fought to breathe, paralyzed by her grip. Everything inside of him burned to life. She pulled her hand from his chest, allowing his flesh to weave itself back together.

Every part of him ached. His heart raced, faster and stronger than it had in millennia. Memories, scents, sounds, and *feelings* overloaded his system. It was as if he hadn't taken a single breath in years. He stumbled back, reaching for his heart as the pain of every terrible, evil thing he had done slammed into him like daggers.

The innocents he had tortured ... the blood ...the body parts ... the cries for mercy as he butchered families, women, *children*. Everything he had commanded Obsidian to do in his name. The torment he had forced his beloved brother Asmodeus to endure, simply because he had allowed himself to love.

Lucifer dropped to his knees as he wept: for the lives he had stolen, the suffering he had caused, the agony he had inflicted on others. And then ... then that golden string snapped into place. His body stretched forward as the bond began to weave itself together, connecting every fiber of his being to his mate. His equal. The one that he had loved above all others.

The tether that had gone dark all those years ago exploded to life. Flashes of a life he had worked so hard to put behind him flickered to the surface.

"I would do anything for you, Lucifer." He heard Talia's voice say in a loving tone.

"You are the first thing I have ever truly loved," he heard himself confess in a memory. *"I never dreamed I'd find someone like you, someone who I ... who I could lose myself in. I love you, Talia. I loved you from the first moment I laid eyes on you."* He heard himself laugh. Vows ... he was reciting vows. *"The moment you tossed that cup of wine in my face, I knew there'd be no escaping you. I wanted you then, and I want you now. Till the end of time, I will always love you. My body is yours; my heart is yours; my power, and everything I am, everything I possess, is yours."*

Image after image of their love flooded his memory. Their bodies, moving as one. The sounds that he drew out of her. The feeling of utopia he found only when he was with her. Happiness ... true, complete happiness. A life and a family they had hoped and planned for. An empire they had built. The power they had possessed.

Then ... so much pain. He felt her in that moment, when she had discovered his plan to kill her and take her power. Her heart had shattered. Her soul was ripped in two. All because of his selfishness.

When in reality ... she was enough. She had always been more than enough, yet he couldn't let go of the past. He couldn't let himself be happy. He couldn't choose her.

His face, wet from the tears of pain turned up to her ... his mate. Talia stood over him, her face no longer masked. Every emotion, every moment of sadness and terror she had lived through was present. Tears fell as she clenched her jaw tightly.

"I would have done anything to protect the life we had planned, Luc ... anything," she said. "Why couldn't I be enough?" she yelled, her anger getting the best of her. "What else could I have done to make you happy? I thought you were happy."

"I was, Ahuvati," he replied in a loving tone. "I was. You made me whole. I had never known true love until I found you. I ... I don't have an answer for you. I'm flawed, Talia. Utterly flawed."

Her fist connected with his face so fast, he didn't see it coming.

"No!" she screamed, fuming with rage. "Tell me! Tell me what I did wrong. Tell me why you threw away everything? Why you ripped out your own soul to steal mine!"

"I couldn't kill you," he replied, staggering to his feet. "I knew with my soul intact, there was no reality where I could take your life and not destroy my own in the process."

"Then why?" she cried. "Why kill me? Why not let me help you find what you sought?"

"I thought it was the only way. You were gifted to me by my Father as a cruel joke. I had broken his heart when I chose power over him ... over his love. He wanted me to suffer as he had when I abandoned him. So, he sent me you ... my mate. The one person he knew I would love unconditionally.

"When I found out you were the key to the power I had searched for my entire existence, it all made sense. He wanted me to choose: either the love I had found with you, or the power I had chosen over him. The same choice he had given me before I fell. I thought it was a cruel joke ... some test to finally become the god I knew I was destined to be."

Talia faced him, her posture stern. "What is the point of building an empire if you have no one to share it with?" she whispered. "What is the point of a legacy with no one to pass it to? Isn't that why you left Heaven in the first place? You've allowed your pride and narcissism to blind you and rob you of a future worth cherishing."

He lunged for her, grabbing her by the shoulders. "We can still have that future, Ahuvati," he exclaimed. "We can have it all." He looked into his lover's eyes, overcome with the need to kiss her, to taste her. "I am so sorry, so terribly sorry, for all I've done. I've lived these past years empty and dead inside. I've learned my lesson. I've lived without you, and I never want to be parted again. Not for another moment."

She forced herself to look away as more tears spilled out. "Lucifer," she whispered.

"I'm serious, Talia. Please. Please give me another chance. I remember ... I remember every single moment together. We were happy, so incredibly happy, and we can have that again." He brushed her hair away from her face. She leaned into his touch, and his knees weakened at the familiar action.

"Father, I love you," he whispered tenderly, allowing his heart to feel. "I am so in love with you. You are incredible. Better than me in every way. You make me better, Talia. We were made for each other. You are my best friend. My mate." He took her hand and rubbed his thumb over the small white stone that adorned her left ring finger. "My wife."

She pulled away from his touch, taking a step back, shaking her head. "No, Luc. I ... I can't."

"Fine," he said confidently. "Then I will wait for you. As long as it takes, I will wait. I will stay here for a thousand years, as it is prophesied, and then once I am free, I will find you and we will build the life I promised you all those years ago in the desert. We will have our happiness. Our empire. Our family."

Talia was sobbing, holding herself tightly as she continued to shake her head. Finally, she brought her eyes up to his and in that moment, he saw it: what she had planned to do.

"No," he whispered, looking at the cage around him. "Ahuvati, no. You can't, please." He stepped closer, but she backed away. "You have saved me once again. I am made whole."

"It will never be enough, Luc," she whispered, wiping the tears from her face. "I will never be enough."

"You are more than enough. You are my world ... my life."

She took a deep breath, steadying herself. "I want you to know ... I want you to know that I hate you. I completely and utterly hate you for taking away our happiness, and choosing a power that was never meant for you over a love that was made for you. I would have gone to the ends of the earth for you. I would have pillaged, killed, and set fire to any village or empire that threatened your reign. You had me, Luc. Every fiber of my being ... my heart ... my soul was yours.

"In Purgatory, I had a lot of time to think back on our life. I wondered what I could have done to change the course of our story ... but our story was never mine to change. You were always the author, and I was just a character following the path you wrote for me. God, do I hate the story you wrote for us. How different this world would be if you had just chosen me. If you had loved me enough to believe in the power we had together.

"But that isn't how our story goes, and I am angry about it. I have watched for months as your brothers have chosen the love of their mates, even a human witch, over all else. Yet my mate, the most powerful, angelic demon prince in history, tossed his gift aside, willing to execute her for the smallest morsel of power.

She paused, taking another deep breath. Silent tears ran down Lucifer's face. "I hate you, Lucifer Morningstar. I hate your pride, your selfishness, your one-track mind, your stubbornness and blindness. Yet ... I wouldn't have you any other way.

"You are the greatest thing that has ever come into my life. The love you showed me, the love we shared, can never be replicated. You are the most stubborn man I've ever known, and I love that about you. I love everything that makes you ... you. You were my entire world, my reason for breathing ... and you still are."

Lucifer felt a spark of hope. His mouth curved into a smile as he looked into his wife's eyes. "You are mine as well, Talia. Forever and always, you will be mine."

She smiled back at him softly. She took a step towards him, slowly reaching up to his face. The moment her skin touched his, something in Lucifer's heart lit to life. He savored her touch, her scent, and needed more. She leaned into him, pressing her lips against his. He wrapped his arms around her, holding her intimately as they kissed each other with an unmatched passion.

In this moment, it was as if no time had passed. They were back in the deserts of Egypt, surrounded by their coven and armies. They were the king and queen of an era. Their reign had just begun.

He pulled away, looking into her eyes. He felt her love, her admiration and commitment to him through the bond. He didn't care how long it would take ... he would win her back. He had to. There was no future worth living unless she was in it.

"I love you," he whispered, rubbing his nose against hers. He kissed each of her freckled cheeks, running his fingers through her long, beautiful white hair.

"And I love you, Lucifer. Forever and always, I will love you." Talia stepped out of his arms and made her way into the center of the cage. Her face was stained with tears.

Time itself stopped.

Lucifer shook his head in disbelief, trying to reach towards her but she restrained him with her powers ... their powers. With the shackles still in place, he was helpless. Talia closed her eyes, began to recite a spell. Her hair lifted gently into the air as she slowly rose above the ground. A bright white light surrounded her, glowing from deep within.

"No," he said. "Talia, no! Please!"

She ignored him, her lips moving faster and faster. The light glowed brighter, seeping out of every pore of her skin. She burned like a star that had come to life.

Lucifer reached for her, but he was trapped. He cried out, screaming and fighting, trying to get to his mate, trying to save her before she destroyed them both.

A loud boom echoed and Talia's head snapped up towards the sky. Her body extended outwards and a painful scream ripped through her throat. Lucifer felt the pain she was experiencing, her power and lifeforce eating her alive from within. He watched helplessly as blood streamed from her eyes, her nose, and the corners of her mouth.

Her perfect, beautiful body convulsed, the light now raging with the heat of Hell. Lucifer cried out again, folding his hands together as he did something he had vowed never to do.

"Father, please," he cried out in desperation. "Please save her. I will do anything. I will cease to exist ... whatever you require. But please, please save her. Please save my mate. My wife." He screamed, fighting the chains, but there was no use.

The bright light and echoing sound of power faded. Talia looked at him, her eyes saturated with blood. Her face twisted with pain and agony. He looked at his beautiful mate, continuing to pray to the heavens in hopes that she would be spared.

"I love you, Lucifer," she whispered, one final time.

A blast of white light exploded from her, incinerating her body into a million particles of white and gold flakes that sparkled like glitter through the air. Lucifer screamed, every blood vessel bursting underneath his skin. All he saw was red. His body shook furiously as beads of sweat poured from his skin.

The particles fused to the bars of his prison, the precious metal glowing with her lifeforce, trapping him inside for eternity. Lucifer banged his hands on the brimstone floor, breaking the hard surface into pieces as he screamed from a suffering he had never experienced.

The bond that connected them shattered, what felt like thousands of shards of glass crashing through him, tearing him up inside. He fell to the floor, grabbing at his heart as it broke into pieces. He cried profusely, calling out for his mate.

"Talia," he whispered, over and over again. "Talia ..."

The light that was her beauty and essence faded as the bars dimmed into the shadows. Lucifer's mind slithered into a darkness that was unknown even to him. Nothing else mattered but her.

He lay there, left in complete solitude, replaying the love he had selfishly sacrificed. The love his pride and arrogance had destroyed. Tears pooled underneath his cold face while he fought to breathe on the cold brimstone floor. His voice echoed through the barren darkness. "Talia ... Ahuvati ... my Talia ... my wife ... my mate."

CHAPTER FORTY-FOUR

10 Years Later

A cool, crisp breeze danced across my skin, sending shivers down my spine. A warmth quickly calmed the gooseflesh that erupted from the winter breeze. A light tickling sensation trailed down the curve of my back, dipping underneath the covers as fingers splayed on the round rump of my ass. I groaned, nuzzling my nose into the soft silk pillowcase.

Deus held me in his embrace, trailing soft, tender kisses down my bare skin. I moaned with delight, kissing each of his fingers as I brushed my thumb over his wedding ring. Every morning, I woke in his arms, I had to remind myself this wasn't just a dream, it was a reality ... my reality.

"A reality we fought very hard for," he whispered, nipping my earlobe.

I giggled at the sensation. "Snoop," I replied.

"What can I say? I'm a control freak." He flipped me over to my back, pressing kisses along my face, neck, and chest. I laughed as he tickled me in more sensitive areas. Every morning had started like this for the past ten years and I prayed for another thousand more. He was truly my sense of peace. My happiness. My home.

A knock came at the door, but Deus didn't stop kissing me, nor I him. His fingers ran across my body greedily. God, the taste of this man. I would never get my fill.

The knock came again. He pulled away with a grunt while I giggled. "What?" he yelled. The door cracked open and in stepped Gallo.

"My lord, my lady," the goldaburg greeted us. Deus turned towards the creature and began laughing uncontrollably. I popped my head up from the pillow. Gallo stood in our doorway covered from head to toe in paint splatters. His glasses were crooked, one lens cracked. His perfectly pressed suit was ruined. He attempted to clean himself with a handkerchief.

"I like the new look, Gallo," said Deus.

"Yes, your majesty, I am sure you do," he replied unhappily.

"I didn't realize you were so interested in art," I added. Deus laughed into my neck, pressing a kiss against my shoulder. "If I would have known, I would have bought you a different present for the Yule fest."

"I can assure you, my lady," replied Gallo, "art is not a strength of mine, nor an interest, regardless of what your spawn may believe."

Deus pulled a black silk robe from the edge of the bed, wrapping himself in it before handing me a red one. I covered my body, sliding my feet into my slippers just as Gallo was almost knocked to the ground by three bursts of wind.

"Dad," screamed Az, bursting into the room. "They're picking on me again! I asked them to stop just like mom told me, but they won't. I'm tired of being nice. I want to set them both on fire." Az crossed his little arms, his lip pouting. "I hate girls."

"Whining again, big brother," Talia taunted Az.

"Always tattling, this one," added Annalise. The twins looked at each other and snickered.

"I wish you were both boys," grumbled Az.

"Alright, alright, you three," Deus intervened. "Girls, what have we told you about teaming up on your brother?"

They rolled their eyes in unison, huffing together. "We are family," they said together, "and family sticks together. We protect one another no matter what."

"Exactly," said Deus. "And Asmodeus, what have I told you about letting them get under your skin?"

"That I need to build a thicker hide," little Az replied. The girls jumped into bed next to me, their long black ringlets bouncing.

"You two need to be nice to him," I whispered. "We outnumber them, you know. Plus, us Salvo girls can be a handful."

"Understatement of the millennia," Deus added.

I sent my tendrils of darkness towards him, smacking him in the rear. He jumped in surprise. The girls laughed. He turned back to me with his devilish smile, and I returned the gesture.

"You were saying?" I asked. He approached the three of us, leaning down on the bed. "That you Salvo women are a gift from above and worth all the riches and lands in the world," he said, kissing each of us on the head. The girls threw their arms around his neck as he picked them up, spinning them around in a circle.

Laughter erupted from all three. I couldn't help but smile, taking joy in the sight of their bond. Deus had outdone any expectation I had of him as a father. He was kind, gentle, protective, and so incredibly loving. The children wanted for nothing. They had no knowledge of the demon their father had once been. All they knew was that he was the most loving and gentle man in their lives.

Asmodeus Jr. looked up to his father, idolizing every step he took and idolizing every word that came out of his mouth. The girls were confident and secure in who they were. They never once feared him or his power. He was the kind of man they would someday look for in their own spouses. Az jumped onto the bed next to me, leaning his head full of black hair on my shoulder. I kissed him and bopped his little nose, which was covered in freckles. His beautiful crystal blue eyes looked up at me.

"Don't let them get to you," I whispered, pulling my firstborn into me. "Remember, someday, this will all be yours."

"And the first thing I will do is sell them both off to the highest bidder," Az replied in a bitter tone. I had to force myself not to laugh, ruffling his thick hair.

"No son of mine would do such a thing," I said while we both giggled. I looked back at the three of them. Deus now had the girls on the floor, tickling them so intensely they were turning shades of blue, fighting to breath. "Alright, alright, time to get ready to go to Castle Salvo."

"Thank Grandfather," Az said, sliding from the bed, storming out the room. The girls jumped up from the floor, running for the exit while Deus chased them. Their screams echoed through the halls.

Deus reentered the room, beaming from ear to ear while he began to dress.

"The girls are going to be the death of him," I said.

Deus laughed. "He'll learn to appreciate women soon enough."

I looked at him with an expression he knew to fear. "He's eight, Asmodeus. I don't even want to think—"

He pulled me into him. "I'm kidding, my love ... just kidding. Who knows what power they'll possess, or what it will take to fuel that power? We have plenty of time until we have to start worrying about all of that."

"The girls are already six. Six more years and it will start. I'm not ready for that."

He brushed my hair back, kissing me on the head. "And we will both be here to guide them down the right path. We have no clue what to expect. A demon prince has never borne offspring, nor has a vessel. Regardless of whatever may come, they will be supported, protected, and they will be loved. And to top it off ... extremely powerful."

We got ready, taking each other in the shower before making sure the children were dressed and ready to go. The halls of Castle Resnov had changed. The sounds of sex and fornication that once filled the corridors were replaced with toys, bicycles, and the laughter and pitter patter of our children chasing one another down the echoing halls of our home.

Our family gathered together before shifting to Castle Salvo. We made our way to Nonna's room, now Aunt Thora's. The children burst through the doors, greeted by our family. A large festive tree stood on the right side of the fireplace. It was snowing outside, dusting the balcony with a layer of white powder.

"Nonna!" the girls screamed, racing towards Aunt Thora.

"Oh, my bambinas," she replied, kneeling to their level just before they barreled into her.

"Brother," Mammon said, greeting us at the door. Deus smiled, embracing him joyfully. "Ah, and your better half," Gluttony added, moving towards me.

"That she is," Deus added.

"Yuletide greetings," I said to Mammon as he pulled me into a hug.

"Merry Christmas," he replied.

"Finally," Giana said, bouncing towards me. "There are so many wedding plans I need your advice on." She embraced me firmly.

"Thank Father you're here," Gor approached, rolling his eyes. "I don't know how many times I have to tell her, I don't care about floral arrangements or color swatches."

"And apparently my opinion doesn't matter, even though I've planned three weddings at this point," Frankie's voice came from the side.

I looked over at my beautiful cousin with my niece on her hip. My smile beamed from ear to ear at the sight. I reached for little Lucia instantly. She laughed, bouncing out of her mother's grip, lunging towards me.

"How adorable are you," I said, kissing her little chunky cheeks profusely. Frankie hugged me tightly.

"I've missed you," she said softly.

"I've missed you," I replied. "I think we need a girl's weekend soon."

She exhaled. "Aradia, please," she groaned. We both chuckled, pressing our foreheads together. Levi appeared, looking half dead. Little Rosetta cried, pulling at his long hair as her face turned bright red.

Deus reached for her. "Oh, my poor niece," he said, shushing while gently swaying her from side to side. "What has my horrible brother done to you?"

"Done to her?" Levi gasped, the skin under his eyes bruised. "More like what she's done to me. I'm delusional. I can't eat, can't sleep. I can't remember the last time I showered or ate anything other than a microwavable meal, and I'm the bad guy here?"

We all laughed. Rosetta calmed in Deus's arms, resting her chubby face against his chest while he rubbed her back in circles, tilting his head against her brown hair. Each and every day I found a new reason to love this man.

Does that mean you want another? he said in my mind, watching me while he smiled.

"Absolutely," I replied. He pulled his head slowly from Rosetta's, like he was seeing me for the first time. He pressed a firm kiss to my lips.

"Tonight," he promised. I smiled as the butterflies took flight inside of my stomach.

"For heaven's sake, you two," I heard Belz say. "Can you at least try going more than two hours without banging each other?"

"Jealous, brother?" Deus replied.

Belz looked at my aunt, who watched the girls opening the presents by the tree and smiled. She caught his eye and blushed. "Not in the slightest," Belz answered, not taking his eyes off Thora.

Gor popped his collar with pride. "Called it," he said.

Mammon rolled his eyes. "Yes, yes, go figure, the Prince of Sloth would win by picking the longest timeline possible for those two to finally shag."

Gor shrugged. "What can I say, I got time to spare."

We all laughed.

"And the wait was completely worth it," Belz said, kneeling next to my aunt and kissing her on the head. She blushed again and smiled up at him. The two of them had finally stopped fighting their affection for one another about six years after the war. Aunt Thora, being Aunt Thora, wanted to take things slow, not trusting him completely because of what he was. But, yet again, a Prince of Hell had proven us all wrong. Belz had fallen completely in love with her before she had even agreed to have coffee with him. She fell shortly after. It was the most normal relationship any of us had been in.

Az strolled over to the window where Satan and Lilith sat at the large, rectangular table. To my surprise, Satan had become Az's favorite uncle.

Satan had begun to teach him the art of the sword, while Lilith was training him in hand-to-hand combat. Az looked up to the Prince of Wrath and idolized him almost as much as his father.

I strolled over to them, embracing Lilith. She stood awkwardly, still uncomfortable from the affection.

"Merry Christmas," I said to both of them. Satan nodded, going back to showing Az a new knife he had acquired.

"Merry Christmas," Lilith replied, holding Lucia's little hand. "Though, I still can't understand why the Christians celebrate the messiah's birth in December, even though he was born in the blistering heat of July."

I laughed. "Always the critic."

She shrugged, looking at Deus. "Critics get a bad reputation. We're right and others can't handle it."

After the war, Deus had refused to speak with Lilith, even after I explained that she was only following my orders. She was bound to me by oath and had no choice. Yet, he still blamed her for the shield and locking him out. He had only begun to acknowledge her presence in the past two years.

It had killed her. Deus had become family to her, a best friend even while she served his court as Malphasia. I felt awful about the distance between the two. I had apologized to her, but she never admitted to being anger or cross with me. I had to believe that time would heal all wounds. Time ... something we now had so much of.

"So, when are you going to start trying for another?" Deus asked, bouncing Rosetta on his hip, causing her to giggle. "The twins are almost one."

Levi gawked. "When I get a solid month of sleep," he answered.

"Demon baby," Frankie said, smacking him in the shoulder.

Even after their wedding, the mating bond never snapped into place, but the two of them couldn't have been happier together. About five years ago, Frankie had undergone the same process Lilith had, becoming part demon to make her immortal. She had willingly gifted her soul to the prince of envy. I was happy about the decision, knowing I would never have to live without my soulmate.

My aunt had not yet made that decision, but I hoped someday she would. We had lost too much ... losses that still haunted me. Nonna and Mamma. Their lives in exchange for mine.

When we all returned after the war, Frankie, Thora, and I found letters from both of them addressed to each of us. I don't know if those letters made things worse in the end or better. All I knew was that I missed them each and every day.

I wished they could have been there the day Frankie got married. The day Deus and I found out about Az. The day the twins were born. They had missed so much. I had hoped I'd be able to see them when I crossed souls over to the other side, but they never came. I was thankful each time I got to see Orion who was now reunited with Delphine, but my heart longed for my family ... my bloodline.

I looked around the room as our family members laughed and teased one another. Antonio and his parents greeted everyone as they entered. Tony had started dating a young witch from Eau Coven. It was new, but I was happy to see him finally moving on. He seemed joyous and fulfilled.

I placed Lucia on the floor next to the girls. They doted over their cousin, tickling her playfully. They would be wonderful big sisters. Something inside of me couldn't wait to get home.

"We can go now," I heard Deus say in my mind. I caught his eyes from

across the room, shaking my head while I chuckled to myself.

Lucifer remained in the cage his mate had built for him. Deus and I had gone there once to make sure the magic had held him. He was unresponsive. He didn't eat or sleep. He just lay on the stone floor, his eyes peeled open while he rambled to himself. The brothers had concluded that he had finally gone mad. No one could make out what he mumbled, but there was a moment that I swore the name *Talia* left his lips.

I stood against the fireplace wall, looking out at the beautiful picture of our family. Aunt Thora and Frankie joined me, taking in the sight.

"How beautiful is this?" I whispered.

"It's something I never thought I'd see," answered Frankie.

"You and me both," I replied, taking her hand in mine. Aunt Thora smiled at us and then at our children spread throughout the room.

"The Salvo women survive," she whispered, a tear escaping her eyes. She looked back at us. "The two of you have strengthened our name ... our line. I am so damn proud of you both." She embraced us, kissing our cheeks, then pulled away, wiping the tears from her face. "I just wish they were here to see this. To see what they sacrificed their lives for."

"They are," Frankie said, taking her mother's hand.

"I feel them each and every day," I added.

Aunt Thora fought back more tears. "So do I, sweetheart," she whispered. "So do I."

We all turned to the picture frame on the fireplace. The last picture the five of us took together, at my wedding. All of us smiling from the joy of that day, from the love we had for one another. That bond, nothing would ever be able to break. Not even death.

Acknowledgments

The ending of this series is such a bittersweet experience. This book, in particular, has been incredibly personal to me, with so much of my own reality woven into the characters, struggles, and plots you've read and experienced along the way.

Writing it has been a healing journey — a process of reflection on where I've been and how far I've come.

I am deeply grateful to my wonderful editor, Kara, for helping me revise, problem-solve, and flesh out this storyline. Your insight, patience, and unwavering support have been invaluable, and I cannot thank you enough for helping me bring this world to life.

As always, this is dedicated to my mom. The bond between a mother and daughter is sacred — untouchable — and it has been a constant source of inspiration for me.

To every woman in my life: thank you for inspiring me, challenging me, supporting me, and loving me in ways that words can barely capture. The strength and power I have found in my relationships with you are a true testament to the woman I have become.

Thank you for walking this journey with me.

ABOUT THE AUTHOR

Jessica Ann Disciacca, an Italian American from Kansas City, Missouri, holds a Master's in Educational Leadership from Northwest Missouri State University (2023). Graduating in 2015 from Park University with a diverse Bachelor's degree, she now pursues a career in educational administration while teaching.

Beyond her professional life, Jessica is an avid artist and writer, finding solace in family moments. Her lifelong passion for literature and storytelling led her to debut as an author with "Awakening the Dark Throne."

facebook.com/authorjessicaanndisciacca

instagram.com/authorjessicaanndisciacca

JessicaAnnDisciacca.com